ROMANTIC SUSPENSE AT ITS BEST!

Praise for the novels of Cherry Adair . . .

"Cherry Adair writes for those of us who love romantic-suspense fast and hot."   —Jayne Ann Krentz

"Adair leaves readers eager to dive into the next novel in her Cutter Cay series."   —*Booklist*

"*Undertow* is the beginning of an exciting and witty new series enriched with fun characters and action-packed drama. I literally could not put it down!"   —*Fresh Fiction*

"Adair returns to her romantic suspense roots with an underwater treasure hunt that is thrilling and hazardous! Nonstop action plays off the treachery and danger. When you add in the sensuous sizzle you have the full Adair package."   —*Romantic Times* (4 stars)

"Grips readers and never slows down as the protagonists struggle with perils, including to their hearts, with every nautical mile they sail. Fast-paced, Cherry Adair opens her Cutter Salvage series with a strong sea saga."
                        —*Genre Go Round Reviews*

"Full of action and suspense! Cherry Adair did such a great job making the reader feel as if they were part of the experience. I felt like I was right there diving into the water looking for the buried treasure with Zane and Teal."
                        —*Hanging with Bells Blog*

"A relentless page-turner with plenty of enticing plot twists and turns."   —*Seattle Post-Intelligencer*

Also by

CHERRY ADAIR

Undertow

Riptide

Vortex

Stormchaser

CHERRY ADAIR

PAPL
DISCARDED

St. Martin's Paperbacks

This is a work of fiction. All of the characters, organizations, and events portrayed in this novel are either products of the author's imagination or are used fictitiously.

STORMCHASER

Copyright © 2017 by Cherry Adair.

All rights reserved.

For information address St. Martin's Press, 175 Fifth Avenue, New York, NY 10010.

ISBN: 978-1-250-01634-8

Our books may be purchased in bulk for promotional, educational, or business use. Please contact your local bookseller or the Macmillan Corporate and Premium Sales Department at 1-800-221-7945, ext. 5442, or by e-mail at MacmillanSpecialMarkets@macmillan.com.

Printed in the United States of America

St. Martin's Paperbacks edition / March 2017

St. Martin's Paperbacks are published by St. Martin's Press, 175 Fifth Avenue, New York, NY 10010.

10 9 8 7 6 5 4 3 2 1

One

The day didn't *look* like secondhand revenge. Instead of ominous dark clouds hanging low over a pewter sea, the hot Greek sun reflected glittering sapphires off the Mediterranean. The wake of the motor launch frothed blindingly white as it carried marine archaeologist Dr. Calista West to the megayacht *Stormchaser*, anchored in open waters south of Crete.

Salt spray cooled her bare arms and legs as the *Riva Iseo* cut through the dark water. The sleek, twenty-seven-foot Italian work of art, with yards of glossy mahogany, soft leather, and sleek lines, looked like something straight out of a James Bond movie. Expensive and ostentatious. Draco Thanos, the short, wiry forty-something chief engineer of *Stormchaser* sent to collect Callie from Heraklion, controlled the fast tender with all the deference of a guy handling a sleek sports car.

Callie wasn't even sure what day it was anymore. A short flight in yet another ostentatious, expensive toy, a private plane from Athens. A twelve-hour flight from Miami, an hour flight from Athens to Crete, and another two hours by luxury tender. She was hardly at her best to deal with Jonah Cutter.

Tuning out Thanos, who'd kept up a steady conversation

in broken English for the duration, she spread her feet, bracing her hands on the rail as they hit some chop. Her stomach did a somersault that had nothing to do with the waves. The closer the motor launch carried her to *Stormchaser*, the harder Callie's heart pounded.

Anticipation. Fear. Excitement.

Thanos pointed unnecessarily. The massive ship was freaking impossible to miss. "There she is."

Callie's fingers tightened on the rail as the ship loomed large against a sparkling backdrop of calm azure water and robin's-egg-blue sky. Brilliant sun bounced off acres of white paint and gleaming brass. *Twenty, thirty mil?* Callie guesstimated, put off by the unnecessary flaunting of the Cutters' wealth.

"Spectacular, isn't she?" Thanos said proudly as he slowed the tender, angling it sideways to dock aft next to the wide dive platform where a guy sat reading. He got to his feet as they approached, lifting a hand in greeting. Callie waved back.

She used both hands to tuck any loose hair back into the neatly tucked French braid on the back of her head, even though she knew there were none. She was too controlled to have flyaway hair. Her penchants for order and organization were perfect for her chosen career. She'd come by them the hard way. By now the traits were ingrained and comfortable.

Without the fine cooling misted spray of the water, and wind generated by the fast movement over the sea, the sun beat down unrelentingly, drying her damp clothes in minutes.

"She's something, all right." Too big, and far too fancy for a *dive* boat, but wasn't that the Cutters all over? A family of modern-day treasure hunters, they flaunted their wealth like robber barons or nouveau riche Internet millionaires, with total disregard for anyone daring their ownership of the seas.

For a moment Callie had a niggle of misgiving for what she was about to do. Jonah Cutter hadn't done anything to her personally; she'd never even met the man. Never met *any* of the Cutters. But they adversely impacted people she loved.

She was uniquely qualified to balance the scales.

Straightening her shoulders, Callie grabbed her duffel before Thanos could reach for it. Ingrained and as sure as her dark hair and green eyes was her independence. Drawing in a salt-laden deep breath, Callie let it out slowly as the tender bumped the edge of the wide dive platform where the older man, dressed in cargo shorts and a yellow polo shirt, waited to grab the rope.

And the game begins, she thought, braced to disembark, her fingers tightened on the bag's handles.

Lying was against everything she believed in. Been there, spent a lifetime perfecting the skill. Just because she was good at it didn't mean she liked doing it. But not only did she have to lie through her teeth for the duration, she had to be convincing as well.

She reminded herself that these people were *not* her friends. She could not soften and bond with them. Growing to like anyone on board *Stormchaser* would make what she was going to do harder.

She'd known going in that she'd have to keep to herself as much as possible. She was here to do a job. Making friends would muddy the waters and certainly complicate things. And, she admitted, make her second-guess herself—which she unfortunately usually did. She tended to overanalyze things before jumping in. Indecision was, she knew, her worst characteristic. Still, once she'd made a determination, after weighing it from a hundred different angles, she tended to be like a dog with a bone defending the decision.

Her friends tried to get her to be more spontaneous. But it was hard for her. Every decision had consequences, and those had to be weighed and calculated and looked at from every angle.

What wouldn't be hard? Pretending. *That* she was damn good at. If anyone knew how to pretend, it was her. She'd done it from kindergarten on. When she'd learned to lie for her parents. Why they'd forgotten to sign her up for school programs? Why they weren't there to pick her up after school? Why she rarely had a lunch packed, or money to buy lunch? She'd known instinctively that to say her mama was passed out from Jack Daniel's would be bad, and mentioning that sometimes her dad didn't come home would be worse.

These circumstances weren't the same, but she figured she'd honed her acting chops. She could do this by mentally tarring everyone on board with the sins of the Cutters. Which were too numerous to count.

And by keeping as low a profile as possible.

The gray-haired man held out his hand, helping her from the boat to the diving platform. "Saul Pinter." His full, mostly gray beard was neatly trimmed. Fit and athletic, he had a nice smile and firm handshake. "Welcome aboard, Dr. West."

"Thanks, call me Callie." A cursory glance revealed the dive platform geared with the usual dive equipment and a row of wet suits ready and waiting. At least she'd get to do what she loved. Dive. Discover. "Is Mr. Cutter diving?"

Saul shook his head, jerking his thumb toward the ladder leading to the deck above where they stood. "Jonah will have seen you, and be on his way down. Heads up, he'll meet you halfway."

Oh, Callie doubted that very much, but she merely smiled as her heart thumped. Anticipation—no, dread? After all the planning, things were finally happening. "I'm looking forward to seeing our wreck."

"You haven't missed anything. We only arrived late last night ourselves," Saul told her, returning to his chair and the book he'd been reading. "We're all eager to get started."

Was that a jibe because she hadn't joined them two weeks ago? Callie mentally shrugged. Climbing the ladder, she observed in a quick sweep the spotless decks, the gleaming brightwork and shiny brass. *Stormchaser* was spit-polished. She'd heard Zane Cutter's ship was a piece of crap, but so far she couldn't fault his half brother on the maintenance of *his* ship.

Several men, in the whites of crew members, leaned on the rail on an upper deck watching her curiously. Callie lifted a hand in greeting and kept going. It was a perfect afternoon to dive, the ocean smooth with just a slight chop. A light breeze loosened strands of hair off her face and neck and brought with it the faint smells of fresh paint and yeasty baking bread.

Water slapped the hull, and the sound of voices died as the men disappeared from view. A gull cried as it wheeled in a perfect circle overhead, then dived like a jet, skimming the water after some hapless fish.

There wasn't anyone else around, and she walked toward a set of sliding doors just as a man stepped out onto the deck ahead of her. His face lit up as he came toward her.

Jonah Cutter. Callie stopped to wait for him, the sun

hot on her scalp, the glare off the water bright despite her
dark glasses. The opinion formed before the man even
opened his mouth. Her assessment was quick and unflat-
tering. But then she was predisposed to disliking him.

Cocky. Self-assured. Entitled.

Exactly what she expected. Her shoulders relaxed.
Handing Cutter his ass wasn't going to be difficult at all.

The Matthew McConaughey look-alike wore blue,
flower-printed Hawaiian board shorts, a too-tight red T-
shirt stretched over sculpted muscles as if it had been
painted on. She'd heard that youngest brother Zane was
the vain one, but clearly his half brother gave him a run
for his money.

Under six feet tall, sun-bleached shoulder-length hair,
movie-star good looks, and boy, didn't he know it. Cutter
was like a peacock spreading his tail as he removed his
shades to eye her up and down.

Shorter, less attractive, and more smarmy than she'd
been led to believe. And she'd been led to believe the
worst.

Maintaining a friendly smile, she extended her hand
when he got close enough. He was about the same height,
so they were eye-to-lecherous-eye. "I'm Calista West,
thanks for including—"

"Now, aren't you just the prettiest addition to the team,
darlin'?" he cut in with a southern drawl and a heated look
from unremarkable blue eyes. His lingering handshake
was the opposite of firm. Callie disengaged and resisted
wiping her hand on her shorts as he looked at her like a dog
staring at a juicy bone. Raking his fingers through his sun-
bleached brown hair, the better to show off his physique, he
gave her a wide, white smile. "Welcome aboard."

Never had two words sounded so suggestive. Smoothing a hand over her tightly constrained hair, Callie made

sure the sun glinted off the plain gold band on her left hand. Although she suspected a guy like this wouldn't be deterred by a wedding ring, she had other methods to repulse if the ring didn't work.

"Sorry I couldn't make it to Cutter Cay." A calculated delay to avoid the two-week bonding of crew and dive team on the ship's maiden voyage from the Caribbean, where the Cutters lived, to this remote Grecian location.

"You're well worth the wait, darlin'."

"Dr. West, or Callie. Only my *husband* calls me darling." Bud nipped. Not that Adam had ever called her anything but Calista, but he'd been über-protective until the day he died. He'd've been delighted to be a deterrent. "If you'll have someone show me where to stash my gear, I'll chan—"

"*Finally*. The late Dr. West, I presume?" *That* didn't sound very auspicious. The deep, impatient voice came from directly behind her. The man sounded more annoyed than excited. "I see you've met Brody." His voice was dry. "Push off, Turner, I'll take it from here."

Mouth unaccountably dry, Callie narrowed her eyes at Brody. "You might've mentioned who you were when we were talking."

He put up both hands playfully. "Babe, you didn't give me a chance to say anything." Eyes flickering over her right shoulder and well above her head, he gave a mock salute. "Pushing off now."

Callie turned. Oh, shit. *The real threat.* This guy was a whole other ball game. Staring up the length of his tall, lean body, she felt her heartbeat stutter. The brilliant sun darkened, and the sibilant slosh of the wavelets went mute.

And she was a pragmatist. Callie couldn't imagine what some romantic would make of him.

Tall. Dark. Devastating.

This man, whose footsteps she hadn't heard, was practically naked. Just a pair of black shorts and miles of tanned, glistening skin pulled taut over rock-hard muscles. Lightly salted dark hair trailed down the steps of his abs to disappear into black shorts. Dragging her rapt gaze back up his chest, she tried to find fault with his physical appearance, but even his disheveled jaw-length dark hair didn't look unkempt, just sexy and untamed, and insanely touchable. Beard stubble shadowed his face, making him look dangerously like a sexy pirate. Instead of looking annoyingly unshaven, the stubble just made him that much hotter. With his piercing blue eyes and dark hair he looked Black Irish, but there was a subtle hint of the Mediterranean in his voice that was impossible to pinpoint.

He exuded utter self-confidence, and sexual prowess.

She imagined him naked. Tried not to, but then imagined them together in a sweaty, heated embrace. Her cheeks felt hot.

Twisting her wedding ring around her finger grounded her as Callie's eyes locked with his. The shockingly clear, Caribbean blue made her breath snag in her throat. Pins and needles, hot then cold, pebbled her skin, and her heart pounded so hard she felt dizzy. Her physical reaction, lust, not fear, shocked the hell out of her.

Please God, don't let this *be Jonah Cutter.*

He held out a large hand. "Jonah Cutter. Glad you finally made it, Dr. West." His laid-back, sexy baritone held a hint of impatience, resonating through Callie's unprepared body like a tuning fork.

Reluctantly she shook his hand. The slide of her fingers against the callused heat of his made her heart do calisthenics. She released as soon as possible, casually tucking her fingertips into the front pocket of her khaki shorts. "Call me Callie."

He had a swimmer's body, tall and lean, with broad powerful shoulders and long, strong legs dusted with dark hair. "You must be beat, but I'm eager to fill you in before I let you grab some z's. Give me an hour, and I'll let you go get some rest."

"Actually I'm not that tired, I slept some on the various flights." She'd been too excited to sleep, and now she was too overstimulated to even think about closing her eyes.

"Excellent."

God help her, there was no mistaking this man for a pushover. His eyes said, *Been there, done that. The hard way.*

Okay then, more of a challenge than she'd bargained for, but God only knew, challenges were a daily occurrence, not grounds to turn tail and run like hell. Despite the strong temptation.

Steeling herself, Callie told herself she was overreacting and she'd better get her shit together before she said or did something out of character and plain stupid. Still, the *Riva* hadn't left yet. She could hear the soft purr of the engines over the rapid-fire beating of her heart. Not that she would turn tail and make a run for it, but it was always good to have options.

Bare-chested and in-your-face male, Cutter gave her a narrow-eyed stare when she just stood there as if turned to stone. Or all her mental fuses had blown. "Are you okay?" He of the crystalline blue eyes, easy smile, and Holy-Mother-of-God broad chest sounded a little cranky, and looked—well, he looked good enough to eat. Or if not *eat*—lick all over.

I'm not impressed. I am not impressed. I am so not impressed.

Steady eye contact, expression bland.

He was just a guy. Just a drop-freaking-dead-gorgeous guy with X-ray eyes who seemed to peer directly into her lying brain. Callie straightened her shoulders and gave him an easy smile. A smile she'd perfected over the years until it felt almost natural. "Just getting my sea legs."

The hot breeze ruffled his shoulder-length, almost black hair around his head and lashed dark strands across his throat. He shoved his fingers through it, pushing it back absently; it fell in shaggy perfection around his face. The beautiful hair in no way softened his features.

"Won't take long." He flicked a glance over her head at the other man. "You're still here." Brody walked away backward, grinning.

Cutter shook his head as he returned his attention to her. "I'll take you down to your cabin to get your gear stashed, then you can play catch-up and meet the others. Hungry?"

Hungry enough to lick the salt off his hot, satiny skin. She shook her head. "They fed me on the plane." She drew in a breath, smelled clean male sweat, and met his gaze while her heart did calisthenics. "Give me directions, I'll find my way." She didn't want to be in close confines with him. He exuded sex appeal, the dangerous kind of bad-boy sex appeal that most women found irresistible. She'd get over the immediate rush of physical attraction and re-gain her equilibrium in a minute. But she needed that minute to kick her own ass.

"Is that it?" He indicated the duffel she held in a death grip.

He bent to reach for it. Their faces were mere inches apart. She almost tasted the coffee on his breath. When their fingers brushed, an electrical shock zinged up her arm, resonating like a tuning fork in her chest. Tightening her fingers around the strap she straightened. "I've got it."

He slanted her an amused glance, and extended his arm in invitation. "This way."

Said the spider to the fly.

Jonah was paying a boatload of money for Dr. Calista West's services. He hoped to hell she was worth it. He was chomping at the bit to get started.

Fairly tall and slender, she was attractive rather than pretty. Even though half her face was covered by dark glasses, she had interesting features. Straight nose, fuller lower lip. Girl next door. Fresh, naturally sexy. *Married*. Still, there was no rule to say he couldn't look. So he did. His fill.

Khaki shorts and a white shirt flattered her slender body. Good legs, small breasts. A fancy braid constrained her hair on the back of her head. Her slicked-back hair gleamed the glossy brown of bitter chocolate shot with intriguing golden highlights. Clearly the loose strands blowing across her cheek were annoyingly out of place as she firmly tucked them behind her ear. She looked serious as a heart attack, and about as humorless.

As long as she did what she was there to do, Jonah didn't give a flying fuck about her personality.

She smelled like warm coconut.

Dr. West stared back at him behind the security of her shades as he led her toward the sliders into the salon. The harsh sun struck her face at a slight angle, and he noticed the faint scars on her lightly tanned skin. A quarter-inch white line cutting into her upper lip, another just under her left eyebrow. Both so faint only the change in light made them visible. Jonah wondered if her husband was a beater.

Fuck, he hoped not. Men beating up on woman were dicks. He made a mental note to find out. For her, but also for the safety of the others on board. He couldn't have some homicidal maniac showing up and possibly endangering them all. Although as far as he knew abusers picked on one target to make their lives a living hell.

"I didn't expect *Stormchaser* to be so . . ."

"Big. Luxurious?" He could tell from the tightening of her rather luscious lips that she didn't approve of *Stormchaser*'s amenities. Too bad. Everyone else had gotten used to everything the ship had to offer pretty damn fast.

"Both. I'm used to spending months on end on salvages sleeping three to a cabin like sardines. No privacy, and barely enough space to get away from anyone for five minutes. The space here is worth hiring on for all by itself."

It had taken seven months of haggling to convince her to join the team.

"Everyone has their own cabin." Jonah indicated the slider. "She's designed to give everyone a private luxury space for their downtime. We have a five-star chef to feed us, and a crew large enough to leave us plenty of leisure time."

"Sounds like a luxury vacation."

"It has been for a couple of weeks, but everyone is ready to get started." The maiden voyage had given everyone time to get to know one another, and to iron out any kinks on board. "We'll work hard, I assure you. This salvage promises to be long-term, and I want everyone to want to stick around." Would this prove to be as lucrative, as lengthy as the salvage of the *Atocha*? Jonah suspected he and his divers would be anchored right here for the next ten years and still not uncover all the secrets of what he'd discovered.

Dr. West was married. He wondered what kind of marriage it could be when she was here and the husband was presumably back in Florida. Not his problem. If this turned out the way he expected it to, everyone on board would get ample shore leave, and their families were welcome to come visit if this turned into years not months.

Anticipation thrummed through his body in a pleasant rhythm at odds with the calmness of the glass-smooth Mediterranean surrounding his ship, and the brilliance of the sun beating down on his bare shoulders.

He slid open the door, and she preceded him into the main salon with its wraparound windows and adjacent dining room. She gave a quick glance at the comfortable, crisp, white slip-covered furniture, the accents of chrome and charcoal, and the bold splashes of color provided by oversized paintings on the teak walls as they walked through the room.

"You have my equipment? None of the containers were damaged, were they?"

They'd picked up the crates in Miami on their way. "Everything looked to be in good order." He indicated the stairs, and she headed toward them. He enjoyed the view of her shapely ass and long, sexy legs. "I gave you a dedicated space on the other side of the galley. Nothing was unpacked per your instructions."

"Good," she said over her shoulder. "I'd like to unpack those before I do anything else."

God. He didn't remember when last he'd been this excited about anything. But he'd waited this long to get started; a few more hours wouldn't kill him. "First things first. I'll show you down to your cabin so you can change."

She paused on the landing. "Change?" Her lips twitched as she removed her dark glasses, exposing eyes the color of the shallow water surrounding Cutter Cay. A soft, clear green. And another tiny, almost imperceptible scar on her nose, millimeters from her right eye. "Into what? A ballerina?"

Okay, so there was a sense of humor lurking under the serious facade. He didn't care. But damn it, the scars bothered him. A *lot*. "Change into your swimsuit. I have your dive gear ready."

She arched both dark eyebrows "I flew halfway around the world, and only just arrived. Surely a dive can wait until tomorrow?"

Jonah backed up a step because the area was narrow and the scent of her skin was making his mouth water. A wholly inappropriate and completely unexpected reaction to the woman who very possibly held his future in her hands. "You can kick back for thirty minutes before we suit up."

"It's not safe to dive when—"

He edged past her to lead the way, expecting her to follow. "It'll be a quick dive, then I'll bring you back and you can rest up." Glancing over his shoulder when she remained rooted to the spot, he used his shoulder to indicate she keep moving. "This way."

She started down the stairs after him. "We might want to establish some ground rules. You're paying for my services—"

"*Very* well."

"Nobody held a gun to your head or forced you to pay four times my customary fee," she said pleasantly, a thread of *fuck you* in her tone. "*You* wanted *me*, and outbid someone else who also had need of my services. I'm here. I'll do my job, but I refuse to be pressured into unsafe diving practices. I need time to decompress from traveling halfway around the world. I won't dive today. End of conversation."

Jonah knew she'd been offered a job at the same time by Rydell Case, the Cutters' nemesis. It had given him and his brothers a great deal of satisfaction stealing Dr. West from under Case's nose. "You'll understand my eagerness to get you under the water when you see what I have to show you."

"And I'm eager to see *Ji Li*," she assured him. "*Tomorrow*. There are dozens of things for me to do right here on board until then. I like to have my environment in order before I get started." Her lips curved. "It's better for me not to drown. The red tape with the Hellenic police would tie you up for weeks."

He bit back a growl of frustration, hardly amused that she'd balked at his first order of business, but gave ground because she was right.

"Fair enough." But it ticked him off that she was being stubborn when he'd been counting the seconds waiting for her arrival. Okay, she was right, damn it, diving jet-lagged and as tired as she must be would be dangerous. Still—

Jonah took her downstairs and shoved open the door to the owner's cabin. "Here you go. I'll wait and take you up to meet the others. Unless you'd like a couple of hours . . . ?"

She stepped inside. "I won't be long . . . Whose cabin is this? Yours?"

Jonah had no idea how she knew that. The luxuriously appointed room was empty of personal effects. He'd cleared out his crap and given her the slightly bigger room.

"Y-yours." Jesus, he hadn't noticed up on deck, but in the lights in the corridor he saw the gleam of the thin white scar that seemed to run from beneath the short sleeve of her shirt down the length of her left arm. What the fuck had the sick son of a bitch done to her? Sliced her up? Jonah felt a sick rage against a man he didn't know for a crime he wasn't sure the guy had committed. All he knew was he didn't like seeing the scars she wore. Didn't like them a fucking great deal.

"Thanks, but I prefer a smaller space."

Jonah dragged his gaze away from her arm. No use arguing. She was making it clear that she was a by-the-book, no-detours kind of woman. "Fine." He just wanted to get out of there. "You can have the cabin I commandeered. For now go ahead and use this one to wash up." The slightly smaller cabin was across the corridor. But it was full of his own stuff, stuff he didn't necessarily want her to see. She was already a pain in the ass; he didn't want her asking questions. "I'll wait out here for you."

She shut the heavy door in his face. Jonah leaned his shoulder against the mahogany paneled wall. There could be a problem: Both of them wanted to be in charge, and that wasn't going to work.

The door opened two minutes later. "Ready." She hadn't changed a thing as far as he could see. But her hairline was damp, and she smelled more strongly of coconut. Probably sunblock. It had never smelled so mouth-watering.

"I understand your rationale for not diving right now, but I can't wait to share what I discovered with you."

"I look forward to seeing it tomorrow. I presume we'll gather as a group beforehand for a briefing?"

He doubted she had a less-than-brilliant bone in her body, but damn was she stubborn. "Yeah. I wanted to wait and tell everyone together." He started walking down the narrow corridor back toward the stairs. "I'll introduce you to the others, then I'd like to discuss my findings with you in private before I fill them in in the morning."

"That sounds intriguing." She waited for him to move so she could follow him down the companionway.

"You have no idea." Jonah glanced at her over his shoulder. "I've waited two weeks to have you in my hot hands. Once I fill you in, you'll be even more eager than I am to dive and see for yourself."

This find blew everything else out of the water. Or could, quite literally.

"If you were any more excited your tail would be wagging," she said drily. "I can certainly look at pictures. Lead on, Macduff."

Annoyed at her lack of enthusiasm, he paused at the stairwell. "It's tail-wagging news," Jonah assured her.

"Right. Tell me about your beautiful new ship."

Stormchaser was his if he wanted her. At some point this trip he had to decide if he wanted this new life, or if he was ready to go back to his old one in Spain. "*Refitted*, but they did a good job."

As a marine architect he would've enjoyed designing his own salvage ship, but that would take time—time he didn't have right now. He'd been fooling with design ideas for his own vessel for years. "The hold was specially constructed," he told her as they headed back upstairs. "Reinforced et cetera for this salvage—"

"You're anticipating a lot of what? Gold?" Her brow quirked and he wondered at the mostly concealed bite in her tone.

"The *Ji Li* was one of the thousands of ships traveling the Silk Road between China and the Mediterranean in the thirteenth century. She carried silk and spices, of course, but also a boatload of gold, emeralds, and silver coins."

"I've never worked with a Chinese ship, but I did some research on the flight. This'll be fascinating."

Ji Li held a king's ransom in treasure, but she wasn't what had him so excited. No, it was what lay *beneath* the Chinese junk that had kept his heart pounding and his mind racing for months. Now he was so close he could taste it. Even one more day waiting for the marine archaeologist to confirm his finding was a pain in the ass.

"You have no idea."

Two

"Have you set up the grid yet?" Callie asked, walking up the inside stairs beside him. He was distracted by her. Not good. The scars. The shape of her neat ears, the no-nonsense way her hair was not only firmly braided, but then tucked up tighter than a miser's purse, no hair out of place.

Her lashes were thick and dark, not long, but they made her pale eyes look as if they'd been set by a smudged finger. He didn't think she wore perfume, but her skin smelled delectable. Fresh. Tropical. Thank God she was married. His lusty thoughts could remain merely thoughts. A romantic involvement was always a bad idea in the close confines of a ship where everyone pretty much knew when someone else rolled over in their sleep. Not that they didn't happen, they just tended not to end well.

"Nope. Dropped anchor here late yesterday. Gave everyone shore leave for a couple of days beforehand while we waited for you." He'd dropped in to visit his grandmother in Spain while the others had spent the weekend in Athens. "We'll start setting up grids tomorrow."

"This really is a spectacular ship."

He stroked a hand along the mahogany paneling lining the companionway. "Yeah, she's a beauty, isn't she? My new home away from home. Hundred and twenty-eight feet, two hundred and thirty five tons, cruising speed eighteen knots. Crew of ten. Six divers, seven with you. We added a heavy-duty winch and some cool updated toys."

He'd captained for his half brother Nick for two years, but on this salvage he wanted a clear head and no additional crap to deal with so he could focus on the task at hand.

He'd hired Maura Sennett, an old college friend, to captain *Stormchaser*. They'd met at Webb Institute when they'd both received their master's degrees in marine science. Both had gotten their captain's stripes at about the same time, too; the rest had been on-the-job training. Jonah trusted her. Maura was more than qualified to take care of a thirty-million-dollar ship and everyone on board. Her wife, Gayle, was first mate, which worked out well for everybody.

His first solo trip was going to be a case of sink or swim.

Jonah's half brothers had their superpowers. Zane with his charisma and natural ability to make everyone love him. Nick with his special dialect skills, Logan with his phenomenal ability to make money. Jonah wanted—hell no—*needed* to earn their respect and find his place with them. And in the Cutter family there was only one way to do that—impress the hell out of them.

This salvage would do just that. He was banking on it.

"Sorry I couldn't join you from the beginning," Dr. West told him briskly as they walked back through the main salon. "I had another project to complete before I could join you."

Jonah had flown everyone in to Cutter Cay so they'd have a few weeks to learn one another's rhythms on the five-thousand-nautical-mile journey to the Mediterranean. "It was a good way for the team to get to know one another and bond. You have a bit of catching up to do."

"Don't worry. I'm used to being the one slightly out of step with the rest. I'll work it out."

It was an odd comment. "Parents in the military?"

She gave him a surprised look. "No. Why do you ask?"

"I just presumed you moved around a lot as a kid."

"We did, but it wasn't because my father was in the service. I tend to keep to myself, and frankly, I've always been more in tune with artifacts and history than with people."

Great. That was going to make for some fucking awkward dinners. Antisocial and not a team player. He hoped she'd be easier to get along with after a nap. "Your other job was with Rydell Case?" he asked, already knowing the answer.

"No, actually," she said mildly. "He wanted me the same time you did."

Which was fine. He already knew he'd outbid the Cutters' nemesis to get her. He just wanted to hear it again from her. But that wasn't the only reason he'd hired her. With her background she was going to be the MVP of the salvage, and was worth every damn penny and more. "You've worked with him before?" Jonah asked as they climbed the stairs to the next deck. The ship was luxuriously outfitted in white and a neutral gray. He'd added artwork collected from his travels for splashes of color here and there. *Stormchaser* might be a working ship, but as he'd told her—she was also his home.

"Several times." She gave him a pointed look. "Cutter Salvage usually uses Maggie Berland, right? Why didn't you bring her instead of hounding me so relentlessly?

Why do you want me here? Neither junks nor the Silk Road is exactly my field of expertise."

Jonah decided she'd understand better once she saw the pictures. In fact, he looked forward to a nice long apology from her royal crabbiness. "No, you have other fields of expertise that will come in handy this trip."

He led her up to the third deck and slid open the ceiling-to-floor doors. A glass table with four comfortable chairs, shaded by a gray-and-white-striped umbrella, sat on the smallest of the ship's decks. The nearby hot tub was covered, and a couple of Jet Skis were secured to the railing.

She looked around. The midafternoon sun sheeted the water with glistening silver. The sounds of male laughter drifted up from below. The coastline of Crete was a blur on the edge of the horizon, and a tiny, uninhabited volcanic island seven or eight miles away seemed to float, a tiny dot, off their port side like a green mirage.

"Why the mystery? Surely your team knows about the *Ji Li*?"

He hid his excitement behind half-lowered lids. "*Ji Li*, yes. Be patient, I'll show you."

She pressed her lips together. "I don't like surprises."

Of course she didn't. "I thought all women like surprises."

"Not me. Not unless you plan on proposing to me with a ten-carat diamond, which *would* be a surprise— especially to my husband."

A timely reminder. "He's okay with all the travel you do?"

"Clearly, since I'm here." Her tone said, *None of your damn business*.

A project like this could take months, if not years, shit—if not *decades*. Not that she had to be there for the duration. But she hadn't stated a time limit when she'd signed on. Was her husband okay with *that*? None of his business.

Now that he'd seen the scars he couldn't unsee them. Was her husband responsible? Also none of his business. But a fucking shitload better than acknowledging the energy he felt like an electric force field when he looked at her. "Fair enough. Want something cold to drink?"

She glanced around. "Sure."

She checked out the rest of the deck while he called down to have someone come up with refreshments. "Who're you sending up?" he asked Tina, their chef. He needed some shit from his cabin, but didn't want everyone knowing his business. Not yet anyway. "Great, have Agyros go to my cabin and bring my iPad and the metal box beside the desk first, will you? Yeah—a snack would be great. Thanks, Tina."

He disconnected and strolled to the rail to join the good doctor, leaning over to rest his forearms on the rail. "That's the extent of my host duties." Some of the dive team were swimming and goofing off in the water. It looked inviting. He'd get in another swim later.

"So—what's this big surprise?" Beside him, Dr. Calista West turned to mimic his slouched posture, forearms over the rail. On her it was downright provocative, even though her khaki shorts covered her lightly tanned legs almost to her knees, and the white T-shirt wasn't formfitting. There was nothing in the least provocative about her. But somehow Jonah felt . . . provoked. His eyes went to her mouth. Jonah noticed a hairline scar over her left eyebrow, another faint one on the edge if her upper lip. Now that he knew where to look, he saw multiple tiny, almost invisible scars on her face and throat. His gaze landed on her arm. How had she gotten them? Hell, the injury must've hurt like hell. The long, thin scar on her arm looked like she'd been cut open with a can opener.

She turned her head so he could see himself reflected in her dark glass. "A *big* secret then." Her tone was a little snarky, but he let it go.

She turned her attention to look out over the water. "I suppose this isn't a bad spot to wait. There's something magical about the light in Greece that I've never found anywhere else. I love it here." Bright afternoon sun glinted warningly off her wedding ring as she leaned forward to drape her crossed wrists over the rail.

Jonah was not the kind to waste a single motion; everything had a purpose, and if it didn't, he ditched it. He'd learned in the last few years the advantage of biding his time. Right now stealth chaffed. When he inhaled the salt-laden air, he got a brainful of the good doctor's fresh scent as well. Endorphins flooded his synapses and he was pathetically grateful when Agyros arrived with a tray carrying glasses with crystalline cubes of ice and a pitcher of tea so he could stride across the deck, away from the allure of the most important person on board.

Hands off, he reminded himself.

The steward had stopped by his cabin for his iPad and the box on the desk. Agyros placed both on the table with the drinks, then left. Funny that two such relatively small objects could hold so much weight. For now he let them be.

"The *Ji Li* wasn't the impetus for hiring you."

"No?"

"I read your paper on Atlantis."

She raised a brow at the non sequitur. After a moment she said, "I wrote several papers on the *unlikelihood* that Atlantis really existed. To sum up five years of research, my hypothesis is that Plato used a dozen cities to make up his fictional Atlantis."

He dragged in a deep breath. The good doctor's fresh scent and the smell of the sea filled his lungs before he let out the air. "I've found it."

She gave him a skeptical look over her tilted glasses. "Atlantis?"

"Yeah."

Shoving the dark glasses back to cover her eyes, she said evenly. "*Here?*"

"Yeah, here."

"You know there's an enormous probability that you're wrong." Her voice told him he was 100 percent wrong and she was merely indulging him even by having this conversation. Jonah enjoyed a good debate now and then. He and Nick had them all the time. He didn't give a shit which side he was on, he'd argue it with alacrity. Callie didn't debate. She knew she was right, and she wasn't going to waste her time arguing the point.

He leaned on the rail beside her. "All I need is a chance to prove that I'm right. And you're going to help me do just that."

The sunglasses were shoved on top of her head as she looked at him with those pale, greeny-blue eyes. "You want *my* help to prove Atlantis exists, even though years of study in my field have proven to my satisfaction that it *doesn't*? Not to mention, you're a couple of hundred miles off—or according to some, several *thousand* miles off. *If* Atlantis was ever a real place, which, since you've read my work—it wasn't." She sounded skeptical as hell.

Jonah expected her response. Hell, he'd counted on it. Converts were the strongest advocates.

Her official stance was that Atlantis was an allegory. A combination of dozens of Mediterranean towns fictionalized into one utopian city. But if she helped him unearth it, prove that he'd found it, her word would hold a great deal of weight. It would make her name in the field of marine archaeology. Not to mention all of them a great deal of money, fame, and fortune.

He rubbed his chest, staring into the water as if he could see the pillars and walls, the streets and temples . . .

"Calculations and educated guesses are off," he said with utmost confidence. He knew, because *Stormchaser* lay at anchor right over it.

She turned to look at him. Her skin, dewy from the heat, looked flushed—from excitement? And crazy touchable. His fingers tightened around the rail to prevent himself from closing the small gap between them and brushing her flushed cheek with a fingertip. He caught a drift of her scent. The brine of the sea, and the mist of mountains, the creamy fragrance of tropical beaches—

Hyperaware of her, he shifted slightly. But the scent of her skin followed him. Jonah clenched his teeth, breathing through his mouth. *Married.* Yeah, right. He needed to send that information to his dick, which was responding independently, and without his permission, to the crazy, mixed-up lust-inducing smell of her hair. Her skin.

She licked her lower lip as her eyes met his. *Briefly,* before she looked just to the left of his face. She shook her head almost pityingly. "You're crazy wrong. Seriously, you've wasted your money. Concentrate on *Ji Li.* She's a known entity and her treasure will be rock-solid, not pie in the sky."

"The same people who said Atlantis wasn't real claimed Homer's Troy wasn't real, either, and yet—" He waved an expansive hand. The ancient city, featured in Homer's *Iliad*, had also been believed fiction. Then they'd discovered the city in 1865. "I'll show you what's sitting right below us, and you can see it for yourself."

The professor gave him a look, something between amused and skeptical, that made his hackles rise. Yeah, better to be annoyed with her than what he was really feeling. Pure, unadulterated lust, the kind that tightened his balls and made his hands itch to touch. Her face. Her hair. Her—

For God's sake. Get a fucking grip. The woman's married. Worse, she's under my protection.

Decency and self-control was going to become his mantra for the duration.

She gave a noncommittal shrug. "Go for it."

Now, *that* was a challenge if he'd ever heard one.

Callie knew the chances of Jonah Cutter unwittingly tripping over Atlantis were a gazillion to one, but God— despite her outward nonchalance, she was intrigued. Smart move of him to hire someone who'd already claimed no such place existed. A skeptic's word would bear even more weight than a true believer's.

Ancient cities were her thing, and discovering Atlantis in particular would make her name in the marine archaeology field. Hell. *Any* field. Publishing and name recognition were everything if an archaeologist wanted to keep funding coming in. Truth was, discovering a new ancient city, even if it wasn't Atlantis, still held the promise of fame and fortune.

And doing so would also make her assignment here easier to perform. A win–win–win. Atlantis? She didn't dare get her hopes up. The most sought-after of ancient cities held worldwide appeal, and for Jonah to discover it when nobody else had? Callie shook her head. "Doubtful," she muttered.

She walked a slippery slope. For Jonah to trust her, she had to appear trustworthy. The fact that she was going to betray him, hand over his findings to Rydell Case, gave her conscience a mild twinge, which she shoved out of sight. She'd heard about the Cutter brothers en masse for years, and had learned not to trust or like any of them from the first.

Is this why Rydell had encouraged her to take the job? Callie wasn't sure how he knew about what Jonah thought he'd found. Jonah said he hadn't even told his dive team. Ry wasn't clairvoyant, but he was obsessed with bringing the Cutter empire to its knees. Maybe he didn't care what it was Jonah was diving for. Just that he could take it from under the Cutters' noses.

Callie would do anything for her brother-in-law, short of murder. *Anything*. It hadn't taken a lot of persuading for her to agree to infiltrate a Cutter ship and report back on any findings. What Rydell was going to do with the information she didn't know, although she suspected he was going to turn the tables on the Cutters as they had done to him off the coast of South Africa last year. He'd keep them tied up in red tape and bankrupt them as they were trying to do to him.

Callie shivered in the hot sunshine. Ry was more than her brother-in-law, he was *family*, and, she knew, a formidable opponent. She'd hate to be the one in his crosshairs.

He knew her very well. He'd bet that the second she heard the Atlantis connection, she'd be hooked. As usual, he was right. Atlantis or not, whatever Jonah Cutter had found was something no one else had seen. *That* alone was enough to intoxicate her. Callie agreed to join the Cutter dive. The pay was stellar, she adored Greece, and the diving was always fabulous. What was there not to like? Other than risking exposure, and Jonah Cutter, of course. She'd known him all of an hour, while Ry had had years of business dealings gone sour because of the Cutters.

Time would tell. A tiger rarely changed its stripes.

Jonah leveraged himself off the rail. "Come on. I'll show you some of the images I have, just to give you a taste before we go down and you can see and touch for yourself."

She joined him at the table, dragging out a cushioned chair to sit in the shade of the huge, square umbrella that matched the fat light-gray cushions on the seats. She removed her sunnies from the top of her head, setting them on the glass-topped table, and gave him an expectant look. "I'm all ears." And apparently all hormones for some reason. Just looking at Jonah Cutter made her feel hot and jumpy all over. Nerves, of course.

Instead of sitting in one of the other chairs, Jonah picked up an iPad, then crouched beside her chair, resting his bare arm on her armrest. The fine hairs on her arm lifted in a static electric connection between them.

Unfazed, Jonah handed her the tablet. "Take a look."

Callie took the proffered tablet. Their fingers brushed. So brief, so slight, she was sure he didn't even notice, but the effect on her was profound. Everything inside her stilled for a moment until it passed, leaving in its wake a ripple of hyperaware disquiet. Such a reaction to a man, any man, was so out of character, so profound, she wanted to examine it and analyze it so she could dismiss the feelings scientifically.

He was so close she smelled the soap and salt on his skin, felt the heat of him through her T-shirt. Didn't the man own a shirt, for God's sake? He stretched out his hand to slide an image of *Stormchaser* aside, his arm grazing her breast. Damn it, he was so close she smelled coffee on his breath and saw the fine lines beside his incredible eyes. She quickly refocused on the screen.

Stormchaser, she thought, trying to get her concentration back and quickly.

The next image was underwater, fairly deep as indicated by the deep-blue wash over everything. She angled the screen away from the sunlight. "Rocks?" Now her heart skipped several beats for another reason. One she fully embraced and understood.

"Lava flow."

Narrowing her eyes, she scanned the image. What she was looking at *could* be pumice . . .

"It's well documented that there was considerable seismic activity in this region all the way back to the Minoan eruption in the mid-second millennium BCE. The catastrophic eruption reached all the way to Egypt, and even China, so this lava flow and what looks like pumice, here and here, are certainly possible."

Probable? Not really.

"Myths and legends were written about it." Callie paused. "I've done my research. Believe me, I want to believe in Atlantis, God only knows it would make my decade. But it doesn't exist."

"Okay. Stick to that until I prove to you that's what we have. Right here"—he pointed—"is a wall." He slid the next image across the screen. And brushed her breast again. Her nipples went hard. Oh, for God's sake! She had to get herself together. Focus, damn it.

A close-up. Not rocks. Square, rough-hewn. Symmetrical. Human-made. Callie's pulse raced as it always did when she discovered something few had seen in hundreds, if not thousands of years. Of course it wasn't Atlantis, but a new discovery of any kind fired her blood like nothing else.

Of course, she realized with relief. She wasn't hot for *him*, it was the possibility of the new discovery. The thrill of uncharted possibilities. And as Rydell often told her, "*Callie, I love you, but you take life* way *too seriously*." She tore her gaze away from the tempting picture for just a moment and stared at Jonah, realizing his eyes were a stunning clear blue that matched the water in the photograph.

She swallowed, her throat dry. "Where was this taken?"

He pointed at the deck beneath their feet. Or at the impressive bulge in his black shorts depending on one's point of view, Callie thought, as he rested his arm on his knee.

They were practically shoulder-to-shoulder, nose-to-nose. Too hot for two strangers to be sitting so close to each other. There were three other very comfortable freaking chairs. Why didn't he sit in one? "International waters?" she asked, shifting a little to break what appeared to be a seal between her bare arm and his.

"Oh, yeah."

She subtly used her shoulder to block Jonah from reaching out to slide the next image into view. Callie did it herself. With her ring finger. The dull glow shone like her personal body armor. She refocused on the screen. Another close-up of the blocks on the wall. She pinched the image, then spread her fingers wide to make it larger. Definitely a wall, and spilling over the edge of it was what looked like a hardened flow of volcanic rock.

The area was known for its volcanic action. There was a small island fairly close by that looked as if it had an extinct cone on it. Nothing to get excited about. Plato had written about a massive eruption followed by tidal waves. Both things known about and reported from ancient time.

Tons of small islands and atolls, volcanic rocky out-crops, and even a few calderas lay between Greece and Turkey. Any of the larger islands could potentially have had a small city or town swallowed by volcanic action and or tidal waves. But was what lay beneath her feet caused by the Minoan eruption of Thera? The idea that this could possibly *really* be Atlantis was mind boggling.

"These are satellite images taken six months ago."

Callie narrowed her eyes at the screen. What appeared to be grid-like lines resembling city streets, perhaps walls . . . certainly human-made. He slid through several more similar images.

Despite her skepticism, Callie's heart leapt. "Was someone taking bathymetric data at the time?" Bathymetric data was collected from boats using sonar to take measurements of the seafloor. "Because you know that these lines could reflect the path the boat took to gather the data?"

"No boat."

"You're sure?"

"Look at the rest. You tell me."

The next image wasn't from a satellite. This was a photograph under the water. A long shot. The wall was about three feet high and stretched into the dark water beyond the lights of the camera. Her heart leapt into her throat. "Do you have anything else?"

"Next image. What do you think?"

A pillar. An honest-to-God temple order. Simple—indicating ancient . . . no capital, but she'd search the ground below and see if it sat flat on the stylobate, with no base, indicating a Doric style. The fluting on the column didn't appear to match the sharp-edged requisite twenty-four grooves on a typical Doric column. But neither did the grooves have the slight flattened spacing between them of an Ionic column structure. It was neither. Because rather than being concave the grooves moved in an almost wave-like continuation around the column, dipping in and out. Something she'd never seen before.

"God . . ." Giddy with excitement, Callie slewed her eyes to his. "How big?"

"What you see here is forty feet high, ten feet in diameter. Almost intact. Once you see it for yourself you can let me know how tall the building was. There are more, half a dozen almost fully intact, many more broken, some missing."

"A temple," Callie said with reverence, almost forgetting that he was so close. An almost intact temple of undetermined era and origin. The diameter and length of the columns indicated an enormous structure.

"And this—?" He leaned against her to point to the tablet. "A mosaic floor . . . check out the colors."

Callie wasn't ready to leave the temple, but by the same token she was eager to see more. The camera light showed an intricate design of multicolored tesserae. The small pieces looked like glass, stones, perhaps clay or pottery pieces; she couldn't tell from the picture. God—she needed to be there to see all of this for herself.

She realized she had her hand over her chest as if her heart might explode with excitement. "This is incredible . . ."

He grinned, his eyes sparking with the same excitement singing through her veins. "There's more."

"I want to see all of them. About twenty times, then go down to see everything for myself—"

"Yeah, and you will. Plenty more pictures in the meantime," he told her, his voice filled with brimming excitement that was infectious. "But wait—there's *more*—"

"You have a Ginsu knife somewhere?"

His smile—damn it—was contagious. He got up from his crouch to lean across the table. He brought a shoe-box-sized metal box back to his position beside her.

"Maybe you'd be more comfortable in a chair?" Callie suggested tartly. Between Cutter's close proximity and the pictures—the evidence—she was seeing, her blood pressure and respiration were off the charts.

"Here's good," he said absently, crouching beside her chair again, and placing the box on the deck between his feet. The lid creaked like a rusty hinge when he opened the metal box. "Hold out both hands and close your eyes."

Callie quirked a brow as Rydell had taught her to do. "Seriously?"

"Close."

Callie obediently held out flattened palms, closing her eyes. With one sense turned off, she was more aware of the smell of Jonah's skin, of the scent of polish on the deck, of sea, and salt, and fresh air. Of *Jonah*. Damn, damn da—

"It's heavy," he warned. Something rough, and indeed heavy, was placed gently on her palms. Fortunately, Jonah had his hands beneath hers, because the weight almost made her drop it. Eyes still closed, Callie let her thumbs explore the object. "A rock? Thanks."

Rough, heavy. She hefted it. Twelve or fourteen pounds at least. Jonah's hands cradled hers. The sooner she got free of him, the better it would be for her equilibrium. "Can I look?"

"Go ahead." He sounded both excited and amused as he said, "What do you think it is?"

"A rock? A chunk of coral?" God. Could it be . . . ? "A piece of the *Ji Li*?" A small scratch in the surface where the outside crust of oxidation and surface accumulation had been removed revealed a metallic sheen that was too orange to be gold, but not yellow enough to be brass.

"*Orichalcum*," he said the word as if it tasted sweetly delicious.

No such thing. Orichalcum, a metal mentioned in ancient writings, was considered second only to gold in value, and said to be mined only in Atlantis. "Impossible." Her eyes rose to meet his six inches away. Callie felt like iron filings to his magnetism. "Plato was a romantic, and creative." Her face felt hot. Hell, her body felt hot. Jittery, as if she'd consumed too much coffee.

"No metal matching his description really exists," she continued, not recognizing her own voice, it was so thick and raspy. "And even if it did—anything found in Greek waters can be seen but not brought to the surface, so keeping whatever you've found is illegal as hell."

"It's not in Greek waters."

Of course Plato's Atlantis, if the mythical place existed, was in Greek waters. Damn, she now wished she hadn't dug her heels in about diving today. Giving her this tantalizing clue made it hard for her to remember common sense. And a deep immersion into cold water would help her sexually charged heat flash.

"I told you, we're anchored right over the city, and over who knows how much of this." He tightened his fingers around hers.

"Here. You'd better take it before I drop it." Callie maneuvered the rock into Jonah's broad hands, then sat back. "Does anyone else know about this?" She absently twisted her wedding ring again.

He shook his head. "Me. You."

Rydell Case? "The rest of the dive team?"

"Not yet."

"Your brothers?"

"No."

"Why not? A discovery of this magnitude will make Cutter Salvage's name go down in the history books." Whatever *this* was. No way could it be Atlantis. But whatever it was would still be an amazing and thrilling find.

"Dr. Calista West is one of the world's authorities on Atlantis. Should she be the one to discover the actual location of the Lost City, she could write her own ticket in the future. So—" His eyes, so blue they looked fake in the sunlight, met hers. "Yours, too."

"Mine, too. That looks very uncomfortable, why don't you sit over there?"

He gave her a wicked smile and rose lithely to his feet. Making her eye level with his—dear Lord, was this what it was going to be like working with this man for the next few weeks? Callie had never experienced anything like this insane, raging lust for a man in her life. She didn't like it one bit. Thank God, pretending to be married would keep them both in check. It had to. This much lusty thought was going to make her implode if it didn't abate pretty damn soon.

She waited as he poured ice and tea. "Thanks. Why haven't you told your brothers about this?"

He leaned a hip against the table right beside her. It was as though he were tethered to her by an invisible, very freaking *short*, cord. "Zane's wife, Teal, is pregnant with their first child and has hyperemesis gravidarum. They have enough on their plate to think about. Nick has a massive salvage on his hands, and Logan is dealing with a problem in Cape Town. Let's just say everyone has their hands and minds full. This is my baby, and I'm going to tie it up in a bow and present it to them as a fait accompli."

Callie knew well and good that the "problem" Logan Cutter was "dealing" with in South Africa was Rydell. "And you want to do—*what* if it really is the lost city of Atlantis?"

"That's the question, isn't it?"

Three

The dive team had had several weeks to get to know one another on the maiden voyage from Cutter Cay to the Mediterranean. Callie was the odd one out.

After he'd made his big announcement and shown her what he claimed to be orichalcum, they went downstairs together. She could contain herself until tomorrow, when rest and a clear head would ensure she saw what Jonah wanted to show her with a scientist's eye.

Jonah gathered the members of the dive team on the second deck to make introductions. He wasn't quite as conspicuous among them, most of whom were shirtless and in shorts. "Some of you met Dr. West when she arrived this morning."

The problem was, Jonah was . . . he was *more*. More good looking, more commanding. More sexy. More everything than anyone else. It was as though everyone else were in faded sepia, and Jonah in Technicolor. It was odd and, frankly, disconcerting as hell. She smiled at the group, seated around a large teak table, with comfortable rattan chairs. "Callie, please."

Jonah introduced the deeply tanned, athletic-looking blonde in her early thirties as Leslie Scott. The flirty Matthew McConaughey look-alike, Brody Turner, she'd met when she arrived, as well as Saul. A hugely tall, dark-haired guy named Vaughn Leader, who seemed the quietest of the bunch, gave her hand a shake with paws as big as hams. Callie wondered how he'd ever found scuba gear to fit.

A compact, dark-haired young woman, wearing the white shorts and golf shirt of the *Stormchaser* crew, came out on deck carrying a tray of sliced fruit and freshly baked chocolate chip cookies. "I've brought sustenance," she said cheerfully, indicating where she wanted the platters placed on the table.

Jonah smiled. "One of the most important members of the crew, this is our chef, Tina Hamilton. Anything you need as far as food and drinks go, she'll find for you. You'll meet our captain, Maura Sennett, and our first mate, Gayle, at dinner. Okay, now that the people are squared away, and everyone about to be fed and watered, let's recap for Dr. West so she's up to speed."

Jonah reached behind his chair, pulling out a wide, shallow drawer from the crisply painted white sideboard behind him. Callie enjoyed the play of muscle under his smooth bronzed skin as he moved. She realized she was staring and jerked her attention to his hands. But that didn't help the heat coursing through her body much.

She crossed her arms to hide the peaks of her nipples.

God, she was a mess. This hyperawareness was disconcerting and uncomfortable and, damn it, wrong six ways from Sunday. It felt as though her blood were hot as it pumped erratically through her veins. *This* was a complication she'd never dreamed of.

Please God, let her be over it by morning. Or sooner. Because attraction to the enemy was not only unprecedented—she wasn't prepared for it—but also the very last emotion she wanted to feel for a Cutter.

She didn't do well with out-of-whack emotions. Not *anyone's* and especially not her own. She tried to anticipate chaos and did everything in her power to master it. She'd corralled, as best she could, all the drama her parents had thrown at her. She'd learned their triggers; she'd figured out how to minimize the madness.

She'd never—not in a million years—considered herself a sexual being. Sex with Adam had been good. Sometimes really good. But . . . calm. Rational. Never in her life had she experienced this heightened awareness, *this* kind of visceral reaction to a man, when she thought of nothing else *but* sex.

Even the tantalizing prospect of discovering an ancient city wasn't enough to redirect her thoughts. Unprecedented on every level.

Oblivious to her chaotic thoughts and rampaging hormones, Jonah spread out a nautical chart. The location of the *Ji Li* wreck circled.

"X marks the spot." He grinned, then unrolled a hydrographic chart on top, weighing the corners down with four leather paperweights to deter the gentle breeze drifting beneath the awning.

The breeze played with his too-long hair. Damn it. She wished he'd at least pull on a shirt.

"And this is our girl." Everyone shifted in the seats to lean forward for a better look as he layered a sheaf of color photographs on top. "The *Ji Li* is a Chinese junk. She's pretty much intact." He slid out each photograph and pointed. God. He had gorgeous hands. Strong, long fingers, mouthwateringly masculine. Just looking at his tanned hands made Callie practically feel the skim of them learning her body. *Shut up!*

She poured herself a glass of lemonade and held the

pitcher aloft to see if anyone wanted some. Vaughan took it from her, poured a glass over ice, and passed it to Brody, leaving Callie to take a long draft of the tart, frosty drink. It quenched her thirst at least.

"The poopdeck is in one piece, just as it was in 1252. The long rudder is whole, too. She's resting on—" There was an infinitesimal pause. "—on a bed of lava and pumice. Other than her sails, it's as if she went straight down and is beautifully preserved, just waiting for us." He grinned, encompassing his team in his excitement.

What, Callie wondered, would their reaction be if they knew he'd been about to say, *resting on the Lost City of Atlantis*?

"Except for a massive hole in her hull," Saul said drily, grabbing five cookies as if they'd disappear in seconds. "We have no record of survivors. From a written account of someone on the island over there"—he pointed to a small smudge off to the north.

Jonah picked up the answer. "The volcano erupted, spewing lava and ash. Everyone aboard must've been asphyxiated by the ash. The hole is probably from a projectile from the volcano."

"*What* volcano? The closest active, or even *in*active, volcano is thousands of miles away. Are you talking about a submarine vent?" Callie asked Saul, her gaze skimming briefly over Jonah sitting between them. His dark hair was tousled as if he'd just slunk out of some woman's bed.

"There's a small extinct volcano on the island here." He leaned back, taking the filled glass Leslie handed him. He took a drink, his strong throat working as he swallowed. Callie's temperature spiked. "We believe it last erupted seven hundred years ago, sinking our junk."

Sinking his junk sounded obscenely suggestive to

Callie, who'd never had an erotic thought before meeting Cutter. She picked up her glass and rubbed the condensation across her forehead.

It was pretty handy that the wreck and the underwater city were in international waters. The Cutters were a sneaky bunch, and Callie had no doubt that Jonah hadn't shared his information with any of the authorities who should be informed. They could dive out here, in the middle of nowhere, for months, without anyone being the wiser.

"Who was she registered to?" she asked, adjusting her depth of field so he was a blur.

"China, but sold to Greece, so provenance is in dispute," Jonah shrugged his broad shoulders. There was nothing soft or vulnerable about this man. He exuded strength and a raw masculinity that should've infuriated her, but instead turned her on. Even blurry.

"The purchase paperwork is being thoroughly researched. We'll take our cut and Greece and China can fight over ownership long after we're gone."

Color her surprised. "You've filed paperwork?"

"China, Greece, and Turkey, hell, even Spain is making noises," he informed her. "Everyone wants a chunk of whatever we find."

"You don't seem particularly concerned by it."

He shrugged again. "That's what lawyers are for. We'll do a fantastic job, retrieve and preserve, and enjoy the hell out of the experience."

He wasn't being blasé or altruistic. *Ji Li* wasn't his focus. The city was.

"To a fun and lucrative salvage!" Leslie toasted.

"Hear hear." Everyone clinked glasses. Their excitement and enthusiasm expected at the start of a salvage.

Callie pulled one of the large photographs toward her

on the table. "She's resting on what looks like a magma flow, but the rock formations here can be deceptive." She frowned. "One volcanic eruption below her, and another brought her down? Doesn't seem—" She looked around the table. "So she was unfortunate enough to be caught in a volcanic eruption, and just coincidentally also happened to sink on top of another? Call me skeptical, but that kind of coincidence is highly unlikely. All we have are vague references to an eruption, *possibly* at the time she sank." She took another sip of her drink, then put her glass on the table. "Nothing before. Not localized here."

The divers just stared at her as if she'd spoken in tongues.

"I know a volcanologist," Callie said into the silence, her tone conciliatory. "I'll check with him, see what the likelihood of that was." If Jonah was right, the volcanic rock and pumice *beneath* the Chinese junk correlated to the Thera eruption that was purported to have felled Atlantis.

"Chinese records describe an eruption in the late seventeenth century BCE, and document the collapse of the Xia dynasty there due to a 'dim sun, then three suns, frost in July and famine'—indicating volcanic action. But that was *thousands* of miles away from where we are currently anchored." Callie glanced—*briefly*—at Jonah. "Are you planning to move us?" Was he playing some kind of elaborate shell game to distract anyone from stealing his thunder?

Callie wondered if the *Ji Li* crossed the known world, not to deliver silks and spices, but to search for Atlantis? The possibility was intriguing.

"No. We're staying put," Jonah assured her, his impossibly blue eyes glittering with the secret knowledge they

shared. Callie damn well didn't *want* to be in on the
secret.

"What does your husband think of you being away for
months on end?" the athletic blonde asked with more-
than-casual interest. *Leslie*. Actually glad for the non sequitur, Callie automatically twisted the plain gold band
on her finger and shrugged, aware of Cutter's intense blue
eyes watching her from across the table.

"He knows I love what I do, and appreciates me when
I come home." Adam *had* loved her, and whatever ful-
filled her and made her happy had made him happy. He'd
have totally understood why she continued wearing her
wedding ring four years after his death. And why she was
doing this for his brother. Rydell had been more like a
father to Adam, even though the brothers were only three
years apart in age. Like Callie, Rydell had been the one in
charge of his family. He'd taken her under his wing, too.

"How long have you been married, then?" Leslie asked.

They'd been married for six years. Adam had died four
years ago. "Our tenth anniversary is in a couple of weeks."

"Any kids?"

God, the woman was like a dog with a bone. "No, not
yet." Not ever. Plenty enough bonding for Callie. "That
reminds me, I need to call him to let him know I arrived
safely." Shoving her chair back, she got to her feet. "Excuse me."

Not running, but walking at a fast clip, Callie climbed
several ladders and stairs to get to the top deck where she
and Jonah had been earlier. A quick glance showed that
no one was around to overhear her. She punched Ry's
number on speed dial.

"Are you on board?"

"Just got here." She hesitated. "Are you okay? You
sound . . . strained."

"Just a shitty connection. I'm good, honey." She didn't expect Ry to say anything else. He took stoic to a whole other level. "Are you going to be all right to do this?"

"I told you I would," she assured him. "I don't know how you figured it out, Ry," she said when he didn't respond. "But you were right to send me. Jonah Cutter claims he's found the Lost City of Atlantis. If it's true, I'll tie it up in a bow and deliver it to you on a silver platter."

Otherworldly.

Spellbound, Jonah observed the sinuous descent of Dr. West as she floated down from the shimmering surface a hundred feet overhead in their first, early-morning dive. Lithe grace, smooth powerful strokes, lean silhouette of a mermaid. Sunlight shimmered through the dappled ceiling of their silent blue world, illuminating long tendrils of dark hair drifting over her head and wrapping around her body like seaweed—okay, the floating hair was a figment of his imagination.

The good doctor had all that shiny dark hair tucked away and pinned, he was sure, within an inch of every strand's life. Still . . . a man could fantasize, couldn't he?

She was covered from head to toe in skintight black neoprene. Fins, not a fishtail, but watching the glide of her body through the water conjured up some pretty racy thoughts. She paused above him, then slowly floated down to the rocky seabed about fifty feet from his position.

Aw, hell, everything about her challenged and aroused him, which wasn't good. He reminded himself that she was skeptical, uncooperative, and cold.

And, go figure, he wanted her anyway.

Sand puffed around the tips of her fins to hang in the clear water as regulator bubbles climbed toward the surface. Not so much as a wave in greeting. Her people skills could do with a little work. But with the way she moved in the water? He'd bet she warmed up just fine.

Jonah couldn't quite get a bead on her. Not much of a sense of humor, but he'd seen suspicious glimpses of drollness, so maybe it took her a while to relax around new people. She seemed a little too buttoned-up to blend well with his rowdy dive team, which was something of a disappointment. Spending long days together was easier if the team meshed. Time would tell. He pointed to the ocean floor with a thumbs-up.

Visibility was incredible but would be shot once they started running the blower. For now Jonah enjoyed the crystalline view. Did the doctor appreciate the scenery? Or was she going to remain all-business?

Ji Li, a worn stone path, mostly hidden beneath sediment and rock, and the bonus of the mermaid. Yeah. A good day to be diving. An even better day to be sitting on top of the discovery of the millennium.

Yesterday, after Calista left the meeting to call her husband and then retire to her cabin for the night—at two in the afternoon!—due to jet lag, Jonah listened to the crew's opinion of her. Excited to have someone of Dr. West's credibility, and willing to put her lack of personality down to sleep deprivation, was the vote.

While they talked he'd had his drafting table and other crap moved back to the larger owner's cabin, and her one bag moved into the smaller cabin. Problem was, he'd slept in that double bed the night before, and when he climbed into his king-sized bed, all he could do was imagine Dr. West sprawled in the same bed—

Crazy.

Married.

Verboten.

Yeah. He got it. Too bad his body wasn't getting the memo.

Maybe it was precisely because she was out of bounds that he found Calista West so damn appealing. Still, it was like being attracted to a prickly sea urchin. Pretty to look at, but a lot of pain if touched.

Since his attraction to Dr. West was a non-issue, Jonah put it aside. He reminded himself that it was good to want things one couldn't have. It built character. He suspected his character was going to be muscle-bound and ready for the Ironman Triathlon by the end of this salvage. He grinned behind his full face mask. If the worst thing that happened on this trip was being attracted to an unattainable woman, he was golden. Turning her back on him, she swam over to the others—again, without a wave or any sort of communication. Should he join them? He loved scuba diving. Diving, hunting for ancient treasure: It was in his blood. His father had taught him when Jonah was almost too young to walk. His heart did its usual ping of pain when he thought about the dichotomy of how his father had been with *him*, and how that same father had been with his three legitimate children. Night and fucking day.

Not his fault. Still—Jonah found himself constantly trying to make up for his father's lack of—*everything*—with his half brothers Zane, Nick, and Logan. It was as though their father bad been two completely different men. A loving, hands-on family man with Jonah and his mother, a drunken dickhead, cheating son of a bitch with his legal wife and sons. And never the twain should meet. His marriage to Jonah's mother was, of course, invalid. But they hadn't given a shit. Well, his mom probably gave a big shit, but she'd never said anything after she'd discovered that he had another family halfway around the world.

Jonah's and Nick's birthdays were only a few day apart. Same month, same year. Good old Dad had been a busy man.

Not here, not now, Jonah reminded himself. Atlantis was going to be his Holy Grail offering to his brothers. His payment for the shit they'd endured while he reaped the benefits of their father for all those years.

Callie did a graceful flip and joined Vaughn and Saul near the wreck where they were reconnoitering for the first time. A look-see before work began.

Ji Li was some four hundred long and sixty feet wide. She lay on her starboard side half on, half off a ridge of rough lava rock, coral, and pumice, and about a hundred feet away from where Jonah had been taking pictures of an amazing floor, inlaid with something shiny, that looked like gold.

The doctor broke away from the others to swim around the square bow, then drifted up to circle the poopdeck, using her hands as well as her eyes to explore, the way he did. Some things were just meant to be touched.

The azure water was top-lit with barely penetrating rays as Jonah breathed easily through his regulator, admiring the scenery. It had taken months and months of paperwork, permissions, legal crap, and putting this team together—but he'd been patient and methodical. It was all about to pay off.

Dr. West had been the last piece of the puzzle. A piece, unfortunately, that he didn't feel quite fit the rest of his carefully vetted group. She'd alluded to not being a team player, and while he was all for being innovative and daring, he was now a little skeptical that his marine archaeologist was the right woman for the job. What if her cynicism wouldn't allow her to see what he saw? What if she wasn't willing to go the extra mile and suspend her disbelief?

His chest tightened. It was too late to find someone else with her excellent qualifications. Hell, her *exact* qualifications. He wanted *her*.

Wanted? Hell no, *needed* her.

Dr. Calista West's stamp of approval on this salvage was paramount.

After all her papers insisting that Atlantis didn't exist, her report on the finding was going to be what kept the world's attention riveted on this find as no fly-by-night rumor but the genuine article. If he was right, and he'd bet everything he had that he was, they'd need more investors. Dr. West's word would bring that weight to bare.

He envisioned their salvage and observations taking *years*. How was a woman going to be separated from her husband for that long? Hadn't she said something about children? He couldn't remember. He'd been too sucked into looking at how his team interacted with her to listen to every word.

He started swimming to join the others.

He was being ridiculous.

He didn't have to like her; the dive team and crew didn't have to like her. Sure, it made life easier, but they could all be professional. He'd be happy as a pig in shit if she did her job. Period. The rest was immaterial.

For a moment he suspended his qualms about her and gave into the fantasy. He was intrigued by his strong physical response to her, because she wasn't particularly beautiful or out of the ordinary. Attractive, yes. But so were hundreds of other women he'd met in his travels.

He enjoyed the rush of adrenaline he felt when she was nearby. He enjoyed the hell out of the smell of her, something both ocean and mountain. Fresh. He liked looking at her. He liked all that. Attraction without a payoff in sight was something new, and rather intriguing, for Jonah.

Bringing the underwater camera up to his mask, he clicked off a dozen shots of her, his artistic eye framing her against *Ji Li*.

Maybe not a traditional beauty, but damn, she had an engaging face. He adjusted the focus on the camera for a close-up. She turned her head, saw what he was doing, and scowled directly into the camera. Jonah grinned, turned on by her clear annoyance.

Suddenly a sharp, bone-shattering buzz sounded, sending an electrical current jolting through his entire body. It sounded, weirdly, like giant pistons, getting louder and louder and more intense, as if a train were speeding overhead.

"What the fuck?" He had no idea where the sound was coming from, just that there was stunning high-volume noise and pressure as if someone were taking a plunger to each ear and pushing in and out.

Sand swirled up from the seafloor. A school of small silver fish flashed by, the sand and fleeing fish obscuring his divers for a moment.

The startling physical reaction to Dr. West was followed immediately by a loud, tooth-jarring noise that seemed to come at him in surround sound. The far-too-close, extremely *loud* noise of a large engine rattled his bones. Jerking his gaze away from his high-priced marine archaeologist, he looked up to see if *Stormchaser* was in trouble. Or about to come plummeting down to join the *Ji Li* on the rocks, since he was pretty sure there wasn't a train anywhere about.

He'd been so busy fantasizing about wrapping that long

hair around his . . . Shit. Had he screwed up and inadvertently floated directly up under the giant propellers?

Nope. He was still levitating a few feet above the sand. He bit back a half laugh. Honest to God, for a nanosecond there he'd thought his attraction to her had caused the sensation.

Idiot.

He cast an all-encompassing look through the blue world at his team, all of whom floated nearby. They were looking around nervously as well, so clearly they heard and felt whatever it was. *They* weren't reacting to their new team member.

"Earthquake," Dr. West said calmly into the lip mike inside her dive mask and therefore directly into Jonah's ear. The comm crackled with interference. "Surface *now*."

Her husky voice sent a different kind of vibration through Jonah, but he didn't like it any more than the one a few seconds before. "It's over," he pointed out as his observation and the cessation of the bone-buzz and the hellishly loud noise vanished, to be replaced by the rhythmic-Darth Vader saw of his own breathing.

"And there could be another, stronger quake any moment," she said unequivocally, heading to the surface. This close up and personal, her voice sounded far too sexy and way too intimate.

He had a strong aversion to being told what to do, and when. But he wasn't going to argue with an expert, especially if it meant putting his people at risk.

"Better safe than sorry," he told the others, indicating they follow suit. His philosophy was pretty much the opposite of better safe than sorry, but he couldn't go off half-cocked when the lives of his people depended on him making sound choices.

As he and the rest of the team drifted to the surface,

he tried not to let her voice conjure images of rumpled sheets and tangled sweaty limbs. If ever a woman was out of bounds, off limits, *prohibido*, it was this one.

Privately lust after? Sure. But too important to mess with.

The four of them pulled themselves up onto the dive platform, legs dangling in the water as they removed their masks and tanks.

"That was kind of freaky." Vaughn Leader shoved his mask off his face and slicked back his long hair with one hand.

Saul undid his tank and stared out over the water, his limbs jumpy with fading adrenaline. "That was freaking cool—I've never been underwater during a quake before."

Neither had Jonah. "It wasn't that powerful," he pointed out, standing to strip off his wet suit. He dumped it in the freshwater tank before hanging it up on the rack. It was barely eight in the morning, and the sun felt good on his skin.

"Anyone on board feel the quake?" He hadn't factored in earthquakes, never even crossed his mind, but now that there'd been one he had to consider if this was going to impede his quest in any way.

Brody and Leslie, waiting their turn to dive on the lower deck, shook their heads, then glanced in unison not at *him* but at the archaeologist. "Stay put or go back in?"

Jonah told himself not to knee-jerk a response to them looking to someone else for direction. They were all working together for the first time. He had to keep his propensity to jump headfirst into things to a minimum until he'd felt his way with the team.

Sunlight gilded Callie's lightly tanned skin and highlighted the curve of her cheek. He looked away. Over the calm water. Not a sign of the quake up on the surface, but there had been plenty of action down below. And he wasn't just thinking of the earthquake.

"Doctor?" Leslie repeated.

Swiveling his head to see what the good doctor had to say, Jonah was grateful he still held his suit, about to hang it up. Sitting on the edge of the platform Callie was in the process of picking apart the wet strands of her braid and using her fingers to untangle her hair. Waist-length hair. There went his fantasies. Holy shit, that *hair*—wet and slick as melted dark chocolate—clung to her body all the way to her shapely ass and pooled on the deck. The woman had weapons that were going to make his sleep fitful to say the least.

Pulling her hair over her shoulder, she wrung out the water. "I'd give it an hour or two, just to be on the safe side. That might've been a precursor to a bigger one." He wanted to bite her soft, pale mouth, with its cushiony bottom lip.

"Or a mild tremor and the end of them," Jonah countered, rubbing his chest, feeling . . . antsy for no good reason. Yeah. There was a reason. He never lied to himself. He was annoyed with himself for being so drawn to her. Not to mention he hadn't given a second's thought to her being so strongly resistant to his Atlantis project.

For some dumb-ass reason he'd expected her to fall all over the news and be thrilled. Instead she was dismissive and argumentative, which raised his hackles. Fucking annoying as hell to have his bright new balloon pricked before he could even tie a string on it.

She shrugged, her delectable mouth unsmiling. "Or that. But why push it if there's no hurry? There isn't a hurry, is there?"

"Time's money out here." Ridiculous thing to say, and everyone turned to him with various degrees of surprise on their faces. *Great.* He'd known her barely a day and she'd reduced him to behaving like a horny adolescent. Not her fault. *His.*

"Sorry. You're right of course."

She'd worked on salvages before. She knew there were investors, sponsors, and assorted other people waiting for their investment to pay off, or for their museum or other institution to get some of the spoils found.

Jonah knew he had to get a grip, but he seemed to be caught in some weird sensual spell that wouldn't let go.

"No—safety first. Since we're waiting out another quake, let's have a quick meeting. I have something important to share."

He'd planned on telling the others about Atlantis the night before, but he'd wanted the doctor to be there when he told them. Once again she'd been the missing component.

They were all together now. "Ten minutes. Deck two."

Four

"We're fortunate the submarine quake was small," Jonah was saying as Callie slid the door to the salon shut behind her. She couldn't ignore the team, and decided to join them for the briefing on the second deck, where they'd gathered around the long table.

Everyone acknowledged her in their own way. Leslie waved and smiled. Brody leered, Saul grinned, and Vaughn nodded. Jonah continued talking as she pulled out the only empty chair—beside *him*—and sat down.

The smell of Jonah—salt, male, soap—mixed with her coconut sunblock made a heady combination that rushed to her brain as if she'd guzzled wine on an empty stomach. Acutely aware of him sitting mere inches from her, their arms just inches apart, she shifted in her seat to put another inch between them, then in desperation swirled her wedding ring around her finger as a reminder.

She'd gone to her cabin to pick up her camera and make a few calls. Now she felt as though she'd walked on stage in the middle of a play as everyone stopped the scene to stare at her.

Gathered around the teak table under shade, they all wore sunglasses. The sun beat down on the white paint-work and reflected off the glassy water surrounding them, making dark glasses a necessity. Fine with her. The less Cutter read in her expression, the better.

"Didn't feel small while it was happening," Vaughn told those who hadn't experienced it. He leaned back, rocking his chair on the back two legs. Like the other men, he was bare-chested and very tan. He was a big guy and took up a lot of real estate, yet Jonah's presence was more powerful, and impossible to ignore. Callie gave it her best shot.

"The fucking noise was hellacious," Vaughn continued as he rocked, a deep frown evident above his dark glasses. "Was it only me, or did everyone have a crackle problem with your comms? Mine had major interference."

"Mine, too."

"Thanos is taking a look at them now," Jonah told him. "Always something with new equipment. Don't worry, he'll get the bugs out before we go down again."

Thanos was the engineer who'd brought her to the ship.

"My life flashed before my eyes," Vaughn continued, clearly enjoying his drama-filled moment. "I thought we'd be buried under *Ji Li* for all eternity." His delivery was a bit dramatic, but he got the point across.

Callie motioned for Saul to hand her the jug of ice-filled whatever-it-was as she tried to appear engaged. Conversation about the quake eddied around her.

Sometimes detaching was appropriate—like when her mother tried to set herself on fire, or the time her father had jumped out of her moving car on the freeway as she hauled his ass back to rehab for the eleventh time.

Oh, yeah, good times.

But here, and now. She had to be in the present. Had to bring her A game. Had to figure out if Cutter was telling the truth, or only the truth as he knew it.

Focus. Be here.

". . . thought we were under the propeller, about to be chopped into sushi," Saul said half seriously.

". . . same thing," Jonah told them. "Thought *Stormchaser* was about to descend on top of us. Fortunately, there was no harm done."

"Other than scaring the crap out of all of you." Brody stretched his arms out, resting them on the back of Leslie and Saul's chairs. "I wish I'd been there to experience it. New experiences are always good, right?"

No. New experiences are not always good. Callie lifted the heavy, frosty glass jug. Her arm dipped, and she brought her free hand up underneath to support it. Jonah reached out without a word, taking it from her, filling her glass as if he did it every day. His arm brushed hers, setting off white-hot, jagged electrical sparks that she was afraid everyone present could see despite the glare. All her girl parts, dormant for seven years, jolted to life, and she jerked her hands away, almost upending the jug from Jonah's hands.

Seeing her own mulish expression reflected in his glasses, Callie evened out her scowl. "I'm quite capable of pouring my own drink—"

His lips—firm, sensual, tempting—quirked. Not a smile. It really wasn't. "Thanks, Jonah," he prompted, his soft husky voice dripping over her already overreacting hormones like gasoline over an open flame. When he was around she constantly felt like a cat with its fur being rubbed in the wrong direction. Her physical reaction to this man puzzled as much as it annoyed her. Jonah Cutter—*all* damn Cutters—were the enemy. And if that wasn't sufficient reason to get her libido in check, she wasn't in the market for a fling. And that's all it would ever be with a Cutter.

She'd never experienced anything even remotely like

this and prayed the jittery overstimulated feeling would pass after she'd been around him a few days. Please God . . .

After leaving a message for Ry, and another for Peri, her best friend and sister-in-law, she'd hurriedly rinsed the salt off her skin and hair, and donned khaki shorts and a short-sleeved, apple-green T-shirt. Since the men were practically naked, and Leslie wore a racer-style black one-piece suit and a tan, Callie felt slightly overdressed for the occasion.

Inclined to be a loner, she'd learned to interact with groups. But her serious demeanor and lack of conversational skills—not that she couldn't chat up a storm, she just chose not to—made her appear antisocial.

She wasn't antisocial . . . exactly. She just preferred her own company, and she wasn't gregarious, which made her frequently feel invisible. Not great in social settings, but frequently a very good thing. She'd learned how to be the peacemaker, the rational one, projecting calm and rationality while her parents did the crazy shit. She'd been the island of calm in their turbulent ocean.

She felt the weight of Jonah's gaze on her face. He murmured, "You're looking more serious than usual, Doctor."

"Talk about the pot calling the kettle black," Callie snapped before she thought it through. Like Vaughn, she was being overly dramatic because her heart thumped uncomfortably, and she felt as though Jonah's X-ray eyes could see her inner workings. She modulated her tone. "You take *inscrutable* to a whole new level."

Leslie laughed. "You just described yourself. When's your birthday, Callie?"

Callie frowned at the non sequitur, but was only too happy to swivel her attention to the other end of the table. "August twenty-ninth, why?"

The other woman grinned, flashing very white teeth. "A Virgo, interesting. Jonah's a Scorpio."

Callie had no idea how to respond to that. Great? Wow? Who knew? Who cared? "Quakes on the ocean floor can cause tsunamis." Leslie clearly didn't require a response to her observation. Callie took a sip of her drink, mulled over the taste. Not lemonade, but something fruity and not too sweet. She didn't feel as though she was being too cautious warning them not to go back into the water, despite what she'd just learned.

"That might well be, but there wasn't even a ripple on the surface," Jonah pointed out as he got up, restoring her ability to drag oxygen into her starving lungs.

Stretching out, he snagged a creased, faded-blue T-shirt from the other end of the credenza and yanked it over his head, tugging it down over black board shorts. His damp hair clung to his throat and cheek, and he absently combed the dark strands back off his face with his fingers as he talked. Tanned and fit, he was so damn, annoyingly sexy, Callie wanted to push him overboard.

He rested his butt on the glossy white cabinet, stretching out long runner's legs. The filtered sunlight tipped the hair on his legs with gold. He looked like some pagan sun god surveying his kingdom as he leaned back on his arms. Entitled, arrogant *jerk*. Her thighs, fortunately hidden under the table, clenched.

Oblivious to her idiocy, Jonah said, "Sennett's looking into it now."

The *captain*? Callie bit back a sigh of exasperation, dragging her gaze away from his physique, and only too freaking grateful that he'd released her from whatever it was his pheromones were doing to her pheromones.

She was the marine archaeologist onboard, and had the contacts necessary to find out exactly what had occurred earlier. Why couldn't he at least pay her the courtesy of asking her professional opinion? The man was as bullheaded as . . . Rydell Case. The fact that she mentally compared the two surprised her.

"I spoke to a colleague at the European-Mediterranean Seismological Center," Callie told them, not attempting to make her tone anything less formal and stick-up-herbutt sounding. It was too hard to be personable while her hormones were all over the freaking place. As a *group*, not speaking directly to Jonah. Just *looking* at the man annoyed her. Damn it. She annoyed herself.

"Dr. Fotopoulos is a seismologist of some repute. He assured me there was *no* seismic activity—not even a small reading—in this area. The closest activity was forty-three minutes *earlier*, a one point three in the Kermadec Islands near New Zealand."

God, she sounded as stiff and unanimated as so many of her colleagues. "Clearly the time and strength of what we felt was not a direct correlation. Whatever we felt had no reading." *Almost as bad.*

"Oh, yeah?" Brody muttered, ignoring the fruity drink as he reached over to grab a beer out of a nearby cooler. "Maybe we should invite your friend down there to experience the non-event with us the next time." He popped the tab and drank.

"He's looking into it and will contact m—us as soon as he knows anything." Dr. Apollo Fotopoulos was a man in his mid-seventies, an expert in his field and someone Callie trusted. If he told her there'd been no activity, there'd been no activity. And yet, unlike Brody, she'd experienced all the signs of a seismic shift first hand.

"Clearly it sure as shit was *something*," Jonah said. "We *all* felt it. Unless you think we all suffered from mass hysteria? No? Well then, it was a quake. A small one to be sure, but a quake. Your friend will call you back to confirm. Since we were on hand to experience this non-event." His voice was dry as he pushed off his perch to stand.

"I have something to share with all of you. I wanted to wait until Dr. West was with us to give you the news. We spoke briefly yesterday because I wanted her expertise on the findings to ensure I wasn't just imagining what I saw in the prelim photos."

Leslie leaned forward, her arms crossed on the table. More, Callie suspected, to get Brody's hand off her shoulder than because she was fascinated by Jonah's words. "Photos of what?"

Jonah held up a hand. His grin was open and so appealing Callie started to lean in like the other woman. She pressed her spine into the seatback. "I'm getting there," Jonah teased.

"Get there already!" Vaughn shot back with a laugh.

"We're floating over *Atocha Two*?" Leslie offered with a wide grin.

The *Nuestra Señora de Atocha* wreck, found thirty-five miles off the Florida Keys in 1985, was the Holy Grail of sunken treasure. The salvage continued to this day. An estimated $450 million cache had been recovered, and there was still more beneath the sea. If they were salvaging such a wreck, the team's cut would be in the multi-millions of dollars.

"From your mouth to God's ear!" Saul told his fellow diver fervently. "I'd be more than happy to stick around here for thirty-plus years if *that's* the case." He turned to Jonah and raised an inquiring brow.

"Good," Jonah said cheerfully. "Because I think we'll have Mel Fisher beat." He pulled open a drawer beside his hip. Taking out the maps and photographs he'd shown her the day before, he spread everything out in the middle of the long table "Ladies and gentleman, I give you Atlantis."

"You aren't serious—" Leslie looked from Jonah to Callie and back again. "Atlantis isn't *real*, is it?"

"That's a matter for some debate." He looked so damn pleased with himself, so brimming with barely suppressed excitement, that Callie was starting to feel like Scrooge at a Christmas party. "But yeah. I've been down several times. Took these—" He fanned out a sheaf of glossy prints. "Whatever is down there, it's real. Look—this is part of a wall, here, a dozen pillars, mosaic floors, and that's not even scratching the surface. I've already started mapping the area. It's huge. I haven't found an outside perimeter yet. But I'm confident that we'll uncover the whole city."

Callie's lips compressed. So far they weren't asking her. And while she *was* the expert, this wasn't her salvage. Jonah could tell his people anything he liked. All she had to do was sit back and wait to make her point.

She tamped down the little—the teeny-*tiny* spark of hope. She was too practical to dream. And finding the Lost City was a dream way too big, and so far out of the realm of possibility they may as well be discussing Area 51 and the discovery of an alien spacecraft.

Saul leaned his hands on the table. "What about *Ji Li*? If we work on Atlantis, what happens to our *wreck*? And frankly, not to be a dick about it, Jonah, but on the ship there's a pretty much guaranteed treasure on board. An ancient city—whether it's Atlantis or not—isn't going to make us any money. Or if it does, not for a hellishly long time."

"True," Jonah admitted. "But we have funding for several years. And the possibility of being kept afloat for many more after that. We're still going to salvage *Ji Li*.

It'll be slower going, time-wise, but we'll work in alternating teams. One on the Atlantis project, the other on *Ji Li*, then switch off, so everyone gets a shot. Spoils, and names in scientific journals—" His grin was wide, white, and boyish. "Shared and divided equally. It's a win–win, and an incredible opportunity to make history."

"How much do you think Atlantis is worth?" Brody asked, eyes glinting.

Everyone worked on a percentage of the salvage. Finding a city without a cache of gold, silver, or gems might net them zero dollars. "Financially, nothing unless we discover gems or precious metals," Jonah admitted. "Perhaps nothing in monetary value, but the historical impact will be off the charts."

"They spent millions before finding the *Titanic*," Saul pointed out. "Do we *have* that kind of long-term backing?"

The Cutters had investors, of course, as did Rydell. They also had incredibly deep pockets of their own, although Ry had assured her that the Cutters didn't appear to use their own money on iffy salvages.

Jonah nodded. "Anyone who doesn't want to be in on the exploration of the city is welcome to stick to *Ji Li*. But know that, as I said, everything will be divided as per your contracts. Every find split."

Leslie resumed her seat, giving Jonah a wide smile. "Then I'm in for the duration. Whatever's down there is worth our best effort."

Vaughn shrugged his massive shoulders after a few moments of internal debate. "Guess I'm in for the long haul, too."

The group as a whole fell for Jonah's story, and his "proof," like starving dogs at a picnic. Chatter and raised voices ran wild as the divers handed off photos to one another and speculated as to what each image showed. Was this really a wall? Part of a palace? Was that a street, or just a rock formation?

Callie picked up her glass, leaning back in her chair, out of the way of everyone who'd now risen from their seats to lean over the table.

She'd spent her life in the middle of whirlwinds and knew how to make herself the calm in the storm. From somewhere outside her body she observed each team member's reaction to the news. Avarice was the number one response when they heard "*Atlantis*." She could see it in the gleam in their eyes.

Not the incredible historical discovery. Not the idea that if this were true, what else in the oral archives of Greek history might also be plausible. What did it matter? She'd only be here long enough to do what Ry wanted her to do. Ascertain if Jonah's finds were correct.

Once Rydell was done with the Cutters, Atlantis—or whatever it was down there—would be tied up in the courts unable to be touched for years and years and freaking *years*! A fitting revenge for what they'd done to him.

But damn it, Callie thought, shoulders and neck stiff with tension. What Rydell planned for the Cutters was one thing, but she bet Ry hadn't thought through what he was doing to keep the *world* at bay from a discovery of this magnitude. Nor, a small voice pointed out in her head, had he considered depriving his sister-in-law of the benefits of something she'd spent a lifetime researching and debunking.

For just a moment she considered what the ramifications would be if this whole pie in the sky *were* true. Either she'd be a laughingstock because she'd staked her professional career on debunking the legend. Or she'd become world-renowned for being instrumental in discovering the Lost City. On the one hand, being ostracized from the community she loved. On the other, being feted, with her name in history books. Both with the same unpleasant end result of putting her too far in the spotlight.

As much as she wanted—no, fiercely *yearned*—to be part of the excitement, she was a pragmatist. It hurt to want unattainable things. It was better not to want *anything* that badly. It never ended well. Not to mention, she just had to be here long enough to tell Rydell what he needed to know. Then she'd be gone.

Chest heavy, Callie's eyes stung. She shook it off. "I hate to burst bubbles here, but Plato wrote about Atlantis three thousand years ago." Her words dropped into the heated voices like a cool, smooth stone. Someone had to be rational and practical. Usually her. All eyes turned her way, and the giddy chatter ceased.

"And according to him, Atlantis thrived *nine thousand* years before that, so we're talking a city that would be *twelve thousand* years old. His is the *only* historical source of information. There's absolutely no collaborating writings—"

"That they've *found*. Doesn't mean they don't exist, right?" Saul pointed out.

Here we go. "There have been dozens of locations proposed for Atlantis. I worked with my colleagues on documenting a sunken city off the coast of Italy two years ago." One she'd secretly believed would refute her research and prove to actually *be* Atlantis. Of course her hopes had been dashed when they'd found Roman writing.

"Finding Scylletium was a *major* archaeological discovery, but it's turned out to be a Roman colony from around 124 BCE, *not* Atlantis. In fact it would be hard *not* to trip over ancient sunken cities and towns up and down the Mediterranean. Greek, Roman, plus any number of other diverse cultures that thrived throughout history in this area.

"So is there an ancient city down there? Probably. Is it Atlantis? I strongly doubt it. According to Plato it's supposed to be in the Atlantic Ocean. And dare I point out— even if it *were* somewhere off the coast of *Spain* or *Greece*, or the Bimini Islands, none of the possible sites are in this area, not even close. Plato said it's at the Pillars of Hercules. That's the Strait of Gibraltar—that's seventeen hundred miles away. There's not a single shred of evidence. No collaborated site photographs, no aerial images, not even a Google Earth shot. Nothing."

Too much? She looked at the blank expressions of her colleagues. Her pronouncement silenced the jubilant energy like the proverbial wet blanket.

Determined to make them see reason, she continued in crisp tones. "Don't you think with satellite technology being what it is and able to find hidden cities in the jungles by their outline alone, they'd have noticed an entire city sitting this close to the surface of the ocean? It's not like we're down thousands of feet."

She could feel the disappointed heat of Jonah's stare as he studied her, and the effects of her speech on his crew. Then he flattened his hand on top of the prints and gave them a tap. "If this isn't a convincing enough start, you'll have collaboration with your own eyes soon enough." Expression inscrutable, he stuck his fingertips in his back pockets.

"But what if it is Atlantis?" Leslie asked, bitten by the curiosity bug. The woman diver looked from Callie to Jonah.

A teasing breeze combed Jonah's drying hair. Too long, too silky looking for a man who had the rugged face of a warrior and the body of a Roman god. "Dr. West doesn't believe Atlantis exists," he said, accepting her opinion while dismissing it with a shrug. "Fortunately, I know what I've seen. I've touched the pillars, seen the mosaic floors . . . I saw several white-colored plinths about a meter high last month when I was here, and plenty more stone blocks of various sizes scattered about. I haven't measured yet, but the ruins are—*enormous*. Huge." He leaned back.

"Atlantis is right below us, just waiting to be discovered."

"The story of the Lost City was a cautionary tale," Callie tried again. These people were doomed to disappointment, but they were looking at her like little kids whose candy she'd just ripped out of their sticky little hands. "Atlantis is a myth. But I don't doubt for an instant that Jonah has found the remains from another ancient city. Exciting. Thrilling, really. Even if it isn't Atlantis, right? It's certainly worth investigating."

Her chest ached with suppressed emotion. God. She wanted this to be true. But if it was Atlantis, Rydell was going to make sure the Cutters weren't the ones to find it. Whoever uncovered and explored what lay beneath the ocean, it wasn't going to be part of her future.

If her time, with *whatever* was down there, was finite, she wasn't going to waste a second worrying about an earthquake that wasn't an earthquake, or a debate over which city it was.

Her chair scraped across the wood deck as she launched herself to her feet. "Let's go down. See what you found."

"Now?" Jonah asked, bewildered by her switch of mood.

"Yes!" Brody yelled, racing for the stairs down to the dive platform like a kid let out of school on summer break.

He sounded like a herd of elephants as he ran across the deck and thumped down the ladder.

Chomping at the bit, and barely able to keep herself from racing after the Matthew McConaughey look-alike, Leslie shot a look at Jonah, her tone tentative. "We can't all go in at the same time, right?"

"Sennett has her PADI, I'll have her spell us. And, sorry Brody," Jonah raised his voice. "You had a beer, you'll have to sit this dive out." He glanced over at Callie and cut off Brody's half-assed protests from the deck below. "If the doctor says it's safe enough for us to go back in?"

Their excitement was contagious, and Callie went with the flow of almost believing herself. "I'm willing to risk it."

Jonah grinned as he shoved his chair back and stood. "Go ahead and suit up then. I'll go get the captain, and we can introduce ourselves to the past and our future."

Five

On this dive, Jonah was far more interested in Callie's re-action and response to what she was seeing than looking at the structures and floors himself.

With *Ji Li* a dark indistinct shadow in the distance, he took her directly to the mosaic floor. Vaughn, Leslie, and Saul were hot on their heels. It wasn't as crystal-clear now as it'd been earlier that day. Possible the quake had churned up some sediment, but still, visibility was good for a dozen or so feet, and pretty damn good when one was standing right on top of the thing he wanted her to look at.

"Well?" he said into the mike in his mask as he shone the powerful flashlight at the ground. Blue, green, and gold mosaic glittered back. *Refute that, Dr. West!* "What do you think?"

Crouching, she ran both hands over the surface. Sand drifted up and hung in the water, leaving a larger surface for her to inspect. "It's . . . spectacular."

"Is it Atlantis?" Leslie demanded, kneeling beside Cal-lie to get a better look.

"It's a stone carpet." Callie's voice was choked with emotion and broken up some by static. "Beautifully preserved—God, look at the colors in this peacock—"

She traced the bird with a fingertip. "This was a small temple, or someone important's home . . ." She glanced around, eyes intense behind her mask. "That could've been a wall. Did you measure?" she demanded, turning back to pin Jonah with an intensity he found sexy as hell.

He smiled. "Sixty feet by twenty-eight."

She was only a foot away from him, and the sheer joy on her face almost knocked Jonah on his ass. Her eyes, the same deep turquoise as the surrounding water, seemed to be lit from within. No fucking fair. Her smile, unexpected and without artifice, lit up every dark corner of his soul. Her breath sounded sexy as hell right in his ear. "A public building, then."

Jonah had stood exactly where she was standing, and seen the animals, birds, and plants on the mosaic carpet when he'd come down to inspect *Ji Li* for the first time. It was as spectacular and exciting seeing it through Callie's eyes as it had been a year ago. "Here, come and take a look at this." Taking her hand, his fingers engulfing hers, he pulled her effortlessly through the water, swimming south about a hundred yards. Everyone followed like ducklings. He pointed to the bathing human figures illustrated by the mosaic glass tiles on the floor.

"A bathhouse!" she marveled, drifting to her knees to get a better look. She waved him closer, without looking up, then grabbed his wrist to angle the light for better viewing. Instead of letting go, her fingers tightened around his wrist.

"Oh, my God—look at this!" These mosaics depicted mostly naked human figures in various stages of bathing. At the crumbled edge the regular, circular shapes of clay piping typically used to deliver hot and cold water, and

to heat bathhouse pools, could be seen sprouting from beneath the floor's edge.

"Breathe," he told her drily when her regulator bubbles
stopped. Wanting her was like a drug coursing through
his body, making him needy and guilty as hell. Jonah left
his arm where it was, enjoying the hard grip of her fingers. Clearly she wasn't even aware she was clutching his
arm like a lifeline. Would she be this intense and focused
in bed?

Would her eyes have the same intense gleam and be
filled with the same almost otherworldly glow?

Yeah. Probably.

He'd never know.

"I found a pillar over here," Saul said excitedly in his
ear just when he was enjoying the sound of Callie's uneven breath. Jonah glanced up to see where the others
were. Leslie was nearby, but Saul and Vaughn were far
enough away that they were a murky blur through the
water. "It looks to be about thirty feet high! Jesus, this is
amazing!"

"I wish I could be in a dozen places at once," Callie
whispered reverently, walking on her knees to inspect the
floor close up, and inadvertently tugging Jonah along for
the ride. He grinned, enchanted by her enthusiasm.

"Jonah?" Maura Sennett's strained voice said directly
in his ear.

"Yeah?" The last damn thing he wanted was to be
brought back to the real word with a thump. A man should
be able to fantasize about a beautiful woman in private
and for as long as possible. "What's up?" His captain
wouldn't contact him in the middle of a dive unless it was
important. Shit. "Are they predicting another quake?" He
could deal with that and still stay down here.

"We have visitors." Her voice crackled in and out. Damn, Thanos had to get the damn comm system fixed sooner than later. "Get your butt topside ASAP."

Maura waited for him on the dive platform when Jonah pulled himself up beside her, leaving the other divers below to continue exploring.

"Who's on board?" he asked, squinting up at her as he stripped off his gear. Late-afternoon sunlight angled white across the surface of the water, bouncing off the crisp white hull. Not a cloud in the robin's-egg-blue sky, and visibility good enough to clearly see the peak of a mountain on a small nearby island that had been no more than a smudge earlier that morning.

A twenty-foot fishing boat, in fairly decent condition, was tethered to his ship.

Maura, dressed in her formal whites, shrugged. "No idea. They showed up in that—" She indicated the boat. "I saw them coming in from over there." She indicated the small island. "Wouldn't talk to me, my being *female* and all." She rolled her eyes. "Wouldn't tell Thanos what they wanted, either. Just insisted on speaking to the man in charge. I put them in the library and sent Gayle in to watch them. Tina brought refreshments, but they won't even sit down."

"The island's inhabited? Might be worth our while to take a tender over there. Convenient for supplies." Jonah pulled his T-shirt on over damp skin, mildly annoyed that he'd been taken away from something profoundly important to have a chitchat with the locals. He was looking forward to the good doctor eating crow.

"There's no indication on my charts that that island is inhabited. It's too small to have a name. But you can ask our guests. Trust me, not fishermen," Maura said obliquely, indicating that he should go up the ladder first. "It's a Mexican standoff."

Jonah quirked a brow. "Intriguing. How many of them?"

"Three."

"Let's go see what they want. I don't want to waste the last few hours of good dive time today playing host with the most."

"Is everyone blown away?" Maura asked enviously as they headed for the second deck and the library.

He couldn't help but smile. "Yeah. It's pretty damn amazing. Where's Brody? I'll have him take watch, and you can come down for a bit if you like."

"God, I'd *love* to. As for Brody . . . Let's leave that conversation for later, okay?"

Jonah wished he'd ignored her request and stayed under the water. He could do without conflict to fuck up a great day.

Together they entered the small library where the men waited. Gayle gave Jonah and Maura a relieved look when they walked in. At an inquiring look from Jonah, she gave a small puzzled shrug.

The library with its two long tables, computers, monitoring devices, and neatly rolled charts was where they'd be cataloging the salvages in the coming months. It was a comfortable, book-lined room, with a big television set, excellent sound system, and deep, comfortable seating. A great place to relax and Jonah's favorite room on the ship.

No one in the room looked in the least bit comfortable or relaxed.

"Jonah Santi—Cutter." Jonah offered his hand, catching himself with his last name. He'd been Santiago—his mother's last name—for the first few years he'd worked for Nick, before his connection to the family had been revealed. Dropping his hand when none was offered in return, he inspected the three elderly men. "What can we do for you gentlemen?" He directed the question to a tall, thin man who appeared to be in charge.

He couldn't quite figure out if the men were priests or some other member of the clergy. Dressed from head to toe in unrelieved black robe-like garments, they were tall, medium, and small in height. Swarthy skin, black eyes, strong features. Greek? Turkish? Possibly Egyptian? Hard to tell. Definitely not fishermen.

"Coffee? Something cold?" Maura offered, defaulting into hostess role, even though she was as unlikely a host as Jonah. She indicated the tray on a nearby table. The chef had brought slices of chocolate cake, a pot of coffee, and a pitcher of juice into the library before Jonah arrived. Nothing was touched.

"No refreshments, thank you." Tall took the chair Jonah offered with an invitational wave of his hand.

Jonah suspected this wasn't a social call.

"I am Achaikos Trakas," Tall said, his voice almost hypnotically serene as he arranged the drape of his robes about his legs. He had a heavy lantern jaw, and a prominent nose took up most of the real estate on his deeply lined face. Wispy hair lay flat and transparently pale against his scalp, and his hooded black eyes seemed to be burned into his skull. Jonah guessed his age to be somewhere between 80 and 150.

Bodyguard-like, Small stood beside Tall's chair as he murmured his name so quietly Jonah barely heard him. "Bion Eliades." He must've been hitting the high eighties as well. He was about as wide as he was tall, which wasn't very. Lipless; his hangdog eyes looked terrified. He looked, to Jonah, a little like a well-fed trout. Eliades eyed the plate of cake like a sex offender at a porn show, but made no move to take a slice.

"Lysistrata Demetriou," Medium said smoothly, clasping bloodless fingers tightly in his lap as he perched, ramrod-straight, on the edge of his black leather chair.

Definitely not relaxed, Jonah thought, amused at the theatricality of the men's demeanors. Three black crows, beady eyes watchful. They were so . . . odd, so out of place, Jonah was—if not intrigued, at least *curious*.

The men's stress level permeated the air like an invisible sticky fog, brushing Jonah's damp skin with skeletal fingers. Rubbing the back of his neck, he shoved the overly dramatic image away.

He'd hear them out, then send them on their way with a go-box of Tina's excellent chocolate cake.

Their heavy accents were more international than country-specific, but the names sounded Greek. Not much of a clue.

Jonah, his captain, and her first officer sat down. Eliades, still standing, folded his hands inside the sleeves of his robe and stared—rather creepily—into the middle distance.

Jonah paid attention to his instincts, which said the men's relaxed pose was surface-deep. "I repeat, what can we do for you, gentlemen? We're in the middle of a salvage. I want to get back to my dive team."

"What is it you are salvaging, *Kyrie*?"

Greek, then. Jonah leaned back in the deep leather chair. "Not to put too fine a point on it, Trakas, but who are you, and what business is my business to you?"

"You did not make a request to do any salvage in this area. To do so you are required to ask permission from—" There was a slight hesitation, before he finished. "From

Kyrie Spanos. You have been anchored in this location for twenty-four hours, and have not yet done so."

"Permission? No, I haven't," Jonah responded, letting the chill seep into his tone, and peeling back another layer of annoyance. "Who is he, and why do I need *anyone's* permission to salvage here? This is open water. *International* waters."

There was a small, horrified gasp from Demetriou. But a sharp look from Eliades made him blink, then lower his gaze.

"Kallistrate Spanos is—How you say? Acting grand master of *Nησí* Fire."

"Fire Island?" Jonah glanced at Maura. She raised her eyebrows to indicate she'd never heard of it, either. "Okay. I'll bite. Where is this Fire Island, since it isn't even listed on any map, and why does this 'grand master' think he can dictate what and where I salvage?"

"*Nησí* Fire is seven miles due *west*, *Kyrie*. *Kyrie* Spanos is . . . *caretaker*, if you will, of this . . . area. He asks that you come with us to the island, and report your findings and intentions."

"Yeah. I don't think so. We're more than seven miles off your island regardless. According to international law, you have no jurisdiction beyond three miles off your coast, regardless of what your big guy thinks." Jonah rose, and so did the two women.

"Thank Spanos for the invitation, and let him know I politely declined."

Trakas and Demetriou also got to their feet. Eliades shook his head as if horrified by Jonah's response. Tough shit.

"You—you cannot refuse, *Kyrie*! It is not done!" Demetriou whispered, horrified.

"As I said, you have no jurisdiction over me or my ship,

gentlemen. If we find anything I think might interest you, I'll be sure to let you know. Now, if you don't mind, my team is waiting for me."

Trakas gave Jonah a flat stare and said in ominous tones, "If you do not comply and come with us, we will be put to death."

Whoa. The hair on Jonah's nape paid attention. He huffed out a laugh, which died when he looked at three terrified pairs of ancient eyes. "You can't fucking be serious."

"We are not permitted to fail," Trakas told him grimly, a muscle ticking in his lantern jaw. "If we do, we will die. If we die, others will take our place. You *must* obey our directive. There is no other choice."

"No other choice? You must be shitting me. I have a plethora of choices. One of which is tossing your bony asses overboard."

"What nonsense is this?" Maura demanded incredulously, cheeks flushed. "Which country does Fire Island belong to? I'll contact the Greek authori—"

"We are an independent state, and belong to no country," Demetriou cut in, looking to Jonah as if it were he who'd spoken.

"You're the Monaco of the Mediterranean Sea? And put people to death on a whim? Man, I'd hate to live on *your* island."

Demetriou's face went starkly pale, and he spoke through tight lips. "This is no joking matter, *Kyrie*. A dishonorable death in our culture is just punishment for failure. If you do not come with us to speak to *Kyrie* Spanos, it will impinge on our honor. Once honor is lost, our lives will be forfeited."

"I've never heard such bullsh—this is ridiculous!" Gayle told Jonah. "I'll escort them off the ship. Let's go."

It was as though the captain and first mate weren't even in the room, as Trakas addressed only Jonah. He pressed a skeletal, freckled hand flat against his own chest as if holding in pain, and said through bloodless lips, his voice stark, "You refuse to accompany us?"

It was highly unlikely the men were telling the truth about being killed if he didn't tag along, but *they* clearly believed it. Jonah plainly saw the strain on the old men's faces. All he needed was one of them keeling over from a heart attack or stroke while on board his ship. The red tape alone would delay them for months. "How about if I come over and meet this Kallistrate Spanos tomorrow morning?"

Maura's head whipped around. "Jonah—"

"It's okay. I'd like to see the island for myself. Sounds like a real fun place."

"You swear on your honor that you will come, at first light tomorrow?" Demetriou demanded, not looking any healthier than the tall guy. "We have your word?"

"Not at first light, I need at least three cups of coffee before I function. How about midmorning?" Jonah was curious, not fucking compliant.

The three men exchanged looks. Eliades looked as though he was about to pass out. He opened his mouth to protest, but Trakas made a slight hand gesture and the shorter man subsided, his face also bone-china-pale, hands shaking. He hastily tucked them inside his voluminous sleeves and bowed his head.

"We have your word?"

Fuck. "Sure."

Callie remembered her mom coming in to kiss her good night. She'd been about ten. She thought her mother looked like a fairy queen that night. Her parents were going to some fancy function, and her mother wore a black velvet dress, diamonds at her throat and wrists. Tonight the sky looked just as magical as that dress, sprinkled with diamonds.

She held on to the visual memory of a ten-year-old, because it was pretty much the last time she'd believed in magic. The dress had probably been cotton, and the "diamonds" were most assuredly zirconia.

The adult in her remembered the stink of booze on her mother's breath that not even a liberal gargle of mouthwash and a dousing of J'adore ever covered.

She had no illusions anymore.

". . . must've swum at least a hundred yards inside. It was massive . . ." Vaughn was talking about the lava tube he'd discovered that afternoon. Callie let the conversation drift around her as she cradled a long-gone-cold cup of tea, staring out at the glittering water.

Jonah hadn't come back down after the captain had called him to return to the ship this afternoon. Whoever the visitors were, he hadn't joined the rest of the crew until dinner, and he'd been preoccupied for the rest of the evening, his face more shuttered than usual.

Who were the mysterious visitors, and why had they come? Jonah hadn't had much to say about anything. He'd asked a few questions of Vaughn and a few of Leslie when she asked what they'd be bringing on board.

She longed to get back to the lab to spend more time with the small artifacts and bits of glass mosaic she'd brought back on board with her. She'd already cataloged them and done the paperwork.

The dive team had enjoyed a terrific meal under the stars, lingering over coffee as they discussed what they'd seen and how they wanted to proceed, who was going to work *Ji Li* and how they would divvy up the city so nothing was missed. Familiar talk. Conversation she was comfortable with.

She liked remembering her parents from when she was too young to know they were drunks. There'd been good times, she was sure. But they'd been few and far between. She'd been the adult before she was in her teens.

As the child of alcoholics, she was a stereotype: She'd perfected lying because she always had to cover with the authorities, she was too critical of herself, a perfectionist, and she found it hard to have fun just for the sake of having fun. She'd proven she was crappy at relationships, and she always felt . . . different.

The people around the table hadn't known one another for more than a few weeks, yet they'd already formed a bond she wasn't a part of. It was such a perfectly beautiful, serene night, for just a second she closed her eyes and wished upon a star.

"Penny for them." Jonah murmured, once again sitting next to her. Callie wasn't sure how that had happened since he'd been seated at the other end of the table when she'd arrived for dinner.

"My thoughts are worth a lot more than a penny," she said lightly, draining the last cold drop of tea for something to do with her hands and mouth.

He always needed a shave, and tonight was no exception. The scruff looked good on him. Sexy. Bad-boy sexy. The kind of man a woman like her rarely, if ever, attracted. She was too by-the-book, and she suspected that Jonah had thrown away the rule book in his teens.

"Is your ring too big?" His voice only carried the eighteen inches between them. "You might want to keep it in the safe, I'd hate for you to lose it."

"It's insured."

A warm breeze made the small white lights dance and

sway overhead, leaving it hard to read him. The smell of him made her hormones sit up and pant. It was ridiculous that soap could turn her on like this. Maybe she should just use it herself and get over it.

"You smell like the tropics," he said.

God . . . "It's sunblock." Eager—more than eager—to change the subject, she raised her voice to include the others. "Who was your visitor this afternoon?"

Jonah's half smile was annoying. "Are you aware Fire Island is inhabited?"

Realizing that she was listing to the side, Callie straightened in her chair. "I don't know about *inhabited*. People go there to climb the volcano or camp, I think. I've never been there, and that's about all I know. Why? Were your visitors from there?"

"Three of them showed up unannounced."

"That was very neighborly."

"Who's this?" Saul asked from the other end of the table.

Jonah filled everyone in on the three elderly men who'd showed up, and made light of what sounded to Callie like a rooster fluffing its feathers to scare off the fox.

"Are you saying," she asked, amused, "that three old men threatened to *kill* themselves if you didn't go over there tomorrow?"

"Nope. They tried to impress on me that if I didn't show up, their lives would be toast—but not voluntarily."

"Senile dementia," Vaughn suggested, refilling his wineglass, then filling Leslie's. Without missing a beat, Jonah moved the bottle well out of Brody's reach. Vaughn continued, "For all we know it was spies from another salvage operation coming to see what we've discovered. You didn't tell them about our city, did you?"

The mention of a rival salvage company coming to

scope them out sent a little shiver down Callie's spine. Like a fox in a henhouse, she was sitting right in the middle of them, having enjoyed a pleasant meal.

Jonah shook his head. "I'm supposed to report to their head honcho. Tell him what we're doing here. None of their business, but I'll go because these geezers really seem to believe they're in danger."

"If they th-think they can just waltz in here and grab our treasure, *fuck* them!" Brody said.

Besides her natural distaste for sloppy drunks, Callie gave Jonah props for cutting Brody off. Drinking and sailing didn't mix well and put them all at risk.

"Maybe they'd heard rumors about the sinking of *Ji Li*, and want a cut if we find anything?" Callie put the mug down because she was fiddling. Loosely clasping her fingers together, she rested her hands on the table. "Then they most assuredly know about the ruins under her."

Jonah leaned back in his chair, not looking in the least concerned that someone else was trying to horn in on his salvage. "What they know is immaterial. They have no jurisdiction over us, and we have the right to salvage what we've claimed."

"Do you think they'll make trouble of some kind?" Saul looked concerned.

"Maybe fifty years ago," Jonah told him lightly. "They're ancient and harmless. Hell, my *abuela* could take all three of them. I think they're curious, and bored. We're something new in the neighborhood and we offer some summer entertainment."

Jonah had just revealed two things. He had a grandmother. And she was Spanish. "You have a *grandmother*?"

Rydell had told her the Cutters had no relatives other than themselves. Jonah had been a surprise. A half sibling. Clearly accepted by his brothers, since they'd handed him a multimillion-dollar ship with all the bells and whistles.

He cocked a dark brow. "Why so surprised? Did you think I was hatched?"

"I—no."

He smiled. "She's a spry eighty-two, and lives in Cádiz with seven cats and her boyfriend, who happens to be a younger man of seventy-three."

"Is that where you're from? Spain?" She hadn't noticed before, but there was a breath of an accent on certain words now that she listened for it.

"Born there, went to school in England, then got a bachelor's and a master's in marine science from Webb Institute. That's where I met Maura."

"You have degrees?" She didn't mean to sound quite so incredulous.

"Marine engineering and naval architecture. Before I signed on as Nick's captain, I was designing ships."

Designing ships? Rydell hadn't mentioned that Jonah had even gone to college, let alone that he was a marine architect.

"Nick?" Callie knew all about Nick Cutter. He'd scuttled his own ship with a fortune of diamonds on board to elude the authorities. He was as crooked as his brothers.

"My middle half brother. Same father."

Callie glanced down the table, but everyone was listening to something Saul was telling them and not eavesdropping on Jonah's story.

Daniel Cutter, the man who apparently couldn't keep his equipment in his pants, had lived with his wife and three sons on Cutter Cay, in the Caribbean. He'd also lived and been "married" to Jonah's mother. Callie wasn't sure if he'd been legally married to two women or not. "Does your mother still live in Spain?"

"She died three years ago. Heart failure. She was only fifty-four. Her death was the impetus for me to seek out Zane, Nick, and Logan, see if we could make a connection. Be a family."

"And?"

"It's as though we didn't grow up thousands of miles and cultures apart. I'll do anything for them."

She nodded. "To prove yourself." Rydell and Peri, his baby sister, were her family, too. They loved her, and she'd been married to their younger brother, Adam, for six years. There was nothing she wouldn't do for either of them. All they had to do was ask. Which was why she was here.

She understood Jonah's need to gain his brothers' trust and approval.

"Nah. Don't need to," Jonah said, unwittingly echoing what she was thinking. "We're family. How about you?"

"Nope," she said, keeping it light. "I've been an orphan for many years." She shrugged. "My parents, ironically, were killed by a drunk driver. *Both* drivers were blitzed out of their minds."

"That sucks."

"I don't mean to sound fatalistic, but it was inevitable. Driving drunk was a favorite pastime of theirs."

"Is that where you got this?" He reached out to run a light finger down the length of her arm, tracing the worst of the scars. Nobody had ever touched her there other than at the hospital, and Callie felt that brush of his finger in every pulsing cell in her body as if it were a live wire.

The symbol of her survival, and so much a part of her she rarely gave it any thought. She jerked out of reach, picking up her empty mug as if it were a blastproof shield that could protect her. "Not in the accident that killed them, no. This happened when I was fifteen." The last time she'd ever gotten into a vehicle with either of them. "No one died that day, but they had to get us out of the car with the Jaws of Life. I was just grateful when I woke up in the hospital and saw the bandages after surgery and knew I didn't lose my arm."

He was quiet for a long time. The conversation at the other end of the table was petering out, and people were starting to tune in to their conversation.

"No grandparents?"

"No," Callie said, feeling uncomfortable divulging anything more personal—she'd already overshared. "Both sets died before I was born."

"Ah, man, that fucking sucks!" Brody yelled too loudly. "Do you need a hug? I'll give you a hug." Spreading his arms wide, he hugged the space around him. "Come 'ere, darlin'." Wiggling his fingers for her to come to him. "Big bad Brody'll give you some lovin'."

"Big bad Brody is going to get his ass kicked," Jonah said with a little heat. "Sit down and shut up. One more warning, and I tear up your contract. No more drinking on board."

"On that happy note, I'll say good night." Callie got to her feet. Men like Brody were easy to handle. And since the only man she knew who was remotely like Jonah was Rydell, she knew she had to get out of his force field before she did something foolish. "It's been a full day, and I still have some jet lag to sleep off."

She'd shared more with Jonah than she'd ever shared with any man other than Adam. Not even Peri or Ry knew some of the things she'd told Jonah tonight.

"The offer of the safe is open if you need it."

She was twisting her wedding ring around her finger again. This time unconsciously. "I'll keep it in mind. 'Night, everyone."

"Let's all go tomorrow and check them out. Going by yourself is ridiculous. If they've got a problem with you, then they have a problem with all of us," Leslie suggested.

Callie didn't hear the answer as she headed downstairs to her cabin.

She didn't call Rydell to report as she'd agreed to do. In part because he had bigger fish to fry at the moment, but more because, first, before she gave him more details on Jonah's city she wanted to have all her ducks in a row, and second, just because she'd been related to Rydell once upon a time didn't mean she was under his command and unable to think on her own.

Callie grinned at her mixed metaphors.

Ry could wait. Just because this would be short-term didn't mean she'd rush the process. There was a right way to do this and a wrong way. And no matter who was going to end up with the spoils, as long as she was involved, every *i* would be dotted, every *t* crossed.

Callie kept her own counsel. So far they hadn't seen anything that could be easily transported. The mosaics should've been left where they were until she—or someone—went over them with a fine-tooth comb and sucked every bit of information out of them, documenting every inch along the way. But she hadn't been able to resist bringing a few samples to the surface.

Don't get too invested, she cautioned herself, sliding her palm down the smooth surface of the highly polished brass rail as she navigated the stairs to the lower deck where most of the cabins were located. Prizes had a tendency to be whipped from beneath a person's feet when they least expected it. She merely had a loan of the Lost City. A temporary taste.

Despite sunscreen, she'd gotten a little burnt. It felt amazing to be out in the field, diving again after months in a classroom. She loved teaching at the University of Miami, her alma mater, but nothing beat the silent beauty underwater.

What she'd seen that afternoon was incredible, and she was eager for what the next morning would bring. She'd make notes and look at the photos she'd taken down there before hitting the sack.

Hearing footsteps behind her, Callie turned to see Jonah heading to his cabin as well. Since their doors were opposite each other, unless she ran into her cabin and slammed the door in his face—which she admitted to herself was a huge temptation—she was going to have to interact with him sans the buffer of the other divers.

Six

Sucking in a deep breath, Callie held it for a calming moment, shoving her keycard into the lock for a quick cowardly getaway at the earliest opportunity.

Jonah stood a little too close for comfort, eyes amused. "Sorry about Brody. I've already given him a warning. I'll talk to him again in the morning." The deep rumble of his voice rolled through her, sending vibrations of awareness to her nerve endings.

Her unsteady breath came a little too fast. Whatever it was that Jonah had, it was her kryptonite, which worried her. "I appreciate it. I don't like drunks, but I can handle myself."

The smile left his eyes. "You're under my protection. You shouldn't have to."

She opened her eyes wide and turned to face him. "Under your protection? Wow, that's very medieval of you. I've been fighting my own battles since I was five."

"Must be exhausting." The corridor was narrow and dimly lit as he came abreast of her. "It was a good dive this afternoon."

"Fascinating. I can't wait to go down in the morning. 'Night."

"Wait—" Jonah's voice too was low; the silence of the

lower deck, the insulating, barely there hum of machinery, made the space far too intimate. Especially since the closer he was to her, the more aware of him Callie became.

It was a strange chemical reaction she had no control over. She gave him an inquiring glance as she pushed open her door. Her feet might be planted, but inside she was running like hell. He'd showered earlier and still carried a trace of soap on his skin. He was one of those men who looked sexy with a day's growth of stubble. She wondered how abrasive it would feel brushing her skin. For a nanosecond her overstimulated brain was filled with the image of Jonah skimming his lips down her body . . . She imagined the prickly softness of that stubble, she almost felt the delicious damp skim of his mouth.

His eyes were a deep, marine blue in the dim lighting as he took the half step necessary to bring them face-to-face. Thick, short black eyelashes masked the color for a moment, and when he met her gaze again something hot and raw flared between them.

Breath snagged painfully in Callie's lungs as Jonah reached out to touch her cheek. "You got too much sun today."

His finger remained, cupping the curve of her face, making her cheeks burn hotter than any sunburn. His touch was light, a butterfly's kiss, but she felt that touch in every atom of her body.

Her tongue stuck to the roof of her dry mouth. "I forgot to reapply sunscreen when we got back. I'll be more careful tomorrow." She should step backward into her cabin and shut the door. *In a moment.* Tension stretched between them like a rubber band.

His thumb, light as a wish, skimmed across her jaw, then lingered at the corner of her mouth. Her lips parted automatically. His pupils flared. "What is it about you that makes me want to touch you every time I see you?"

Ditto. "I—" *I want to jump your bones, Jonah Cutter.* Apparently she didn't have to like or respect the man to want him with every fiber of her being. She'd never, never *ever*, felt this way in her life. It was—unsettling.

She swallowed around the lump in her throat, forcing herself not to lean into him. Attempting not to inhale the clean smell of his skin—which was like catnip to a cat—and forced *rational* between tingling lips. "I'm married, remember?"

The heated glint in his eyes vanished, and he gave her a cool, mocking smile as he shoved his fingertips into his shorts pockets. "Which is why I'm not already kissing you and hauling you into my cabin like a caveman right now."

"Married or not." Callie dragged her gaze away from the tent in his shorts, magnified by his hands bunched in his pockets. "The answer will always be no. I never was interested in Neanderthals. Besides which, I love Adam, and would never cheat on him."

Taking his keycard out of his pocket, he flipped it end over end between long, tanned fingers. "He's a lucky man."

"I tell him that every day."

He frowned. "I've never slept with a married woman—"

"Good for you," Callie said drily, grateful to have something to hang her annoyance on. She used it like a shield. It was all about self-preservation. "I'll alert the media in the morning."

"You didn't let me finish."

"I have no plans of letting you get started," she shot back.

He leaned in, his mouth a breath away from her own.

Close enough that the energy buzzing between them made her lips feel as though he were kissing her. "I've never slept with a married woman, and I don't intend to. Ever. You don't have to worry about my actions, they're strictly honorable. I believe in monogamy. As much as I loved my father, he couldn't keep his dick in his pants. I was lucky— my brothers accept me for who I am. But I'll never do to a woman what Daniel did to my mother and the mother of my brothers. Your virtue is safe from me, and your husband can rest easy. I won't poach."

Her eyes were so fixated on his lips, she noted the almost-smile that lifted the corners ever so slightly. Hell, she could feel the damn movement of his mouth. "'Night, Callie. I'm glad you agreed to join us."

Without responding she slipped into her cabin and shut the door, then sagged against it weakly, her heart pounding. She slid to the floor, leaning her head against the door, and squeezed her eyes shut. Dear God, the man had powerful mojo. "Please let this feeling go away, please."

She sat there for several minutes, too wiped out to move.

Then she heard the door across the corridor quietly close. He'd been standing mere feet away the whole time. Probably had heard her muttering to herself through the door.

Callie dropped her head to her knees and groaned. She was in deep, deep trouble.

After enjoying three cups of coffee with his breakfast, and a pleasant hour online reading his daily fix of news, Jonah was as ready as he'd ever be for Fire Island. Going was a pain in the ass. He, like everyone else, was eager to get started on the salvage, and this delay, while not earth shattering, was annoying and inconvenient. But a promise was a promise.

As much as he'd loved his dad, the man was the king of promise breaking. Of course, it was hard to juggle two families a world apart. But at the time, Jonah, and his mother, had no idea about the other half of his father's life.

His father had taught him a lot. Sailing, love of the sea, a passion for salvaging . . . and not to break promises, and never to cheat on a woman. The good, the bad, and the ugly of Life's Lessons taught to Jonah by the late, great Daniel Cutter.

Thanos brought the tender up to the dive platform where Jonah was meeting Vaughn and Saul, as Callie and Leslie were suiting up to go down.

Callie was in the process of tugging on her wet suit, but since it was only at her knees, he had the opportunity to enjoy the view. Her long legs were toned and sleek from years of swimming, her narrow waist just the right size to circle with both hands. The sight of her breasts, although flattened by the racing-style black swimsuit, made his mouth water.

The scent of coconut would always be associated in his mind with silky skin, pale Caribbean-turquoise eyes, and a sassy mouth he wanted to nibble.

Bent over, Callie glanced up to see him standing there like a teenage boy, dick in his hand. If not literally, certainly metaphorically. The tender bumped the platform with a soft thud. Vaughn and Saul seemed to have materialized beside him, but he'd been so busy eating up every inch of Callie, he'd been oblivious to the activity around him.

She frowned at him.

Jonah smiled back. He didn't regret telling her he wanted her. It was true. He'd hoped, however, that it would clear the air a bit. Negatory. The way she looked at him was still distant and closed.

"Last chance to meet the crazies on Fire Island," he offered, keeping his tone light with effort as she efficiently finished getting into tight black neoprene. Almost as good as seeing her naked. Except with no skin showing.

Nope. Not nearly as good as naked, but as close as he'd ever get.

The thought was depressing as hell.

As she pulled the cord to draw up the zipper in back, she said under her breath so only he could hear, "Stop looking at me like that." Decidedly unfriendly.

He gave her an innocent look. "Like what?" *Like I want to strip you naked?*

"Like—" She hesitated, but he imagined he saw the thought of them together in the heated flash of her eyes. Wishful thinking, Jonah knew. "Never mind." She lowered herself to sit on the edge of the platform beside Leslie.

It was the fact that she was so damn unattainable that made Callie so alluring, Jonah knew. Being this aroused, for this long, around a woman was unnatural and—damn it to hell—painful. He had to get his hormones in check. He hadn't taken himself in hand this much since he was thirteen and discovered his dick.

It had to stop. He had to *make* it stop. "I can't modulate how I look as well as how I think."

Shit. And not flirt.

Callie turned her head to give him a cool look as she got ready to pull on her mask. "Even a five-year-old can multitask, Cutter. Give it your best shot." She turned to Leslie. "Ready?"

Leslie looked from Jonah to Callie and back again. "And miss the show?"

"There isn't any show. We just rub each other the

wrong way. Eventually we'll get used to each other's hot buttons and not get on each other's nerves."

Leslie swung her crossed ankles over the water as she adjusted her mask before putting it on. "Is that what it is?"

Callie shrugged. "Oil and water."

"Ready to rock-and-roll?" Saul asked Jonah, already seated with Vaughn on the smaller boat.

No surprise that the two women didn't want to accompany them to Fire Island. The last thing sh—*they* wanted to do was go ashore. She wanted to go back down and get started on documenting the city, and Leslie had decided to stay and get another dive in, too.

Brody hadn't been given any options. Jonah was trying to decide if it was worth keeping him on. He was an excellent diver, and would be an asset if he'd get his shit together and stop drinking. Drinking and ships did not mix. One misstep and a drunk could drown without anyone noticing his absence until it was too late. A life lost and a fucking headache of a liability.

Logan would be righteously pissed at all that paperwork. Jonah grinned. Yeah, better not piss off his new big brother just yet.

"I hope that smile doesn't have anything to do with a certain married lady," Saul ventured as they headed out away from *Stormchaser* toward the smudge of the island in the distance. "She doesn't seem like a woman who takes her vows lightly."

Jesus. He was *that* obvious? Not cool. "As a heart attack. I'm good with that." Good thing he wasn't Pinocchio. His nose, as well as his dick, would be a yard long by now. "Strictly hands off, but it doesn't hurt to enjoy the scenery, does it?"

"Better keep those sunglasses on when you're around

her, then," Saul suggested drily, sitting on the padded bench in the prow. "The way you look at Dr. West is enough to melt Gorilla Glass."

"I'll have to train my eyes to be more circumspect from now on," Jonah said with a slight frown. It was unconscionable that anyone knew how badly he lusted for Callie. It wasn't fair to either of them, but especially not to her. He'd never cross that line in the sand. The last thing he wanted to do was make her feel uncomfortable.

He was uncomfortable enough for both of them.

It didn't take long to reach the small island. It rose this morning, a clearly visible cone of black rock covered in a skirt of verdant green, from the slight ripples on the sun-dappled water. But then the clarity underwater would be spectacular, too. He immediately imagined Callie gliding through the water, the ultimate water nymph—seductive as hell.

Promises, he reminded himself. Hands off. But despite her directive, and Saul's astute observation, Jonah knew he couldn't keep his eyes off her. Bad as it was that he had his nose pressed to the candy shop window, to close his eyes and cut off that treat was beyond him. Sunglasses would be required for the duration of their voyage. He just had no fucking clue how he was supposed to accomplish that with a goddamn dive mask on.

As they got closer, Jonah smelled the tangy scent of wild oregano, peppery and sharp. Three swallows dipped and drifted on the thermals alongside the boat for a few minutes, then peeled off like the Blue Angels, heading for the island.

Hilly, lots of trees and shrubs, but no structures he could see save for the small cement breakwater-dock combo they angled toward. The place was pristine. Au

naturel. Deserted. Except for the small fishing boat bob-
bing on the water. Thanos angled the *Riva* behind it.

Jumping out of the boat, Jonah caught the line and
proceeded to tie up as Vaughn and Saul joined him on
what passed for a dock. The air smelled strongly of an old
catch mixed with brine and oregano and a hint of wild
thyme.

Heat shimmied up from the concrete structure and it
was barely nine a.m. He'd rather be underwater right now.
They hadn't been long enough at sea for a trip to shore to
be appealing. Still, the old guys had aroused his curiosity, and he could spare an hour to see what they were all
about.

He finished tying up to the cleat on the dock. "Stay
put," he instructed Thanos, who waved his okay and sat
on the bench seat to wait in the shade of the canopy. "This
shouldn't take long."

Sunlight bounced off the water. A deep, dark blue here,
not like the crystal-clear turquoise waters at Cutter Cay.
The same color as Callie's eyes.

I need to get laid. Jonah mentally riffled through the
women he knew within a thousand-mile radius. Dr. West
was fast becoming an obsession, and wanting, no matter
how badly, wasn't getting. He could control the lust by
taking the edge off. Maybe that would negate the strong
feelings he had for her. God, he hoped so.

He'd get out his little black book when he got back to
Stormchaser.

"Not exactly a bustling metropolis." Saul pulled his
baseball cap down to shade his eyes as he looked around.
"You sure those guys said this island?"

Jonah looked around. "Maybe there are buildings on
the other side."

Vaughn shoved his hands in the front pocket of his

shorts and looked around, as unimpressed as Jonah. "Maybe."

The island was small, ten, fifteen miles square at most. No buildings that he could see. The land sloped up, a series of gently rolling, tree-covered hills, toward the flat-topped volcano slightly off center, surrounded by dense vegetation.

"I had an old prof who used to say, '*Beware a quiet volcano*,'" Saul said, indicating the one in front of them.

Vaughn glanced that way and shrugged. "Looks pretty dodo-ish, doesn't it?"

"Couple of centuries, give or take," Jonah agreed. "If anyone lives here they're keeping a low profile. Most people would build their home here on the leeward side on that bluff overlooking the water. Perhaps my elderly visitors are *visiting* Fire Island. Although I can't begin to imagine those guys camping. Let's get to the top of the rise and see what we can see."

In retrospect, it was pretty damn funny that he'd been spooked by the old men's visit yesterday. Here, with the smell of the sea, the sharp lemony scent of thyme, and the sun already promising to be hotter later, he realized that surprise had made him more susceptible to their superstitious behavior than his normal pragmatic self.

"I see a particularly aggressive shrub over there. Maybe we *should* have come armed," Saul teased, falling into step with Jonah and Vaughn. Maybe not everyone on the island was as old as Methuselah. They'd discussed bringing some heat, which Jonah kept in a safe on board, but in the end opted not to carry weapons.

The hair on the back of Jonah's neck prickled as if sensing danger. But if that was the case it sure as shit wasn't evident out here in the open. The day was clear, sunny, and decidedly nonthreatening.

He suspected the whole Callie/married/off-limits/horny-as-hell thing had all his senses wound into a tight overimaginative knot. Throw in some woo-woo old guys dressed from head to toe in black. Mix in some dire threats to their safety, and he had a recipe for his imagination to take flight.

Rubbing the back of his neck, Jonah forced his shoulders to relax. "This all feels rather anticlimactic after their big buildup yesterday—" Two figures emerged from the tree line some two hundred yards ahead.

"Three o'clock," Vaughn said quietly.

"Got it." Jonah had seen the black-garbed men moments before the others noticed them. "How's your Greek?" He only knew the basics.

"I speak some." Vaughn took his hands out of his shorts pockets as if he was getting ready to defend himself.

Saul looked ready to head back to the tender at a run as he said, "I understand it better than I speak it."

The men made no move to approach them, merely stood stoically, hands tucked into voluminous sleeves of their black robes as they waited at the tree line.

Jonah continued walking up the dirt path at a leisurely pace, Vaughn and Saul flanking him.

"You notice there's not a damn thing here but rocks and trees, right?" Vaughn observed, looking around.

"They came from somewhere." Jonah kept his eye on the men waiting for them. It had taken a good ten minutes to walk up the slope, but they still hadn't moved. "Those aren't the guys who came on board."

They came abreast of the old men. "Greetings, *Kyrie* Cutter." The man's rheumy eyes flicked to Vaughn, then Saul, then back to Jonah. "There is transportation. This way."

"Is it far?" Jonah asked as one man fell behind them

while the other led the way. It was slow going. Like the others, these two were well into their eighties, at least, and the one in front moved as though every bone in his frail body ached.

Jonah raised his voice. "How far do we have to go?" Since the man didn't respond, he figured he was extremely hard of hearing, or didn't speak English.

The transportation, as he saw when they breached the rise, was three moth-eaten-looking donkeys. The men exchanged a few words, and the leader gestured for them to climb aboard. Jonah wondered if they'd known he was accompanied by Vaughn and Saul, or if the three beasts were for the two of them and him. When the old men made no move to mount up, he figured the donkeys were for guests only. Whoever their employer was, he was a jackass to make these old coots walk their guests to wherever the hell in this heat. "You'll walk?"

One of the old men shook his head, the cowl of his heavy robe half shading his face. "Stay."

A glance around showed exactly what they'd seen ten minutes ago. Hills, vegetation, sky, volcano. "How will we get to where we're going?"

The guy who'd brought up the rear pointed. "*Gaidaro* know."

"The donkeys know the way?"

The man nodded.

"Okay, let's see where they take us." Jonah flung a leg over the beast, a small cloud of musty dust rising from its back. "Jesus—" he laughed, trying to fold his long legs so they didn't drag along the ground as the animal took off with no urging from him.

He grabbed the scrubby mane, a stiff broom-like ridge along the donkey's neck, and held on for dear life. It was like riding a particularly odoriferous dirt bike—with no shocks. The damn thing trotted along the path at such a quick clip that his teeth slammed together. His spine was getting a workout. He'd ridden a horse three times in his life. And this wasn't even close. He hadn't enjoyed riding a horse, but at least that had some kind of a rolling gait to it. This was just bone jarring and he was pretty damn sure he wasn't going to remember this ride fondly, either.

"Either of you ever ridden before?"

"Not one of these," Vaughn said, his voice vibrating with the uneven ride.

"Outside the mall when I was about si—Whoa! Whoa, I tell you! Whoa, you little shit!" Saul's donkey decided to take the lead, jogging ahead, and his voice drifted over his head as he galloped past Jonah and Vaughn. "Holy Mother of God, are these things *trying* to kill us?"

"Think they're that smart?" Jonah said, amused. He'd never father any children after this. He'd definitely opt to walk back. All three animals slowed after cresting a rise. In the shallow dip of a narrow valley below was a cluster of mud-colored houses.

"We've arrived. And other than sprained dicks, all in one piece," Jonah marveled, tone wry. He dropped his feet to the ground, leaving the donkey to its own devices. "I'm walking from here." Jonah shoved his donkey's head away from him as the beast tried to nuzzle his neck.

"Christ, I thought we'd never get off these damn things," Saul groaned, swinging a leg over his donkey's back. He bent over, hands on his knees.

"Looks abandoned," Vaughn observed, not looking back as his mount hightailed it over the hill the way they'd come.

The village, consisting of several dozen houses, was tucked neatly between valleys. Unlike most Greek or Turkish homes, which were painted in stark white or brilliant hues, the buildings here were made from, or coated with, the local soil, camouflaging the buildings into the terrain.

"Yeah," Jonah agreed, heading down the hill, his feet kicking up dust, the two men on his heels. Waving away a buzzing fly, he wondered why the sight of the sleepy settlement made the hair on the back of his neck stand up.

Seven

Excited and awed, Callie examined a large roundish object, severely corroded and covered in a cement-like concretion, which she'd just uncovered on the seafloor. God—the day couldn't be more perfect. Ideal diving conditions, and the discovery of artifact after amazing artifact. Idiotic, but she wished Jonah were there to share the finds with her. So far this morning she'd discovered a fully intact marble head, indicating the body was some-where. A dozen amphorae, several utensils, and this large—intriguing—*something*.

She peered at it more closely. Holy crap! Was that a *gear wheel* mostly hidden by the concretion? She flagged the location for later collection. She was dying to get it into the lab to clean it and see exactly what it was.

"Les? Come and see this . . ." It took Callie several seconds to realize Leslie wasn't close by. Looking around, she didn't see the other woman anywhere, al-though the water was clear and visibility good. "Where are you?" she said, not bothering to keep the censure out of her voice. She might've been distracted, but Leslie shouldn't have gone off on her own. She'd put both of them in danger by doing so.

"You know the cave Vaughn found yesterday?" The

other woman's voice was high with excitement. "Well, I'm inside, and you won't beli—" The feed crackled and died.

"Damn," Callie said more to herself than to her dive partner. As focused as she was, if her partner was in trouble, she had to find her PDQ. Remembering where the lava tube was that Vaughn had mentioned, she swam in that direction. Diving partners were always supposed to stay within sight distance of each other. It was one the basic rules taught to get an open-water dive certification. Callie had been so distracted she hadn't even noticed her partner's disappearance.

They were both to blame.

"Leslie?" She waited a minute for a response. Nothing but static. Thanos had to get these mikes to work and soon. "Can *you* hear Leslie?" she asked Maura, who was on board monitoring them through her mike.

"Negative."

"I'll find her. Stay tuned." Since it was an open mike, Maura could hear anything the divers said, but Callie said it anyway.

She cast a regretful glance backward. The treasure-filled ruins pulled at her like a powerful magnet would metal filings, but she kept swimming until she found the entrance to what looked like a giant cave in the cliff face. The small underwater mountain was a giant lava deposit that had cooled, then been covered over and over by hot magma. The opening near the base was at least twenty feet high, at least half that in width, and ridged with "bath-tub rings." It disappeared into the darkness up ahead.

A lava tube wasn't nearly as interesting as what she'd just left a few minutes earlier. "Leslie?" Callie skimmed her powerful flashlight around the opening. The golden circle bounced off the rough curved surface of the tube but couldn't penetrate the darkness at the far end.

The channels were conduits through which an active, low-viscosity lava flow developed a hard crust as it traveled beneath the heated lava. Some channels, she knew, were forty or fifty miles long. She hoped Leslie hadn't taken it upon herself to explore on her own.

"Come inside and see!" Leslie's voice fuzzed in and out.

Callie had seen hundreds of lava tubes. She didn't need to swim into one to know what it looked like. Viscous rhyolite lava flows formed knobby, blocky masses of rock throughout the area, under and, in many places, over the city's various structures. *That's* what she wanted to see.

"No thanks. I'm waiting right outside."

Crackle.

"Damn it. Les, can you hear me? Maura?"

Neither responded. Callie swore again, then swam into the dark entrance, strafing her light to lead the way and illuminating the silver flash of a small school of tiny picarel heading the same way. The cave entrance was a lot bigger than she'd expected. The floor was sandy with a few piles of rocky outcroppings, breakdown from the ceiling. Long streamers of vegetation swayed in her wake. No sign of Leslie, however. Not even the bounce of light up ahead from the other woman's flashlight.

A few minutes passed as Callie swam through the darkness, lit only by the bright beam of her flashlight. Particles in the water drifted in and out of the beam like dust motes. "Keep swimming," Leslie's voice crackled in her ear. "About five hundred feet . . . there's a right-hand bend."

"Leslie, stop and wait for me." All she got was static in reply. Mildly annoyed, she desperately wanted to get back to the ruins in the open water before daylight began to fade. Callie followed the tunnel almost vertically now before rounding the corner, her powerful light leading the way.

Three *Dentex macrophthalmus* swam toward her, veering left only when she stayed put. The large-eyed dentex's pinkish scales looked phosphorescent in the beam. The darkness became less dense the farther she went. She realized that she could see the striations in the magma, see the progress it had made in its slow path as it cooled in the sea. How many thousands of years ago? There was no longer any need for her light, and she switched it off.

The chamber was, if not flooded with light, certainly bright enough for Callie to see Leslie sitting perched on the edge of a rocky outcrop, ten feet above the water, mask in hand.

A grin lit her face. "Whatcha think? A cave! How frigging cool is *this*?"

What she thought was that her dive partner was wasting productive time exploring and pulling her away from her own work. Callie swam closer, then rested a supporting hand on the rough rock below Leslie's swinging fins. She lifted her mask. The air was a bit musty smelling, but fresh.

"Impressive." Her voice echoed in the vastness of the cavern. "But not a cave, a *lava* tube." She pointed up at a variety of speleothems, stalactite forms: shark tooth, splash, and tubular. "See the tubular lavacicles?"

"Lavacicles?" The shifting reflection of the water contorted her features ghoulishly as she grinned. "Like icicles? Amazing. We must be really close to the surface, right? This air is pretty fresh for an air pocket, and it's so light."

"I agree. How'd you get up there?" Callie indicated the rough, vertical cliff face high above her.

"There are steps cut into the rock over there." Leslie gestured to the right. "We aren't the first humans to find this place."

Callie doubted the steps were human-made, probably the ebb and flow of the water and tides over centuries eating into the hardened lava rock. Drain tubes commonly exhibited step marks on their walls, which marked the various depth the lava had flowed through the tube.

"I didn't realize I'd come so close to the surface." The arched ceiling of the cavern was covered with algae and sea creatures. Clearly it filled with water—consistently, as indicated by the intermittent drips from the rough ceiling some thirty feet overhead.

"Did you go farther in?" Sometimes the lava flowed in an unchanneled fan as it left its source. Those tubes tended to be much narrower, and were frequently blocked by debris. Just out of curiosity, she swam to where Leslie had indicated she'd find the "stairs."

"No, but it looks as though it goes quite a way in behind me. I ventured in a bit, but the rock's rough as hell. I don't want to cut my feet."

"Another time th—Holy crap!" Callie breathed. "These steps *are* human-made!" There was no mistaking the crudely carved and chiseled steps in the blacked lava rock face. Human-made, and smoothed by the water. Someone had, at some time in the far distant past, used tools to cut seven uneven steps from one level to the next. The number seven had been the perfect number, lucky and magical to the ancient Greeks.

People had known about this entrance to the sea, had used the stairs to access the water. The thought boggled Callie's mind, and the lava tube was suddenly interesting. Had people centuries after the drowning of Atlantis discovered a path to the Lost City via lava tube? There was certainly no way an average person could have held his or her breath long enough to free-dive the length of the lava tube to this cavern.

Who? When? Why? Most important, how?

"Time," Maura said in her ear.

Callie, about to remove her fins to start up the steps, mentally cursed. She hadn't even glanced at the time. "On our way. Leslie?"

The other woman got awkwardly to her feet. "Time already? But this—"

"We'll come back and explore in a couple of hours." Had Jonah known about the lava tunnel? Callie wondered as she waited for the other woman to descend the narrow, precariously angled steps, fastening her mask as she went.

"Mind blown?" Leslie asked via the headset as she slipped into the water beside Callie.

"Boggled." To say the least.

Silently, they swam down the tube and back into the open water. She wanted to stay there all day, now torn between wanting to get back to her newly discovered artifacts, and the tantalizing hint of a street, and possibly a sewage system.

Despite her disappointment, Callie reminded herself it had all been right here thousands of years. It would still be here in a couple of hours.

"Mr. Cutter, welcome." Smiling, hand extended, the man strode into the small parlor followed by Tall and Small, and a stunningly beautiful young woman clinging to his arm.

"I'm Kallistrate Spanos—Kall, if you like." Mid-forties, with a pleasant, craggy face and an open smile, the man extended his hand in welcome. Like the other men he wore enveloping black robes, but he was at least forty years younger than the ones Jonah had seen when they'd been escorted through the small house.

The woman who stood beside Spanos had to be his mistress. Dressed as she was in skintight jeans and a white tank top that hugged her body and bared her shoulders, and black spiky-heeled boots that came almost up to her knees, she was a jarring counterpoint to the black-robbed men.

If the dramatic difference in clothing hadn't been enough, the large gold hoop earrings, dark eye makeup, long dark-red nails, and abundance of long curly hair certainly made her seem as out of place as a hooker in a nunnery. Or in this case, a hooker in a monastery. She couldn't have been more overt if she tried, and she'd tried very hard to look as outrageously, overtly sexy as possible. All she needed was a FOR SALE sticker on her ample cleavage.

"This is the light of my life, my little sister, Anndra, and you've met Trakas and Eliades. Demetriou will be distressed to have missed you."

Jonah couldn't imagine why, but he shook the man's hand, introducing Vaughn and Saul. Pleasantries exchanged, their host indicated a group of deep, brown leather chairs near a bank of windows overlooking a small enclosed courtyard. The room looked and smelled like an antique book store, with leather-bound books stuffed into ceiling-to-floor bookshelves three deep. The furniture was old, the area rug worn.

The place smelled of musty paper, candle wax, and dust. Dust motes lazily drifted in the streams of sunlight coming through the windows overlooking the stone-paved courtyard. No plants, no fountain, nada. There wasn't anything green to be seen. The walled yard was the same stone as the floor. Just a ten-by-ten walled nothing.

Not only did the homes here have no ocean views, apparently they didn't want *any* view.

Trakas and Eliades, both forty or fifty years older than the rest of them, remained standing by the door in the shadows while everyone sat down in the pool of sunshine. Jonah reached for his sunglasses, then realized it might be rude to conceal his eyes and left them in his pocket. Vaughn and Saul also squinted into the brightness.

"Your men made an immediate visit sound imperative," Jonah told his host, keeping his opinion of their methods to himself. "Refusal of the invitation sounded dire. I was curious." Not particularly curious, not when he had all sorts of interesting things to uncover on— *beneath* his ship. But now that he was here, he could see that the ominous threats of yesterday had been no more than theatrics.

Spanos smiled. "Overly dramatic. Still, it's always pleasant to have company. So few people visit us here on Fire Island."

"I wasn't aware that anyone lived on the island. It doesn't look inhabited at all. Do you and your sister live here permanently?"

"No, we are frequent visitors, however. Our forefathers have always lived on Fire Island. We consider it, even if we are not permanent residents—home."

"And where is home?" Jonah asked.

"Unfortunately, I spend most of my time in hotels around the world. You can see why coming home to Fire Island's natural beauty is so desirable."

"Hotels?" Jonah rested his ankle on the opposite knee,

but he was far from relaxed. He still had no fucking idea why he'd been summoned, and for what purpose. He had about ten more minutes of pretending to be interested before he got the hell out of Dodge. "Is that the business you're in?"

Spanos smiled. "Hotels? No. I am in the cosmetic industry. Product development and some sales. A great deal of travel."

Jonah looked at the guy's sister. If those were the cosmetics, the guy must be in the poorhouse.

"Anndra has her own path." Spanos stroked her knee. "Don't you, my dove?"

"I'm a student," she said in an accent that sounded more British than Mediterranean.

Jonah rubbed the back of his neck. "We thought this was a deserted island. There's no indication of civilization from the sea at all."

Four more minutes for someone to get to the point and he'd be adios.

"That was by design originally. Our forefathers valued the seclusion, and built this small village away from prying eyes. It's become a habit for the inhabitants to be equally private, I'm afraid. A sore trial to my dear sister who chafes at the restrictions of a small community such as this." His gaze slid over to Anndra. "Isn't that so, my dear?"

Anndra Spanos, perched on the arm of her brother's chair, one slinky leg crossed over the other, exposing a strip of spiked, buckled leather circling the ankle of each boot, smiled into Jonah's eyes. He had the oddest impression that the smile was no more than a facade. In fact she, out of everyone in the room, gave the impression of a small, pretty, but deadly spider watching a plump fly flounder in its web. Jonah blinked away the bullshit.

Achaikos Trakas flushed, then stepped back farther into the shadows by the door. "*Oxi, Kyria*," he murmured, in a small, sullen voice.

No, *mistress*?

"Naughty, Anndra," her brother said, squeezing her jean-clad knee in a decidedly *un*brotherly way. "Behave please, *agapi mou*, we have guests."

"*Vevea, tha simberiforthw, agapimene mou adelfe.*" The woman grinned, showing straight white teeth as she flung her arm around his shoulders and rested her cheek on top of his head.

Didn't look particularly sisterly to Jonah, but then he'd never had a sister, so what the hell did he know? "We'll be anchored for several months, would it be possible to get fresh produce here instead of going all the way to Crete?" Jonah asked. There was a slightly . . . *off* atmosphere in the sunlit room. Something he couldn't put his finger on, but he trusted his gut and listened.

"Of course," Kall said, smiling as he reached up to stroke his sister's dark hair. "We don't have our own beef here, but sheep and chickens, and of course fruits and vegetables. In fact—" He snapped his fingers. "Bion, make a, how you say, care package for our friends. Include some of those delectable strawberries we had with breakfast."

Small bowed himself out, sideways because of his girth, disappearing into the shadows before disappearing from the room.

"What is it you do out there, Mr. Cutter?" Anndra Spanos sat up, leaning forward so that the shadow of her cleavage emphasized the firm swells of her breasts. Her eyes were black and deep-set, with long spiky lashes he found a bit distracting. She oozed sexual attraction designed to snare the attention of every man in the room the way a Venus flytrap oozed sweet sticky liquid to trap its victims. Her appearance and actions did just the opposite to Jonah.

He glanced at both Saul and Vaughn. Both men were mesmerized by her overt sensuality. Perhaps they all needed shore leave and some R&R. But since, while waiting for Callie, they'd only been back on board for a few days, he figured they'd all have to take their blue balls in hand.

"*Stormchaser* is a salvage ship," he told Kall. "I tracked down a Chinese junk from the twelve hundreds. Since there have been people living on Fire Island for centuries, I'd be very interested in any local legends. Any mentions, actually, that might shed more light on her."

Kall waved an expansive hand. "You are most welcome to peruse my library. I have many books and scrolls going back hundreds of years, also some that refer to documentation and stories from even further back than that. I haven't, as yet, read them all, so I have no knowledge of what you might uncover. It would be an interesting pursuit, and one I'd enjoy assisting you with. How did this junk sink, do you know?"

The offer was too tempting to refuse. Perhaps those documents mentioned the city beneath the wreck. Callie would love to get her hands on them, Jonah was sure. And while he was painfully aware of the hands-off nature of their relationship, he'd enjoy having some time alone with her off the ship. A win–win.

"I'll take you up on that offer," Jonah smiled. "I know our marine archaeologist will enjoy going through any old documents you have."

Spanos inclined his head. "He also will be made welcome."

"*She*," Jonah said with a smile. "Dr. Calista West is well known in her field."

"Do you know how this junk sank?"

The man was focused, Jonah thought, answering his repeated question. "From all indications she was caught in the debris of a volcanic explosion, but we'll know more as we salvage more of her."

Spanos looked to Achaikos Trakas.

The old man shot him an unfathomable look from rheumy eyes, his heavy jaw clenched as he addressed Jonah and the others. "Our volcano most recently erupted in the early twelve hundreds." His broken English was clipped. Damn it to hell, Jonah and the others were only here at Trakas's invitation. If he was pissed they were taking up Spanos's time, he shouldn't have insisted Jonah come.

"Ah." Spanos looked pleased. "Possibly the killer of your ship?"

"Possibly. Your papers may very well answer that question if there were eyewitnesses on the island who kept records."

"What an exciting project," Kall said enthusiastically. "I'm very much looking forward to helping you uncover answers, and if not answers, *clues*. I presume, since you are here, that the ship carried something of great value?"

Jonah was no fool; he'd done his homework, and had a legal team all over the *Ji Li* and who might lay claim to her. The same attention to detail that Cutter Salvage gave all their finds. The inhabitants of tiny Fire Island couldn't waltz in and stake their claim. Still, what the junk carried was none of the other man's business.

"She traded goods from mainland China to Spain and Portugal. We only found a partial manifest of what she carried," Jonah said. "Let's leave the speculation until I have something in my hands."

Anndra's black eyes gleamed. "Treasure!" She clapped her hands, making the heavy gold charm bracelet on her wrist jangle. She looked to her brother. "That is *most* exciting. Kall, may I be permitted to go and see what Jonah has discovered so close to our shores?"

Permitted? How about somebody fucking well asking *him*, seeing as how it was his ship? He tamped down his irritation. "We haven't found anything other than the junk at present, but you're welcome to come on board when we have something to show you."

"Tonight?" she asked eagerly.

"There's nothing to see," Vaughn pointed out. "But—" He slewed his gaze to Jonah. Jonah shook his head slightly, and Vaughn finished. "—as Jonah says, it'll be more exciting to show you the treasures when we have them aboard."

"Oh." Her shoulders slumped for a moment, and then she straightened with a smile. "I could come for dinner, no? I could bring you the delicious strawberries Eliades grows in his garden." She turned back to her brother, grasping the inside of his thigh. "Say yes, Kall, *please*? I am going mad with nothing to do and no one to talk to with just all these old people about!"

Their host shrugged, spreading his hands. "What is a brother to do? This would be acceptable to you, Jonah? I would not like my foolish sister to impose."

Crap. The last thing Jonah wanted was strangers on board. Beside the intrusion factor, besides the necessity to remain as low-key as possible about the underwater city, he and his team were still bonding. Not to mention he had a feeling none of the women on board would particularly like overtly sexy Anndra.

"Perhaps in a week or two when we have something worth your whi—"

"The produce has been taken down to the dock, *Kyrie*." The little fat guy was back like a ghost, hands inside the sleeves of his robe, plump face glistening, breath erratic as if he'd jogged the distance.

"Knock before entering, Eliades," Kall scolded gently. "Remember?"

Jonah had had enough. He had work to do, and paying social calls to the locals wasn't getting it done. He got to his feet as the old man bowed his head obsequiously. Saul and Vaughn rose as well. "Thanks for your hospitality." Although now that he thought about it, there'd been none. "But we have to get back to our project. I'll let you know when we have something of interest for you to see."

Kall and his sister also got to their feet. "Yes, that would be most agreeable. I am sorry to see you go, I'm sure we'll meet again very soon. And if you don't mind, I will accompany my sister to see what you discover at a more convenient time."

"Sure. Both of you will be welcome when we have something to show off."

"And I will give you my personal number and you may call here anytime." Spanos handed Jonah a thick, cream business card. "I will be interested in knowing what progress you make with the sunken ship."

"I'll walk you out," Anndra offered, tucking her hand into the crook of Jonah's arm and effectively pressing her breast against his biceps. The heated scent of her spicy perfume drifted to him from her velvety cleavage, and her long hair brushed his chin.

"Perhaps I can do more than dinner," she whispered

once they were out of the line of sight of her brother. "Perhaps you would let me stay the night, no?"

God only knew, she was exactly the diversion he needed to keep his eyes, hands, and everything else away from Callie, but instead of feeling even a mild attraction, Jonah was slightly repulsed by her. Go figure.

Just when a man thought he'd have to search far and wide for a chance to relieve his pent-up frustration, an opportunity placed herself squarely in his lap. Odd then that his sudden windfall made him uncomfortable as hell.

He didn't want the woman offering herself to him like a deli sandwich, and he couldn't have the woman he wanted.

He was well and truly fucked.

Eight

Brody lugged over another tub filled with the muriatic solution to wash the coins they'd brought to the surface earlier. Callie, Leslie, and Brody had tagged and assigned ID numbers to this morning's artifacts. They'd logged the DGPS coordinates, as well as bottom terrain and depth, then entered everything into the Cutter Salvage database. The squared centers were lined up to be photographed in individual, labeled clear-plastic bags before they packed them to ship.

Brody came up behind her, resting his hand on Callie's shoulder. "Hungry?"

He smelled strongly of beer and mouthwash. She shifted out of reach, concentrating on the task at hand. Washing the silver and gold pieces from the junk's storeroom was a mindless task. But there were a lot of them, and they'd be the first thing transported back to Cutter Cay in the morning. The rest of the artifacts would need days, if not weeks more processing so she could actually *see* what she had. The artifact with the gear was her top priority. She couldn't wait to dig into it and uncover what centuries had hidden. "The sandwiches will hold me until dinner," she said absently. Her hands moved independently from her mind, which was on what the object could possibly be.

Ji Li.

"I thought Jonah wanted you to work exclusively on Atlantis." Brody leaned his hip on the table beside where Callie worked, watching her fill individual cups with the muriatic-acid-and-water solution to begin dissolving the concretion around the next batch of coins.

The room suddenly darkened as if someone had pulled a blind over the sunlight streaming through the window. She didn't care for Brody, no matter how hard she tried to push aside old prejudices. "I get paid either way, and we don't know what city that is. Not yet. And I enjoy exploring a shipwreck just as much as you guys do."

She'd spent several hours diving the *Ji Li* with Leslie, and in turn Les had joined her nearby as she searched for artifacts from the city.

Callie found nothing nearly as exciting as the statue head and the gear—*lump*—but Leslie had handed her a shard of pottery she found, and Callie had it propped up on her worktable to admire the still-fresh colors. Now it was safely photographed and documented and out so she could enjoy it as she worked. The blue swirls and images of birds on the creamy background were a fragment of a vase, she thought. Part of some ancient *someone's* daily life.

Now that she'd found some real, datable artifacts, she felt as though she was earning the exorbitant amount Jonah was paying her.

It was possible that the coins came from spillage from the *Ji Li*, but as encrusted as they were it was impossible to tell yet. The junk, for now, was far more orderly and concrete than some amorphous city that may or may not be the fabled Atlantis. Callie knew she'd go kicking and screaming until she had absolutely undeniable proof that the city was Atlantis.

Until she cleaned the rest of her artifacts, the coins and the broken piece of vase were precious finds and she was going to enjoy every moment she had with them.

"No city?" Brody raised a brow. "Roads, sewage systems, and courtyards? Even to my untrained eye that makes up, if not a city, a civilized town."

"I didn't say it isn't a city. I'm still not convinced it's Atlantis," Callie pointed out, her gaze out the window at the unexplainable dusk. "Is that fog?" She rubbed her arms, suddenly chilled. It had been eighty degrees a few hours ago when they'd come back on board.

Brody twisted his mouth in disbelief, then turned to the window before looking back at her. "Yeah, it is. Thick, too." He leaned his elbow on the sill, peering through the glass. "Holy crap, did you see that?"

"No. Was that lightning?" The crack of lightning snapped and she mentally counted, waiting for a clap of thunder, but it never came.

Looking concerned, Leslie joined him at the window. "Weird. Unusual for this time of year, isn't it?"

"Unusual for the time of year, the time of day, and the temperature, sure." Callie settled a coin in each container. "Brody, will you go ask the captain if there's a weather front coming in? Maybe we should lock things down." Suddenly the fog lit up with a bluish glow; this time, she *did* see it.

"Well, that answers the question. Electrical storm." She carefully rinsed a silver coin with a worn edge.

Leslie stepped back from the window. "What if we get hit?"

Callie watched the jagged blue streaks light up the clouds crowding against the window. "Salt water is an excellent ground. I wouldn't go on the top deck holding aloft a golf club, however," she told the other two drily. "If you stay clear of the window you'll be fine. It's actually quite lovely."

"I hope the guys get back soon." Leslie perched on one of the long tables nearby. "I want to show them the lava tube cave and get Jonah's take on those steps."

Callie pulled off her gloves, tossing them near the plastic container. In her experience, storms like this one never lasted long. Beautiful, deadly if people lacked common sense—something Jonah Cutter had in spades. She wasn't worried about them. Not really. Not a lot. Hardly at all.

She wished Jonah would get back; she didn't like thinking of the guys out in a storm in the relatively small *Riva*. She slid off her stool. "Why don't we talk to the captain—see on the weather station how big this thing is."

"I like a good plan," Brody said with alacrity. "Let's all go and see what she has to tell us."

In the few minutes it took to get to the wheelhouse, the white fog grew so thick Callie could see neither the stern nor prow of the ship. The flashes of light in the clouds grew more frequent and spectacular.

"Wow. Hi, Captain, ever see anything like this?" Callie asked as they walked in to see Maura and Gayle talking. It wasn't a romantic chat if their posture was any indication.

The captain and first mate might be married, but Callie hadn't seen Maura and Gayle display any overt romantic gestures beyond a look.

Maura frowned, pulled away from their discussion. "The only time I've seen fog like this was in San Francisco a couple of years ago, remember, Gay? It shouldn't be here."

"That was fog and low-lying stratus clouds," Gayle pointed out, tapping the instruments as one would kick a car tire. "Lightning storms at sea are really rare," she told Callie and the others. "Except when you're in coastal water twenty or so miles from shore. This is a first for me, too. Let's get Thanos up here to run some diagnostics when this is over. Hopefully all systems will return to full functionality. If things are wonky afterward, someone will have to go and get parts."

"We have the backup generator if we need it," Maura reminded her. "But let's see how the storm plays out. This might only last an hour or three. Thanos is with Jonah and the guys, remember? Let me call Dell up here to see if he can figure out what's wrong." Dell Quist was both deckhand and second engineer.

The captain called him, then turned to lean against the table. "*Wonky?*" she repeated, a smile in her voice. "Is that your professional opinion as my first officer?" Maura's pinkie brushed her wife's for a second as their hands lay side by side on the mahogany table edge.

It was a sweet gesture that spoke volumes about the two women's relationship.

"Look how dense it is. It's as if we dropped off the end of the world," Gayle observed.

"I'm more worried about the electrical component. It seems to be impacting our instruments," Maura muttered. The fog pressed against the windows, obliterating everything beyond the glass. Streaks of condensation trailed rivulets down the windows, and blue bolts of light streaked like veins through the white outside.

Even though it was warm inside, Callie shivered, the small hairs raising up on her skin in reaction to the electrical energy circulating in the air. "It's very horror movie, isn't it?"

"Oh, please!" Leslie shuddered. "That just freaks me out more than I am already. My God, is it hot in here?"

Callie smiled. "Don't lose it, this isn't the Twilight Zone. It's water vapor, not cement—Holy crap!" She jolted as electric blue light filled the room. The wheelhouse was plunged into semi-darkness as every light went out. Her ears buzzed.

"Hell, there go our instruments! The Carnegie curve?" Maura asked Gayle.

"Wrong time and place, but certainly seems like it."

"What's a curve?" Brody asked.

Maura tried to get the control panels back online, but the screen remained dark. She cursed under her breath then turned to face the others. "It's the rhythm of the electrical heartbeat linked with the earth's rotation, and the way thunderstorms build. But it usually occurs at around seven p.m. GMT when the earth's atmosphere crescendos to an electrical peak across the globe. Right now it's not damn well anywhere close to seven p.m., we are *not* twenty miles off the coast of California, and this fog shouldn't *be* here. I have absolutely no explanation for this. I don't like not knowing things."

"As Callie said, we aren't in some weird paranormal warp," Gayle added. "It's an electrical storm that will pass. Once it's done, we'll see where we are. Switch to auxiliary power, Captain?"

Maura shot her a smile. "Sure, go ahead."

A second later the lights flickered on. But the instrument panels remained dark. Callie didn't like the look of *that*.

"Have you heard from the guys?" she asked. The captain and first mate were cool, calm, and collected, but she had her doubts about Leslie. And Brody also looked spooked. She kept her voice calm, but knowing Jonah and the others were out there, in the relatively small *Riva*, worried her. A lot. "They have instruments on board, but can they return to *Stormchaser* blind, with only their instruments to guide them?" Callie wondered what would happen to the much smaller craft if their instruments went wonky, too.

"All four of them are excellent sailors," the captain assured her. "And I'd trust my life to Jonah to get me out of any tight jam at sea. They'll be fine."

"It'll blow over pretty fast, right?" Brody leaned over the controls to peer outside, as if his vision would part the fog and they'd see blue sky any minute.

"It came in fast," Maura said. "Hopefully it'll dissipate just as quickly."

Day three. Everyone was restless, eager for the weather to get its shit together. Wasn't happening. There didn't look to be any break in the dense fog, or any abatement in the electrical storm, and they were stuck inside with no AC, no lights other than those hooked up to the generator, and no communications.

Jonah had hoped the fog would dissipate within hours of their return to *Stormchaser* three days ago. It had been no fun running blind. They'd hit the fog four miles off the coast of Fire Island. One moment it had been hot and sunny, not a cloud in the sky, the next they had zero visibility.

Far from dispersing within hours, it was just as thick and mystifying three days later.

Worse, the electrical storm shorted out all their instruments, leaving them functionally useless. *Stormchaser* was a literal sitting duck at sea. Without GPS and electronics to help them map the city or the wreck waiting down below, or to refill the tanks and gauge depth, all they could do was sit and wait. Riding out this oppressive pea-souper was like floating on the ocean inside a cotton-filled shoe box.

Jonah didn't share with the others the captain and first officer's concern that their instruments might not come back online when the storm did finally blow over. Some-one was going to have to navigate through the fog, and communicate with the outside world.

He picked himself. The entire dive team had spent the day before processing coins, tagging and assigning iden-tifications numbers in Callie's lab while she soaked and chipped away a large clump of something mystifying. It was painstaking work weighing, measuring, document-ing, and cleaning, but everyone participated despite the thin tempers.

They all wanted to get back under the water; there were things to see and be discovered. Jonah was intrigued by the description of the lava tube and stairs, and was just as eager as everyone else to go down and explore. But he didn't want anyone outdoors or in the water until the weather changed.

Once the coins spent ten minutes in the acid bath, they were rinsed in water and ready for three or four days in the electrolysis tank, which required a low-voltage current provided by the generator.

Among them, and with Callie looking over shoul-ders, they processed all the coins they'd found while he was gone. There were several more steps in the pro-cess, but that wouldn't come for days. The crew was restless *now*.

He strolled across the room, where Callie stood, hair piled in a neat, braided coil on top of her head, up off her neck, he supposed, in deference to the heat. As he came up behind her, Jonah was tempted to run his teeth along the delicate tendons of her nape, and taste the lightly tanned skin on her shoulders, which looked soft and silky. The smell of her damp, coconut-scented skin was like a drug. He shoved his fists in the front pockets of his shorts instead.

"Spanos has an extensive library of ancient documents," he said quietly as he stepped up beside her. "I need to get somewhere out of this s—"

"Yes!"

Jonah smiled. Because just looking at her flushed cheeks, glowing with the heat, and the way her water-cool eyes lit up was enough to make a rock smile. "You don't even know what I was going to suggest." But whatever he suggested he knew *yes* would always be the correct answer.

"We're going to Fire Island?"

"We'll try there first," he cautioned, not wanting to get her hopes up. The island was more than likely socked in just as they were. "If this weather extends that far, we might have to travel all the way to Crete."

"I'm game." She glanced behind him, where the coin cleaning was winding down. "What about the others?"

"They're better off here. I have no idea what we're going to encounter out there." Not that he wanted to go back three days after being on the island, but the second he mentioned the ancient documents he suspected were in that dusty library back on Fire Island, Callie was going to be like a dog with a bone.

And damn it, it was an opportunity to be alone with her. No funny business, just . . . alone. So sue him.

Pulling off her gloves, she wiped her hands on a towel. "When do you want to go? Now?"

"Too late. The weather might clear tomorrow, which will be safer. Either way, we'll go in the morning."

"Perfect. Then while we're hanging around here with idle hands, start attaching these electrodes to those coins over there."

Kallistrate Spanos had given Jonah his phone number. But the freakish electrical static in the air put paid to using the phones, and the radio didn't work. Still, seeing as how Spanos had offered them hospitality to come and get their fresh food from the island, he wasn't going to wait for an engraved invitation.

Hopefully when he and Callie showed up unannounced, he'd be just as generous with offering the use of his library.

"Callie and I are going to Fire Island to see if we can get some outside communications, and get some parts the captain thinks she'll need when this blows over," Jonah told the others the next morning after breakfast. They were sprawled on the deep sofas in the salon about to watch a movie on the giant screen thanks to the generator. *That's* how bored they were.

Callie pushed to her feet. "Now?"

Watching her eat a slice of jam and toast for breakfast earlier had given Jonah a low-down ache that wasn't going away. If watching a woman eating breakfast turned him on, his mind boggled at seeing any more of Callie than what her T-shirt and shorts exposed. Her hair was braided and hung in a bumpy, glossy rope down her back, neat and no-nonsense, except that the paintbrush tip of said braid almost reached her narrow waist, and seeing it made him think of crumpled sheets, hot sweaty skin, and a mile of silky dark hair wrapped around his body. He was almost tempted to take Anndra up on her offer. Almost.

"It's as good a time as any," he told the object of his fantasies. Diving would help. A huge ocean between them would help, physical activity would help, a fucking frontal lobotomy would help. Being on the ship blind and incapacitated did *not* help.

He'd already logged more miles jogging around the deck than if he'd been in an Ironman race.

Callie's face lit up. "Give me five minutes to get my shoes." She dashed out of the room on silent feet, braid bouncing down her back, and Jonah's scrotum tightened as it always did when she was around. He was starting to get used to the uncomfortable feeling, and the annoying heightened awareness she always brought with her. He was the lamp, Callie the electrical plug.

Everyone was good-natured about the two of them going off without them. Jonah could've let any of the others join them Callie. He trusted his chief engineer to get her to and from Fire Island safely. But if anyone was spending the day with her, it would be himself.

He was a glutton for punishment.

By the time Callie got back—a good fifteen minutes at least—Thanos had the *Riva* running and ready to go. Not that they could even see the smaller boat. They got down to the dive platform more by instinct and feel than by seeing where the hell they were going. Every time they touched metal, they received a snap of electrical charge for their trouble.

"Ouch!" Callie sucked on her thumb and Jonah briefly thought about just tipping himself into the water to cool off.

The generator had allowed Maura and Gayle to electronically contact someone on a weather channel, apparently. "Any updates from that weather services today?" Jonah asked Thanos as they moved through the eerie whiteness of the fog. Even with the retractable hood up as protection from the elements, the fog felt like small, cold, damp, *unpleasant* fingers trailing across his skin. Static electricity pinched when he touched anything conducting electricity.

The whole trip was turning into an interesting character study of himself. He didn't do a lot of belly-button psychology. He'd never been superstitious, never had a particularly active imagination, unless it had something to do with a ship he was designing. Nor did he usually get "feelings" from people or places. But apparently his imagination was working overtime on this salvage.

"It wasn't a weather service," Thanos grumbled. "I think the captain managed to get ahold of some kid on a shortwave radio. Whoever he is, he said he'd check." Thanos pulled his windbreaker collar up around his jaw and hunched his shoulders. "He got back to us half an hour ago. Line was crackling, and sounded fried, but the gist, according to him, was that three reporting stations say there is *never* this kind of fog bank in this area." He sounded very Greek as he spoke. He was spooked, and attempting not to show it.

"Someone should come and see it for themselves," Callie said into the oddly muffling miasma. Moisture beaded on her hair and made her skin look even dewier than usual. She'd changed into jeans and a royal-blue windbreaker, which made her eyes look more deep sea than shallow water.

Jonah wanted to snuggle up with her in the protection of the hood. He wanted the right to hold her close, and warm her body with his . . .

Fuck. He stared blindly into the blank white world through the windshield. It was good to want things. And God only knew, one rarely got what one wanted, not without a boatload of hard work. Which he'd be more than willing to do, if there wasn't the small matter of a loving husband waiting for her back home.

Too bad all his wants and needs would have to go un-fulfilled. *Live with it, buddy.*

He stuffed his hands into the pockets of his own jacket and hunched his shoulders, hands fisted to prevent the overwhelming need to grab her. "It's probably just an anomaly, too low lying to register."

"It *should* register," Thanos said mutinously. "It should alert the weather people. It's odd, and while unprece-dented, their instruments surely should have registered what we can all see plainly with our own fucking eyes. Excuse me, Doctor."

"Can't last fo . . ." Jonah stepped forward. "Well, shit, look at that." Fire Island appeared ahead of them like a mirage, bathed in brilliant sunshine from a clear, cloud-less sky.

Callie looked over her shoulder. "Look behind us."

Jonah turned. The fog was like a solid mass behind them, yet he felt the heat of the sun hot on his face.

"I've never seen anything like this." Callie came to stand beside him, her sleeve brushing his. "We *are* in the Twilight Zone."

"Weird, all right. Let's ask our host about it. He's lived here all his life. If anyone knows it'll be Spanos."

The ancient-looking fishing boat was tied up where it had been a couple of days before. When the craft bumped the cement wall, Jonah jumped out, then held out his hand to help Callie.

"We're probably going to be here awhile," he told Tha-nos. "Want to hang out here in the sun, or head back to *Stormchaser*?"

The chief engineer scanned the hillside, then glanced back at Jonah. "*Mè kheíron béltiston*," he said drily.

"And that means?"

"The least bad choice is the best. I'll head back. How long you think you need?"

Jonah glanced at Callie, who was looking around, taking it all in. "Four hours?"

"A whole library? At least."

Jonah glanced at Thanos. "Four hours, but bring something to entertain yourself in case we stay longer."

Thanos saluted, then angled the boat away from the cement dock. The *Riva* was clearly visible until it was . . . not.

"We head this way. Watch your step, the ground is sandy and littered with rocks." He would've taken her hand. A chivalrous gesture Jonah would've offered his mother or grandmother. Callie was neither. And if he got hold of her hand he'd never fucking let go. He kept a cautious eye on her as she picked her way up to where scrub grass and shrubs made footing safer.

Callie shaded her eyes to look up at the off-center volcano. "When did your new friends say that last erupted?"

"Spanos didn't appear to know. He deferred to one of the old guys. *He* said twelve something."

"So it *could've* sunk *Ji Li*. You said Spanos didn't know about her sinking, right? Then why do you think there could be writing about it in his library."

"Frankly, I'm not even sure it *is* his library."

She looked over at him, so Jonah saw himself reflected in her glasses. "Why wouldn't it be?"

"He said he and his sister consider this home, but he's hardly ever here. And I get the feeling the old guys don't much like either Spanos. He was pretty vague about what we'd find in the books, and from the amount of dust on the shelves, I doubt anyone has opened any of them in years. Maybe more than a few years. But that's not what interests me, and you know it. I want to see what we can find about our city. If it *is* Atlantis, people living this close to it would know about it."

"Especially in those days." Callie paused to look around, skin dewy with perspiration. "If Atlantis existed, and if that is Atlantis down there, it would've been a major seaport. Trade ships would've been coming and going. Any writing or verbal histories passed down through the generations would have descriptions and details. God, I can't wait to see what we uncover. It'll be incredible if he allows us free access."

If Spanos didn't, Jonah figured he'd have four hours alone with Callie on a picturesque island. He'd had worse days.

"I think he's trying to buy my favors so I take his sister off his hands," Jonah said drily, observing the two black robed men waited for them at the top of the hill. They must be lookouts.

"Is she eighty like the men who visited the ship the other day?"

"Nope. Mid-twenties."

Callie shook her head. "What twenty-something woman wants to live on an isolated island in the middle of nowhere? Are there any other women living here?"

Jonah shrugged. "Didn't see any, now that I come to think of it."

"No wonder he wants you to take her off his hands, poor girl."

Jonah frowned. "I'd reserve judgment on the '*poor girl*' until you meet her. Our transportation is waiting up ahead."

Callie looked up to see the men and the donkeys. "Cute. But I'd prefer to walk."

"Same here."

The two old men insisted that they ride, but Jonah was equally insistent that they walk. He remembered the way, so they wouldn't get lost. After several minutes of back-and-forth in his poor Greek, the men agreed to let them walk.

"Is everyone who lives here as old as Methuselah?" Callie asked as they started off up the first incline.

"Everyone I've seen so far, except for Spanos and his sister."

"Doesn't look as if *anyone* lives here."

"There's a small settlement tucked between the hills at the foot of the volcano. Maybe twenty houses. They seem self-sustained. They have communal plots for fruit and vegetables. Some chickens and sheep. Clearly they fish."

"Doesn't sound like the kind of place a man would bring his sister to live. How old is he?"

"Forty, maybe? I'm not great at judging someone's age, but he's about four decades younger than anyone else around."

"I wonder what he does with himself here?"

Jonah shrugged. "Not a clue. We'll ask. He's some kind of cosmetics-something."

"This is an odd place for a cosmetics-something to hang out, isn't it?"

"It's *all* odd," Jonah told her drily. "Ever hear of Hebe Cosmetics? He's listed as CEO on his business card, with addresses in Athens, New York, and London."

"Never heard of them. But that doesn't mean anything. I don't wear makeup that often. And all those addresses don't mean anything, either. With an Internet connection and a mailbox, anyone can look like a mogul."

"Yeah. Exactly what I thought."

It took less time to get to the small village the second

time. Certainly it was quicker on foot than on the donkeys.

"This whole place looks like it's camouflaged," Callie
observed quietly as they walked up to the front door of
the largest house on the island. The house was right on
the dirt path, with just a narrow skirt of weedy grass
where a chicken pecked for its breakfast.

"Have you noticed how quiet it is?" Callie's voice was
pitched low. "No sounds of humans, or animals, or even
birdsong."

"My thoug—Anndra, good morning." It was barely
nine, and she was wearing a low-cut, glittery black sweater,
gold jeans, and high-heeled sandals.

"Jonah. I was so happy when they told me you were—
Who is *this*?"

Callie held out her hand. "Dr. Calista West. It's nice
t—"

"You didn't say you'd be bringing a woman." It sounded
both accusatory and petulant. She ignored Callie's out-
stretched hand.

"Callie is our marine archaeologist. She has an even
greater interest than I do in your brother's papers. Are you
going to let us in, or should we wait for your brother out
here?"

Wordlessly, Anndra widened the heavy wood door and
stood back. Jonah ushered Callie ahead of him.

"Kall is busy. We're both busy. But I'll let him know
you are here. Wait in the library," Anndra said flatly, all
fake niceties gone. "You know the way."

"Charming," Callie said under her breath. "She might
be best in show, but she needs her distemper shots."

Jonah grinned.

Callie looked around, clearly having already forgotten the other woman. "I wonder how old this house is?

Architectural design hasn't changed much in this region for hundreds of years, if not thousands. This looks as if it's been here for centuries."

"I suspect so," Jonah said quietly. There was no one around, but walls always had ears. They strode down the dark hallway, but after turning a corner ran into Small.

"Good day, *Kyrie* Cutter. You are here to visit my— Kallistrate's very fine library?" Small asked, his voice cordial enough.

"We are. And happy to be allowed to do so. Callie, this is Bion Eliades. Dr. Calista West from Miami."

"*Despinis.*" Eliades bowed his head respectfully, then gestured with a pale, plump hand for them to follow him. He was wide enough to plug the corridor ahead, which meant they plodded slowly behind him. The hem of his robe made a soft, rasping sound on the tile floor, and his sandals made a small *snap* as he walked.

Jonah stepped closer to Callie as the hair on the back of his neck lifted for no apparent reason.

Nine

"You don't need to stay if you have something better to do," Callie told Eliades softly in Greek. Spanos and his sister hadn't made an appearance. A good thing: She didn't want anyone hanging over their shoulders all morning. The old man was there, but mostly dozing in his chair, emitting a small throaty snore every now and then.

Already covered with dust, she and Jonah stood in front of one of the ceiling-to-floor, wall-to-wall bookcases, going through the volumes. The leather-bound books, and thousands of loose-leaf manuscripts, were piled high on every shelf, higgledy-piggledy, three and four deep. It was laborious, dusty work, and she loved every magical second of it.

Callie knew if she dug deep enough into this gold mine of information she might find the gems she needed to decode what lay beneath the aqua waters of *Stormchaser*'s hull. She wished she had a month alone in the book-lined room. But even with just the few hours they had, the old man remained in the library with them, a corpulent, sleepy guard.

The poor old guy, seated in one of the comfortable, deep leather chairs, kept nodding off. His head jerked up at the sound of her voice. Blinking several times, he cleared his throat. "I am quite content to sit here and let my old bones soak up the sunshine. Don't let me disturb you."

"Can I get you anything?" Callie asked softly. Dressed from head to sandals in dense black wool, he couldn't be comfortable sitting in the blistering sunlight streaming through the window beside him.

The damp folds of his plump face creased into a sweet smile. "In my own home? It is I, Doctor, who should offer you *my* hospitality."

So the house was his, not Kallistrate Spanos's? She met Jonah's brilliant blue eyes to see if he'd caught that. He gave an infinitesimal nod. "Thank you n—"

Pushing himself up from the chair, and moving surprisingly fast for a man in his eighties who was at least a hundred pounds overweight, Eliades nodded his balding head as if remembering his hosting duties. "I will bring."

Callie waited until the sound of Eliades's surprisingly light footsteps faded to another part of the house. She'd palmed her cell phone in her jean pocket as the old man shuffled out of the room. The second she could no longer hear the snap of his sandals, she was already carefully flipping pages and taking pictures.

"Here," she whispered, pausing long enough to slide Jonah another tome the size of a phone book from the piles she'd sorted in the last two hours, ready for the time the old man left the room. She'd learned long ago never to ask. The answer was invariably no, and it was easier to beg for forgiveness than permission. She suspected that the sweet old man would not take kindly to them taking pictures of his books.

Keeping her voice low enough so that only Jonah, standing two feet away, would hear her, she instructed,

"Take pictures from the middle to the end, as fast as you can, before he comes back."

"Find something?" Immediately opening the heavy manuscript to the middle, Jonah slipped his phone from his back pocket. He didn't ask any more questions, just started taking pictures and turning pages.

He needed a shave, of course, but at least he wore a black T-shirt over black shorts this morning. He looked disreputable and sexy. The thick fog on the boat ride coming over had put a bit of curl in Jonah's dark hair, which had since dried. It should've softened his face, but instead the slightly shaggy, rumpled strands made him look even more masculine and appealing. Callie had been itching to comb her fingers through his hair for hours. But instead she kept them busy flipping the heavy vellum pages that smelled of dust, leather, and age.

She loved how focused he was, even though he had no idea what he was looking at, or for. He had a smudge of dirt on his cheek as he took a picture and flipped the pages. Rugged, masculine to the nth degree, and heart-poundingly sexy, Jonah Cutter was every fair maiden's wildest sexual fantasy.

But she was no fair maiden, and having sexual fantasies about a man she was going to screw out of his discovery of a lifetime made her feel like more of a bitch than ever.

She hadn't told Rydell that when she'd talked to him at the crack of daybreak this morning. She'd mentioned the strange fog, and the head, and the mechanical whatever-it-was. She'd told him about the silver and gold coins; she'd briefly discussed the lava tube, and the tiled floor. She hadn't mentioned the owner of *Stormchaser* or his natural allure.

Click. Turn page. Click. Turn. Click.

"Let me put it this way." Callie spoke softly as she finished taking shots of the book she was holding. "I'm guardedly freaking excited." An understatement of epic proportions. Inside she was doing a happy Snoopy dance, yelling *Holyshit! Holyshit! Holy. Shit!* at the top of her lungs.

Click. Turn page. Click. Turn page.

She spoke and read Greek, both modern and ancient, but the faded, spidery writing in the manuscripts was more ancient than ancient, and very hard to decipher. "I need more time to identify and analyze the structure of the morphemes—"

Click. Turn page.

"Which is?"

Click. Turn page.

The linguistic skill called morphology would help her ID linguistic units so she could better understand what she was reading. Or rather, trying to read. It seemed like a root dialect. Something akin to Greek, but also Latin. "Implied context, root words, intonation," Callie told him absently, taking pictures as fast as the cell phone camera would allow, and as fast as she could turn pages while being careful not to tear the delicate vellum.

No gloves; books left out here in the open, in a dusty, brightly sunlit room. The scientist in her cringed at such carelessness. These documents were invaluable. Priceless.

"Dear God . . ." Callie shifted the phone so she could better look at a newly opened page. This time her heart didn't race, it stopped with a hard thump. "I hope what I *think* I'm reading is really what I think it is—" Lord, what was she doing? No time to speculate—*Go. Go. Go. Before the hefty guard gets back*, her brain screamed.

Click. Turn page.

She repositioned the phone so she could take more pictures. There'd be plenty of time when they returned to *Stormchaser* to look and analyze. But, oh! She wanted to sit down, the large book in her lap, and try to read every intriguing, tantalizing, ancient word. "I can't wait to get back."

"Me, too, if it gets you this excited." Jonah's soft chuckle caused the already overstimulated little hairs on her body to stand up even more. Which showed how powerful her attraction to him was, because despite the incredible findings in her hands, she was still hyperaware of Jonah. All the time.

Callie heard the chink of china before she heard Eliades's shuffling gait heading back to the library. She glanced over at Jonah, who was already slipping his phone into his back pocket.

Quickly and reluctantly returning the two heavy books to their previous spaces, she stacked other books in front of them. Exactly as they'd found them. She hoped.

Taking a later manuscript with her, Callie sat down just as the old man trundled in, carrying a large, tarnished silver tray with cups and a tea-stained cozy-covered pot.

Jonah strode over to take the clearly heavy burden from Eliades's gnarled hands, then set it on what looked like an eighteenth-century Oeben marquetry mechanical table, which was probably worth double what her condo in Miami cost.

"You will take tea with an old man?" Eliades addressed Callie first, then looked to Jonah. "I would very much enjoy the company."

"We'd be honored," Callie responded, also in Greek. She didn't want to waste time sipping tea or chatting. What she'd seen so far had her too excited even to sit still. But she got up to pour three cups of almost black-colored tea, passing them out before returning to her chair with her own cup and mismatched saucer.

The tea was far too strong and bitter, but she politely sipped it anyway. Jonah set his cup and saucer on the table beside him and crossed one ankle over his knee, stretching his arms out on the wide curved arms of his chair, looking perfectly relaxed. "We appreciate you allowing us access to your library. There is material here, I'm sure, we couldn't find anywhere else."

"There have been people living on Fire Island for centuries, possibly longer. What you see here is an accumulation of writings passed down from the oldest son in each family for generations. This scriptorium has been here as long as my ancestors were alive. A very, very long time."

"This room was originally a scriptorium?" Callie asked, cradling her tea in her palm.

"What's a scriptorium?" Jonah asked.

"In medieval monasteries it was a room devoted to the copying of manuscripts. Are you an order of monks, *Kyrie* Eliades?" It would certainly explain the black robes and isolated living, and the fact that she hadn't seen any women other than Anndra Spanos. Callie suspected the young woman was the exception to the rules.

"No. Not monks. A different, more ancient order. You do not speak Greek, Mr. Cutter?" Eliades asked over his cup, sipping his tea.

"Only the most rudimentary words and phrases, I'm afraid. But I understand more than I speak. Dr. West is fluent, however."

The non-monk smiled. "Yes," he said in heavily accented English to Callie. "You have an excellent ear for my language." He waved an expansive hand around the book-lined room. "You have found what you were looking for? So difficult in a room of this size with so many works to choose from in a small amount of time."

"I think I have, yes." She indicated the book on the table beside her. "Have you lived here all your life," Callie asked, her eyes going to the hundreds if not thousands of dusty manuscripts and texts she was dying to get her hands on.

"I have, yes. Many, many years."

"And Kallistrate Spanos? Has he lived here all his life?"

"He left sixt—many years ago, and returns every few months to—to rejuvenate himself. This time we are fortunate to have his young sister visit as well. We hope that he will adjust once again to the simple life and teachings of Fire Island, and make his permanent home here with us again."

"I haven't seen any women. Are they too shy to come out?" Callie asked in a teasing tone.

"Other than Anndra, there have been no women here for many years. We are . . . caretakers of the island." He rested the cup on his knee. "Did you find anything of interest?"

Callie nodded, tamping her enthusiasm. "I think I've found a written report of a story from the correct time period. It mentions a Chinese boat being swallowed by the fire from the volcano. I'd like to ask—would it be possible to borrow some of these books for a few days? I promise to take excellent care of them, and return them as I find them."

"That book." He pointed a gnarled finger. "No more."

Disappointed, Callie reminded herself that they could come again, take more photographs. "Thank you, I'll be very careful with it. May we come back soon to look at more?"

"Here. Yes."

It was lovely and warm sitting in the sunshine pouring in through the dusty windows, but she wanted to get back to the ancient texts, which predated the sinking of the *Ji Li* by hundreds of years.

"We've encountered a strange anomaly in a localized area near where *Stormchaser* is anchored," Jonah said easily. "A dense electrical fog that's scrambled our equipment. The weather bureaus are insisting there *is* no fog. Is this something you've ever encountered?"

The old man shrugged even as he confirmed the oddity. "This is something no one has understood for centuries. The fog comes and goes. Once, twice a year. No one understands it. It is never wise to question God's will, yes?"

When it was obvious that the old man had settled in for a pleasant afternoon with his company, Jonah signaled Callie, and they both got to their feet. "Thank you for your hospitality, and for lending me the book."

"You may keep it as long as you want to," Eliades said magnanimously, pushing to his feet as well.

Callie topped his height by at least a foot. "I'll take the tray to the kitchen and then be on our way."

The old man wouldn't hear of them carting the tray off, so they said their goodbyes and stepped outside into the sunshine. Eliades stood outside the front door, hands tucked into his sleeves, watching them leave.

"I wonder what happened to your little friend Anndra?"

Jonah shrugged. "Probably off somewhere doing her nails, or curling her eyelashes."

"She's stunningly beautiful."

"I guess."

Callie glanced over her shoulder as soon as they were clear of the small group of houses. Jonah had just taken his phone out, presumably to call or text Thanos, when

Callie grabbed his forearm with both hands. Barely able to control her excitement, her words ran over each other. "Holy *crap*, Jonah! I can't wait to get these images back to *Stormchaser* to see what we have!"

His eyes narrowed. "You pulled those two documents from the back of the bookshelf. How did you know what was in them?"

"I didn't. But when I looked at all the shelves when we first walked in, I noticed how the dust was pushed back in several places. Those books were hidden from us in plain sight. Someone with not very good eyesight moved them to the back, and pulled others forward to block them from view."

"Will you be able to decipher what you got?"

She'd studied—briefly—the discipline of reading, deciphering, and dating historical texts. But it would take more than her basic skills. "Maybe. I hope I can at least get an idea of when they were written, and see how much I *can* read. The style of alphabet in every language evolves constantly.

"One has to know the various characters as they existed in various eras. I only took a semester of the study of ancient writing, but I have a friend in Spain who's a specialist in palaeography. Miguel's made it his life's work, and he's amazing, I'll send him what we have right away and see—"

Jonah put his hand on her wrist as she took out her phone. "Let's wait until you take a look yourself. If those texts allude to Atlantis, I don't want anyone else knowing about it until we're ready to announce it to the world."

Callie frowned, her anticipation fueling her agitation at Jonah trying to stonewall her efforts to decipher the images. What would take her weeks, maybe even months, would take Miguel only hours or days at most.

"If the images we have allude to Atlantis, chances are I won't *know* because I can't read them!"

"Let's wait until we get back to the ship and your lab and go from there, okay? No point going off half-cocked asking for help until we know how much and who we can trust."

She pulled her tingling wrist out of his grasp. "I trust Miguel." She didn't want Jonah touching her. Overreaction caused her heart to thump and her nerves to jump. Maybe she was running a fever?

"Then you'll still trust him in a few days when we see what you can do with your one semester of palaeography."

God the man was stubborn. "Two days."

"A week."

Ridiculous when a find of this significance was at their fingertips. "Three days."

"Four."

Callie crossed her arms, clutching the book she'd borrowed to her chest like a shield in battle. "Okay, but on the morning of day four I'm sending these images to Miguel to work on."

"Fair enough."

"Your buddy back there said several very interesting things today." Callie stared ahead as they picked their way down the winding path through the rock and brush.

"Like?"

"He referred to the library as *his* before he caught himself."

"Yeah, I noticed that. Perhaps Spanos and his sister are nightmare houseguests who never left."

Callie locked her gaze on Jonah's piercing blue eyes. How could such a cool color give the impression of so much heat? She imagined his gaze was hot—for her.

Translated that look into the feel of his hands touching her all over. She shivered in the hot sun.

It was a mistake to look at him directly like this. It was as if those eyes were tractor beams, holding her immobile while her pulse raced and a dull ache radiated from between her legs to throb in her breasts.

"Before he caught himself," she said, adjusting her depth perception, focusing on a shrub over his left shoulder, "it sounded as if he were about to say Spanos left *sixty* years ago. Is he that old? I thought you said he was in his early forties."

His gaze dropped to her mouth. "Maybe he's just well preserved. Left when he was a baby."

"Sure." That was possible. But Callie's gut told her that just like the hidden books, there was more being concealed here than just a few dusty tomes.

Jonah copied the images off their phones to his computer's hard drive, as well as a thumb drive, then backed everything up twice more.

Fortunately, all the systems knocked out by the electrical interference were back in working order as if there'd never been a problem once the strange fog disappeared. And that had disappeared as suddenly as it had appeared.

Still suspicious, Jonah called one of the most reliable weather stations in Europe, and spoke to their head meteorologist, Robin Waugh. Jonah trusted Robin, still enjoyed her company all these years later, and on hearing her sultry and very unscientific voice again seriously considered making a quick trip to Paris for a booty call.

He'd debated for all of thirty seconds as he watched Callie talking to the others while he was on the phone. Her elusive scent spiked the air in the cabin, making him all too aware she was within touching distance if he just reached out and . . . Not going to happen. He told Robin he'd catch up with her the next time he was in Paris, but they both knew he meant over coffee, not in the sack.

Robin checked back records and confirmed what Eliades had told him: The electrical storms and fog were intermittent, coming and going without warning. According to her weather station's records, the anomaly went back to the 1950s and, she suspected, giving it an educated guess, further, way further back than that.

"Jonah?"

"Sorry. What were you saying?"

Seated on the comfortable sofa in the salon, he and Callie looked at each page of text up on the big-screen television. They'd been at it for six hours; everyone else had hit the hay a while ago. The aroma of coffee lingered in the air despite their cups having gone cold.

With the lights dimmed for better viewing, the room was far too intimate. Callie was curled up at the other end of the deep sofa, but she didn't look the least bit relaxed as she leaned forward, holding a pen and a notebook, eyes fixed on the image in front of her.

She pointed with the pen. "See how this passage is written in a consonantal form from left to right?"

Jonah tipped his head to the side, still unable to make any sense of the squiggles and smudges. He was amazed she could identify anything resembling language there at all and now completely understood why she had wanted her friend's expert help.

"I'll take your word for it. It all looks like chicken scratches to me." How could she tell something this old and faded had been written left to right, or upside down? He wasn't even sure that he was looking at letters and not ancient fly guts. "Don't get me wrong, I'm as eager as you are to see if and how this relates to Atlantis, but my eyes are crossing, and my brain is about as thick as that fog."

"Go ahead and go to bed then," she muttered absently, chewing the corner of her lip as she leaned forward, elbows on her knees, staring at the screen. "I think I can figure out the next passage . . ."

Jonah loved watching her think. The twin lines of concentration between the wings of her eyebrows, the way she nibbled at the corner of her lower lip. He could almost hear the wheels turning. He bet she wasn't even aware he was sitting three feet away, watching her, or that leaning forward like that gave him a mind-numbing view of her cleavage. Who the hell could concentrate on a page of ancient text when something so delectable was on display in the same room?

"This appears to be written in Linear B syllabary, which was always on clay tablets. *Mycenaean*. The earliest Greek writing." Her voice rose with excitement, and she leaned forward, eyes fixed on the screen. "I've *never* seen it on parchment, and *never* like this. Holy crap! This appears to be *prose*. It's always been held that Mycenaean literature was passed on orally, because nothing was ever written down. Or not anything ever found anyway. Linear B doesn't lend itself to the sounds of Greek."

"Hmm."

"This is remarkable . . . The only Linear B documents ever discovered were prosaic lists. Mainly for trade. Inventory. They think perhaps some poetry. Never prose. But isn't a list—see—there aren't any short lines, which would indicate word dividers. That's *prose. Prose!*" She scrolled to the next image and dragged in a breath. "Linear A. Hieroglyphic script. I've seen it on seal stones, but those have yet to be deciphered.

"My God, Jonah . . ." Callie turned shining eyes to

him. Pale as peridot, and filled with wonder. She said with quiet awe, "The few pages we have from just two manuscripts could be the Rosetta stone of ancient Greece."

Jonah heard the wistful bliss in her voice, he understood the magnitude of the discovery, but in that instant his entire world shifted on its axis, and it had fuck-all to do with ancient writings.

She kept talking, her excited voice a sensual hum in his ears. He wanted to lie with her on a field of green grass under the sunshine so he could look at every inch of her body. He wanted to touch and taste, and linger while he did it, and then start again. He wanted to pick up that thick rope of braid and slowly unravel the strands, and spread them out around her in a dark silken blanket.

The light caught the long shiny scar on her arm, and Jonah's heart twisted in empathy. When she'd told him about the car accident, he'd been furious with her irresponsible parents. His father had been a drinker, too. More when he'd been around Zane, Logan, and Nick than he'd ever been around Jonah. But even as a kid, he'd had a problem with his father's social drinking.

It was fascinating to Jonah that while he and his brothers had lived a world and life apart, none of them drank more than one beer. He noticed Callie didn't drink at all.

"How old were you when your parents died?"

She blinked him into focus, her frown deepening. "Wow. That's out of the blue. What made you think about that now?"

"I was looking at your scar. It's hellish, and a badge of your courage. You said they were alcoholics. My father also had a drinking problem. More so when he was with my brothers, but he drank a lot."

She frowned, the light of discovery dimming in her

eyes, crowded out by more unsavory memories. Interestingly, she made no move to cover the scar, as most people
would do when mentioning what they perceived as a flaw.
Callie wasn't most people. "We have that in common
then."

"I don't think so. My mother was there to protect me
from the worst of it. I never saw him anything more than
slightly tipsy. But my brothers have told me some of the
stories, and it's like he was another man when he was with
them."

Callie rested her chin on her knees. "Are they alcoholics, too? It's not uncommon."

"No, none of us drink. No more than a beer once in a
while." He paused for a moment. "So how old were you?"

"Seventeen."

"Who took care of you after your parents died?"

She gave him a surprised look. "I took care of myself.
I became an emancipated minor right after the accident.
Their life insurance paid my way through college. I was
fortunate I didn't have to go into debt."

Her life didn't sound fortunate at all. "Is that when you
met Adam?"

Callie nodded. "His sister has been my best friend
since junior high, so I've known him since I was thirteen.
I spent a lot of time at their house. He has an older brother
who was basically the man of the family. Their mom
was more a mother to me than my own mother ever was.
I was more devastated by her death than I was when my
own mother was killed. I'm still close to them all.
They're family, and family is everything."

"Another thing we have in common then," he said, giving her an easy smile he didn't feel, especially when all
he wanted to do was wrap himself around her and take
her mind away from all those memories that had stolen

the light out of her eyes. "We both found family when we didn't expect to. I'm glad you weren't alone."

She sat up, her back straight, and leveled her gaze at him. "Even if I had been, I would've survived."

"I know you would've. But having people who love you makes pretty much everything in life better, right?"

Her eyes narrowed. "You've never married?"

The powerful need to see her naked, that silky dark hair loose around her shoulders, wrapped around him . . .

Dios. These thoughts *had* to stop. He was many things, but, unlike his father, he'd never stoop so low as to seduce another man's wife. And even if that *were* a faint possibility, if he lost all sense of honor and reason, he'd despise Callie almost as much as he'd despise himself for giving in.

Man, he couldn't fucking well win.

"Almost." He kept his thoughts well hidden. "Somehow I let her slip through my fingers. Young. Stupid. Blind." He shrugged. "She's the woman I called at the weather station earlier. Robin Waugh. I thought at the time that she was the love of my life. I had no idea." Because what he felt for Callie, if not love, was as powerful, as motivational as love and sure as hell made whatever he'd felt for Robin feel like a school yard crush in comparison. And his hands were tied.

It was some sort of cosmic joke that when he was ready, really ready, the woman was unavailable.

"Is she still single? Maybe you could rekindle what you had."

Jonah sat back, deliberately putting himself out of reach of her soft, tanned skin. "No, that ship sailed years ago. Plenty more fish in the sea, right?"

She covered a yawn with her hand. "Not always."

His gut twisted. Yeah. There'd never be anyone like

Callie. And letting that particular ship sail just out of reach was killing him.

"Let's give it another hour, tops," Jonah said, longing to take her in his arms, to carry her downstairs to his cabin and make love to her slowly. "If you want to dive tomorrow you need a decent night's sleep."

"I just want to run through all the pictures to get a sense of what we have here. I think . . ." Trailing off as she thought to herself, she picked up the remote control and brought up the next picture from a different book—the one that he'd been photographing. "This is Old Aramaic script." Brow furrowed, she squinted as she tried to read the faded text.

Jonah was having a hard time multitasking. Focusing and keeping his hands off her. "That was the international trade language of the ancient Middle East, right?"

She nodded. "It originated in modern-day Syria between 1000 and 600 BCE. What we're looking at here is the ancestor of present-day Arabic and Hebrew . . . Damn it, Jonah! I can't decipher this. It's like having something on the tip of my tongue. *Please* let me send this to Miguel."

It made complete sense to send it to an expert. But even if it didn't, her eyes looked so green, so pleading, that damn if he could deny her anything.

"If you send it now, can we go to bed?"

Ten

Maura agreed to spell them, so all seven divers went down together to explore the enormous lava cave the next morning.

The headset worked just fine on the surface when she tested it, but once again, as soon as they went deep, all Callie heard was faint, annoying static. She tapped Jonah on the shoulder, pointing to her ear. Her wireless communications headset wasn't just malfunctioning again. It appeared to be completely offline. Not that she minded; she enjoyed diving in silence.

Jonah shook his head. His didn't work, either.

With hand gestures he checked with the other divers to see if any of the communications devices worked. None did. The masks were expensive; Jonah should get a refund.

Divers used a sign language of their own for instances like this, so they could communicate just fine without the head mike. But having the mikes in their face masks made it easier and faster, and meant they didn't have to be facing one another to communicate. If not for the dead air in her ear, Callie was exactly where she wanted to be. Calm, serene, tranquil blue water.

No pressure. No lies. No looking over her shoulder. Jonah locked up tight in his wet suit, mask covering his face. It wasn't even a case of *look but don't touch*. There wasn't much to see. Feeling as though she'd been released from a strong force field, Callie could, ironically, finally breathe freely.

The words he'd spoken so matter-of-factly last night throbbed a persistent beat in her brain. *"Can we go to bed?"*

He hadn't of course meant it in a sexual way. But her body, so sexually aware of him, so primed and on edge already, leapt at the suggestion. She was in a constant state of annoying, bewildering, heightened awareness. Primed and ready for sex.

Jonah hadn't touched her, and yet she felt as though the last week had been one intense bout of foreplay.

She was a scholar, a scientist. Practical. Down to earth. She hated the muddy swirl of strong emotions, and had avoided them like the freaking plague as far back as she could remember.

She didn't *do* lust.

She didn't know who this sexual being *was*.

Sleepless the night before, body sensitized and aching, she seriously contemplated seducing Jonah. Something she'd not even considered when he'd hired her. Hence the reason for the wedding ring. Protection from any hunting male.

But this distraction had to stop. She could barely do her job because her days and nights were filled with images of herself and Jonah having hard, driving, hot sweaty sex.

Get him out of my system. Sleeping with Jonah can't possibly be as good as my imagination.

Men rarely turned down the offer of sex. It shouldn't be too hard. God only knew, having sex with the man might stop her thinking about it 24/7.

Callie had lain there in the darkness, knowing Jonah

was merely across the hall from her cabin. Did he sleep naked as she did? God . . . Her skin grew feverishly hot.

She couldn't now admit that she'd lied. That Adam had died four years ago, and as a widow she was more than free to have sex with him.

Confessing that lie would dredge up her reasons for doing so. And she couldn't do that to Rydell, who was already putting plans in place to usurp Jonah's finds and make them his own.

Would Jonah sleep with a married woman? Other than Adam and Rydell, most men of Callie's acquaintance would have no compunction about having sex with another man's wife. Would Jonah balk if she offered herself to him? It would have to be just before she left *Storm-chaser* once and for all, and before he realized that she'd deliberately set him up so Rydell could steal everything he held dear out from under his nose. As payback. Revenge. The Jonah whom Rydell had told her about should have no problem satiating her desires despite the wedding ring. But she was beginning to doubt Rydell's clear-cut version of Jonah.

The timing had to be just right. And God only knew, Jonah might not want her and reject her desperate offer out of hand.

But hey, what the hell was a little humiliation when she was so aroused she couldn't catch her breath when she was near him? It had been so long since she'd felt anything—who knew when she'd feel this way again? If ever?

They swam around the hulk of *Ji Li*, and over and around several temple pillars, which she had already photographed every which way from Sunday. Callie ran a hand over one perfectly intact beauty as she swam by. *I'll be back.*

She hadn't wanted to tell Jonah last night, not until
Miguel confirmed what she suspected: The pages they'd
captured might be more profound than either of them realized when they were on Fire Island.

Miguel had promised to look at the images right away,
but Callie knew he was thorough and precise, and he
wouldn't report until he was absolutely sure. So as much
as she was dying to know, she had to be in the present and
explore the caves with the others.

Callie had learned at an early age how to compartmentalize.

Pushing the ancient texts off to the side, tucking the
future exploration of her city into a neat pocket of her
brain, she focused on what they might discover in the lava
cave. The only thing she couldn't seem to compartmentalize was Jonah. Was he friend or enemy? Competitor or
lover?

The beams of their powerful dive lights led the way
through the wide entrance into the tube. Small shoals
comprising thousands of tiny transparent fish swam
around them, flashing like bits of glass in the aura of the
lights.

Charmed, Callie wanted to tell Jonah they were in a
traffic jam, but of course couldn't do it in sign language.
But as she was thinking it, he turned his head, eyes smiling mischievously. He made a steering wheel motion with
both hands so the beam from his light danced around the
walls.

For a moment, suspended between ceiling and floor,
as tiny fish swarmed around them, as the others swam
ahead, there was just the two of them. Callie struggled
to breathe through the burning ache in her chest. It felt so
tight, so strong, that for a moment she forgot how to
breathe and saw dancing particles of light in her vision.

Unrequited lust.

God. Her own stupidity made her sigh.

Why did she have to meet a man like Jonah Cutter now? Under these circumstances?

Why, damn it, was she *this* close to finding the discovery of a lifetime?

Everything she'd ever wanted was inches from her outstretched hand.

And she couldn't have any of it.

Suck it up, Calista, and move on. Life is seldom fair.

Vertical, and maintaining his position, Jonah, as if sensing her sudden mood change, frowned at her through his mask. He gestured *OK?* Callie circled her fingers, *OK*, then resumed swimming after the others, leaving him to fall in beside her.

The ache in her chest didn't go away, and she had to blink the sting from her eyes before she fogged up the inside of her mask.

Grateful she could do something meaningful for Ry, she'd sworn to do anything to help him best the Cutters, but she'd had no freaking idea when she'd made that promise that everything she held dear, everything she could love, would be ripped away from her in the process.

The lava tube cavern was a lot bigger than Jonah realized. Masks off, and depositing their tanks, fins, and buoyancy compensator units high on the stairs, the entire dive team clambered up the rough-cut, uneven steps to the thirty-foot-deep ledge high above the water.

"Quite a view." Brody sounded awed at the eerie beauty of the auditorium-sized cave as he looked around.

Reflected ripples of the water danced on the lava rock ceiling forty or more feet overhead, stalagmites dripped dramatically over their heads, and the dark water bounced the streams of light from their flashlights across the surface.

"There's more." Leslie indicated a black opening large enough to drive a car through off to the right-hand side in the craggy rock of the back wall. "I only went in a couple of hundred feet the other day, but I think it goes back much farther than that."

"Sometimes these lava tunnels remain intact for centuries." Callie walked gingerly on the rough, uneven floor to peer over the edge. Twenty feet down. One slippery misstep and she'd plummet to the water and rocks below. Jonah's heart did a little hop-skip of fear. He planted his feet. She wasn't his to worry over. Not officially. She was a grown woman. Brilliant. Savvy. Married to another man.

He willed her from the edge anyway.

As if she'd heard him, she returned to the group, gathered a good ten feet from the sheer cliff down to the water. "The tube might be open and navigable all the way up to the source. Personally, while I see that humans forged those stairs for some purpose, which begs the question who and why, I'd prefer to concentrate on the city and *Ji Li*. Those two salvages and explorations are enough for thirty or more people, and we're only six. I think we should concentrate our endeavors and limit our exploration to those. There aren't enough of us to waste going spelunking or exploring."

"I agree, to a certain extent." Jonah addressed the group instead if looking directly at her. Callie sounded stiff, and more formal than usual. Did the cavern freak her out like it did Brody? "This *is* historically relevant. Those steps were carved to serve a purpose. Perhaps they had something to do with the city. We won't know until we look to see if there're any clues farther in. I think we should explore for a couple of hours, and see how deep the tunnel goes. Then we can get back to business. All in favor?"

The ayes had it.

They all wore water shoes inside their fins for this dive, and the flexible rubber soles made walking on the rough, porous pumice rock a breeze. Their combined flashlights' powerful beams lit up twenty feet ahead. Rough walls, rough floor. But easily navigable.

"Notice the smell? Or lack thereof?" Leslie's voiced echoed in the tube as she picked up the rear of the group with Brody. "Fresh air must be coming in from somewhere."

Jonah's brain was currently filled with the warm coconut scent of Callie. Whether real or imagined, it was a powerful aphrodisiac. They were in the lead, and she was a few steps behind him. In this confined space he was ultra-aware of every breath she took, and he found his own breathing rhythm matched hers after a few minutes.

"Vented somewhere for sure." His head didn't touch the ceiling, but still, he kept wanting to duck. Stretching out his arms, he found his fingers just missed touching the walls on each side. Six feet wide give or take. What he hadn't figured on was Callie walking into him when he stopped to measure.

They came wet-suit-to-wet-suit. Not exactly full-body contact, but the touch of Callie's body down his back was electrifying. "Sorry," she murmured, stepping back as he resumed walking.

"*No hay problema.*" Which was bullshit. It *was* a problem if the accidental brush of her body caused his heart to race and his mouth to go dry. "Now, isn't *this* interesting." Jonah put up his hand to indicate he was stopping this time. "Just a guess, but I'm thinking this is human-made, too."

Their lights illuminated a massive, rusted metal door blocking their path.

"What the—" Callie's mind boggled at the unexpected sight.

A door? It was so out of context she stared at it for several minutes trying to compute what she was seeing. Approximately eight feet high and six wide, the door was *huge.* No markings, no ornamentation, no handles of any kind. Just an incongruous, riveted, rusty monolith obstructing the way.

The seams fit tightly into the surrounding rock, so snug, she doubted a piece of paper would fit between rock and door.

Her flashlight beam joined Jonah's as she pointed it directly in the middle. "Amazing craftsmanship."

"Open it," Saul ordered.

"How? I don't see a handle, do you?" Leslie murmured.

Brody shouldered his way closer, jostling for position with Vaughn. "Need some muscle?"

Callie shared a look with Leslie as the guys tried to wrench and shove open the door, using their combined body weight. "Are you going to *kick* it next?" she asked drily.

"We need a crowbar," Brody suggested. "Or a nice big stick of dynamite."

Callie shook her head. "Always good inside the tightly confined space of a lava tube." She took her opportunity to squeeze between Vaughn and Brody to get a closer look. Of course Jonah was standing right *there*, so she had to be right beside him. Not on purpose, but it felt right.

Together they shone their flashlights in unspoken unison from left to right along the seam where door met rock.

Across the top, down the right-hand side, across the bottom, up the left side.

A large family of barnacles decorated an upper corner, and a piece of dried-out vegetation clung to the bottom edge.

Jonah's eyes were stunningly blue, even in the iffy light from their various flashlights. It was always a shock seeing that piercing azure gaze focused on her. "What do you make of it, Doctor?"

I make of it that I could fall into your eyes, and never come out. Her attraction to him was getting worse, not better. She'd prayed propinquity, and her own common sense, would kick in. But that wasn't the case. And thinking about case reminded her of Rydell Case. The man who'd put the wheel in motion. If she did what she'd promised Ry she'd do, Jonah would *never* forgive her. If she did what *she* wanted to do, Rydell would—no he'd never hate her, but he'd be disappointed. And that would almost be worse. She worshipped her brother-in-law. Loved him as if they were blood. She owed him. She'd promised.

Callie rubbed a fist across her sternum where the pain of the unattainable, and the urgent need for Jonah, collided until the ache was almost unbearable.

"Pressure in here getting to you?" He took a half step toward her, hand raised as if he was about to touch her arm. He dropped his hand. "We can head back if there's a problem."

Leave it to Jonah to notice her discomfort.

Damn it. His voice turned her on. Callie couldn't think of a worse or more inappropriate time, and she didn't want to feel like this about him. She wanted to feel nothing for this man with his piercing blue eyes and six o'clock shadow. The only thing she was grateful for was that he was covered from neck to ankle with black neoprene.

Skintight, muscle-defining, bulge-outlining black neoprene.

She conjured up the memory of being in the hospital after being jettisoned through the windshield when she was a kid. Remembered the fear and pain that even the medication-induced numbness couldn't quite mask. The memory was powerful and visceral, and her stupid hormones backed off to a low simmer.

"Callie?"

She was going to have to have sex with him. Soon. She couldn't go on like this, she really couldn't.

"I'm good." *Now that I've made a decision.* Reaching out, she ran the flat of her hand across the rough patina. "I thought it was wood, but it's metal. Heavily corroded and rusted, but solid." She banged several times. "I suspect this is really thick, and look at this." She pointed. "Water marks. Indicating that the cavern fills, probably with the tide."

Jonah's light strafed the door. "How can it have *tide* when we're a hundred feet under the surface of the ocean?"

How can the tube and cavern not be filled with water, would also be an interesting question, begging an answer. "I'm not an oceanographer. This is illogical, but clearly the tide rises, as indicated right *here*. And here. And here. And these marks—" Callie shone her flashlight directly on the marks she wanted Jonah to see. "Probably made by a large starfish. You can just make out, here and here, the outline of its five arms, and the marks from its tube feet. The water down there rises all the way up here."

"This doesn't make sense." Jonah ran his hand over the metal, then rubbed his fingers together when his hand came back dusted orange with the rust. "First, why would anyone have gone to such elaborate lengths to seal off the tube from the surface, and from this cavern? Why come down here at all? Some sort of ritual, do you think?"

Intrigued, Callie shrugged. "I have no idea. This door could date back to medieval times, if not earlier." A *lot* earlier. *Like around the time of Atlantis?* "Or the Iron Age." Her heart was racing now for a different reason than sexual tension.

"*Iron Age?*" Leslie repeated. "Are you saying this door has been here for more than two thousand years?"

"Or longer. *Three* thousand years? They certainly had the skill and tools to make something of this size."

Everyone took a moment to process that.

"There's no point hanging around, since we have more questions than answers," Jonah told them. "Clearly we aren't going to get it open with an 'Open Sesame.' We need to document this, which means cameras and better lighting. I also want Thanos to check the malfunction in our headsets." They decided Brody and Saul would go back to *Stormchaser* and grab the cameras, while the rest of them worked on salvaging more coins from *Ji Li*.

They returned through the tube to the deep landing. Jonah put his hand on Callie's arm, holding her back when the others started down the stairs to get their equipment. She felt his light touch on her forearm all the way through her wet suit, her skin, muscles, and tendons all reacting in unison to one giant ache. That light touch effervesced through her vascular system like hot Champagne.

How had she ever doubted? The outcome was inevitable.

A muscle ticked in Jonah's jaw when she jerked her arm out of his light hold. "We both know the implication if that door's been here as long as both of us believe it has."

"*We* don't know anything until we've had it carbon-dated, and someone confirms the age and material. You know that. We can't jump to conclusions, Jonah. That's neither scientific nor wise." She heard the splashes as the others hit the water at the base of the stairs.

The cavern seemed immeasurable, the silence throbbing, a low heavy heartbeat against her stretched-taut nerves.

"Join the dots, Doctor. Atlantis was sunk by a volcano. We're in a lava tube. Someone carved those stairs. Someone built that door. None of *that* is speculation or wishful thinking. You like facts. *Those* are facts."

Callie started walking toward the top of the stairs as he talked. Jonah walked beside her. Their steps perfectly synchronized. Her heart was doing the fight-or-flight calisthenics. Coward that she'd discovered she was, Callie chose flight. She wanted her tank, her BC, and her face mask, and she wanted to be swimming, without communication. She wanted to swim anywhere. Away. Just away.

She realized she was staring at his mouth and dragged her gaze back to his face. His eyes burned hot, the color at the base of a flame. She felt the insane and erratic pounding of her pulse beneath her cold fingers when she put a hand to her throat. Mouth dry, she chewed the corner of her lower lip for a second to steady her frazzled nerves.

This was stupid. Inappropriate. Wrong on every level. If Jonah realized, by word or deed, how powerfully he affected her, her wedding ring was not going to fend him off. He'd take what she offered and to hell with the consequences.

Isn't that what you've already decided you want? a little voice mocked.

The hunger she felt for him made her body yearn and

ache, and she had to do a course correction as she swayed toward him. She kept her gaze steady with a great deal of effort, and said calmly, "N-none of that proves our city is Atlantis."

Clearly distracted by the importance of what he was saying, his gaze remained fixed to her mouth, which in turn made her lips tingle and her heart beat too hard.

"None of this proves our city *isn't* Atlantis." His husky voice rasped along her nerve endings. "Too much of a coincidence that this is *here*, and pretty much right outside this cavern is a giant city underwater. Would you at least give me the *possibility* that we've found Atlantis?"

She dragged in a deep breath and held it, her gaze dropping to his mouth. Were they still talking about Atlantis? "I'll give you a definite *maybe*."

"*Dios*, you're stubborn wom—Damn it, Callie, don't fucking look at me like that."

Her focus jerked from his mouth to his eyes. Her heartbeat stuttered at the intensity of his gaze. "I wasn't—"

"To hell with it!" Yanking her against the hard plane of his chest and belly, his steely arm circled her waist. Taking her chin in his hand, he tilted up her face and kissed her.

Hard.

The moment his mouth crushed hers and his tongue passed the barrier of lips and teeth with ease, Callie was lost.

He set a match to her banked and primed fire and it roared out of control. Not a tentative kiss, not a getting-to-know-you kiss. This was carnal, erotic, and incendiary. There was an inevitability to it that made her sink into it and forget the consequences.

She wanted to rip their wet suits off right where they

stood, or at the very least crawl inside his with him. She craved the feel of his skin against her skin. Wanted to feel, with no barrier, the heat they were generating. She was done waiting. Done pretending that this wasn't exactly what she wanted. God help her, exactly what she needed.

Shuddering, she sighed into his mouth as his tongue danced around hers, teasing and enticing. Callie's fingers tightened in his cool, silky hair; her other hand gripped his back, holding him against her. Pressing him against her aching breasts, and the liquid need in her center.

She wasn't aware of moving, but his muscles flexed and rippled under her touch. Her entire body, from the top of her head to the soles of her feet, jangled with surging adrenaline as his arms tightened around her tight as steel bands.

Held in check by his wet suit, the ridged length of his penis nevertheless pressed against the juncture of her thighs. Her short nails dug into the small of his back, then went on an exploratory dance over the tight globes of his butt. She'd never hated neoprene more.

His fingers gripped her hips in a vise-like hold, as if he needed to hold her still. The friction just torqued the pulsing throb at every point of contact to an even more unbearable pitch.

Wrenching his mouth from hers, Jonah whispered a hoarse curse, then dropped his forehead to hers. His breath sawed ragged and uneven and his body—or was it hers?—trembled.

As if an invisible force was ripping him away from her, and he couldn't let go, his fingers tightened on her hip bones with bruising force. After too short a time, he released, stepping back. He wiped the back of his hand across his damp mouth and closed his eyes as if in pain.

"That shouldn't have happened, I know." His thick voice was pitched low as he opened his eyes to meet hers. "I've never wanted a woma—You're *married*! I have fucking well got to get the hell out of your gravitational pull. It won't happen again."

Dear God, she knew exactly how he felt because she felt the same wrong-in-more-ways-than-she-could-count way. She'd made a decision based on nothing more than this.

"Jonah, I have t—"

She reached out, but he jerked his arm out of reach as if he couldn't bear to touch her. "Have mercy. Not now, Callie."

Turning away, tension in every line of his body, Jonah took the uneven stairs at a dangerous jog. He picked up his tank without looking back. "Forget this happened. Tomorrow will be business as usual," he gritted, slinging the strap of his tank over one broad shoulder. "Suit up."

A Greek tragedy of epic proportions.

Dr. Calista West filled him with so much ridiculous, impossible, *forbidden* need that Jonah was going fucking insane thinking of anything else.

Lust and insanity, Krazy Glued together, tied him in Gordian knots.

"You, Jonah Santiago Cutter, are a fucking dick." He shut his eyes. "A stupid, *inconsiderate* dick."

He'd given in to one taste. One small taste to compensate for the avalanche of pent-up horniness that had nowhere to go. One *fucking* taste.

He'd decided against it. Ignored the clamoring of every hormone in him. Ignored it, until those big blue-green eyes dropped to his mouth.

Then all goddamn bets were off.

His dick had done the thinking. Had made a convoluted interpretation that she wanted him as badly as he wanted her.

The smell of her coconut-scented skin fused with his synapses. A low-down subversive trick that clouded his judgment and made him stupid.

He was *not* his father. Fuck it. He was the *opposite* of his father.

He had to make this right.

How exactly *did* one apologize for ravaging a married woman? Because while to an outside viewer that kiss was just a kiss, Jonah knew it was a damn sight more. His intentions hadn't been in the least bit honorable right then.

What should he say? *Sorry, Callie, I was a madman because you lit my fuse the moment I first laid eyes on you, and it finally burned all the way down to the TNT, so an explosion was inevitable?*

He'd held on to her so tightly, he must've left fingerprint bruises on her hips. Kissed her so hard, so ravenously, her lips had been bee-stung and reddened when he'd managed to unglue himself from her. He thumped his head against the headboard again.

Impossible for her to miss his hard-on, even through two layers of neoprene.

He'd wanted to strip them both naked and fuck her brains out right there on the ledge, on the rough lava rock.

He'd imagined that her lips had clung for an extra heartbeat before he broke contact, and regained his brain, even if it was reptilian at that point.

He'd needed a break from the unbearable tension of wanting her. Jonah squeezed his eyes shut. Fuck. Fuck. Fuck. He'd chosen poorly.

But, admit it, it had been worth whatever punishment she was going to mete out tomorrow. Worth it for those few minutes when nothing else had mattered but the feel and taste of her mouth, and the lash of her eager tongue dueling with his.

Stretched out on his wide bed, sweat-dampened, Egyptian cotton sheets rumpled by all the too-wired-to-sleep tossing and turning, he needed to kick his own ass. Intermittent moonlight streamed pure white light over the foot of the bed, making dragons and water nymphs out of the random pattern on the carpet.

He stared blindly up at the ceiling. Sleep? Shit. Probably never again. Was Callie sleeping? He glanced at his watch. Two a.m. Yeah. Probably. He was going to have to figure this out so he could talk to her first thing in the morning.

Her mouth had been hot and wet, slick and eager. What other parts of her might also be that way? Jesus. He couldn't afford to wonder about it.

A Pavlovian response to the wildness in his kiss, he was sure. Callie wasn't the type of woman to cheat on her husband.

He admired her for it.

He hated her for it.

He hated himself even more for acting on something he was old, and wise enough, to keep under wraps. He'd behaved like a randy schoolboy. And with about the same amount of finesse.

I. Am. Not. My. Father.

He was confused as hell and didn't know what the fuck to do with all the pent-up lust and frustration surging through his body like a fucking riptide.

He was sucked in, and sucked under, and didn't know what the hell to do about it.

He gave his hard head another clarifying thump on the burl wood behind him. "Unacceptable." *Yeah. Got that.* "What the fuck will I do if she's pissed enough to walk? What the hell will I do if she *doesn't*?" He scrubbed his palm over his stubbly chin.

That kiss. Had he ever kissed a woman quite like that? Not just no, but hell no. The melding of their lips had rocked him to the core, short-circuited his synapses, and made him uncomfortably rock-hard. All that. Just from a kiss.

Christ, and he'd pretty much taken everything he could, with not a single thought to the consequences.

He was a dick *and* an asshole.

His phone rang. His heart leapt into his throat. *Callie.*

Lunging off the bed, he raced to the chair where he'd thrown his shorts when he'd come down after dinner. A dinner Callie had not attended. Probably packing to return to her loving husband. Fuckshitdamn.

Scrambling, all thumbs, he managed to fumble his phone out of his pocket, her name on his lips.

"Jonah? Maura. I have a Dr. Miguel Ebert on the line for Callie."

And his captain presumed a married woman was in his cabin at two a.m.? *Fuck.* That just compounded the situation.

"I imagine she's sleeping the sleep of the pure and innocent in her *own* cabin," he told her, not feeling friendly or diplomatic. He scratched his chest as he sat on the foot of the moonlit, messed-up bed. That was his current situation, a bright spotlight on the messed-up idiocy of his poor choice and lack of self-control. *Way to go, Cutter.*

"He says it's urgent, and she's not answering. Want to take it, or should I tell him to call back tomorrow?"

At least it wasn't the perfect Adam calling to make sure Jonah was taking good care of his wife. *Shoot me now.*

Jonah fell back on the bed, repressing a groan. "I'll talk to him, patch him through." What the fuck else did he have to do at two in the morning?

Eleven

Two in the morning and Callie sat wide awake, and dry-eyed, the ache in her chest unrelenting. Feet tucked under her butt, she rested her chin on her knees and squeezed shut her eyes. The tray Tina had sent down hours ago sat untouched on the desk by the door.

Callie had come—at a brisk walk, if not a full-out cowardly run—belowdecks after the kiss in the cavern. No excuse, just said "See you tomorrow" and fled to the safety of her cabin. Now she could add *coward* to *indecisive* and *aroused*.

"Who the hell *am* I?" she asked the room. Callie let out a frustrated groan, because the answer was embarrassingly clear. "A horny, indecisive chicken, *that's* who. Snap the hell out of this, Calista. You don't like it? *Fix* it."

She'd been giving herself the same damn pep talk for nine freaking hours as she tried to formulate a workable plan.

She liked plans. And lists. And goals checked off.

Methodical was good. Rational was good. Not taking a giant misstep was not only good, but also smart.

But the situation with Jonah wasn't as easy as writing down the pros and cons. Although God only knew, she'd done that a dozen times, too.

Having sex with him would have consequences far beyond momentary pleasure, she knew. Far-reaching repercussions that, when the heat and excitement cooled, could very well destroy what she'd built of her life.

Was a roll in the hay worth the aftermath?

After that incendiary kiss, she'd *started* to tell him the truth—"Partial truth," she corrected. "And he didn't cut you off, *you* chickened out." Lying to herself wasn't one of her faults. Brutal honesty might hurt, but it shone a spotlight on all her failings, making them impossible to ignore. More faults than she'd realized she possessed, apparently. That sucked. She'd thought she was all things pretty damn fabulous, until now.

Child of alcoholics and bucking the stereotypes, a self-made woman. She had close friends, and colleagues who respected her.

"You didn't try hard enough because, despite your earlier decision to seduce him, you're *still* conflicted." Still afraid. Still talking to herself like a frightened child.

Rydell had always assured her that her caution was wise. That not thinking things through, acting impulsively, could do her reputation harm. His sister, her best friend, bitched about her indecision and kept telling Callie to go for it. By the time she realized she'd made a mistake, if that was the case, she could make a U-turn and do a directional correction.

Callie chewed her lip. She wasn't a woman who jumped into dangerous situations blindly. She didn't take risks. Life was hard enough as it was without asking for trouble. But this couldn't go on. Not without her internally combusting.

Clearly he'd be receptive. She should be happy. She could take what she wanted.

Why did it feel as though she were several different

people and each of them wanted something different? She hadn't always been quite *this* indecisive. She'd known how and when to get her parents into rehab, how to drive the car when her feet barely touched the pedals, to go get bandages when her mother beat the crap out of her father in one of their drunken battles.

She'd known to go to Peri and Rydell's mom when the war zone of flying fists and bottles prevented her from sleeping at her own house next door.

She'd received her high school diploma on determination and focus, and her degrees the same way.

She wasn't wishy-washy. She wasn't a pushover. She made sound, intelligent decisions every damn day of the week. And damn it, she refused to be afraid. Had always refused to be afraid. And those situations had been a lot more dire and dangerous than an obsession for a man she shouldn't want.

Maybe that was the problem.

This was something *she* wanted. A personal decision that only affected herself. And Jonah.

Confessing she was a widow was the least of her transgressions. If he discovered her connection to Rydell Case, and why she was on board *Stormchaser*, he'd never forgive her.

And if she didn't deliver on her promise to Ry, she'd be betraying him. He was family. He and Peri were all she had.

She couldn't be loyal to both men.

Staring sightlessly at the dark window she knew, no matter which way she looked at it, she had to tell Jonah that she was widowed. That letting others assume her husband was still alive was a deterrent from people like Brody hitting on her on a long-term salvage. That was certainly the truth. Even if it was only part of it.

She didn't have to tell him about her connection with Rydell. And at the moment, Rydell didn't have to be filled in on anything. Her response to Jonah was no one's business but her own. She'd still do what she was there to do.

"It would just be sex, right?" It was a waste of time talking to herself. She'd tried calling Peri for several days with no luck. Who knew where her friend was off to? Talking to herself was the only game in town.

Sex was sex. No one would get hurt.

A tiny, annoying voice in her head reminded her that of course someone could be hurt.

Actions had consequences. If anyone knew *that*, it was she.

No pain, no gain.

Mind made up, and every scenario analyzed and turned inside out, Callie tossed off the throw and got to her feet. A quick glance at her watch showed it was well after two. Would Jonah still be awake? She'd knock on his door lightly—see if he answered . . .

She hoped he didn't. That she could skulk back to her cabin and have time to make a better decision.

God, she hoped he *did*, because she wasn't sure she could go through all this angst for the rest of night.

Should she change from the soft cotton shorts and tank top she wore? She wasn't going over there to seduce him. She put a bra on under the multi-times-washed pink tank. Better. When she confessed, she didn't want Jonah to think she expected him to sleep with her. Just the facts. Done. Return and slide into her still neatly made bed.

A quick glance in the mirror to see if she looked as she normally did—hair confined in its usual French braid tucked up tightly on the back of her head, no makeup to make her eyes look more sultry, no lipstick on her pale mouth to tempt him.

Of course, Jonah didn't need a damn thing but himself, his almost-smiling mouth, his shaggy hair, his constant need for a shave. His abs. His shoulders . . .

Callie sucked in a bracing breath. Procrastination wasn't getting the job done.

As her clammy fingers reached for the door handle, she heard a soft knock. Her heart jumped into her throat. "Wh—"

The quick mechanical sound of a keycard, and Jonah filled the doorway. Hair rumpled endearingly, wearing shorts and a brown T-shirt pulled on inside out, his eyes blazing in not a very friendly way.

He didn't look as if he'd come over to deliver good news. He looked, Callie thought, like a cable at snapping point, and she couldn't imagine what might have set him off at this time of the night. Jonah wasn't the kind of man who lay awake brooding about a simple kiss ten hours earlier.

"Good." He stepped into the cabin, the heavy door closing behind him with a dull thud, making Callie flinch. "You're awake."

As much as she wanted to retreat, because he looked very large and threatening standing there in his rumpled clothes and shitty attitude, Callie stood her ground. "What's wrong?"

"Who said anything's wrong?" His eyes skimmed her neatly made bed then slewed back to her.

"You just burst into my room unannounced at two in the morning, what's *right*?" She could tell from his tight expression that reaming him out for coming into her room without her permission would throw the match on what was clearly a short fuse.

"Your friend Dr. Ebert just called."

Callie's shoulders relaxed slightly. He was pissed

because he'd been woken up. Reprieve. "Other than inconsiderately waking you, at an ungodly hour, what's so urgent?"

"He was able to decipher the text you sent. He discovered some pretty mind-boggling information, and thought it important enough to share. Is he your lover?"

"Wha—Of course not!" The question, apropos of nothing, disconcerted her for a moment. Like a monolith standing in the middle of the cabin, Jonah took up a lot of space. The room, spacious five minutes before, was suddenly cramped. "What did he say?"

"What *I* want to s—" He cut himself off with a deep breath. The kind of inhalation Callie used to ground herself when shit was hitting fans. "He's intrigued by the few pages you sent." Jonah's voice was modulated low and cool as he changed course from what he'd been about to say. *What* he *wanted to say . . . ?*

"Wanted more pages right away. Said half a dozen of the pages you sent indicate a secret, magical society—"

"Papyri Graecea Magicae?" Astounding news. Enough to divert her stress about him for a moment.

Stuffing his fists in the front pockets of his black shorts, Jonah shrugged. "Those weren't the words exactly."

"But he said *magical* and *society*, right? If we have pages from the Greek Magical Papyri—my God. This is amazing! I have to call him back." This was a million miles and a thousand times better a conversation than she'd anticipated. She felt as though she'd been given a stay of execution, and let out a ragged breath.

"He's in the field." Jonah looked around the cabin. "He'll call you tomorrow when he gets back to camp."

There wasn't anything personal to be seen. Her few belonging were stashed away neatly. The only things she had out were the blue-and-white shard and a few unusual mosaic tiles she'd cleaned and cataloged and wanted to keep nearby, in a glass bowl beside the bed.

"Did he say anything else?"

"Like what, Calista? It was all Greek to me."

"Funny." But he wasn't being funny. He looked grim, and annoyed, and apparently relaying the message wasn't making him less irritable. The news was exciting enough to temporarily allow her to ignore his annoyance.

When Jonah didn't move from his position in front of the door, she asked, a little desperately, "Did he mention defixionesor binding spells?"

Other than cranky, his expression and demeanor told her not a damn thing as he scrubbed a rough palm over his unshaven jaw and practically snarled, "Know what, *Doctor*? Why don't you ask your friend all about it tomorrow?"

Callie narrowed her eyes as her temper spiked. "Damn it, Jonah. I'm sorry Miguel called so late, but it's not *my* fault. Why are you so freaking cranky?"

"I could tell you," he said shortly, reaching back for the door handle without turning away from where he had her pinned by his unwavering gaze. "But then I'll have to kill you."

Annoying, annoying man. "Thanks for relaying the message. Feel free to leave now."

He hesitated, eyes hot. A nerve ticked in his jaw. "We'll talk in the morning."

Not if Callie saw him first, unless he got a grip between now and then. With that attitude, he was making her decision a lot easier. "Fine, don't let the door hit you on the way out." Stupid to respond like Pavlov's dog. Just because he was in a foul mood didn't mean she had to antagonize him further.

Gasoline, meet fire.

Callie was being childish and she knew it. She let out a breath. *Tell him. Now.* "Jonah, wait—"

"Tomorrow, Callie. We have a lot to talk about."

They were together practically 24/7, what could he possibly want to talk about? The kiss at the lava cave? Because if so, she *really* didn't want to talk about *that*. Not until she told him the truth. *Part* of the truth.

Conflicted enough for two people, she bit her lip as he wrenched the door open hard enough to rip it from its hinges.

"Sure," she said softly to the space he'd occupied, which seemed to still vibrate from his presence. "Night."

The door would've slammed loudly, Callie was sure, if it weren't on hydraulic hinges. Feeling hollow and guilty she stared at it as it closed between them.

She was a coward and a fool.

Before she weighed every nuance for the zillionth time, before she tried to see it from every side, *again*, Callie wrenched her door open. The corridor was dimly lit and smelled faintly of cleaner. The faint hum of machinery was a throbbing counterpoint to the almost painfully hard *thump-thump-thump* of her heart.

"I have to talk to you—"

He paused, shoulders tense, gripping the door handle, half in, half out of his own cabin.

"Seriously?" White-knuckled, his fingers tightened, but he didn't turn. "Not now, Callie."

When she placed her hand on the small of his back, electric sparks shot from his body to hers. Her breath snagged, then stuck in her throat.

About to jump into a swimming pool from a dizzying height, it was time to find out if there was cool, clear water below, or if she'd just dived headfirst into cement. "I'm a widow, Jonah."

The stiff planes of his face were in stark relief as he turned his head. With an intensity that only made her fires burn hotter, his cobalt eyes ate the meager light as he stood, unresponsive and grim.

What was he waiting for?

The hot need inside her burned her skin and made her blood course through her body like fountains of pāhoehoe lava. Mouth dry, every nerve and tendon in her body poised on a precipice of need, she waited for his response.

He still didn't move. His eyes glittering like icy sapphires, and a muscle jumped in his jaw as he reanimated. "*What* did you say?"

"I'm not married. I'm a widow."

"You talk about Adam, you talk *to* Adam twenty times a day." His voice was low and lethal, his expression hard to read. "You're wearing a goddamn *wedding* ring, Callie!"

His fingers were wrapped around her upper arm, but the bruising grip loosened somewhat, although she wasn't going anywhere unless he allowed it. She hated being restrained, but Callie realized dimly that it wasn't Jonah holding her in place, it was her own fingers gripping his T-shirt. The hard thud of his heart pounded against her palms, or maybe it was her own erratic heartbeat pulsing in her fingertips.

Biting her lip, she shook her head as she sucked in a breath to steady her jittery nerves, then let it out in a shuddery rush. "Adam died."

"How?" There was no softness in the question.

"Leukemia," she said in a small voice, knowing darn well that wasn't the correct answer.

"Four *years* ago!"

"I have a good reason. It's more practical to tell people that I'm married than get into a situation that's untenable."

Half the truth. "I'm frequently the only woman on a salvage. Wait—*What* did you say?"

"You've been widowed for four fucking *years*."

"How did yo—*Miguel* told you."

"He casually mentioned flying out for your husband's funeral. And in case you haven't gotten the memo, Doctor, I'm not *people*," he gritted between clenched teeth. "Do you even comprehend, even a *little*, just how badly I've wanted you, and how controlled I've been since you arrived?"

Of course she knew. Was he doused with an aphrodisiac? Why was her physical reaction to this man like being consumed by a tidal wave of lust that she was helpless to resist? "Why didn't you say something when you barged into my room a minute ago?"

"I wanted to see if you'd confess before I dragged it out of you."

Fair enough.

Bending his head, he skimmed his mouth on her throat. Goose bumps roughened Callie's skin as adrenaline surged through her body, making her dizzy and weak-kneed. Grounding herself, her fingers tightened in the fabric over his heart.

His hot breath brushed the corner of her mouth, her lips parted in anticipation. She tasted his breath—hunger, coffee, uniquely Jonah. Hypnotized by his voice, by the scalding heat of his gaze, Callie longed for what she knew she shouldn't have. But oh, dear Lord, the temptation, the driving heated *urge*, made her forget reason and logic.

"How seeing you every day in that wet suit, watching you swimming—imagining . . . *this*. Goddamn it, Callie, I've been in physical pain twenty-four seven since you got here."

A fission of fear mixed with heady anticipation swept through her. Now was the time to call a halt to this before irreparable damage was done. She shifted in his hold. Needing to break free, but lingering for just one more moment. The smell of him came to her. Musk, male, testosterone. She loved the way he smelled. "I'm sor—"

His mouth crushed down on hers, instantly wild, rough, and unchecked. *Abandon hope all ye who enter here—*

The time for talking was over. Callie's response was immediate as he slanted his lips over hers, plunging his tongue into her mouth, where she met it with her own.

She reveled in the taste, the heat of him, giving back as good as she got. Fingers tangled in his hair, she held his head in place, winding one leg around his, returning his passion with every pent-up emotion she'd tried to hold in check since the moment they'd met.

It was amazing kissing him. This afternoon had been little more than an appetizer. Jonah's tongue dueling with hers gave her a brain melt. He kissed her as if he were drowning and she was his lifeline. His mouth on hers was rough to the point of pain, deep, hurried, ravenous, and so hot Callie was already starting to internally combust.

Moving against him, Callie pressed her aching breasts against his chest. It wasn't enough. The brush of his large hand skimming up under her shirt made her tremble. Hot. Electrifying sensations exploded inside her. Clever fingers encountered her cotton bra, ignoring the barrier as if it didn't exist as he slid his fingers beneath the thin cotton to cup her breast. Arching her back with the exquisite pleasure of his touch, Callie moaned low in her throat as his tongue explored her mouth, tasting and teasing, driving her mad with lust as his hand learned the shape and texture of her breast.

Everything inside her pulsed with a need so powerful she wasn't sure she could wait another moment to feel him inside her.

This was insane. They stood between their cabins. Out in the corridor, where anyone returning to their room would see them. Privacy was just feet away. This was lust. Lust and insanity wrapped together in a tight grip she was incapable of resisting. She'd *tried*. But she didn't want to resist this anymore. She no longer cared. About anything, *anyone* other than the two of them, in this moment in time. Let the bubble break later. But for now . . .

Breathing harsh, he dragged his teeth down the tendons of her arched throat as he circled her nipple with the rough pad of his thumb.

Breathless, she tried to put some distance—some sense—between them. "Jonah—"

"Three seconds to tell me no," he whispered raggedly, his face a taut mask. "Then all bets are off."

Yes. A thousand times yes. "Yes."

Eyes primal, skin pulled tight over his cheekbones, he grabbed her upper arm in a vise-like grip, yanking her inside his cabin, then kicked the door shut behind them.

Callie got a brief impression of the black-and-white room as her spine hit the hard door with a thump. Then her vision filled with Jonah Cutter. All six foot three, two hundred pounds of unleashed sexuality. Focused on *her*.

"One hundred percent sure about that?" he murmured dangerously, coffee-scented breath hot on her face as he crowded her against him. His voice, intimate, rich, seductive, and lethal, made the hair on her body stand to attention and her pulse race into overdrive.

Sexual intent burned like blue flames as his eyes locked on her face.

Every part of him was hard, his chest, his thighs, the

ridged length of his erection. Callie had never felt more
female in her life. Her senses went haywire as she was
pressed between the door and his powerful body. Pulse
throbbing in places she hadn't thought about until she met
Jonah, she wrapped her arms around his neck. "Ye—"

Jonah slid his tongue into her mouth. Not gently, not
coaxing, but a full-on assault to her senses. Raw posses-
sive male. The hot devouring kiss was unlike anything in
her wildest imagination. Callie fell into it headlong, drunk
on the taste and smell of him, intoxicated by his heat and
strength and the implacable grip of his hands grasping her
hips with steely strength.

Already painfully aroused, she couldn't take much
more foreplay. She wanted Jonah inside her. *Now.* Swal-
lowing a moan of intense need, she was barely aware of
the hard fingers gripping the elastic waistband of her
shorts until she heard the loud *rip*. The fabric resisted for
a moment, then tore, taking her underwear with it.

Tilting her head back he deepened the kiss as he cupped
her bare butt. Then slid his other callused palm down her
thigh to cup the back of her knee. The solid bulge behind
his shorts pressed against her pubic bone, throwing a
match on a fuse that had been drenched in gasoline.
Clenching her fists in his hair, the ache inside her was
strong and powerful. Her body shuddered with need.

Her hard, aching nipples pressed against his chest, but
that wasn't enough. She wanted his hands and mouth on
her. Every part of her body had its own unmet demands;
she wanted it *all*.

Jonah shifted his hips away for a disappointing second,
then he pulled up her knee, opening her damp heat to the
cool air in the cabin. Hot–cold ripples chased across her
sensitized skin. Breath erratic, pulse pounding, she canted
her hips, welcoming him. She felt feverish, jittery, heat

suffusing her body in electrifying waves. Her nipples ached and her knees went weak.

Every nerve and tendon in her body was on high alert. Oh, Lord, she was going to come fast, she knew it, and nothing she could do could hold it back as it surged through her in pulsing waves she wasn't able to control.

He pulled his mouth from hers, then said harshly. "Lose the ring."

Moaning with dismay, for a moment she had no idea what he was saying; then the words penetrated her sex-hazed brain. Callie wrenched the gold band off her finger, throwing it blindly behind him, then fisted her fingers in his hair. "You're *killing* me, J—"

With a heated thrust he filled her to the hilt.

Nothing but unadulterated sensation, she climaxed so hard, so fast, she went deaf and blind.

Twelve

The moonlit room spun in pinwheels as, still deep inside her, Jonah swung her off her feet. Wrapping her legs around his waist, her body still spasming, Callie landed on her back. His welcome, heavy weight trapped between her parted legs. It was shocking, a little scary, and utterly intoxicating to feel him deep inside her.

The hot length of him resumed pumping as if there hadn't been that momentary break. Skin hot, then cold, she let go as one climax rolled into the next, until her toes curled and her head thrashed on the pillow. She barely registered the pain of her tight braid being pressed into the pillow. On fire, already dewy with sweat, barely able to drag air into her lungs, she lifted her knees, canting her hips to meet each hard, measured thrust. Locking her ankles in the small of his back to anchor herself, she allowed the intense pleasure to take her to even higher peaks.

Callie buried her face against the damp crook of his neck. Everything about Jonah—the smell of his skin, the touch of his hand, the color of his eyes—encapsulated the one place in the world that always brought her peace and sheer happiness. The world beneath the waves. Jonah smelled of the ocean. Wild and free. He was immersion in watery blue. He was swimming through the glorious colors of a reef. He was finding a piece of shard, the first person to hold it in centuries. That was the *exact* smell of him.

She wanted to inhale him, drink him so deeply inside herself that they'd cast one shadow.

Taking both her hands from around his neck in one of his, he stretched her arms over her head. His smile was sexy, predatory as he held her gaze, stroking his hand down her body and then up again, skimming the soft cotton tank top over her breasts.

Her thigh muscles clenched around him in response. "This, you don't need." An expert tweak, and the cups parted as he released the front clasp of her utilitarian bra. Plain cream cotton. There wasn't even a rose on it. For the first time in her life, Callie wished she had beautiful sexy underwear.

"That's rude, don't you think?" He probably couldn't understand her, her breath was so labored, her body shaking so hard she could barely understand herself. The next climax hovered a stroke away. She urged him deeper with a twist of her hips. This was a night of firsts for her.

There was no rushing Jonah Cutter. The strokes were measured and infuriatingly controlled. At least his breathing was rough as he murmured, "Rude to tell you how exquisite your breasts are?"

Her bra disappeared as if wished away. "How *small* they are."

"More than this, and I'd go into full cardiac arrest." Large, callused fingers cupped her breast. The rough stroke of his thumb over the hard tip made her jolt as the sensation speared through her already oversensitized body.

"I love the soft, shy pink of your nipples, and how boldly they respond to my touch."

Bringing her hands down, because she had to touch

him. Loving his soft moan of pleasure, she slid her hand up the back of his neck, then tunneled her fingers through the dark silk of his hair, holding him to her breast.

She loved the feel of him, the taste of him—God.

It had been so long since anyone had touched her, and no one had ever touched her like this.

The sensation of him tending to her nipple while he was deep inside her put her over the edge again.

He was still inside her, still slowly stoking the fires when she was replete and incapable of moving a muscle in response. "You. Can. Give. It. A. Rest, Cutter." She barely had the energy to speak, let alone reciprocate as he continued moving his hips. "I'm a limp noodle." Nothing was going to get another rise out of her. "I'm done. Kaput. *Terminado. Hecho.* I've used up the next decade's worth of orgasms. Maybe we can do this again in a week or two?"

He laughed. "I love how responsive you are." His rich, dark voice trailed over her naked body like a fur glove. She dragged in a shaky breath, and forgot to exhale as he kissed her. He sucked the air right out of her lungs.

"*Dios,*" he said reverently, eyes closed as he savored her breast, his Spanish accent thick and sexy. "You're even more gorgeous than I imagined."

"You can't see me." Callie smiled, pushing his damp hair off his forehead, taking a moment to enjoy looking at him without him looking back. Sweat ran down her temples into her hair; her thighs screamed, begging for mercy from being held apart by his hips. She tightened her ankles around him and reveled in the discomfort, because he was so tightly melded to her she didn't know where he began and she ended. She ran her fingertips over the rasp of his beard stubble.

Tears stung her eyes. Overemotional, she knew. But

she'd never in her life felt this connected to anyone. It was wonderful and terrifying at the same time.

Wanting to run, she was compelled to stay.

"Your eyes are closed," she told him, voice thick.

"My hands can see you. My lips can taste you. Gorgeous is an understatement."

She hissed in a breath as he adjusted her legs around him. "Damn." He opened his eyes. "Uncomfortable?"

"It wouldn't be for the first seventy-two times we made love, but after the seventy-third ti—" Callie laughed as he rolled them both over so she sat astride him.

He arranged her legs with care, draping them over his muscular thighs, leaving her open and vulnerable to the heated intensity of his gaze. The look he gave her banked her own fires impossibly hotter. "Better?"

"Much more comfortable. That's an amazing feat to be able to—"

"Lift you?"

She punched his arm. "Stay inside me while doing other things."

"Like this?" He started moving again, helping her gain her rhythm by bracketing her hips with his hands. Callie curled her fingers into the soft springy hair on his chest, feeling the shift of rock-hard muscle and the powerful throb of his heart beneath her palm.

It didn't take long for her to realize that she had all the power in this position. She could make his strokes as deep or light as she liked. Pushing his hands off her hips, she found she had plenty of rhythm. A surprised laugh bubbled out of her as she braced her palms flat on his chest, arching her back. "Oh! I like this a *lot*!"

With a wicked grin, he stacked his hands behind his head. "You're a natural."

"Yes. I think I am." She leaned forward, spreading her

fingers in the springy hair on his chest. She liked this angle even more. She felt him everywhere, his mouth on her nipple, his penis buried so deeply inside her their heartbeats were one.

"Make yourself come."

"Make myself—" Her eyes widened. "I don't think so."

"You've never touched yourself? Never given yourself an orgasm?"

"In private. When I'm alone."

"We're alone in private."

"I'm—"

"Open? Pink? Juicy?"

Her slowly pistoning hips faltered, and Jonah brought his hands back to help her. When she returned to a slow rhythm, he put his hands beneath his head again.

Jonah's eyes darkened to slate. "Play with your pretty nipples."

"Why don't you?" she challenged, face hot. Despite moving slowly, she could feel an aching spiral twisting inside her as her muscles contracted around the spear of his penis. "Too lazy?"

His lips twitched. "Enjoying the view. Touch yourself. I double-dare you."

She huffed out a laugh and playfully cupped her breasts. "You're incorrigible." The problem was, her breasts, so sensitive, already painfully aroused, weren't in on the joke. Callie's nipples pressed insistently into her palms and she felt a sharp spear of pleasure right through her core, where she and Jonah were joined.

She squeezed her eyes shut, imagined his hands on her. Imagined him squeezing her nipples to the point of pain. Backing off, doing it again. Rolling the tight buds between her fingers until the spiral blazed a path through her body and she cried out with the pleasure jolting her body.

Pulling her down, he kissed her until her head spun. Digging his fingers into her hips, he changed the speed and rhythm until she was nothing but pure sensation.

He kissed her again, making it impossible to breathe or think. His hips driving against her, relentlessly, without pause or mercy.

She couldn't take any more. Her nervous system was on overload. "*¡No más!*" She needed a moment to catch her breath, a moment when her body wasn't electrified. A minute when her senses and emotions weren't on overload.

"*Sí, mucho más,*" yes, more, he murmured against her damp forehead. "*Tenemos toda la noche, mi amor.*"

"Can I die of pleasure?" Voice ragged, heartbeat off the charts, skin flushed. Callie could barely drag in another breath as the next, surprising, *shocking*, climax rolled through her. Sharp and achingly sweet, the sensation traveled through her like an electrical current. She was sure if she opened her eyes she'd see her body lit up like a Christmas tree.

"*La pequeña muerte.*" The little death. His voice was as uneven, his breath as raspy as her own. Holding her gaze, Jonah cupped her face. "We go together, sweetheart."

They were both slick with sweat, their bodies glued together. His heartbeat syncopating with hers, a hard driving rhythm, an erratic, primal drumbeat, filling the room.

Callie dimly wondered if a woman could die of pleasure.

And then she didn't care.

Limp and exhausted, she allowed Jonah to rearrange her body so she lay on top of him, his ankles draped over her. Her face was pressed against his sweat-damp neck as he stroked her back in long languid sweeps from her butt to her nape and back again as their respiration and heart rates slowed back to normal. Although Callie doubted she'd ever be normal again after this. Hell, she'd be lucky if she could walk after this.

"Thank God," she said weakly. "Eventually even Superman has to take a break."

He traced the curve of her butt with a lazy finger. "You think I'm Superman?"

"I didn't say *you* were Superman. I was hoping he would swoop in and rescue me from your lecherous clutches." She turned her head slightly to kiss under his jaw. The dark stubble felt prickly soft, and she tasted his sweat-dampened skin with the tip of her tongue. "If that's supposed to be soothing? Just an FYI? It's not."

"No?" He trailed his fingers up her spine, then she felt him delving into the surprisingly still-intact braid on the back of her head. He found several pins and pulled them out. She heard a few pings as they hit the floor. "Is that so?" Untucking the end of the French braid, he unraveled the three dented strands. *Slowly*.

It was as if every skein was attached to a corresponding nerve, making her shiver. "God, when you do that . . . Every hair follicle is attached to a nerve, and every nerve runs from there, to here, and here." Since she couldn't move, and had no intention of doing so, he had to figure it out on his own: breasts, and juncture of her thighs.

Jonah spread her hair down her back, arranging and smoothing it like a silken cape. He brought a handful to his face, inhaling deeply so she felt the shift of his chest beneath her. "I've been fantasizing about doing this since you came on board."

So had she, Callie thought, loving the feel of his hands drifting through her hair, scooping it up, and then letting it fall like water from between his fingers. The cool feel of the strands on her sensitized skin made Callie wiggle against him. It felt almost painfully good, and she ground her mound against him, enjoying his responsive hiss. "I'm in no hurry."

"Maybe I am."

Not. Married.

Holy fuck, the news was better than his birthday and Christmas rolled into one giant, mind-blowing present.

Jonah stretched his arms over his head, watching Callie wrap a towel under her arms covering her nakedness. A crime to rewrap what he'd so enjoyed unwrapping. Lying on the wide bed, he was bare-ass naked and still rampant as the first morning rays of sun warmed the walls of his cabin.

Hell, he should be satiated. They'd made love for most of what had been left of the night. He'd come, and brought her to release, so many times that he'd lost count. But seeing her as she was now, with those yards of dark, glossy hair loose down her back, looking like a pagan goddess, he was horny all over again.

Glad she'd kept that magnificent hair a secret, Jonah figured any red-blooded man seeing that silky mass hanging nearly to her waist would want her naked 24/7. He knew what those strands felt like everywhere on his body, and he wanted her back in bed, wrapped around him. To hell with diving.

"Do you have to?" he asked lazily, loving the way the golden morning light gilded the hills and valleys of her body.

Her smile was part sleepy, part seductive. How had he ever thought her cold? "Go?" she asked, tucking the fabric more securely between her breasts. "Or wear this towel?" Her legs looked a mile long, the strong sleek muscles covered by skin so soft, so silky, his mouth watered. He'd kissed her everywhere there was to kiss. It wasn't enough. He already ached to do it again. He felt a little guilty for leaving red marks on her skin. She'd assured him he didn't need to shave. And she'd certainly not complained when he'd rubbed his stubble on every delectable inch of her skin.

"Both."

"I have to shower and get ready for the day, and your clothes won't fit me. And the towel is because, unlike you, I'm not an exhibitionist, and people will be stirring soon."

"I'm very stirred right now," he murmured, tossed his legs over the side of the bed, then walked the few feet to her side. "I'm sure we can get you all stirred up, too. Why don't we do something about it?" Tunneling his fingers through the silky strands of her hair with both hands, he cupped her face, tilting her chin so her lips were inches from his.

The hard peaks of her nipples pressed against his chest, and the cool, silky weight of her hair draped over his arms as he backed her against the closed door.

The scent of hot coconut and the musky, arousing aroma of sex drifted from her skin. "Let's say to hell with everyone and stay right here." He kissed a trail across her cheek to linger at the corner of her mouth.

Her breath hitched, and she rose to her toes to press her body to his. Wrapping her arms around his neck, she whispered a firm, "No."

"Cruel."

He kissed her. A lingering melding of mouths that had intimate knowledge of each other. He loved the instant, hot, slick caress of her tongue against his, and her full-body shiver when he tightened his fists in her hair.

Her lips slid from his, and rather than waste a moment, Jonah skated his teeth gently down the tendons of her neck, making the shiver turn to a shudder. "Practical," she whispered, arching her throat for him. "I s—God, Jonah! I spent the last six hours using muscles I d-don't think I've ever used in my life. I need a period of recuperation."

"Really?" he said, pleased, looking up from where he was kissing the length of her biceps. She tasted delicious.

Dropping her arms from around his neck, she laughed. "Lose this smug look before anyone else sees you, Cutter.

"You lost your towel. I'll get that for you—"

Callie dipped to retrieve it herself. "Na-ah. If you're down there, I'll never leave this cabin."

"You say that like it's a bad thing."

Straightening, towel in hand, she reached up to pull his head down for another kiss, then wrapped the terry cloth beneath her arms again. "See you on deck?"

He took a step backward so he didn't reach for her again and do what he wanted to do. Have his wicked way with her before breakfast. Of course, he'd said that the last time they'd made love, and the time before that. Instead of grabbing her, he smiled. "Yeah."

A second later she was gone.

Chest tight, balls aching, Jonah stared at the closed door for a moment.

Not married.

Damn, life was good.

With a new outlook on the day, he took a quick, cold shower before dressing and leaving his cabin. And almost ran into Callie, who paused on the bottom step of the stairwell like a 1950s pinup girl to wait for him. White shorts, long tan legs, and a heart-levitating smile. Her hair, wet and scraped back off her beautiful face, was in its customary tight braid, the plait tucked up efficiently on the back of her head.

His secret to know and fantasize about for the rest of the day.

His brain, his hands, and his body knew what those mile-long, cool silky strands looked like loose down her back, knew what they felt like wrapped around him, knew the texture as they sifted between his fingers.

Stern and humorless she wasn't. He wasn't afraid to acknowledge when he was wrong. And he'd been *very* wrong about Callie.

There was no sign of the strategically placed beard burns marking her soft skin. Makeup? Jonah knew where to find each one, and although he regretted leaving his marks on her, he loved knowing he'd left them on her where no one but himself would see them.

Which reminded him, he'd better delete some of the video from the corridor feed before the captain looked at it.

"Morning." Her soft green eyes heated to remind him of what they'd shared earlier. She wore a T-shirt the color of the lavender growing in his *abuela*'s garden in Cádiz. She smelled of soap and coconut. Good enough to eat. Again.

"And a damn fine morning at that," Jonah agreed, resisting the urge to skim his fingers up and down the satiny smooth skin on her arm. They had to be circumspect. He wasn't ready to share this—whatever *this* was—with anyone else at the moment. Discretion in such close confines would be difficult, but hopefully not impossible.

That's what they'd decided an hour ago, lying naked and close to each other. Now? He could barely keep his hands to himself.

"Stop looking at me like that!" she whispered sternly.

"You look a little tired," he teased, feeling buoyant and energized just looking at her even though they'd been together barely twenty minutes earlier. "Restless night?" Neither had slept more than an hour.

"Not at all." Her voice was cool, her peridot eyes hot as she said sweetly, "I slept like a baby. I want to talk to Miguel as soon as possible, see exactly what he has for us. And I already know that we need to get back to the island to take more pictures, and get the documents if possible. Although I doubt our request will be considered if what Miguel and I think is true, *is* true. If the old men are—what? Priests? Caretakers? Will they let us come back and do some more reading, do you think?"

"I guess we'll find out. Here." He handed her the plain gold band he'd stepped on when he'd gone to get dressed.

"Thanks." Callie took it from him, then stuck it in the front pocket of her shorts as they walked.

"You're going to tell the others?"

"It's time, I think."

They got to the top of the stairs, and Jonah leaned in and kissed her. It was quick and sweet, and her lips clung to his for a moment before she gave him a cautionary look and continued upstairs.

"And if the old men *are* some kind of island caretakers," she said as they walked across the salon side by side, "what are Spanos and his *sister* doing there? I doubt *they're* taking care of the land. Not in those shoes."

Turning, she waved at Saul, who waited for them near the sliders. "Morning."

"They don't exactly fit the profile."

"Profile of what?" Saul slid open the doors and preceded them out to the deck.

The day was already hot but still hazy, the water a

little choppy. The short, shallow waves, white-tipped and active, musically splashed the hull. Somewhere out of sight, a crew member was painting the railings, and the pleasant, clean smell of paint mixed with that of the sea, and the rich aroma of freshly ground coffee.

And under it all: the erotic scent of coconut.

Callie pulled out her chair and sat down. "The Spanos siblings don't fit with the old guys on the island."

"I don't know which one I find creepier," Saul admitted. "Him or his sister. She's a barracuda, and that's insulting all barracudas."

Agyros was setting the table, as Randy, the second steward, laid out fruit, coffee, and pastries. Jonah was a proponent of excellent food on board. He'd paid a premium for Chef Tina Hamilton, swiping her from a ritzy restaurant in Portland and including her in the bonus program. Everyone was happy with the arrangement. Feeding his divers and crew well made the long days on board without shore leave bearable. A happy crew was a productive crew. He'd learned that from his brother Nick.

The pale, cloudless sky indicated it would get even hotter later in the day. Jonah was eager to get under the water. Or go back to bed. He met Callie's eyes as he sat down, and saw the same heat he felt.

"She's an odd one all right." She drank half her orange juice then held the glass to her chin. "I don't mean because she's so blatant. Although, yeah. That, too. I also find it peculiar that for a woman whose family is in the cosmetics business, she trowels on her makeup like a sixteen-year-old going to a rave. On an island where the only men are eighty years old? That's incongruous to say the least."

Their eyes met across the table as if magnetized. She narrowed hers in warning, which made him smile as he poured straw-smelling green tea into her cup, then fragrant coffee into his favorite mug.

He wasn't sure what the hell to make of the Spanoses, nor the old men. The old guys seemed harmless, while Spanos and his sister clearly had another agenda. Spanos seemed like an okay guy, and his sister was oversexed. But did that make any of them dangerous?

As long as everyone on Fire Island kept out of his way, he didn't give a flying fuck *what* their agendas were.

Jonah was dying to call his brothers and tell them about his discovery, but those calls had to wait until he had something concrete to report. Still, he felt as anticipatory as when he'd been a kid waiting for his father to come home from a distant salvage. Or, as reality showed, back to Spain from his *other* family in the Caribbean.

Another man might resent that reality, but Jonah felt nothing but love for his father, and gratitude that he now had three brothers he considered friends. He was a lucky guy, and never forgot it.

And now Callie . . .

Jonah requested an enormous breakfast, Callie decided on fruit and her tea, and Saul said he had to wake up before he put anything in his mouth. Jonah shot Callie a wicked look, which she pointedly ignored.

"I'm dying to hear what Miguel has to tell us." She sounded both excited and her usual controlled self. Typical Callie.

Damn she was sexy as hell, with her flushed cheeks and full mouth slightly swollen from hours of his kisses. He appreciated her supreme efforts to keep things nonchalant. Casual. He skimmed a glance to Saul, wondering if he bought it. Of course, Saul had his own romantic interest to pursue.

"I'm going to try him before I eat." She licked a drop

of OJ off the tip of her thumb. "Would you like me to put him on speaker?"

Attention fixated on her mouth, Jonah muttered, "What?"

Lifting her hip, she took her phone out of the back pocket of her shorts. "I'm calling Miguel."

"Put him it on speaker."

Callie's cheeks turned a dusky rose, as if she could clearly read his thoughts. She gave him a stern look, which made his dick stand at attention.

Leaning back in the comfortable seat, he rested an arm over the empty chair beside him, crossing an ankle over the opposite knee. He could look at her all day. Hardly productive, but a man had to do what a man had to do.

"*Hola, mi amigo*," she said in greeting, her Spanish as excellent as her Greek. Jonah wanted to get her back in bed and speak his native Spanish to her, to whisper hot words in her ear knowing she'd understand every nuance.

He was obsessed.

He left it to Callie to explain her marital situation to the others. But that explanation better come soon. While they'd try to keep their intimacy discreet, the ship was too small to keep the relationship a secret. And he sure as shit didn't want anyone thinking he'd fool around with a married woman.

Callie's soft laughter made an ache form in the pit of his belly. How much of a friend *was* this Dr. Miguel Ebert? Crap. Was he *jealous*?

She switched to English. "Is it okay to put you on speaker so the others can hear you?"

"Certainly. But Calista—" The man lapsed into rapid-fire Spanish, his excitement evident. The hair on the back of Jonah's neck came to attention, and he leaned forward in his seat as he caught snippets of Dr. Ebert's monologue.

Fire Island. Guardians. Atlantis . . .

Callie shrugged and mouthed *Sorry*, then took her phone off speaker as the others arrived and pulled out chairs. While she talked, they ordered breakfast, poured coffee, and popped bread in the conveniently placed toaster.

Jonah indicated Callie and the phone. "Dr. Miguel Ebert."

Vaughn shot a smile in her direction, though she didn't see it. "Ah. Good news apparently."

Breakfast was served and eaten by everyone while Callie's tea went cold, and her sliced fruit lay untouched. She listened to her friend with mounting excitement. So excited, she got up and started pacing as she talked.

Jonah grinned, enjoying the flash of her long legs and the expressive, very Mediterranean way she gestured as she talked. A warm breeze played with fine strands of dark hair, teasing them around her face. She brushed them away impatiently, her entire focus on the conversation. Jonah bet she was completely oblivious to the others seated at the table watching her. Of the sound of the lapping water, or the clouds scudding across the sun.

He spoke the language of his mother fluently, and he loved listening to the musical notes coming from Callie. She spoke beautiful, colloquial Spanish like a native. He preferred listening to the sound of her voice rather than the one-sided, clearly thrilling conversation.

"We only got sixty some images," he murmured to the others as he poured a third cup of coffee, then reached over to take Callie's filled cup. Dumping it in a nearby empty bowl, he refilled it with hot tea as soon as he heard her winding down.

He grinned when she started asking questions instead of saying goodbye. He gestured. "Like an Italian opera."

"This is the guy she sent the images from the books, right?" Leslie asked, pushing her chair away from the table so she could put her crossed ankles on the chair beside Jonah. Odd that from the first Jonah hadn't felt an iota of sexual attraction to his diver. She was attractive, exactly the kind of woman he enjoyed. Tall, athletic, blond—not a spark.

He looked back at Callie. More than a spark. A fucking volcano.

Just then she glanced up. Her pupils dilated, and a pulse throbbed at her temple as her eyes locked with his as she returned to the table. "*Sí, gracias, Miguel.*"

Resuming her seat, she placed the phone on the table. "'*Groundbreaking*' is what Dr. Ebert says," she said, addressing everyone. "Miguel believes the pages from the books we photographed were copied from fragments of ancient papyri. Similar to Papyri Graecae Magicae."

"Similar? Or copies of the original?" Vaughn asked, leaning his elbows on the table to see around Saul. "Wasn't the PGM an entire *body* of papyri with hundreds of pages of spells?"

"It was, but Miguel doesn't believe what we have is from the PGM. This is something different, and even more ancient. I've known him for ten years, and never heard him this excited by his findings."

"Good God, woman, don't keep us in suspense, what do we have?" Intrigued by her excitement, Jonah had only heard her side of the convo, not enough to piece together all the *¡Oh, mi Dios!* and *¿Está absolutamente seguro?* even though he understood the sporadic rapid-fire Spanish insertions on her end.

"The writings are arcane. And yes, this *is* a book of spells and mystical secrets," she answered Vaughn. "Compilations of spells and magical writings. Miguel says it was incredibly difficult and slow going to decipher the texts we sent. It's written in a mixture of Attic, Ionic Greek, and even some Doric forms. The same word appeared in several forms throughout, as if the writer wanted make sure *everyone* understood what he was telling them, no matter what language they read."

"I'm not sure I understand what that *means*." Leslie rested her folded arms on the table, and Saul moved her plate aside to give her more room.

"He was able to piece together context and intent from the formulaic words and phrases, which were, interestingly, similar to the ones found in defixiones—"

Brody frowned. "De-what?"

"*Curse tablets.* Binding spells. Magic recipes." She glanced around the table. "He thinks the copies were painstakingly transcribed from the original lead tablet forms. Circa sixth century BCE. The letters were incredibly hard to re—never mind, *those* were his findings from the images *I* managed to get. And while those are groundbreaking and undeniably fascinating, they aren't the entire point. It's what was in the pages from the book *Jonah* captured that had something even *more* fascinating and certainly even more intriguing to show us."

It was a little disconcerting to see the same avaricious, excited look on her face for some magical papyri as she'd exhibited an hour ago while they'd made love.

"Hurry, woman." Jonah dropped his feet to the deck, resting his forearms on the table. "I hope you tell us what it is sooner than later. The suspense is killing us."

Eyes shining, she smiled. "The pages you photographed talk of a powerful port city on the coast of a small volcanic island. The city built on concentric rings—"

"No shit?" Saul said. "Are you saying what I think you're saying?"

Jonah's heart leapt to his throat. Conclusive evidence. Proof that his city was *the* city. *Atlantis.*

Thirteen

"Let's not assume *anything*," Callie said drily, but it was evident just how excited she was. She practically vibrated with excitement. Jonah was familiar with those vibrations from the inside.

"The volcano was clearly active at the time of the writings. They say that the people believed it would stay quiet if they made sacrifices and offerings to the gods."

She picked up a sliced strawberry, then merely held it between her fingers as she spoke. "Ships from all over their world traded goods and services there. The city became corrupt with all the wealth and power. The gods were displeased, and to punish them spewed fire and flaming rain, shearing the city from the island, plunging it into the sea. The people tried to flee. Many did, but most perished in the 'red tide.' The epicenter of trade and commerce vanished overnight."

"It isn't an epicenter now, if Fire Island is what the texts refer to." Saul thumbed behind him where Fire Island lay, a vague green-brown smudge in the far distance. "Odd that such a small dot in the Med would be so bustling in ancient times, when Crete is just a hop, skip, and a jump away and much larger."

"Miguel was emphatic that the island referred to was Fire Island, and that it's been protected by Guardians for thousands of years. The honor was passed down from father to son for centuries."

"The old men are descendants of the Guardians?" Jonah mused, not altogether convinced about that part of Callie's summary. "Maybe *centuries* ago, *maybe*. But now? What's to protect on the island? A herd of sheep, an extinct volcano, and some scrub brush?"

"*Flock*. And maybe . . . What if . . . ?" Callie seemed to gather her thoughts. "What if the *Ji Li* really *did* land on top of Atlantis? What if those old men are protecting not Fire Island, but the *city* even now?"

What if I really, really want to take you to bed again? Jonah thought, stunned that getting Callie naked again was of far more immediate importance than a city he'd spent six months researching and documenting. No, maybe not true, but his physical need for her was as addictive as a drug, and he could satisfy the craving for her now. Atlantis would be there in an hour.

Saul raised a brow, then addressed Callie directly. "You're the authority who stated *emphatically* that no such place existed, aren't you? Are you really saying you believe we've found Atlantis?"

This was *exactly* the reason Jonah had snatched her from beneath Rydell Case's nose. When Case heard about this, as he most assuredly would, Jonah and his brothers would enjoy one-upping their nemesis. Hiring Callie was one of the best business decisions he'd ever made. Case should've upped the ante and paid her what she was worth. His loss.

Poker-faced, but far from casual, Callie shrugged. "I'm a scientist. I only believe what I see with my own eyes, and things that are confirmed twenty-seven times from Sunday. All of this new information, plus what we've already seen for ourselves, gives it a layer of credibility, yes.

"Fact: There *is* a city down there. Fact: The buildings and structures *look* to be from the correct time period; they have the markings and landmarks we've read about in various writings through the ages. Fact: The writing Jonah and I found on Fire Island *seems* to substantiate our findings according to another high-level authority on ancient texts.

"*Are* they making reference to what we believe is Atlantis? *Were* they written thousands of years ago?" She shrugged. "I have no idea. And yes, I have convincingly documented my disbelief that a real city called Atlantis ever existed anywhere other than as a myth or parable. But now . . . ? We have fragments of ancient text that talk of circular canals, and enormous temples—"

Her gaze met Saul's. "Yes, I think we very well might be sitting right over Atlantis, and those old men are here to make sure no one tampers with it."

"I think you're all taking these Guardians a little too seriously. They haven't done anything to prevent us from diving. Don't you think if something as significant as Atlantis was down there, they'd be doing more to get us out of here?" Leslie pointed out, holding out her mug for a refill. "Thanks, Randy. They can't be *too* worried."

Vaughn grabbed a homemade doughnut, broke it in half, and held it near his mouth as he said, "Maybe they don't think we've gotten close enough." He took a bite, powdering his T-shirt with white sugar.

"How much closer could we be?" Jonah pointed out, enjoying the hell out of the debate. "We're anchored right over it. Maybe they don't perceive us as a threat?"

"You're not saying that you believe in magic, are you?"

Callie's smile made Jonah realize that she had the power to change the physiology of his every cell until it felt as though he had effervescence in his veins.

"*I* don't. But it's clear, even from the small section of pages we have, that the people on Fire Island did. Or perhaps still do."

"I'm not exactly worried by a bunch of ancient men who use even more ancient donkeys as their only mode of transportation," Vaughn said around a mouthful of doughnut. "That island is about as primitive as it can get. Shit. They didn't come brandishing *Uzis* when they came on board the other day. How are they capable of protecting anything?"

"Hey, I want to believe that's Atlantis down there," Leslie added. "I really do. And maybe it *is*. But I'm not sure I buy that those old guys are protecting it. Protecting it from what, exactly? Everyone who lived there is long, long, *looong* gone. The city is already a hundred and fifty feet under the ocean; what else can happen to it?"

"Good point." Jonah pushed away from the table. "But instead of sitting here debating, why don't we suit up and go down and see what we can find to prove or disprove the writings?"

Vaughn rose, too. "I'm taking a crack at getting through that door. Anyone want to join me?"

More so now than for the months prior to this salvage, Jonah knew it with every fiber of his being: His city *was* Atlantis.

Jonah, Brody, and Vaughn gathered equipment to take with them. A lot of equipment. Men and their toys. Callie and Leslie shared a grin. Acetylene cutting torches, crowbars, and assorted heavy-duty salvage equipment raised the testosterone 150 percent.

Leslie spelled the divers, and Callie partnered Saul. There was no pretense that she gave a damn about *Ji Li*'s cargo. It was the city, and only the city, that interested her, especially now. And since the city was why Jonah had hired her in the first place, that's what she focused on.

Her mind spun like a gerbil on a wheel hopped up on energy drinks and training for a triathlon. Sex—amazing sex—with Jonah was enough to short-circuit any red-blooded woman's brain. Throw in the very real possibility that she was one of a small handful of people to stand on an Atlantean street in three thousand years, and she was giddy with excitement.

Older than the PMG, and older still than the Derveni papyrus, what they had, as little as it was, was sure to be the most important new evidence proving the existence of Atlantis to come to light. And if Miguel was correct, and he always was, they had evidence of Europe's oldest surviving manuscript as the cherry on the top.

It boggled her mind that those arcane writings were just stuck on a dusty shelf in an old man's home with full-blown sunlight allowed in the room and who knew how many years of accumulated dust. She had to go back there, the sooner the better, to convince them of the importance of the documents, and request she be allowed to preserve them.

But that was later. Now she focused on what she suspected had once been a large palace or perhaps the home of a very important man. Fully intact to her eyes, but in reality merely a hint of the foundation's footprint, the ruins indicated a huge and impressive edifice. She could tell the approximate size and grandeur of the building by the rows of pillars and hints of graceful arches. Shattered sheets of marble, half buried by time and tides, fallen from the now gone walls of mud and brick, lay nearby.

Hidden partially beneath the marble sheathing, her flashlight illuminated a portion of an exquisite, ornately pieced mosaic tile floor, depicting people of obvious wealth, which gave her a tantalizing view of life in Atlantis.

"Can you hear me any better now?" she asked Saul, who was wrangling with the blower. While she preferred doing her work in silence, having the full-mask headset made communicating considerably easier than hand gestures. When it worked. But once again it was more static than conversation. Something still interfered with their communications devices as soon as they were underwater.

Since he didn't answer, she presumed he couldn't and swam over to tap his shoulder, indicating how she wanted the blower directed.

He gave her a thumbs-up, then dragged the tube where she wanted it. The partial mosaic floor lay inside what must've once been the wide front door. As the sand particles swirled and eddied, Callie flagged each item, then took pictures and made notes in her waterproof notebook.

As the blower exposed more, Callie held up a hand for Saul to pause so she could investigate something human-made protruding from the sand. The blower caused too much debris to hang in the water, obscuring her vision before it settled.

The slab revealed tantalizing bits of relief carvings, and the edge of a freestanding sculpture. She dug faster, Saul joining her. Possibly the pediment from above the front door?

From the pieces of various building she'd already uncovered, Callie recognized the style as First Empire Romantic.

She cleared sand with her hands, going as fast as good

sense allowed. God, she couldn't wait to see what it was. The more of the fragment was revealed, the more excited she became. A triangle—not a fragment at all—a *huge* slab with *relievo rilievo*, the background chiseled from the stone to reveal a relief sculpture of soldiers on horses. She was touching ancient history.

The tympanum was the triangular area inside the pediment. She'd found an intact, perfect, *amazing* pediment gable.

Reluctantly she stepped back, her breathing too fast, her heart rate accelerated with excitement. She was sucking up the air in her tank too quickly, shortening the time she could stay down in the water, exploring. Determined to stay as long as possible, she slowed her breath and forced her heart rate down.

She and Saul took photographs from every angle. Callie marked its exact location, then noted it in her book. Even though she knew they'd see it much better once it was aboard *Stormchaser*, she wanted to dig out the entire thing *now*. They'd need the crane for this . . .

She wanted to hurry. To get all the answers. To tell the world.

She also wanted to take her time, damn it. To keep it a secret for a little while longer. From Rydell. From the world.

If this city wasn't Atlantis, then it was a close sister.

She couldn't wait to show Jonah.

Jonah.

When had his opinion and excitement become as important to her as her own? When had she lost sight of the fact that Rydell was *family*?

Very soon she would have to decide which it was going to be.

She *had* to tell Ry.

And if she told Rydell, sooner than later, she'd have to tell Jonah about the promises she'd made.

He'd hate her.

Even snug in her insulated suit, Callie shivered.

Saul pointed to his watch. Yes, she knew it was time to head up. Callie held up two fingers for more time. He gave her the okay, and started securing the blower to an anchor so they could leave it where it was and not have it drift in the currents.

She got a few more pictures, loath to leave. Stroking her hand over the relief, she wondered whose eyes had last seem this, whose hands had carved the amazing details—

Thus far she'd managed to ignore the crackle in her ear from the malfunctioning headset, but Saul's sharp cry cut through the static. Callie spun to see what had alarmed him.

Saul was waist-deep in the soft sand and sinking as she watched. His eyes behind his mask were huge, and regulator bubbles tumbled over one another indicating his fear and panic.

Quicksand underwater? Callie had never seen or heard of it. Perhaps he'd stepped over an opening to a building or chamber underneath and his weight had broken whatever barrier there was and he was being sucked down. Regardless, Saul was trapped and sinking fast.

"Arms up!" she instructed. With no way of knowing if he heard her or not, she mimed her words, waited for him to raise his arms before she swam over to the blower. She fought the tie down attached the end, then swam back, dragging the hose with her.

She'd only taken her eyes off him for a minute, ninety seconds at most, but now the sucking sand was chest-deep as he beat the surface with both hands, causing particles to swirl around him and his air bubbles to surge faster and faster as he panicked. She swam over to him and found herself caught in an ocean current she didn't expect. It took all her strength to hover close enough to try to feed him the end of the blower.

The current swept it just out of reach.

She tapped her headset. "Jonah? *Anyone?* Can you hear me?" Her voice was calm, but inside she was starting to echo Saul's panic. "SOS! Repeat SOS!"

Crackle was her only response.

Saul, mouth moving frantically, was now armpit-deep, hands in the air, eyes pleading, clearly terrified.

Callie dropped closer, relying on her buoyancy compensator vest to hold her aloft. She dared not touch the seafloor. The sand surrounding Saul looked the same in every direction. There was no indication how far afield the quicksand extended. Grabbing his hand, she hovered over his head, parallel to the dangerous ground, then closed his fingers around the edge of the blower.

His grip was white-knuckled. Callie gave him the okay sign, then shifted so she could grab his other flailing hand. Securing both hands around the end of the hose, she gripped her hands into fists and nodded, indicating for him to hold on for dear life and not let go. When he mouthed *Hurry* and she heard nothing through her headset, she indicated that she was going to activate the retract mechanism to have the blower pulled to the surface.

The grinding sound of the blower's mechanics retracting filled her ears. Staying as close as she dared, Callie watched the sand fight to hold on to Saul.

He was now shoulder-deep.

If the blower didn't tug him free *right now*, the strong drag of the sand on his arms could dislocate his shoulders. Worse, it would cause his fingers to release their grip.

Callie wrapped her fingers around his, squeezing as tightly as she could. The fingers on his right hand started to loosen. Tightening her two-handed hold on his, she pulled with all her strength, puny as hell underwater, with nothing to brace herself against for leverage.

For a moment she thought she'd lose him. But after a brief hesitation, the blower started dragging them up.

Her breath gusted out in a silvery stream of bubbles and a blast of fog inside her mask. As soon as half his body was free, Callie wrapped her legs around his waist from behind. Her legs were stronger than her arms, and she needed every bit of strength to counter the pull of the sand. Was the retracting blower strong enough to pull them both up? She was damned if she'd let go of Saul, but she didn't want to get sucked down with him, either.

Even as they rose with agonizing slowness, Callie fought the dip of his body as the sand tried to reclaim him and suck him back under. What the hell was under there, for God's sake?

It seemed to take an eternity for them to reach the surface. Behind his mask, Saul's face was gray. As soon as they reached the surface, Callie yelled for help. *Now* the damn communications worked just fine.

The metal door resisted even their most aggressive efforts to open it. Damn. Jonah made a quitting motion with his hand to let the guys know it was time to resurface and regroup. While the intriguing portal through the lava tube was fascinating, they still had the treasures of the *Ji Li* to salvage, as well as the city to excavate. He hoped Callie and Saul were having better luck.

They were nowhere to be seen as he, Vaughn, and Brody circled the junk before ascending into the heat of midday and climbed onto the dive platform.

Hearing the *whop-whop-whop* overhead, Jonah looked up with a frown. "Hell, now what?" The chopper wasn't due to fly out with artifacts until the next morning. The chopper rose above the ship, then headed north.

"Supplies?" Vaughan looked up as he removed his equipment.

Jonah frowned. "Thanos picked up produce from Fire Island yesterday." And returned with a note from Kallistrate Spanos and his sister requesting an invitation for dinner, and to see what treasures had been found, the next evening. *This* evening. It had been more of a directive than a polite request. Apparently there was no need to respond as the answer was a given.

"Jonah!" Leslie stood on the first deck. "There's been an accident—"

His heart leapt into his throat. "*¡Dios! Callie?*"

"No. *Saul.* He broke his leg in three places. We got him stabilized. Thanos and Gayle flew him to Heraklion."

"Where's Callie?"

"In her lab, I think."

Dropping his gear as fast as he could remove it, Jonah stripped down to his swim trunks in record time, then bolted up the ladder. Leslie stepped aside as he hauled ass across the deck.

He burst into the lab to find Callie bent over the table with a magnifying glass, a sweating glass of juice nearby. She turned, her expression serious. "You heard?"

Jonah stalked over to her, wrapping her tightly in his arms, burying his nose against her soft, fragrant nape beneath the tightly controlled braid on the back of her head. "Not the details. Were you hurt?"

Turning, she wrapped her arms around his waist and shook her head, breath warm on his chest. "I'm good."

"Indeed you are." Jonah held her at arm's length to

search her face. He didn't see any cuts or abrasions, thank God.

Tilting her chin up, he searched her eyes. Troubled, but no pain. He dropped his head to taste her soft mouth, a soft warm brush of his lips. She tasted of warm orange juice. Sharp and sweet. Jonah ran his thumb along the heated silk of her cheek. Her skin felt as smooth as rose petals.

Callie's eyes fluttered closed, long lashes black smudges on the high color of her cheeks. Her fingers tightened around his waist, and he urged her more tightly against him with his palm in the small of her back.

Brushing his lips on hers he tasted and nipped, drew the delicate curve of her lower lip with the tip of his tongue, felt her hum of pleasure as he slipped his tongue between her lips to explore her honey sweetness. Jonah kept it slow and soft-focus, but the heat built anyway. He'd been thinking about doing this for hours, days, weeks, hell—his entire life.

He'd stop in a minute. Or three . . .

He lingered, enjoying the moment as he imagined peeling her out of her shirt and shorts, then taking her on one of the high lab tables behind her.

Reluctantly he broke away, smiling at her moan of disappointment as he held her upper arms to steady her as she swayed.

Blinking him into focus, she gave him a soft look. "You have some powerful kissing mojo, Cutter."

"If you keep looking at me like that you'll find yourself spread-eagled on that table back there."

"How do you know I won't have you spread-eagled on the floor?"

"Best out of five?"

She laughed. "Impossible man." Taking his hand, she led him over to the high counter that figured in numerous of his fantasies. He'd have to kick aside the comfortable bar stools that made long hours of late-night reading and research comfortable but restricted them from having wild monkey sex on the flat surface.

"Tell me."

Callie urged him to sit on the stool next to her, then swiveled to face him so their knees touched. "We found some incredi—" She waved her hand as if erasing the words. "We were leaving when Saul stepped into some sort of weird quicksand."

"Quicksand?" he asked skeptically, taking her hands because he couldn't *not* touch her. He didn't doubt Callie's veracity, he trusted her word, but *quicksand*? Under the ocean?

"I know. Weird. But strong. The only thing I could think of is perhaps he broke through to some chamber or cavern and the equalization of the pressure acted like a giant vacuum. It sucked him down so fast I thought I'd lose him. I managed to hang on and get him out. Then Maura, Gayle, Leslie, and I administered first aid. Boarded and tied up his leg. Thank God by then he was unconscious. I must admit, the whole thing scared the living crap out of me."

She'd skipped what must've been the most harrowing part: getting a semiconscious man with a broken limb on board. Getting him up the ladder . . . Jonah's blood chilled. "You're a hero."

"Are you kidding me? I was scared spitless!"

"A mark of a true hero."

"He's going to be okay, thank God. They're keeping him overnight and sending him back tomorrow."

Jonah frowned. "He shouldn't come back at all."

"He insisted. Don't worry, Leslie and I figured where he can sit out of harm's way. We can't exclude him now,

Jonah. Not when things are so exciting! Saul's the bad news, turned into almost good news, but the *really* good news is we found a temple! At first I thought a residence. But it's way, way too big for that. No. A temple for sure. I documented evidence of eight-by-seventeen columns and got tons of pictures to show you. It's not a *naos*—the simplest form of a shrine. It's a *huge* temple. Think the size and scope of the Parthenon. Or the size of a soccer field!" Her eyes glowed. "I estimate it was more than twenty yards in height—not including the roo—"

He slid off the stool. "Do you need a nap?"

Callie frowned at the non sequitur. "Of course not. I'm not five."

He tugged her off her stool. "A cool dark room, a nice soft flat surface . . . I think you *definitely* need a long siesta after your traumatic day."

A glint lit her eyes. "Hmm . . ." Wrapping a slender arm around his waist, Callie nuzzled his throat. "I do feel a little sleepy."

"I assure you, you won't be the least bit sleepy in a few minutes."

Fourteen

Jonah put in a call to the hospital in Heraklion to check on Saul. With pins in his casted leg, the diver insisted he was still part of the team, and assured Jonah he'd manage on board. Set him up in a comfortable spot and he could clean coins all day, while the others did their thing below.

Jonah wasn't convinced it was a good idea to have someone who was physically restricted on board. But he reserved the right to send Saul home later if necessary.

After the brief call, he and Callie had done the opposite of nap. Their calisthenics had strewn bed linens and a side table on the floor with their clothing. He'd reluctantly left her to finish her shower on her own.

Now he felt energized and completely relaxed. Especially since he knew Saul was in decent shape and going to be okay. What he wanted to do was return belowdecks to Callie. What was *required* was being polite for a few hours to uninvited guests.

The Spanos were coming for dinner.

Standing on the first deck, attaching their approach, Jonah pulled a light-blue T-shirt over black shorts and finger-combed his hair. Done and done.

The Spanish-designed yacht *Astondoa* looked brand-spanking new, the Burmese teak gleaming richly in the fading evening sunlight. Jonah had been offered a job by the company several years ago. Though tempted, he'd opted to go on his own. Still, she was a masterpiece of workmanship. He'd like to go on board and check her out more fully.

He hadn't seen the boat docked on the island. Just the old fishing boat the old guys had arrived on when they'd paid their visit. Jonah was a hell of a lot more interested in this yacht than the woman emerging from the fully shaded bridge deck.

Black hair flowed loose and curly around her bare shoulders like a glossy cape, lifted lightly by the breeze. Anndra Spanos was stunningly beautiful, and he couldn't figure out why the hell he was pretty much repulsed by her.

The packaging was certainly there. In spades. It should have drawn him in. Yet he knew it wouldn't have even if he weren't pulled like a lodestone to Callie.

A thin, low-cut white tank top showed off Anndra's tanned olive skin—and not only the shape and size but the *color* of her nipples, as well. Nothing was left to the imagination. Decent legs, muscular and sleek, were shown off by white shorts so short the pockets hung well below the bottom edge. The musky, overprocessed smell of her perfume was an insult to the fresh ocean breeze coming off the water.

Jonah held out his hand to assist her. "Where's your brother?"

"Wait," she instructed the robed man who'd delivered her to *Stormchaser*. Silently the old man bowed his head.

Anndra's fingers tightened in Jonah's, and she kept eye contact in an unnerving way that made him uncomfortable. Not for himself, but for her. Should he tell her she was barking up the wrong tree, or just keep his mouth shut and hope she eventually took the hint he wasn't interested?

"Kall is taking an important business call," she said, voice husky as she stood far too close. "He didn't want me to wait. He'll try and come later."

Too bad. "Another time then. Welcome aboard *Stormchaser.*" Taking a step back, Jonah tried to disengage his hand, but she held on like a limpet. Other than arm wrestling with his guest, he had no choice but to relax his fingers and hope she'd let go soon.

"We're having drinks on the third deck, and dinner will be served shortly."

"I'd like a guided tour of this magnificent ship, may we do that before dining?"

He didn't particularly want to be either alone with her, or in confined spaces. "Sure." Extricating his hand from hers, he indicated she precede him up the ladder to the next deck. "Do you dive?"

"No. I never learned." She gave a delicate shudder. "I don't like to get my hair wet."

Score another hundred points for Callie. "It's an amazing and beautiful world down there, you should try it." *Shit.* Now she'd ask him to teach her.

Instead she asked about the ship, the length, the tonnage, how many crew members, how many people on the dive team. Harmless questions he was happy to answer.

As they entered through the sliding door into the salon he spotted the second steward passing through on his way from the deck above, returning to the galley. "Randy? Ask Tina to hold dinner for twenty minutes, would you? Then take a plate and drink to the man waiting for Miss Spanos."

Anndra put a hand on Jonah's arm. "Oh, there's no need, Christos is used to waiting. There's no need to feed him. He is quite content."

Randy gave Jonah an inquiring look.

"Go ahead and do it anyway. He's as much our guest as Miss Spanos."

He glanced back at Anndra and saw the slight crease of disapproval between her brows smooth away instantly. He held out his hand to indicate their next move. "This way. I'll show you the pilothouse and we can work our way down."

"I'd rather see where the artifacts you've unearthed are being kept." She put her hand on his forearm, the touch light and seductive.

"Anything of any historical interest has already been sent to the Counting House on Cutter Cay. There's nothing much to see."

Anndra pouted. "Can we peek in anyway?"

"It's our marine archaeologist's domain. Why don't I have her come down to meet us? I'm sure Dr. West would be happy to show off her toys." He suspected Callie would be anything but. She guarded that room like a pit bull. "There might be a few small artifacts and coins to look at."

"No. Let's not bother her. You can show me, and save time."

Jonah took her down the hallway and unlocked the large room set aside for Callie's work. Her equipment and long tables were neatly and precisely placed, ready for the artifacts. White, rectangular plastic tubs were lined up on the long table, filled with small, cleaned artifacts. A large magnifying glass with built-in lighting hung from a swinging adjustable extension mount suspended from the ceiling. It allowed Callie to look at any artifact up close and personal while keeping her hands free to take notes and type in data.

One padded bar stool was placed in front of Calista's laptop, and in the far right corner a deep sink with a commercial-kitchen-grade spraying faucet hung from the ceiling. Useful when rinsing artifacts. Soft evening light streamed in through a series of large windows along the portside wall, while the starboard side was covered in locked floor-to-ceiling white cabinets.

Anndra looked around. "Are your discoveries so valuable that the door has to be kept locked?"

Jonah shrugged. "Company procedure. And since my brothers run the company, I follow procedure. Although the more valuable treasure won't be kept on board long. It'll be processed here, then taken by helicopter to Heraklion, and then on to Cutter Cay. Doors on board are all locked, not only for security, but also privacy. Belowdecks we all live on top of one another, so it's practical as well. Potentially we'll all be together for long periods of time, and everyone needs a place to call their own, with the assurance that people won't just come barging in unless invited."

She hitched her butt onto one of the tables, swinging her feet in gold strappy sandals with FM heels. Perfect attire for an evening on board, Jonah thought, amused. He wouldn't think it so damn funny if she joined Saul with a broken leg, of course, or fell overboard in the ridiculous things.

"Tell me what you found on this wreck of yours." She leaned back on her hands, showing off her breasts. "Diamonds? A big amount of money? Oh! Did you find any kind of metal objects?"

"Sorry. No diamonds on board, but we've found a lot of interesting coins." He pointed. "That's what's in the tubs."

She pursed her lips in disappointment. "I thought treasure hunting was supposed to be exciting. No silver bars?"

"I'd be surprised if there were," Jonah told her. "None were indicated on the manifest." Just a king's ransom in coins. The real treasures were being found in the city.

He casually shut the blank screen of Callie's laptop. "Not much to see in here unless someone is cleaning artifacts. Ready to go?"

She slid off the table, then rubbed her shorts-clad butt with her palms as she sauntered around.

"What's inside the cabinets?"

What was she hoping to find? Gems and gold? "Chemicals for cleaning the artifacts. Mild acids and such."

"Anything flammable?"

Christ, was she planning to fucking blow up the ship? The woman was a pain in the ass; he hoped to hell she didn't prove dangerous as well. "No. The most dangerous effect could be unpleasant-smelling vapors if things are mixed incorrectly. But Dr. West takes every precaution to ensure that doesn't happen."

"I suppose." She ran a fingernail along the coins hanging on small wires to dry, making them clink. "What happens in case of fire, or some other kind of emergency? Like someone has a heart attack in the cabin? If they're the only one with access how can anyone help them?"

Jonah couldn't shove aside the creepy feeling crawling up his spine. He didn't know what it was about Anndra, but the less time he spent alone with her, the better.

"We have contingencies for emergencies. Would you like to go up and meet the captain, and have a quick tour of the pilothouse?"

Encompassing the room with a quick sweep, she turned, then tucked her hand against his arm. "I'm hungry."

"Great, because our chef is terrific, and I know she's prepared a special meal for us tonight." He had absolutely no idea what the hell was for dinner.

As he led her to the stairs to the upper deck, Jonah glanced at his watch. Only fourteen minutes had passed. It felt like fourteen *days*. It was going to be a long night.

Callie had seen the boat arrive with Jonah's dinner guests, and been surprised that Anndra's brother hadn't come with her as he'd told the captain when he'd called earlier.

Jonah had asked her to save the seat beside her, which Callie had done. Two chairs had been open halfway down the other side of the table. Maura had opted to stay on the bridge, and Saul was in his cabin resting.

"No. *Here*." Anndra sat down, then patted the empty chair beside her. "Next to me, Jonah."

Barefoot, he walked down to the other end of the table. Kicking out the chair beside Callie, he sat down. His shirt and shorts looked like he'd slept in them, and his hair stood up as if he'd constantly thrust his fingers through it. His sex appeal was off the charts. Callie took a deep breath of soap and salt as his arm brushed hers. All the little hairs on her body seemed to lean over in his direction.

"I'm a creature of habit," he said easily. "This is my usual seat. It would feel weird sitting in Saul's chair."

Anndra pouted. "That is too far away."

Callie caught Jonah's subtle gesture for Randy to remove the extra chair.

Outgoing and gregarious, Anndra didn't sulk for long. Certainly the men found her amusing. Brody in particular couldn't get enough of looking at her, or rather her obviously displayed breasts. She was like one of those little dogs movie stars liked to carry in their purses, Callie thought, pretty, but not very bright.

The outfit she wore was so blatant a come-on that Callie speculated which of the men the woman planned to seduce tonight. Jonah seemed the obvious choice. But then she was prejudiced. He'd be her target, too.

Callie considered Anndra Spanos a sort of artifact, and over dinner tried to figure out what the woman was about. Mentally peeling away the concretion of the heavy-handed but expertly applied makeup and trashy clothing. It wasn't the woman's face she was trying to see behind. It was her motivation.

What was Anndra Spanos doing on board *Stormchaser*? Especially without her brother in tow? And what was her role on Fire Island?

One thing the woman was not, was a girl's girl. She was all about fixing the attention of every man in the vicinity squarely on herself.

Callie sent Leslie, seated across from her, an amused glance as the Greek woman charmed the men, ignoring the two of them as if they were invisible.

They were still seated at the table. Dinner, as usual, was fantastic. Tina made sure the divers and crew were always well fed. Tonight was no exception and they'd all enjoyed the sea bass baked in coarse sea salt, accompanied by a bottle of Moschofilero, a delicious, crisp, floral white wine from the Peloponnese. This was followed by fruit salad with a sinfully rich sauce made from Limoncello, lemon curd, and Greek yogurt.

Callie had eaten sparingly, as was her habit, but she'd cleaned the dessert off her plate and contemplated a second helping.

Leslie pushed her chair back. "That's it for me, guys. Cal? Seven?"

"Perfect." Callie loved diving early before the sun was high enough to cast shadows underwater. She couldn't wait to see what else she'd discover.

Leslie plucked an apple out of the bowl in the center of the table. Saul loved apples. Callie hid a smile. "'Night. See you in the morning."

Anndra rose, too. "I need to use the little girls' room."

Leslie shot Callie a look. *No. Please. Anyone but me.* When no one else offered to be tour guide, Leslie sucked it up and said pleasantly, "There's a bathroom off the salon, I'll show you on my way down."

There was a chorus of good nights as Leslie left, Anndra, tottering on her ridiculous high-heeled gold sandals, in tow.

It was wiser to be polite and welcoming than not. They needed access to those texts. Callie was damn sure that if pissed off, Anndra would slam that door, *hard.* But being civil was hard for all of them. The woman was an unpleasant caricature, and impossible to like. And certainly to trust.

The conversation turned to that day's adventures. Callie loved to talk shop, but the meal, glass of wine, and fresh air, after all the calisthenics in Jonah's cabin earlier, made her pleasantly tired.

Not feeling like another round of Anndra, Callie yawned. "I think your friend is lost," she told Jonah. "Want me to go and see if she fell overboard on my way down?"

"No, I'll—Ah. I hear the pitter-patter of tiny stilettos," he drawled moments before Anndra sashayed out on deck in a cloud of freshly applied perfume.

"The ship is so big, I got turned around," she cooed, passing her own chair and making a beeline for Leslie's vacated seat, on the other side of Jonah. Of course. "Oh. Is that fresh coffee? Pour for me, Jonah?"

Callie did a mental head shake as Jonah obediently filled a cup. Anndra turned her ample charms to Vaughn and Brody and at the same time scooted her chair the extra few inches so that her leg touched Jonah's.

When Jonah replaced the coffee carafe on the table, he scooted his chair a little closer to Callie. "Chicken," she whispered under her breath.

He was a big boy, and clearly not oblivious to his guest's pursuit. Callie allowed her full tummy and the soft music playing to lull her into a sort of hypnotized state of peace. It had been a very long day, and she was pleasantly tired. The day was cooling off as the sun set, and the breeze felt good on her skin.

"Penny for them?" Jonah murmured.

"I'm thinking that if your guest knew where you spend your nights she'd lunge across the table and claw my eyes out."

"I don't think she's that energetic," he said drily.

"Why didn't her brother come out?"

"Some business thing. Do you think it would be rude to excuse ourselves and go below to make out?"

"Only if you want everyone to know about us."

His smile spoke of rumpled sheets and the slide of his damp skin against hers. "You think they don't?"

"If they do, they're maintaining a discreet silence. Let's not ruin the illusion by leaving together. Besides, she's *your* guest. You can't go until she does."

Jonah looked instantly crestfallen. "Crap. Will you wait up for me?"

Callie stifled a yawn. "I'll try, but I'm not making any promises."

"I know it's been a long day. I won't wake you."

"I don't like secrets," Anndra pouted, tugging at his arm. "Share with us, Jonah."

"Believe me, this isn't something anyone else would be interested in."

Before she started laughing, Callie stood. "'Night gang. I'm beat. See you tomorrow. Jonah? Walk me down and you can bring that book up for Vaughn."

"Sure."

The minute they were down the steps he moved up closer behind her, his breath warm on her neck. "I could come in and forget about Anndra. Brody or Vaughn will see her safely back on her boat."

She turned, placing a hand on his chest to ward him away, when what she really wanted to do was pull him into her cabin with her and fall asleep in his arms naked as the day she was born. He should applaud her will-power, if only he knew.

"It's been a long day." And an even longer night. How could a man be so freaking blind? "'Night, Jonah. See you in the—"

He kissed her as if he were a starving man falling on a feast. After several minutes, when she forgot her name, let alone that she just said she was too tired, he lifted his head. His eyes gleamed wickedly. "That should hold you." And he sauntered off.

Jonah went back on deck to have a last drink with the guys. Since Leslie had hit the sack early it was just Vaughn, Brody, and himself. He dropped into the chair he'd vacated earlier. It had been a long day; they were all tired. But he wasn't too tired to make love to Callie. He'd been looking forward to falling asleep with her in his arms. Shit.

He nodded when Brody offered him a beer. He'd nursed one all night, and the half left was flat and warm. "Anndra gone?" he asked, popping the top and drinking a long draft of fizz. It hit the spot. Shit. As host he should've escorted her back to her tender. On the other hand, thank God she'd gone before he had to be that polite.

He put his crossed feet up on Callie's vacated chair, looking out over the moonlit, choppy water illuminated by the running lights, and the small overhead white bulbs swaying gently in the balmy breeze coming off the water.

"Yeah." Brody indicated the barely visible, disappearing wake of her speedboat in the distance. "I gotta say, man, if you aren't going to tap that, I'm going to take a running dive at her myself."

"Be my guest." Anndra. Not Callie. He could be generous as hell. "Hope your shots are current. Better include rabies in that cocktail, buddy."

Brody snorted, then pulled his beer away from his mouth. "Man, don't say that kind of shit when I'm taking a drink. I snorted that beer right up my nose. I'll risk it, she's fucking *hot*!"

"Well, you better be ready to pay up, 'cause she's clearly selling something," Vaughn said under his breath.

They shot the breeze for another half hour, then headed down to their cabins. Jonah was looking forward to another full day of diving. So far it was working out well. Each team member spent half their time with *Ji Li* and the other half with Callie on the city.

She was like a kid in a candy store, he thought, smiling. He only hesitated a moment between his cabin and hers. No. If he went in he'd wake her. He'd already worn her out enough for one day. If he went in, neither of them would get any sleep for a second night in a row. Still, tempting . . . Turning, he inserted his key, opening the door to his dark cabin. Shouldn't *be* dark. The moon shone brightly.

There was a familiar heavily musk smell . . .

Jonah flicked on the light beside the door.

Anndra Spanos lay sprawled naked on his turned-down bed. Her tanned, olive skin liberally covered by sparkly oil, which now covered his crisp white, Egyptian cotton sheets.

"Fucking hell, Anndra! How did you get in? And how did you know which cabin was mine?" That's why she'd been gone so long after dinner: She'd been belowdecks breaking and entering.

"I borrowed your key when we were in the lab before dinner. I found your cabin by smell. You do smell most delicious, Jonah, there was no mistake that this was your personal space. The drawing board, all those maps and charts . . ."

"What do you want, Anndra?" It was obvious what she wanted him to think, but he'd bet that wasn't the reason behind her visit. Her sexuality was merely window dressing. He cast a glance at his personal crap across the room. Drawing board with nothing on it. Rolled charts, some paperwork he needed to get around to—none of it looked disturbed. His gun and a few valuable artifacts were locked in his safe behind a painting of a sea horse he'd picked up last year in Barcelona.

"I think it's obvious what I want, Jonah. I thought I made my desire for you clear at dinner."

"You noticed I didn't respond favorably to your advances. Don't embarrass us both any more. Grab your clothes." Dropped on the floor between door and bed. "And f—leave."

"I'm not in the least little bit embarrassed, εραστής," she assured him, stretching like a cat. For such a petite woman her breasts were large, and a bit too firm. Implants, Jonah figured. Her nipples were large, dark brown, and flat. No arousal there, thank God.

She held out a hand, wiggling her fingers. "Come to me, I can give you pleasure like you've never known."

Jonah stayed right where he was. "I saw your boat leave."

"Christos will have circled back when he saw the outside lights go off. He will wait for me."

"The guy's eighty years old, for God's sake! The last thing he should be doing is ferrying a spoiled brat where she isn't wanted in the middle of the night. You need to leave now, Miss Spanos. I'm tired, and my patience is wearing incredibly thin. I don't want to have sex with you. Not interested. I can't be any plainer than that."

As she slithered off the bed, Jonah figured she'd hang her head, blush, and get the hell out of Dodge, but instead of bending to pick up her jettisoned clothes, she lunged at him, kissing him full on the mouth. As if that would change his mind. If anything, it sealed the deal, disgusting and turning him off, even more if possible.

Jonah felt like an adolescent virgin as he clamped his mouth shut against her invading tongue, and at the same time, clamped his hand over her slippery hips to keep her from grinding against him.

She was like a fucking Venus flytrap. He wrenched out of her hold as her fingers wrapped around his dick, holding on tightly through the thin layers of his shorts. "Enough!"

Grabbing her wrist, he pulled her hand off his dick. Shoving her aside, he raked his fingers through his hair, at a loss. "Lady. Take a hint. *Not. Interested.* You wanna spend the night? You're welcome to bed down in the lounge. You want sex, you're in the wrong place."

"I could *make* you want me." She circled him like a cat around catnip, her long-nailed fingers scoring his chest, her lips brushing his arm, almost as if she were tasting him.

Goose bumps of revulsion sandpapered his skin. "No, you absolutely cannot make me want you." He grabbed a trailing hand and gave her a not-so-gentle shove. "Not today or any other day. Sorry, Miss Spanos, you're barking up the wrong tree."

"You don't like me?"

Not just no, but hell no. "Not particularly."

Throwing herself back on his bed, she stroked a slow hand up the inside of her thigh. "A man doesn't have to like a woman to have sex with her."

"This man does." The others had just returned to their cabins. Hauling her over his shoulder, *naked*, and probably screaming like a banshee was going to cause all sorts of shit to fly. Okay. He had to admit, that would be embarrassing enough. But *Callie* was right across the hall, not four feet away from his door. Jonah could only imagine what she'd think if she saw him carrying a naked Anndra through his ship.

"Are you *αρσενοκοίτης*?"

"I have no idea what that is." Although he suspected he did. Shit, he didn't give a rat's ass if she impugned his masculinity as long as she got the hell off his bed, and off the ship.

She played with her nipple as she watched him from beneath heavy lids. "Queer."

She was no more aroused, even by her own touch, than he was watching her. "No, I'm not. I don't know how I can be plainer than showing you that I'm not attracted to you. In any way. At all. You're making a fool of yourself." He walked over to the bed, intending to yank her to her feet. If she wanted to leave naked, so be it. "Have some dignity and get out before I carry you bodily through my ship and toss you overboard. There. Is that clear enough fo—"

The door cracked open, and Callie slipped inside, turning slightly to close it behind her. About facing, she gave him a delicious smile which, even under the ridiculous, farcical circumstances, made his heart skip several beats.

"Jonah, I was thinki—" Her eyes narrowed like laser sights as she realized they were not alone.

Hard to miss a very naked, sparkly Anndra, sprawled on her back, one knee cocked. Open and ready for business.

Fuck. Fuck. Fuck.

Both Jonah and Callie took aggressive steps forward. Him to intercept, her to—God only knew what.

"What the hell?" Callie said, clearly outraged.

And Fuck.

As if the situation couldn't get any goddamn worse.

Jonah stayed where he was until he could ascertain if she had any sharp implements on her. He put both hands up as Callie walked farther into the cabin. Dark hair hanging loose down her back, she wore the T-shirt she slept in, and he suspected nothing else. Her legs looked silky and a mile long.

"Believe me," he said, with utmost sincerity, not moving from his spot at the foot of the bed. The timing couldn't be worse. Their truce, while hot enough to burn the sheets, was still at the embryo stage. "This is *not* what it looks like."

"Oh, I think it's *exactly* what it looks like." She looked from Anndra to him and back again. "I think a skanky, opportunistic slut slipped into your cabin and lost all her clothes, then waited for you like a spider."

Okay, so far, almost so good. He couldn't quite tell from her closed expression exactly what she thought, but he could most certainly imagine. He took a tentative step in her direction.

Anndra in the meantime made absolutely no move to cover herself. Wearing nothing but a smug smile and some sort of slick oil that made her body gleam like a fish about to be fried, she was as fucking relaxed as a cat sunning itself. Jonah would like to strangle her, but that would require him touching her.

"I was in the process of kicking her out. I'll do just that, and we'll—"

"Oh, no," Callie kept her gaze firmly fixed on Anndra. Anndra smiled like a Cheshire cat and stroked the inside of her thigh with black fingernails.

Callie smiled back. The temperature in the room kicked up by several degrees.

Holy crap. Jonah took a step back.

"Please." Callie's voice sounded silky and menacing at the same time, making the hair on the back of his neck stand up. "Let me do the honors. I'll enjoy it."

Fifteen

Close enough to throw his body between them if Anndra got aggressive with Callie, Jonah retreated to lean against the dresser, arms folded to watch the show. "Have at it. Let me know if you want me to jump in."

Callie shot him an unfathomable glance before bending to pick up Anndra's scattered clothing off the floor, where she'd left a—short-trail. There wasn't much. *Two* items to be exact.

"I suspect her plan to eat you before, during, or after sex had nothing to do with your sexual satisfaction." Callie tossed the clothes on top of the other woman. "Just an FYI, Cutter. This one doesn't consider sex *recreational*. Do you?" she asked Anndra as she walked over and stood closer to the bed.

With one finger she shoved the other woman's bent knee. "Close these. He's not interested, nor is he your gynecologist."

Anndra slapped her legs together and dropped her hand from her breast. Then glared at Callie as if she were the devil incarnate. "I have as much right to be here as you."

Callie's smile was scary. "Not in a million years."

Turning to Jonah, she picked some flimsy piece of clothing off Anndra's belly, forced the fingers of Anndra's left hand open, then shoved the fabric into her palm. Anndra squeaked with pain as Callie rather forcibly closed the other woman's hand around her clothing. "Lady, get yourself dressed or suffer the consequences if I have to do it for you. I'm very generously giving you thirty seconds before I jump right in and see just how fast I can do it for you."

She turned to Jonah. "Just an FYI. I'm saving your ass. This one is a particularly nasty *Phoneutria*."

Jesus. She was magnificent. Cheeks flushed, pale eyes glinting with annoyance, she was a volcano under an ice cap. Fascinating to watch. Deadly as hell. Sexy—man, her sex appeal was off the charts. He grinned. "I'm guessing that's something extremely unpleasant."

"What is this?" Anndra shouted, swinging her legs off the bed, holding her clothing to her chest. She made no effort to fully cover herself; nor did she seem in any hurry to get dressed and run for her life. "I am no murderess!"

"A Brazilian wandering spider," Callie informed him, yanking something out of the other woman's hand, holding it up for inspection, and then pulling the skimpy tank top over Anndra's head. "Wow. The size of your clothing is in direct correlation to your intelligence. Who would've thunk it? Stick your arms through, or be trussed up like a Thanksgiving turkey and sent home to your brother just like this. I don't give a shit."

She crossed her arms as she waited, giving the other woman a don't-fuck-with-me look, until Anndra shoved each arm into an armhole with all the cooperation of a fractious three-year-old.

Not that it made a damn bit of difference. The skimpy bit of clothing barely covered her naked breasts and didn't reach her belly button. The rest of her was still naked.

Callie wrestled the shorts from Anndra's grasp,

dropped them on her lap, then gave the woman's ankle a sharp kick until she complied and pulled the shorts up to her knees.

Callie told her with utmost calm, "I'm quite sure you're practiced at getting undressed and dressed while prone, but get your greasy, skanky ass off Jonah's bed and finish this process. Hurry up, my patience is wearing extremely thin. Although, I must confess, I'm actually looking forward to you resisting so I can throw your half-naked ass into the boat and send you back to the loving arms of your brother."

With a spate of unintelligible Greek, mixed, Jonah suspected, with some Turkish and possibly Arabic, Anndra slipped off the bed and yanked up her shorts, spitting invectives. He straightened in case he needed to intervene, but didn't get any closer. If Callie made a move indicating she needed his assistance in any way, he'd be right there between them. So far she was more than holding her own.

If looks could kill, Callie would be lying in a smoking heap on the floor writhing in agony.

The two women were only a foot apart, because when Anndra stood up, Callie didn't give so much as an inch. Inside, Jonah applauded. Yeah, he suspected he'd pay later, but right now it was a show not to be missed.

"Vicious," Callie continued to him as if they were having a private conversation. "And sometimes hard to identify. Not that I had any trouble. One of the most toxic spiders in the world. Do you need help with that?" she asked politely as the other woman fumbled with the zipper and button on her shorts.

"*Min m 'angízeis, skýla!*"

Ah, don't touch me, bitch. Jonah understood that much. Anndra finally got everything zipped and buttoned. "You have no right to burst in here and interrupt us with your petty accusations."

Callie laughed. "Seriously? You can say that with a straight face? Up and at 'em, Stheno. Hope there's a boat waiting for you, because it's a long haul swimming back to your island."

"This is an outrage!" Anndra screeched, struggling in Callie's hold as she was dragged to the door.

One hand clamped on Anndra's upper arm, Callie pulled open the heavy door with the other. "It most certainly is." With a firm shove, she pushed Anndra into the corridor. "Keep moving."

"My brother will slit your throat for this."

She was dead serious. Time to intervene? "Hey, that—"

Callie held up a hand to shush him as she stopped Anndra in her tracks, spinning the other woman around to face her. She got right in her face. "You listen to me, Spider Woman. You were not invited into my man's bed, *καταλαβαίνετε*?"

Anndra gave her a black look, then swore at her in Greek. Jonah didn't have to know what the words meant; their intent was clear.

"You have a nasty, filthy mouth," Callie told her, then after a pregnant pause continued evenly, "I just gave you two pertinent pieces of information, which you'd be wise to actually *hear*. Let me reiterate those for you: You weren't *invited*. *My* man."

"I want my shoes!"

My man. Silently, Jonah handed Anndra's gold sandals to Callie.

"Good Lord, you have *enormous* feet. To match your ego."

Anndra snatched the heels out of Callie's hand.

"You can put them on in the boat on the way home."

She gave the other woman's arm a not-so-gentle shove to get her moving in the right direction. "I've had all the conversation with you I can stomach. Keep moving."

Callie didn't break stride going up the stairs to the next level, nor when she almost threw the other woman down the ladder to the dive platform.

Fortunately for Spanos's sister, the small boat bobbed on the choppy water. The man/monk/accomplice woke from his nap with a jerk and raced over to assist her. Jonah untied their mooring as soon as her feet left *Stormchaser*.

Anndra grabbed the rail of the small craft, pale face a rictus of fury in the moonlight. "I'm going to tell Kallistrate how you treated me. You'll both be sorry."

"Please have him talk to me," Jonah informed her coldly. "I'll tell him exactly why you aren't welcome on board my ship, and what you offered me—in detail—while you were here. I suspect your holiday will be cut short."

She threw one of her sandals at him. It bounced off the side of the boat, then made a small splash as it hit the water. The sound of the powerful engine muted her screams of fury.

Callie padded over to a towel rack and pulled one down, wiping her hands vigorously. "I have skank glitter all over me."

Jonah wrapped both arms around her waist from behind, resting his chin on the top of her head as they watched the white wake of the small boat head toward the darkness of the distant island.

"Holy crap." Callie wrapped her arms over his. "That woman has *no* boundaries."

She'd been an Amazon for the last fifteen minutes, but now she trembled slightly in the aftermath. Jonah tightened his arms around her waist. "Thanks for saving me from a fate worse than death." He was only half joking.

"When I first met her, I dismissed her as a pleasure-seeking bimbo. But I think she has a whole other agenda. And sorry to crush your ego"—she twisted to look up at him—"but I don't think it's crazy lust for your admittedly scrumptious body. I think Miss Spanos has a different, more unsavory agenda."

He cupped her breasts through her T-shirt, loving the weight and silky glide of the fabric over her smooth skin. Her nipple peaked to greet him. He smiled against her hair. "You think I have a scrumptious body?"

"Is that the only part of what I said that you heard, Cutter?"

He turned her in his arms, tilting her face up. "No, I hear and compute, but right now she's on her way home, and I have you, the moonlight, and an empty deck."

Dipping his head just as she stood on her toes to meet him, Jonah kissed her. A blast of sexual energy tore through them, like a forest fire, so that what he'd intended as a soft kiss instantly turned into a forest fire of need.

He sucked in her gasp of surprise, wrapping his arms around her slender body, loving the feel of her, the taste of her—Hell, he was in deep, deep trouble here.

"What's a Stheno?" he murmured, lifting his head, sliding his hands down to cup the sweet curve of Callie's butt through her shirt. He danced her back against the rail, keeping the press of her small, perfect breasts and the flat plane of her belly against him.

Her legs parted enough for him to bring his erection tight against the juncture of her thighs. He felt her damp heat through his shorts, and got harder still as he wound his hand in her hair.

Annoying thoughts of Anndra faded as quickly as the wake of the rapidly retreating *Astondoa*. He wanted to take Callie right now, right there, on deck, under the stars.

"A Gorgon, and Medusa's nastier sister." She ran both hands up his chest under his shirt, her fingers cool as she paused to circle his nipples with the pads of her fingers. He could've told her it didn't work that way on him—but right now, having his nipples fondled by *her* turned him into a bundle of rampant nerve endings.

Rock-hard, his dick pulsed as if it were a magnet zeroing on true north. Skimming her palms over his sides to his back, Callie ran her hands on either side of his spine in long, languid strokes in a far-from-soothing caress. The feel of her fingers on his body made his dick twitch, and his hair lifted as if electrified. Nipping at his jaw, she arched her throat when he went in to kiss her mouth.

"A vi-vicious female monster with brass hands, sharp fangs, and hair of live venomous snakes . . . Oh—I like *that*." She gave a full-body shudder as he used the edge of his teeth on the taut tendons of her throat, then followed with a slow stroke of his tongue. "She—I feel that all the way down to my—She killed more men than both her sisters combined." Callie finished in a rush, clearly trying to remember how to breathe as he nibbled his way to the shell of her ear.

Jonah slid the long skeins of her hair over her shoulder, loving the silky slip and slide of the dark, waist-length tresses. Having liberated her ear, he ran the tip of his tongue along the swirls, then nipped at her earlobe, pulling her harder into the cradle of his thighs. Her skin felt as soft as heated satin. "Then I'm very happy you burst in to save me." He felt her smile as he explored her eyebrow with his lips.

"I burst in to have wild monkey sex with you."

The skim of his lips felt the flutter of her heartbeat at her temple. "Didn't we do that a few hours ago?"

Callie patted his back. "Aw, did I wear you out, Cutter?"

"Hell no. Seeing you tangle with that Gorgon revitalized me."

"You are such a guy." Smiling wickedly, Callie's sparkling eyes reflected the small lights strung around the deck as she wrapped her arms around his neck. Jonah wanted to eat that smile—and more—all night.

The security cameras placed at strategic points through the ship made anything more than touching out here dangerous. He knew where the cameras were—he'd maneuvered Callie and himself just out of range—but he wasn't taking any chances.

He caressed the firm globes of her ass. "*¡Madre de Dios!*" He bunched the fabric up to get to bare skin. "You went into combat *commando*?"

"That wasn't the kind of combat I went in for," Callie pointed out, kissing his chin. "I could hardly ask your skanky friend to wait while I went back to my cabin to throw on my panties, could I?"

He ran his fingers along the seam of her first-class ass. "Should've trussed her up, gagged her, and had her delivered to her brother."

"How is this going to impact our access to the library? You know she's going to run home crying to him."

"I'll talk to him. Diplomatically, man-to-man."

Callie bit at his lip, taunting him. "Hell hath no fury like a woman scorned. We'd better brace ourselves for attack."

"I'm not worried about her. No woman would keep coming on to a man who flat-out tells her he doesn't want her." Except Anndra Spanos.

"I think she's over the coming-on phase of her agenda

and might go into an even more aggressive mode. Watch your back, Jonah."

He smiled. "I'd rather watch your front."

"I'm not opposed to making out here on deck in front of God and the fishes. But you know Randy is doing his rounds, right?"

He opted not to tell her about the strategically placed cameras on all the decks and in all the public rooms. "Life raft?"

She laughed, grabbing his wrist to pull his hand away from the delectable, silky curve of her butt. "Crazy man. That's what beds are for, and there is a perfectly sized one without oily sheets in my cabin." She slid her fingers between his, palm-to-palm and gave a tug. "Come on, I'll race you down."

The innocent holding of hands was sweet, and shouldn't've been erotic, but still, Jonah felt his need for this woman torque as she jogged him back inside.

"Craziest place you've ever made love?" he asked as they raced through the salon. As he passed, he slapped a palm on the light switch, plunging the salon into gloom while they headed downstairs.

Not that he wanted to know the *who*, but he was intrigued that a bed was the first thing that came to her mind.

"A bunk bed?" Waiting for him to use his keycard on his cabin door, she whispered in deference to the close proximity of the other cabins.

"You're kidding me." Pushing open the door to his cabin, Jonah tugged her inside. "No swinging from a rope?" he asked with mock incredulity, skimming her T-shirt over her head and backing her toward the bed. "No sex while skydiving?"

She punched his arm. "Neither have you."

"I'm going to have to open new horizons for you."

"What?" She pulled his shirt over his head, then made short work of his shorts. "Like making out in a small lifeboat? No thanks, I like being able to stretch o—" She stopped reversing. "Whoa! Not on those sheets!"

"Trust me, nothing happened on those sheets."

Callie's expression was one part sexy as hell and two parts I-don't-give-a-damn. "Her naked butt was on those sheets. I'm burning them tomorrow."

"Ah, crap. Those are my favorites."

"I'll buy you twelve more sets. Burn. You're coming home with me, Cutter. Where's my shirt?"

"I dare you to go just as you are."

"*Naked?* You're crazy! Someone will see me."

"Everyone's asleep."

"Not some of the crew!"

"It's *four* feet."

She bit her lip, then blew out a sigh. "You have to come with me."

"Okay."

"Run!"

He grinned. "Bet you won't run from one end of the corridor to the other."

"Jonah!"

Time to expand her horizons. A little dare might jump-start the process. "Triple dare."

She hesitated. "If you make one sound I'll kill you. Go unlock my door first. I want somewhere to hide just in case someone sees me."

"Us."

"Trust me," she said drily, "I don't give a damn if anyone sees *your* naked butt. It's probably something they have all seen before."

"It's not my butt I'm worried about someone seeing."

"Then let's not do this stupid th—"

Opening the door, he took the few steps to her door, using his master key to unlock it, then propped it open and went back into his cabin. "You know this will only take thirty seconds, right?"

She grabbed his hand. "Run quickly and lightly!"

"With this?" Jonah indicated his rampant erection. "I don't know—"

Callie yanked him into the dimly lit corridor, spun right, then took off down, running flat-out. Her shapely ass was a thing of beauty. Half a step behind her, Jonah grinned, amused as hell that she'd actually taken him up on his dare. At the end of the corridor, they turned and raced back.

Of course no one, other than the camera discreetly tucked in the corner, saw them. And he'd take care of that before anyone saw it. All doors remained closed, and the night watch prowled the upper decks.

They dashed into Callie's cabin, and he kicked the door closed behind them. "You are such a brave girl."

She raised a haughty brow, hilarious since she was naked, and pink all over with embarrassment. "I'll give a pass to the '*girl*' part of that as a onetime compliment."

Jonah pulled her to him with an arm around her waist. The blush made her skin warm all over. "You're all the woman I need."

"Excellent. I'll send your little friend Anndra a memo. Now," she continued firmly, pushing at his chest with both hands, "let me see if you have glitter on your boy parts."

She stepped back to inspect his dick with eyes and hand. "No skank glitter, lucky for you. But I see some serious swelling. I need to get you into a shower immediately."

He backed her against the wall. "How about getting me inside you immediately?"

Callie shook her head and gave him an admonishing look that made his heart tumble head over heels. "You have to be fumigated first," she told him, voice librarian-stern as, frowning, she grazed her hand along the length of his dick and up again. "I'm not sure how long this will take. I have to be thorough."

Jonah made an expansive gesture toward the bathroom. "The decontamination chamber is that way. Let's get the painful process over as slowly as possible. I'll try to be very, very brave."

Sixteen

Jonah showed his excellent navigational skills by backing her into the bathroom while kissing her. He angled past the edge of the bed, tempted to stop right there, then around a chair, and through the narrow door opening to the head. All with his eyes closed.

He'd always enjoyed kissing. The slick, sweet taste of a woman's mouth, the heat and flash of arousal as the kiss got hotter. But kissing wasn't his main focus prior to love-making. It was a delicious hors d'oeuvre before the main meal.

Kissing *Callie* changed the ball game. He couldn't get enough of her, couldn't tear himself away from the taste and texture of her mouth. Kissing her could be enough—it wasn't, but damn, it was so good, it *could* be.

Kissing her felt like magic.

Breathing was highly overrated.

This mad, mindless lust was new to him. He'd always been able to compartmentalize. Not so when he made love to Callie. Brain and body engaged 110 percent.

Leaning his hip against the counter, Jonah pulled her flush against him. Pressed together from chest to knees, he felt the furnace heat of her silky skin, still warm from mortification. He loved that she'd run naked for him, despite her reluctance and embarrassment.

The woman melted his brain cells.

Rock-hard, aching to get inside her, he angled his hips to press his dick against her moist heat. Instantly responsive, she shifted her feet, canting her hips to meet him. The hard points of her nipples pressed into his chest, upped his heat. He liked the small, plump shape of her breasts, the soft, pale pink of the hard tips, loved how responsive she was to his slightest touch.

He inhaled deeply as she moved against him, filling his head with the scent of her. A faint hint of coconut underlay the intoxicating natural fragrance of her skin.

Without breaking their lip-lock—the room wasn't that big—he reached over to twist on the shower. Her short nails dug into his back to hold him to her. "Not going anywhere," he murmured against the corner of her mouth.

She stroked his back, then cupped his ass. "Good." Her nails scored his skin, making him shudder against her. "I have long-range plans for you, Cutter."

His heart tripped quadruple time. "*Long range*" should've scared the erection away. Somehow the words did just the opposite. "*Dios*, you smell delicious, and you *feel* even better. I can't get enough of you. *Te necesito, querido.*"

"You have me."

He shifted her slightly so he could open a drawer in the cabinet behind her. Lifting his lips from hers, he handed her a foil package.

She blinked, then took it from him. "Where did this come from?"

"Bedside table, and, being the long-range planner that I am, a few in here for emergencies." They kept a giant-sized box of condoms in the infirmary for anyone who wanted them when they went on shore leave. He'd grabbed two handfuls, then a third for the hell of it. Her cabin. His cabin. A few in the cabinet near the hot tub, a few more in her lab . . . Yeah, he was a long-range planner all right.

"This certainly constitutes an emergency." Impatiently she inspected the small square to figure out how to open it. "*My* bedside table? How'd it get there?"

"Not it, *they*. I put them there before dinner."

"Sneaky," she said admiringly as she ripped the corner off with her teeth. She took his dick in her palm, inspected it, then used both hands to fit the end over his pulsing hard-on, nice and snug. A shudder shot from Jonah's balls to his brain.

She stuck her tongue out so he could remove the tiny bit of foil since her hands were busy. "You're a man scout."

She gripped his shaft, stroking the lubricated latex down the stone-hard length of him. His dick twitched eagerly in her hand.

"A man s-scout." His fingers clamped around hers to guide her. "Jesus, that feels—Yeah. Just like that."

"Then take your hand off mine so I can keep doing it." Callie admonished tartly, nudging away his helping fingers with her free hand. "This isn't *boy*-sized, but I *do* like a man who's prepared. You do realize this is a little like putting the cart before the horse, don't you? We've made love at least five hundred times with nothing between us but—us."

Yeah. He'd given that a vague thought.

"All done." She gave his dick a friendly pat, which made him grin as he pulled her back into alignment. "Are we done kissing?" she asked demurely, peridot eyes sultry as she shifted her gaze to look up at him.

He smiled against her lips. "Not by a long shot." While

the water drummed like tropical rain, he resumed kissing her slowly and thoroughly. Cupping the back of her head so her hair poured over his hand and arm, a dark, silky waterfall, he went back to the task at hand. Urging her tighter against him with his palm on the small of her back, he let his hand linger there when she shivered and her tongue faltered as it tangled with his. He'd never thought of the small of a woman's back as an erogenous zone, but he already knew it was for Callie.

Sucking her tongue caused her fingers to curl into the hair on his chest as she angled her head and took the kiss to another plane.

Steam swirled around them as he trailed his fingers down the sweet globes of her ass, slid his fingers teasingly down the crack until she moaned.

Gliding his lips down her neck to the rapid, uneven pulse at the base of her throat, Jonah tasted coconut, salt, and Callie. He returned to nip her lower lip with his teeth, smiling against her as she gasped and tightened her arms.

He used his knee to spread her legs as he backed her against the sink cabinet. "You okay?"

"Better than." A hazy green ring circled her dilated pupils. "I have a sweet ache, right here." Taking his hand, Callie pressed it to her mound. "Just when I think you've brought out everything I have, I discover newly woken parts. Teach me more."

He loved the way she let him move her where he wanted her.

He groaned, lifting her onto the sink. She was wet, slick folds opening like a dewy rose. Their eyes locked as Callie wrapped her long legs around his waist, and her arms around his neck. Her knees bracketing his hips, Jonah cupped his hands under the firm globes of her ass to pull her where he needed her, at the same time thrusting his hips forward. He filled her to the hilt, had to pause because the sensation of her tight wetness clamping around him was so good it almost hurt.

Her nails dug into his shoulders as she arched her back. Jonah felt the throbbing pulse of his heartbeat echoing deep inside her. Hers pulsed back, sending a clear message that made his heartbeat thunder in his ears.

He devoured her mouth, pistoned his hips against hers, his hands gripping her taut ass. She devoured him right back, fingers gripping his hair as they gave and took. Took and gave. Until Jonah didn't know where he started and Callie began. Sweat ran into his eyes, and their skin noisily slapped together. Music.

Weightless in his arms, he felt her release cresting, and withdrew just enough for her to cry out and tighten her ankles in the small of his back, jerking him back deep inside her. "More," she demanded, not losing any of the rhythm as she urged him faster with hips and hands. Her mouth swooped up to kiss him. Tongue, teeth, urgency.

She was poetry in motion, on fast-forward as she rose and fell on the spear of his dick. Her breasts rubbing against his chest, her mouth fed ferociously on his.

Synapses firing on all cylinders, Jonah felt like a god. Poseidon at the very least. Nothing in his life had felt as good as making love with Callie. Nothing. Ever. And each time was like the first.

They made love in the shower with hot water pulsing down on them, then staggered out, wet and tangled together, their breathing erratic, muscles limp. Made it as far as the foot of the bed, where Jonah tumbled her sideways across the mattress. Clasping her waist with his big hands, he flipped her so Callie lay on top of him.

Resting her chin on her folded arms, she looked her fill,

his mouth conveniently situated a few inches from hers. His hair was wet, slicked back off his face by her fingers moments before. Her own hair lay sodden and cool down her back, and fell in swaths over her back and around his hips.

She pressed her own hips down lightly. "You know this is anatomically impossible, don't you?" Her breathing had gone from raw and labored to merely breathless.

His eyes looked impossibly blue. "My erection?"

"Your *ninety-ninth* erection of the night. Honest to God, Cutter, I didn't know a man could climax that many times. And I know for a fact that it's impossible for a woman to have that many O's without internally combusting." If anyone told her she could climax that many times she'd call them not only a liar, but delusional.

He stacked one hand beneath his head. "It's a gift," he told her modestly, playing with the wet strands of her hair with his other hand, lifting and dropping the water-heavy skeins onto her back.

God, yes. It most certainly was. "I thought I worked it out of you."

He grinned. "Almost." He sounded highly amused.

She stared into his eyes. "*Almost?*"

His eyes darkened. "If you're tired we can—ah, Callie?"

Callie discovered his body with hands and lips. Her mouth lingered on the drumming pulse at the base of his throat. She kissed her way down him, enjoying the way his belly contracted and his skin pebbled with goose bumps as she explored his navel with her tongue.

"I think I was kidding," he said faintly when she nuzzled the crisp hair at the base of his stone-hard erection. His fingers tightened in her hair.

"Too late, Cutter, I'm calling your bluff." This was another first for her. But she was a quick learner. His erection bobbed right in front of her lips. Thick. Long, Hard. The head flushed, the tangle of pulsing veins along his shaft darkly intriguing. She wanted to taste him. Feel that pulsing energy against her tongue.

He smelled so good. Soap and damp, musky, sexy man. Running her fingers lightly along its length, from root to gleaming tip, Callie was fascinated by how her lightest touch made his penis jerk as it hardened and thickened even more. If soft and slow did that to him—

She cupped him, loving the feel of him pulsing with life in her palm. The smooth length was like iron beneath silken skin. He gave a strangled moan as her fingers slid to the very tip, then moved down to the crisp hair at his groin. Closing her fingers around his shaft, she squeezed, giving the length firm strokes, up then down. Groan guttural, Jonah's hips surged into her hand. The tug on her scalp from his fists was painful pleasure. She loved the unexpected softness of his skin, silken velvet over the over tensile hardness. He moaned as she squeezed, his fingers tight against her scalp.

"I love how you smell," she whispered against his thigh. Hot, salty, musky male.

He shot her a slow, sexy smile.

"God. Yes. Just like that." Callie played with him, running her fingers up and down, feeling him swell impossibly larger. Rubbing the pearl of moisture from the tip, she glided her hand in an ever-increasing grip and speed until he arched off the bed, lashing his hand out to circle her wrist with tight fingers.

"It'll be over before it begins." His breath was rapid, his chest heaving as he struggled to catch his breath.

She lowered her head, closed her mouth over the blunt, heart-shaped tip. She sucked him deeper, reveled in his gasp and the taut arch of his hips. His heartbeat pulsed against her swirling tongue.

Her own heartbeat thudded erratically. His pleasure gave her pleasure. She loved the taste and texture of him, the novelty—the *power* of holding him in her mouth. Hell, it was the ultimate power a woman had over a man. Callie liked it. No. *Loved* it. A lot.

His body gathered, tightening like a too-tight bow-string. *She'd* done this.

One moment she had her face buried against his groin, the next he swung her up and over onto her back and plunged her onto his damp hardness. They came together so violently it left them both limp and incapable of moving. Even her eyelashes felt depleted.

"So much for all those condoms," she muttered weakly against his heaving chest.

Other than his erratic and hard heartbeat syncopating with hers, Jonah was as limp and depleted as she was. "Highly overrated."

She was too happy to give it its due consideration. She figured that ship had sailed the first, second, and eleventh times he'd been inside her.

Callie danced her fingers over the corded muscles in his neck, then skimmed the sweat-damped muscles of his back with the flat of her hand.

"Do you have any idea just how erotic and sensual you look when you do that?" Seductive and low, his voice sounded like hot chocolate on a cold night. Like every dream she'd never allowed herself to dream. Like a sweet that was going to be snatched away any second. Need incarnate made her brain skitter away from grim reality. She was nothing but heat, and light, and a need so power-ful her body shook with it.

His lips traveled over her forehead, then down over her

temple, where she felt the damp glide of his tongue tasting the still-hard-beating pulse he discovered there. "Is running naked down a corridor the most daring thing you've ever done?"

He'd challenged her to see if she'd chicken out. But running down a deserted corridor was the new Callie. "You're joking, right?"

"I don't mean diving, or hang gliding." Jonah cupped her chin, his long fingers caressing her jaw and his lazy lips exploring the contours of her face as if fascinated by the taste and texture of her skin. "I mean something that exposes your vulnerability."

Her thick hair was still wet, and she shivered in the air-conditioning. "You mean like having sex with you?" Her voice was dry, but her heart thudded uncomfortably where her breasts pressed against the hard wall of his chest. She *was* vulnerable. When he found out who her brother-in-law was, he'd see it as a complete betrayal of his trust. And he'd be right.

"*This* is daring?"

"It's not easy for me to trust anyone. I can count on the fingers of one hand the people I trust unconditionally."

And one of them isn't myself, she thought, heart heavy. Rydell and Peri were *everything* to her. She'd known them almost her entire life. She'd known this man who touched and tasted her so intimately for mere minutes in comparison.

She automatically opened her mouth when his lips covered hers. His tongue swept inside to slide over hers, hot, seeking, hungry. Callie forgot to breathe, savoring the moment because it was soon going to be snatched from her greedy grasp, and she'd be left empty and alone.

Jonah pulled away an eighth of an inch, his breath hot on her face, his eyes painfully, startlingly intense, and so blue Callie felt as if she could fall into them and be enveloped in warmth. "I trust *you*."

Oh, God—Callie wanted to yell, *Don't!* "And your brothers."

"Yeah. I haven't known Zane, Nick, and Logan long, but I trust them with my life. *They* trust me with a multimillion-dollar ship, and give me carte blanche to do what I like with her. This salvage—this *Atlantis* find—is my gift to them, my show of appreciation for them putting their trust in me.

"We're close. So close. With just a few more artifacts I'll prove myself to them and to the archaeology community. Everyone will know the name Cutter Salvage after this. A win–win."

And there she had it.

No win–win.

Her loyalty to Rydell was absolute.

Jonah's loyalty to his *brothers* was just as unequivocal.

There was no room for negotiation. No compromise.

Rydell or Jonah?

Only one could win.

The other would lose.

And no matter which of the two men won, *she'd* lose.

"That woman's behavior last night was *really* odd," Leslie said the next morning. Everyone but Jonah had already eaten breakfast and gathered on the dive platform getting ready to dive.

Jonah had showered and gone by the time Callie woke up in her own bed. Showered and dressed, she went up to breakfast, but no one had seen him this morning. She presumed he was with the captain and would join them when he was done. She knew he liked to read his news alone over several cups of coffee, and he might be anywhere on board doing just that until it was time to go down.

"There was no doubt—to everyone here last night—that none of us had any interest in her." Vaughn pulled his wet suit up his legs. "She seemed pretty focused on Jonah, I think. But, intelligent man that he is, he put out a giant NO sign, in neon, like the rest of us."

"Hey, speak for yourself," Brody muttered. "I would've done her in a heartbeat."

"Charming," Callie muttered with a shake of her head. It seemed that every salvage had someone like Brody on board. Brash, and not too bright. At least Jonah had nipped Brody's drinking in the bud. He'd had all the booze removed, not counting on the younger man's willpower to do the trick.

Callie reached up to shove the pins more securely into her coiled braid, squinting from the glare on the water. "Jonah found her in his bed last night."

"Holy crap," Vaughn said, pausing what he was doing to stare at her. "You're shitting me. Is that where he is? In bed with that crazy woman?"

Leslie pulled a disgusted expression. "Ew! I thought I heard something running up and down the corridor late last night. Please don't tell us he took that bitch up on her offer?"

"God, no." Callie shook her head. "I went to ask him something, and she was sprawled naked on his bed in all her bouncy, glittery glory."

"Oh, man, Callie, that's just cruel!"

She ignored Brody's expected response. He was over thirty and had the attitude and hormone levels of a teenager.

"I don't get it." Leslie looked at Callie. "Why was she so damn persistent?"

"Maybe I'm irresistible?" Jonah said as he came down the ladder to join them, dressed in nothing but black shorts and his killer smile. Callie's heart went into overdrive, and the temptation to throw herself into his arms was overwhelming. She picked up her mask instead. He gave her a good-morning glance, brief and hot.

"I'm sure your legion of fans would agree," she told him with just the right amount of humor. "Maybe she wanted not some*one*, but some*thing* on board?"

"To steal something, you think?" Brody demanded. "You were with her most of the night, weren't you, Jonah? You would've seen if she swiped anything."

"I was with her most of the time. Other than an hour or so when I thought she'd left. Then she was God only knows where, doing God only knows what."

"My cabin's always locked," Leslie assured him as she sat beside Callie, their legs dangling over the water.

"Anndra had the master key," Callie pointed out grimly, slipping her sunglasses on since they were chatting instead of diving, and the glare off the water was fierce. Not to mention she was sure the longer everyone sat around at such close quarters, the better they'd be able to see she was a well-satiated woman this morning, and not because she'd gone to bed early and had a good night's rest.

She admired the play of muscles shifting under the bronze satin of Jonah's back as he lifted his wet suit from the rack. "She had full access to every nook and cranny on board." And tried to get into all Jonah's nooks and crannies while she was at it. The skank.

"Yeah." Jonah turned, his wet suit in his hands. "My thoughts exactly. I just talked to Maura about that. She'll check to see if anything's gone missing, and she and Gayle will go through all the security tapes to see if Anndra was up to no good."

Security tapes? Callie narrowed her eyes and looked around. *There are cameras? Oh, crap, of course there are.* Most large ships had them, and especially salvage ships, where danger could come from 360 degrees given the valuable cargo on board. Was there a camera anywhere near where they'd made out on deck last night? What about in the hallway? Wouldn't that be great having half the crew see her running bare-ass naked down the corridor? Maybe it would go viral.

Leslie gave him a glance filled with humor. "You mean even worse '*no good*' than getting into your bed?"

"That alone should be a punishable offense," Jonah told her drily, then cocked a brow at Callie.

"Was it a secret?"

"Nope." He started suiting up and shot her a small, way-too-intimate smile, Callie was sure no one could miss. "No secrets on board *Stormchaser.*"

Callie's heart squeezed. *One* truth revealed, but the sword of Damocles still hung directly over her head. She took off her sunglasses, she didn't want anyone to think she was hiding anything else. "Um . . . one more."

She held up her bare left hand. "I'm actually a widow. Sorry for the subterfuge, but the ring keeps most predators away. I like to wear it until I get to know everyone."

Leslie made a noncommittal hum, but her eyes spoke volumes as she snagged Callie's. "Sorry, Cal, was it recent?"

"Four years. Leukemia."

The other woman gave her a sympathetic look. "Tough on both of you."

"Yes, it was." It was going to take some getting used to having a bare left hand. She'd worn her ring for six years; it would be a hard habit to break. "Adam would've gotten a kick out of me using his ring as a shield. He was one of the good guys. I was lucky, even if it was for such a short time."

"Not that *I* have a problem fending off mashers, but I think I'll make up a fictitious husband," Leslie said drily, making her voice upbeat, for which Callie was grateful. "It's the closest I'm going to get, since I'm never on dry land and my dating pool is extremely . . . nonexistent." She laughed. Saul didn't even crack a smile. "I think his name will be Brad, and he looks like a movie star. That's my fantasy and I'm sticking to it."

"The best you can do for a fantasy is a pretty guy with six kids who *acts* for a living?" Saul demanded.

"It's *my* fantasy, what do you care if he has six kids, or twenty?"

"You should have kids of your own."

Leslie gave him a startled glance. "I think that ship has sailed."

Saul looked at her over his coffee mug. "That ship's in dock."

Good for you, Callie thought, shooting the poor guy an encouraging look before turning to Jonah. "Maura and Gayle are going to beef up security, I presume?"

"The captain and first mate won't let anyone on board until we know what, if anything, has been stolen or compromised. Anndra had some pretty specific questions about things blowing up on board, and mentioned fire. I gave Maura an accurate account of what she asked; she'll ensure that everything is where it should be, and no tampering was done. When we get back from the morning dive, I'd like everyone to check and double-check your personal possessions to make sure she didn't have sticky fingers."

"Well, she left rather unexpectedly, and in a big hurry,"

Callie told them, not making eye contact with Jonah. "So maybe whatever it was she came to find wasn't taken."

"Maybe she got what she wanted and took off." Brody's eyes settled directly on Jonah.

"Maybe she's just a misguided young woman with too much time on her hands." Leslie played devil's advocate.

"Whatever happened, she's not welcome on board *Stormchaser* again, so she better find her entertainment elsewhere. One more thing before we go in. Callie and I are going to investigate the location where Saul was injured. I'd like the rest of you to work on *Ji Li* this morning." Jonah instructed. "Then everyone on the city for the duration, unless anyone wants to keep at *Ji Li*, in which case go for it."

"What duration?" Callie asked, swinging her feet over the tempting clear aqua water, dying to get in. Silence would be good right now. Just looking at Jonah made her want to jump his bones, and she needed to cool off.

"I put in calls for more divers," Jonah told them as everyone finished getting ready. "Ten to start with, we'll see how that goes. If we need more, we'll make that call in a couple of weeks. The new divers will arrive next Thursday."

Brody grunted as if displeased.

Jonah continued. "Two finds of this size can't be handled by six people. It would take each of us seven lifetimes to uncover everything from the city. And while I know that's the most interesting part, right now *Ji Li*'s cargo is what's paying the bills."

"I'm not that happy about my split being split." Hooking on his tank, Brody looked like a sulky teenager.

Callie didn't much like Brody, but she was pretty sure his sentiment must be in everyone's heads. Her concern wasn't how the spoils were going to be divided, but whether any of the new divers would know *her*, or make a connection between herself and Rydell? She'd gone on three major salvage operations with Ry over the last five years. That was a lot of people who knew of their close connection.

Her relationship with Jonah was so new, so budding, it wouldn't take the knock of this information.

God. Now she had something *else* to worry about.

Seventeen

Jonah, the last to suit up, pulled up the zipper on the front of his suit. Wrapping him like a gift in mouthwatering tight black neoprene—a present Callie couldn't wait to unwrap. She hid a smile, even while her heart ached with the knowledge that this couldn't last, wouldn't last. And would probably all blow up in her face a lot sooner than she anticipated.

No regrets.

"I'll use my cut to pay them," he told the team, accepting his tanks from Vaughn, who was dressed and ready to rock-and-roll. "Thanks. The investors will have to take a small hit, too. But they'll be grateful in the end. Don't worry, nothing will change for any of you. It'll just lighten the workload. Get everything to the surface faster. Logan's dispatched a second chopper, which should be here in a couple of days. It'll be based in Heraklion, so we can get artifacts back to Cutter Cay quicker."

He looked at the assembled group, and up to the first deck where Callie and Vaughn had set Saul up under an umbrella with the comm equipment and everything he'd need for an afternoon on board.

"Anyone got questions?"

"Let me know what you find with that alien quicksand,

will ya?" Saul raised his voice as the blower started up. Casted leg propped up on a chair, he looked as fit and healthy as a man could look with a cast from ankle to mid-thigh.

"First order of business," Jonah shouted back.

Saul gave Jonah a thumbs-up.

"Let's do it, people." Jonah dropped into the water, Callie right behind him.

She loved diving with him. Even more so now that she knew his body so well. She'd stroked the muscles he used to pull his body through the water as he swam. She loved the tight flex of his taut backside, and thought his strong swimmer's legs so sexy she'd spent half the night exploring how flexible they were.

Very.

Putting aside everything while she was under the water, she grinned behind her mask.

The others branched off when they reached *Ji Li*, while she and Jonah continued on to where Saul had had his accident. The water this morning was as clear as she'd ever seen it. The same incredible color of Jonah's eyes. As far as she knew, he hadn't ventured nearly this far before. She hadn't told him, wanting to see his reaction when he rounded the corner.

It was a long way away, past the lava tube and cavern, and beyond another "mountain" of deposited lava with tentacles that reached for miles. She and Saul had marked hundreds of artifacts that would eventually be taken on board.

The tender could anchor close to this grid, the smaller boar easier to maneuver as necessary than *Stormchaser*.

It must've been terrifying for the inhabitants of the city to feel the rumble beneath their thin leather sandals, to smell the thickening smoke, to see the fire erupting into the sky. They'd probably believed they'd angered the gods, and this was their punishment. They must've tried running, and gotten caught as the magma swirled around the streets, crashing through brick houses and taking everything in its path in seconds. Evidence of the flow of magma was everywhere, and it was easy, with the incredible evidence before her, to picture what had transpired that day.

Some might've made it if they were fleet of foot enough, or had a boat. No, Callie knew, *no one* would run fast or far enough to avoid being consumed by an eruption of this size. The mountains of lava rock were scattered through the seabed for mile after mile, stretching as far as she could see.

The eruption had been cataclysmic. No one survived. In one way it was depressing as hell swimming through people's lives, imagining their hopes and dreams, picturing children playing in the streets, and musicians tuning their instruments.

Callie was too scientific to be too sentimental. This was history waiting to be written. She wouldn't let these people disappear and leave nothing of themselves behind. She wouldn't let them be forgotten. Over time, she'd piece together their lives. If she *had* time.

Others might see ancient buildings, but she saw lives in the pottery and utensils, in the exquisite mosaics, the amazing detail of the statuary, and the decorative bowls and flagons.

They had art, and music, and culture. They loved and were loved back. The people wouldn't be forgotten; she would bring them back to life for countless generations to come.

She motioned Jonah to follow her around a thirty-foot outcropping of jagged lava rock shaped like a crouching dragon, its tail now part of a cobbled street.

Together they swam with the merest flick of fins and hands through the clear deep-blue water. Drifting with the currents was just as she imagined flying would feel. Callie did a barrel roll, and when she righted Jonah was directly in front of her. His eyes sparked hot enough to turn the entire Mediterranean to steam. Taking her hand, and curving his arm around her back, tank and all, he swirled her around as if they were waltzing twenty feet above the seabed. Around them as they twirled, tiny four-inch, silver-and-pink pandoras flashed their metallic scales in a choreographed dance of their own, parting around the crazy humans and then coming together again in a flash of shimmer and light.

For those few minutes as Jonah danced her through the blue of the water, Callie felt the happiest she'd ever felt in her life. The happiest, the freest. Oh, God—

The most in love.

The smile slipped. Jonah's hand in hers tightened, and he gave her a worried look. *What's wrong?* he mouthed, because the damn comm still didn't work. Forcing a lightness to her features she wasn't feeling, Callie smiled and mouthed back, *Nothing. Excited to show you.*

With a swoop of his arm, he indicated she lead the way. The abrupt movement flipped him head over heels, and laughter went hand in hand with the sudden prickle of tears as she grabbed his arm to help him upright.

How could this happen? Falling in love with the enemy was not part of the plan.

Rydell's enemy, *Rydell's* plan, a small voice reminded her.

The situation was already complicated enough without falling in love.

No.

No. No. No.

Lust. She was in *lust* with Jonah, that was all it was. The best sex of her life. Propinquity.

Jonah, oblivious to the rat's nest that was her brain, and the desolate wasteland that was her heart, reached over, threading his fingers through hers. He lived to dive, loved to swim. He did not love *her*. It was too soon. They barely knew each other . . .

They swam in tandem while Callie's chest ached so badly she could barely breathe. Detaching her hand from his, she indicated it wasn't practical to be tethered together when they were swimming between boulders and rough rocks.

Jonah's eyes glinted behind his mask. *"Later."*

No. There would be no later for them. The only way she was going to survive this was to leave. If Rydell wanted vengeance on the Cutters he'd have to deliver it himself.

She'd just tell Rydell that she'd fallen in love with Jonah. What would he do? Take away her birthday?

Callie couldn't even make light of that in her head. Ry would be disappointed in her. He'd given her so much, done so much for her. He was family. He and Peri were everything to her. He'd asked one damn thing of her. And while he'd claimed it was payback for everything the Cutters had done to him and his business over the years, Callie was afraid it was something a lot darker and more serious than that.

She'd leave tomorrow at first light. Make up some emergency at home.

Leave Jonah and her city behind?

She couldn't breathe. She swam, but her chest ached, her eyes burned behind her mask, and indecision, the bane of her life, reared its ugly head.

Disappoint Rydell.

Lose out on the discovery of the millennium?

Walk away from Jonah?

He enjoyed her. But love? She didn't think so.

Then it was a toss-up between Ry and Atlantis.

Rydell and Jonah.

She was bereft and she hadn't even walked away yet. Her heart already felt the pain of loss.

Better now than in a week, or a month, she told herself bracingly. Better, *much* better to rip off the Band-Aid before it became part of her.

One day.

And if all she had was this one day, then it was going to be the best damn day of her life.

Swimming side by side, arms and legs synchronized, Jonah thought they were as compatible under the water as they were in bed. He turned his head to smile at her, but she was looking straight ahead, concentrating on navigating between the hills and valleys of lava rock, which could cut right through their suits to skin if they weren't careful.

She was beautiful to watch. Sleek as an otter, sexy as a mermaid. Everything about her turned him on, and turned him inside out.

Wide swaths of pale sand, curved in a sinuous river-like path between black islands of rock, showed just how clear the water was today. Light, attenuated more by water than by air, limited the distance one could see. But with nothing to stir up the seabed, the particles and organic matter stayed on the bottom, hardly disturbed as they passed. This morning he could see at least 120 feet in all directions.

Perfection. Just like Callie.

Callie stayed him with a hand on his arm. He smiled at her through his mask. She smiled back, then turned him around to see what she and Saul had discovered the day before. For a moment he was distracted by a shadow behind her smile. He wondered what put it there, or if it was his imagination.

Jonah knew the bulk of city was around the biggest lava flow mountain. He'd seen it from pretty much this exact vantage point last year and almost swallowed his tongue with excitement then. His reaction seeing it again now was pretty damn close.

Buildings and foundations, broken walls, and thick sheets of pale marble—some intact, others shattered. The cobbled street couldn't be mistaken for anything other than what it was. A ten-foot-wide road, with parallel ruts from ancient wheels, worn by foot and wheeled traffic. On either side, drainage ditches could clearly be seen as the road stretched out until it disappeared into murkier blue. The heart of the underwater city.

Callie swam beside him as they moved beneath half a stone arch, which towered twenty feet above the seabed.

She pointed out an almost intact marble statue of a naked young man holding a spear, his cloak draped across one shoulder, then gestured a few feet away, to the head, half embedded in the lava flow. A dozen flags marked various artifacts—mostly household items—swept into piles by the fast-moving magma. He'd seen this last year when he'd first discovered the city. But he enjoyed it even more now, through Callie's eyes.

A half-melted statue of a wrestling boy, toppled on its side, indicated the work of art was made of a soft metal consumed by great heat. Pots, pans, and metal utensils fused into a jumbled heap. Jonah knew Callie would enjoy piecing together the lives of the people who'd used them. She injected the emotions into the artifacts.

Her excitement was evident as she showed him what she pantomimed to be a kitchen, but was little more than a mostly submerged foundation, filled with goblets, bowls, and dozens of amphorae. Jonah imagined it had been a small restaurant or shop. Maybe selling oils or wine judging by the shape of the containers. She'd found a lot of scatted coins and small utensils there yesterday, and flagged them all.

Jonah touched everything with his hands as well as his eyes, the same technique he'd seen Callie use to explore.

After several hours, he indicated they needed a break. Neither wanted to stop; this was just too thrilling, too damn amazing, to stop for any length of time. But they needed to conserve the air in their tanks. He indicated they head back to the cavern, where they could catch their breath and breathe normally, instead of returning all the way to *Stormchaser*.

Callie, eyes gleaming with discovery, reluctantly nodded.

As soon as they climbed the first few stone steps, Jonah reached above her and turned on a small powerful lantern that the guys had left there when they came down to work on the door the day before.

They removed their face masks and unhooked their tanks. Jonah managed to stroke her breasts and belly as he slowly removed her tank. Then he removed his own, setting both against the wall from which the steps had originally been carved.

Smiling ear-to-ear, he ran his fingers through his hair, making it stand up on end in dark spikes. "*Now* will you acknowledge we've got Atlantis?"

He looked adorably sexy in the golden light thrown by the lamp. Callie's heart squeezed as she sat halfway up the stairs. Not willing to concede victory just yet, she exhaled and stretched out her cramped calf muscle. "We should just be ecstatic we *have* a lost city," she told him, leaning back on her elbows.

"Which is *Atlantis*." He started peeling off his wet suit. Why, she had no idea. He'd indicated a *short* rest before going back to explore further. "Come on, admit it. Even if it's just to me."

The lamplight made the blue of his eyes dance and twinkle. She itched to touch him, and since he moved up between her legs, she combed her fingers through his hair as he bent over her. It felt cool to the touch, silky and heavy as she let it run through her fingers. "Maybe."

He bent his head to brush a kiss over her closed lips, his mouth a hot contrast with the cool temperature of his hair. Callie tasted his smile as he murmured, "Definitely."

She shook her head, still not willing to say aloud what she believed in her heart. There were still dozens of ways to prove or disprove if this was the Real Deal. The reflection off the rippling water below danced across the bronze of his skin and sparkled the droplets of water on his shoulders as he finished peeling off the wet suit, then tossed it casually aside. "You have on too many clothes."

"Oh, I so don't think so, Cutter." She put a hand over his as he started tugging down her zipper.

He shut off that thought by kissing her until she was breathless, her mind a swirl of lovely colors. The delicious taste of him, dark and salty and hungry, spiked her own need to fever pitch. Cold air hit her warm skin as he pulled the zipper all the way down and reached beneath the neoprene to cup her breast in his hand. "Arms out, please."

"You're doing such a sterling job of undressing me, do it yourself." She leaned to allow him better access.

"Be practical. I need both hands."

"All right." Callie peeled out of the tight neoprene, and Jonah helped by pulling it all the way off, leaving her in just her thin, racer-back swimsuit, which was no barrier to Cutter at all. Supporting himself on his arms, he bracketed her body with his, so she felt the heat of his body and the hard, pulsing bar of his erection at the juncture of her thighs. She couldn't help but arch against the delicious heat of it.

Using his forearm to lift her off the step, he stuffed the neoprene into the small of her back, cushioning her from the rocks, then came down between her legs, his weight balanced on his arms so he circled her with his body. He bent his head to brush her lips with his.

His eyes darkened, the black of his pupils huge and circled with a thin rim of navy blue. "I can't get enough of you, Dr. West. I'm in a permanent state of arousal, and all I can think about is making love until neither of us can move."

"I can't move right now," she murmured drily as his lips moved with maddening slowness down the cords of her throat. The stairs were barely four feet wide. There was the wall to her left, the drop-off to the water below on her right, and her body encased by the cage of Jonah's body. She'd never felt safer.

Callie couldn't think of anywhere she'd rather be, and then she couldn't think at all as he kissed her.

She loved the way he seemed to be unchecked, that he

didn't hold back or try to temper his passion. She felt it, too, and gave him back everything she had.

Loving the cool, smooth feel of his lips on hers, she explored the hot taste of him as he stroked her tongue with his. While he kissed her, Jonah slid first one strap of her utilitarian black swimsuit, then the other, down her arms until the cool air bathed her breasts and her nipples arched into tight peaks.

"You know anyone can swim in here at any moment, right?" she murmured against his mouth.

"Not likely, everyone's busy, and even if someone was so rude as to interrupt—I'm lying on top of you, they won't see anything."

Ever practical, Callie shifted. He was heavy and barely moved. "We're sitting under a *lantern*."

Reaching up over her head, he plunged them into pitch darkness. Without the sense of sight, her other senses of touch and hearing amped up even more to compensate. The hot brush of his breath against her skin was a caress. She shivered with the quick jolt of her body, and her breath came out in a rush as his hot mouth closed unerringly over her nipple.

Blood swimming, heart thumping erratically, she tightened her grip in the strands of Jonah's hair to anchor herself. Her senses went haywire in the darkness as he made love to her with his teeth and tongue while the throbbing silence of the cavern closed around them like a lover's embrace, and the gentle lapping of water against rock was in counterpoint to the heated surge of her blood.

He closed his lips over her nipple, sucking the hard peak into the warm cavern of his mouth through the stretchy silk of her swimsuit. Drew the cloth back and forth, slowly rasping it across her nipples and bringing them to stiff erection as he tormented her other hardened nipple with callused fingers. Her breasts throbbed, her back arched involuntarily.

Callused fingers skimmed down her side, gliding the top of her suit over her breasts. As his hot mouth closed over a distended tip, she tried to help by wiggling out of her swimsuit while tugging it down to give him better access to her breast.

Jonah pushed her hand aside. "Uh-uh. *I* want to unwrap you." He slid her suit down to her hips. As he kissed his way from between her breasts, the hot wetness of his tongue danced across her nipple, making everything inside her contract almost painfully. Cupping her breast, he twirled his tongue against the taut peak, then grazed his teeth on the tight bud. She lifted against his mouth, offering herself.

He groaned as her back arched, his fingers cupping the cool globe to bring her breast to his mouth. Molding the other breast, he brushed his thumb over the hard, aching peak until Callie's breath snagged in her throat. His mouth cruised down between her breasts, nipping and licking, hot and damp, and leaving a path of icy fire all the way from the base of her throat to her belly. The rasp of his unshaven jaw turned her on even more. Every nerve ending, every atom of her body was so tuned in to Jonah that she was now unaware of anything but the feel of his hands and mouth on her supersensitized body.

Soft lips, sandpapery beard.

She'd lost her mind.

Breath fast and hot, Callie's fingers slipped from his hair to his shoulders as he kept moving down. His muscles shifted beneath his skin as he kissed her belly. She still wore her suit, but it was a thin G-string around her hips. Jonah made fast work of tugging the rolled-up fabric down her legs, then shifting his upper body just enough to pull her swimsuit off completely.

"Don't throw it!" she lifted up on her elbows to warn him. "I can only imagine what people would think when I got out of my wet suit on board and was bare-butt naked. I so don't think so." Taking the wadded-up nylon from him, she stuck it under her head as a pillow. It would probably be more practical to put it under her tailbone, which was in direct contact with the step.

"*I'd* enjoy it."

"You're an exhibitionist. You *like* being naked."

"True. I like you being naked even more."

"Yes, well, we can't—" she started, but got distracted as he extended the tip of his tongue to outline her belly button, making her butt arch off the step and her nails dig into his shoulders.

His callused fingers felt as rough as a cat's tongue against her sensitized skin as he glided his hand into the exposed V. "Soft. You smell so good. Woman and ocean, and sex."

Feeling full and juicy, and impossibly aroused, she tightened her fingers in his hair. The muscles in her legs and butt clenched and released as his slightest touch made her unravel.

Feeling the heavy ache in her lower body ratchet up, tighter and tighter, made it impossible to catch her breath. A flurry of pleasure shook her.

"You were saying?"

"The stairs aren't wide enough—we'll fall off into the water." A ten-foot drop.

His teeth grazed her inner thigh, making her shiver. "We can swim."

She laughed. "Crazy man. This isn't the time or—"

Jonah face's was a mask of tension and desire. "You are so beautiful." His breath scalded her inner thigh.

Her cheeks flushed hot. He wasn't looking at her face, and she wasn't used to a man staring so intently at her private parts.

Smiling, he cupped her mound, teasing the swollen seam with his finger. Already wet, and he'd barely touched her. Callie moaned, tangling her fingers in his hair.

Jonah slid two flingers inside, and her butt levitated off the hard step as he stroked and circled, explored and teased.

She made a harsh sound as his hot, open mouth closed over her, tonguing and teasing, until her head thrashed on the hard pillow of the step. Her knees opened wider to accommodate his broad shoulders as his tongue did amazing things to her clit.

Sound amplified. The slosh of the water at the base of the stairs, the lapping of his tongue delving inside her, seemed shockingly loud. She felt his heartbeat, her heartbeat, right where his mouth teased and tormented her.

Flushed and feverish, her head dropped back as she pushed herself against his mouth. His growl of pleasure reverberated through her. Panting, ratcheting higher and higher, she felt defenseless and at the same time all-powerful.

The tight coil of her braid was the only part of her protected from the stone. The rock was icy cold all the way down her back and legs, his wet suit no longer protecting the small of her back. Callie didn't give a damn if she walked away with one giant bruise from head to toe. This, right now, was worth it.

The aching tension tightened unbearably . . . she cried out as pleasure shuddered through her in pulsing waves as she convulsed around his mouth, and rode the sharp, shuddering wave of ecstasy.

"Sometimes sex is sex. Sometimes sex is making love," he murmured, stroking a hand lazily down her rib cage. "And sometimes it's heat and flash and absolute perfection."

"You did all the work, and I reaped all the rewards."

"As I said. Perfection."

She smiled. "Did you guys get the door open?" she asked, lazily combing her fingers through his hair as his head lay against her breast. She was going to be wearing the marks of these damn stone stairs all the way down her back for weeks to come. She didn't care, and she curved her hand around his prickly jaw to hold him against her.

Jonah shook his head. "Almost. We left all the crap up there. Wanna see if we can do it?"

"Three of you gave it your best shot, with God only knows how much equipment. Are you saying it's like handing someone a jar to open after you've done most of the work?"

"Exactly. Come on." He shifted to turn on the lantern, making her squint into the light. Naked, he held out his hand. "Let's give it our best shot."

Sitting up, she glanced around for her swimsuit. "If the door's been there for thousands of years unopened, what makes you think we have a snowball's chance in hell of opening it now? You'd better get dressed. Who knows what's up there." Picking up her swimsuit, she turned it right-side out and put her feet through the leg openings.

"Won't know until we try it, will we? Damn, I hate to see that go."

Callie stood so she could yank the suit up all the way, covering her breasts. Not that it made much difference to

Jonah, who knelt several steps down. He just leaned in and closed his teeth gently over her nipple. Callie put her hand to his forehead and gave a little push. "Behave."

Jonah smiled wickedly. "Come on, pretend it's an adventure."

"It *is* an adventure." Callie couldn't help laughing. "Are you referring to that"—she pointed to his still-erect penis—"or trying to open the door?"

"Let's go tackle the door."

"What's with you being naked?"

"I like being naked."

"You're an exhibitionist. *I* like being naked only when I'm behind a *closed, locked* door." She pulled the straps over her shoulders. No easy task with Jonah "helping" her. Batting his hands away, she gave him a stern look. "Come on, Cutter, get dressed. You don't want to get that snagged when we open the door, do you?"

"No, ma'am." He pulled on his shorts, then spread his hands for her approval.

With a rueful shake of her head, Callie applauded. She approved the dark hair running down the center of his impressive six-pack. She approved the still-hard bulge behind the black fabric, and she approved the feel of his satiny skin beneath her fingers. She pulled her hands away. "Are we doing this or going back?"

"Don't you want to see if we can get inside?"

"I suppose," she told him unenthusiastically. "But I'm imagining a lot of thousand-year-old bones, or giant spiders, so don't be surprised if I scream like a girl if we do somehow manage to get in." She had her doubts about subterranean spiders, but the ancient bones were a real possibility. She struggled into her wet suit and zipped up the front.

"Don't worry." Jonah mimicked her actions, making

her grin as he struggled to tuck a rock-hard erection into the neoprene. "I'll be manly and protect you. Shit, this is uncomfortable."

"It will go back to normal soon. Be brave." Callie hesitated as they climbed to the top of the short flight. "Wait. It's pitch dark in there, we won't be able to see anything. Why don't we come back another time?" she asked hopefully.

"We left our equipment close by. There are several more lanterns and a couple of flashlights."

"Let's try 'Open Sesame,' " Callie suggested as they got up to the promontory ledge overlooking the water. Grateful they'd worn water shoes under their fins, she nevertheless eased her way cautiously over the rough lava rock.

Jonah took her hand, his warm fingers closing over hers, making her realize she was spooked for no scientific reason. "We tried everything short of a blasting cap the other day." His voice echoed slightly inside the tube as they moved through the darkness preceded by a stream of golden light from the lantern.

"Well, I have no intention of being inside this mountain when an explosion goes off! So let's act accordingl—Look!" Callie lowered her voice to a whisper. "The door's open!"

Eighteen

It wasn't *open* open, but it was about a quarter inch ajar. Jonah immediately turned off the light, plunging them into darkness. Callie suppressed the aforementioned girlie shriek. There weren't any old bones or bodies to be seen. Not yet anyway.

She didn't have a wild imagination. She thought like a scientist. But an ancient door that shouldn't be there, in an inaccessible place, that none of them had opened? Yeah, she gave a second and fifth thought to three-thousand-year-old ghosts and long-lived magicians. Nonsense. But she rubbed the goose bumps on her upper arms that even the wet suit couldn't keep at bay.

No light penetrated the darkness, but whatever was beyond the door was a lighter shade of dark than where they stood. Jonah bent to take something out of the pack, leaning against the rock wall. The rustling sounded loud as he rummaged around inside.

Callie's eyes opened wide, and her whisper barely carried to Jonah who only stood two feet away. "A *gun*?"

"*We* didn't crack this," he whispered back, his voice barely reaching her ears. "*Someone* opened it."

She clutched his strong, steely forearm. "I don't want to see inside that badly."

"Then wait for me outside."

"Are you *insane*, Cutter? You're not going in there alone!" Callie's heart raced, and her eyes felt dry and gritty from straining to see in the darkness.

This was a monumentally bad freaking idea. Really bad.

"Scared? Seriously, go back, I'll check out what's inside and come get you. Five minutes tops."

"What else do you have in there that I can use as a weapon?" Not that she'd shoot at a giant spider, or a ghost, but she'd feel a hell of a lot better with a weapon, or at least a very solid spider-killing shoe.

"Know how to shoot?"

"Probably. Not terribly accurately," she told him grimly. "But enough to point and squeeze the trigger."

"Take this. Safety's off." He closed her fingers around the butt of the gun, warm from his hand. Then bent down. "I have another one. And for God's sake, don't shoot either yourself or me. Stay behind me, and don't turn the flashlight on until I tell you."

Callie gripped the gun so tightly she felt the ridges on the grip bite into her palm. "Hurry up, the suspense is killing me."

Hoping she didn't accidentally shoot him in the back, Jonah used his foot to ease open the heavy door.

No creaking, no grinding. The door opened inward, quiet despite its size and weight. He felt Callie behind him, and to the right. Heart pounding in anticipation, he stepped inside where the temperature was significantly warmer than the lava tube at their backs. The air smelled a little stale, but not dangerous. Nothing to indicate the place hadn't been used in centuries.

Fascinating.

He turned on the flashlight, staffing the beam of light around the room.

What the fuck?

The room was about eighty feet deep by fifty wide, and filled with machinery. *Big* machines. A shitload of institutional, green-painted control boards and electronic panels. Two long rows of them. The place looked like the cockpit of the Starship *Enterprise* circa 1960, complete with hokey pull levers, round dials, and little blinking arrays of lights.

In the corner a hulking machine looked like an industrial-sized generator. The beam lit several flat control panels—antiques from the 1950s or '60s, but nothing over a century old and certainly not thousands of years.

The large, currently dark, flat-screen monitors above the multidial control panels were the only thing that looked this decade.

Callie crowded against his side and stage-whispered, "What *is* this place?"

"Control room of some kind." Jonah scanned the area with the flashlight, searching for a light switch. "Let's see if we can get a better look. Ah. There." One across the room, next to a closed door; another close to where they stood. Callie flipped the switch. For a moment the fluorescent overheads flickered, popped, sizzled, then bathed the area in brilliant white light.

Callie grabbed his upper arm, "Holy crap!"

"You can say that again." They walked farther inside what appeared to be a well-ordered, well-maintained mechanical control room.

Callie ran a finger over a metal surface with hundreds of buttons and dials. She held up the digit for his inspection. "No dust."

"Yeah, got that. This place is getting regular use—

Let's see what this puppy controls." He started flicking switches.

"You're such a guy."

"What can I say?" The monitors lit up like the Fourth of July. *Pop. Pop. Pop.*

Callie stepped forward to look at a live-feed underwater shot of a broken wall, the pillars indicating it had been some sort of temple. She stared narrow-eyed at the fifty-inch monitor. "I don't recognize this area, do you?"

"No."

"What do you think the light indicates?" She pointed to a small, blinking red light on the ground. It appeared to indicate something in, on, or near one of the mosaic carpets.

Jonah shrugged. "There's a light on this one as well." This time the tiny, blinking red dot looked as if it was embedded in a crumbling wall.

Together, they moved down the row. There were twenty-five of the fifty-inch monitors in all, each showing a live feed. It was going to take a while.

"Shit!" The shot of *Stormchaser* was clearly from the air. He turned a few dials and the view zoomed out, so his ship was a white pinpoint in the vast deep blue of the Mediterranean. He tuned the dial the opposite direction. The zoom-in was so clear he saw Maura and Gayle on the bridge. Close enough to see Gayle's mouth move as she talked. Creepy as hell.

"And double holy shit." Callie came to stand beside him. "This is a satellite view."

As with the other views, the image of *Stormchaser* was a live feed. "Yeah," he muttered, tone and thoughts fucking grim. He toggled a switch and the voices of the two women filled the room as they discussed the day's business.

"Dear God." Callie's voice was appalled. "Not only are they watching us, they can *hear* what we're saying? Who *are* these people?"

Jonah frowned. "Hell if I know. At a guess I'd say *Spanos*. But this equipment has been here for at least forty or fifty years, which predates him."

"He could've taken over from someone?" Callie's expression grew angry as she patted the equipment. "*Who*, I have no idea. The monitors and some of the electronics look new, and recent, so he could've taken over and added to it all."

Jonah glared at the screens. "Possible. But what is it they're monitoring? Ships probably don't anchor at exactly that spot every day. They didn't know we were coming, so how did they know to put a satellite in the air to watch us? That's not something you do quickly or without preparation."

"*Ji Li*." Callie pointed to the activity on the next monitor. Vaughn and Leslie loading the basket with coins ready to take on board. They used sign language to communicate.

So they'd known about the ancient junk all along. "This place is why our comms don't work," Jonah said furiously. "They're blocking our transmissions. Fucking hell."

"Jonah—take a look at this." She indicated a flat, four-inch silver dial with words inscribed on it in Greek. "This says *seismos*."

He gave the dial a dubious look. "Are you sure those aren't scratches?"

"It's Greek. *Seismos*. Quake. I'm positive."

"These sons of bitches are responsible for the quake we had on the first dive day."

Leaning over the console, Jonah toggled the aspect on the screen above it to a view of an area he was familiar with. It was a long way from where his divers worked. Once he zeroed in on a line of broken pillars, he slowly turned the dial. The image shimmied. Sand whipped around the pillars to swirl in the surrounding water.

She grabbed his wrist. "Stop!"

Callie's admonishment came seconds too late. The pillars toppled in slow motion like dominoes, dropping to the ocean floor in clouds of sand to obscure their view. With a curse, Jonah turned the dial back to neutral.

"Dear God. This makes absolutely no sense at all. Earthquakes, and elaborate surveillance—to what purpose?"

Jonah cupped the back of his head. "It makes crazy sense if your friend Dr. Ebert is right, and the men of Fire Island are the Guardians the ancient text talked about."

"Maybe. It explains the stairs, anyway. But I can't see those old guys in scuba gear swimming in here to man all this, can you?" Callie waved a hand at the monitors.

"Hard to imagine anyone lugging tons and tons of equipment up those stairs."

"Which means—"

"There must be another way in and out," Jonah finished for her.

"I'm sure there is." She glanced around. "It's not obvious, though."

"There must be one—ah, shit. Check this out." He indicated the area they'd left half an hour ago, the place where Saul had encountered the quicksand. A tiny red light blinked on a tiled floor nearby. "They manipulated the sand when Saul walked over this area."

"I don't think you can manipulate—What am I saying?" Callie threw up her free hand. "Of course they could do any damn weird thing they like. What do you think this is?"

A monitor showed a grid, similar to the ones used by treasure hunters to mark underwater locations. This grid was filled with hundreds of winking red dots. "Whatever these represent, there are hundreds of them. And see these three?"

Callie leaned in closer. "They're on board *Stormchaser*! Something Anndra left behind? Or are they somehow monitoring the artifacts we have on board? Okay, as weird and disturbing as that is, I get it. But we have *hundreds* of artifacts on board now. Why just three blinking lights?"

"The lights mark something specific."

"Sure, but what?"

"Particular artifacts? Locations of . . . who knows." He inspected a reel-to-reel recording device he'd only seen in old movies. When he turned it on, nothing happened. "Broken."

"Here's one that looks like it's out of a sci-fi movie," Callie pointed with the gun she still held. "See if this works."

"Is the safety on?"

She raised a brow. "Of course. Doesn't mean I'm putting it down. Who knows who or what will show up any minute?"

Same shit Jonah was thinking, which was why he, too, carried his gun as they explored. He inspected the recording device. Dates, in chronological order, were written in tiny, spidery script on pieces of tape affixed to the metal background of the main panel beside the recorder. He ran a finger down the list until he got to the day *Stormchaser* dropped anchor.

"Your first day." He smiled as he saw the next date. "God, you were a hard-ass."

"Past tense?"

He slid his hand down the sweet curve of her butt, felt the flex of toned muscles beneath the neoprene. It was warmer in the control room than it had been out near the water, but her nipples were still hard peaks beneath the thin black material. It wouldn't take but a second to peel it off her again, hoist her shapely ass up onto the console, and plunge into her wet heat. He smiled as he crowded her against the edge of the console. "I'm very fond of your hard as—"

"Are you on board?" an unfamiliar man asked.

"Just got here." *Callie's* voice. A brief hesitation. "Are you okay, you sound . . . strained."

"Who were you talking to?" Jonah withdrew his stroking fingers from Callie's ass.

"Just a shitty connection," the man responded before Callie answered Jonah's question. "I'm good, honey. Are you going to be all right doing this?"

"I told you I would." She sounded smug as hell, making Jonah's ire rise to throb behind his eyeballs. "I don't know how you figured it out it, Ry. But you were right to send me. Jonah Cutter claims he's found the Lost City of Atlantis. If it's true, I'll tie it up in a bow and deliver it to you on a silver platter."

"*Ry?*" Her friend's name dripped like an icicle from Jonah's lips. "You work for *Rydell Case*."

Not a question. The bitter tone coupled with his grim expression made Callie's heart ache and her throat swell shut. The immediate retreat of his heated hand from her bottom left her colder and emptier than she'd thought possible. But deep down she knew the hand wasn't the only thing Jonah had already instantly withdrawn from her.

"He's my brother-in-law."

His skin pulled tightly over his cheekbones. "That

wasn't the question. But I suppose that is an answer. So your brother-in-law sent you to spy on me. What's his plan? To stake his own claim on my city, with your insider knowledge?"

She met the intense blue of Jonah's eyes. The anger and hurt she saw there were cold enough to slice straight through to her heart. There was no point in prevaricating. "Yes."

"What was the plan? Throw it in my face? Walk away?"

She lifted her chin. Even that small movement was painful, and Callie felt as though she'd shatter any minute. She swallowed painfully. "Walk away."

"So finding Atlantis takes second place to the loyalty you have for your brother-in-law? And fuck-all loyalty to me, is that it?"

"Things have changed."

"Really?" The look of contempt in Jonah's eyes almost brought Callie to her knees as he said coldly, "I'm dying to hear how. Changed because now you're convinced that *is* Atlantis out there, and the stakes are considerably higher than if it was just some ancient city we'd found? I wouldn't know about your betrayal until after the fact, would I? No fucking clue what you'd done. I would've lain in bed at night wondering how what we had could have gone so drastically wrong. Why my treasure *and* my city were ripped off right under my fucking nose, and how I lost the girl as well. A pretty shitty triple whammy, wouldn't you say?"

Standing there in nothing but a wet suit and water shoes was not conducive to a rational conversation where she could be in control. Of course she'd need body armor for that—preferably Kevlar. And Jonah wasn't saying anything that wasn't true. It pissed Callie off that she didn't have much of a defense. She was wrong for the right reasons, but he wasn't going to give a crap about that.

"Yes," she admitted, voice thick. "Really shitty all around. I had no idea when I agreed to Ry's request that I'd . . ."

"Discover the real Atlantis?"

Fall in love with you. Taking a much-needed breath, she was surprised at how shaky it was. "Have feelings for you."

Her fingers tightened reflexively around the butt of the gun she still held. God. They were both armed. Standing six feet apart, with loaded weapons in their hands. And God knew Cutter was pissed enough to take a shot. Her fingers shook slightly as she slid the weapon onto the console. Not because she wanted to shoot Jonah, but because she was afraid she'd shoot herself in the foot by accident. Guilt mixed with anger made adrenaline surge through her body, making her jumpy and her hands damp.

"Feelings? This." He made an angry swirling motion with his finger. "This is *feelings*? Screwing me, whispering love words in my ears as you sharpen a diving knife to plunge deep between my shoulder blades?"

There was no hint in his expression that he even remembered they'd made love barely half an hour ago. "When I came on board it was out of loyalty to my friend. My *family*. It wasn't personal." God, she was just making it worse. "I didn't know you," she said a little desperately. "Rydell has just cause to dislike your family, and you know it. This salvage was in my purview. I agreed to help him. No one would get hurt, except the Cutters' monumental pride. Then I met you, and I—"

"So your brother-in-law's enemy is your enemy, is that it, Callie? To hell with anyone else's feelings, dreams, and aspirations. Including, I might fucking well add, your own. Ah, I see that thought *did* occur to you. By screwing me, you end up screwing yourself. Because you know damn well that if some court in the land gets a wild hair up its ass, and allows Case to stake a claim for some trumped-up reason, Atlantis will be tied up in court for the next millennium. We *all* lose."

Remembering why she'd agreed to help Rydell, she drew on her buried anger. "Trumped up like what you Cutters did to him in South Africa, you mean?"

"Is that the bullshit Rydell fed you? That my brothers trumped up that claim?"

"Do you deny it?"

Fury burned in every inch of his face. "A court of *law* denied it."

"Then we have nothing to discuss, do we? You believe he wronged you, he believes you wronged him."

"Guess we know what you believe," he snarled back.

The sound of her heavy heartbeat filled her head, and it felt as though an elephant sat on her chest. She wasn't a crier, but God, she'd like to lay down her head right now and have a good sob. Which of course wouldn't fix a damn thing. Her indecision had reared up and bitten her in the ass.

"Are you going to let me get a word in," she asked, keeping her voice even with effort, while her mind went a mile a minute trying to come up with something that didn't sound as damning as it really was. "Or are you just going to stand there and be judge and jury without letting me speak my piece?"

A muscle jerked in his cheek. "You can put your 'piece' in an email when you return to Miami, Doctor. Then go ahead and hit DELETE. I have no interest in any of your justifications."

Maintaining eye contact, Callie swallowed the lump in her throat. Going back home would give her ample time to reorder her thoughts, to come up with something that was the truth, but didn't make her look—No. No matter what she did or said. Jonah had every right to be furious with her. If she hadn't slept with him, maybe there would've been a chance of salvaging this mess. But she had, and there wasn't.

"Then there isn't anything else to be said, is there?" Her voice sounded odd, calm and flat. "I'll head back to *Stormchaser* and pack my stuff. I'll be gone in an hour."

"You can't go back on your own."

Her eyes stung, but she was damned if she'd cry. Especially in front of Jonah. Fueled by shame, her temper spiked. "I can do any damn thing I please, Jonah Cutter. Stay here and watch me on the monitor, but I don't want you to buddy me. Not no—"

"How did you get in here?" Anndra Spanos demanded, staring at them as if they'd suddenly materialized before her. She was wearing scuba gear, and carried a large gun as she stepped farther into the room, her brother hot on her heels. He, too, wore a black wet suit, and held a gun.

Both weapons pointed at Jonah's heart.

The first shot, a warning across the bow, hit the monitor an inch from Jonah's head exploding into hundreds of pieces. He heard Callie's startled half scream and leapt for her, taking her to the floor as large chunks of thick glass and monitor parts rained down on them.

No time for words. Or recriminations. He kept his body curled over hers.

The long console was only good protection if the gun-wielding Greeks didn't come around the back of it. Peering over the top edge, he made out Anndra's forehead and a portion of Kall Spanos's face. He scooted back, trying to make Callie, and himself, smaller targets.

Crouched as they were between two long consoles, they had some protection, but they were also trapped by their location. All the Greeks had to do was walk ten feet, and they could shoot them like fish in a barrel.

Another shot, another monitor shattered to smithereens. The loud, reverberating ping of bullets hitting metal, the sound of glass breaking and bouncing off the cement floor, made whatever Anndra was yelling impossible to understand.

The next shot almost grazed his fingers where he was gripping the console. He felt the wind a millimeter above his knuckles and was grateful his head was lower than his hand or he'd be toast.

Fuck. Bad shots or calculated misses? Whichever, even a bad shot couldn't miss hitting fish in a barrel. Spanos blocked the exit. Motioning for Callie to stay down, Jonah lifted up just far enough to peer over the edge, and squeezed off a shot in their general vicinity. The bullet ricocheted off the metal door behind them with a loud *crack*. Kall screamed at the same time another shot was fired. Followed by two more.

The heavy door shut behind the Greeks. Trapping them all inside. No way would they do that to themselves. Either they were counting on reinforcements, or they had another way out.

Fingers wrapped tightly around his ankle, Callie hissed, "Get down!"

He didn't need the hard tug for motivation. Jonah dropped flat. "What are you doing here, Kall?" Jonah shouted, motioning Callie to crawl beneath the console. He hoped to hell that door across the room wasn't the fucking broom closet.

"You talk to Kallistrate because he is the *man*?" Anndra laughed. "Do you think such weakness should be in charge of an operation such as this? You are all fools." Her next shot was a hell of a lot closer.

There was about an eighteen-inch clearance beneath the console. Jonah hoped they didn't get stuck as he pulled Callie underneath with him.

"What operation?" He motioned Callie to get the lead out and crawl for fucksake.

"My cosmetic empire, Jonah Cutter."

Jesus. That was a ridiculous explanation if he'd ever heard one. He glanced at Callie, who shrugged. "What does any of *this* have to do with cosmetics? Are you harvesting some sort of ingredient that only grows—Where? In the cavern? Near the city?"

"There is no need for further discourse," Anndra snapped.

"I *told* you we were too greedy!" Kall yelled at her. "One ingot, you promised. No one would know, you said! But did you listen when I told you the Guardians wouldn't tolerate us coming back so often? No. You never list—It's all *ruined*! You ruined it!"

"Shut up," Anndra screeched back. "Shut up! You fool!"

All Jonah could see from his vantage point were her feet as she circled around the other way. The Greeks weren't dicking around. They kept firing. Anndra was a great multitasker. Yelling at her brother and shooting at them simultaneously.

"Cover me. Contact the others," Anndra yelled at her brother. "And for God's sake stay by the door, *Now*, Kall!"

Others? Fuck. Double fuck.

Jonah heard Anndra's soft footfalls approaching between shots. He kept slithering on his belly beneath the dusty underbelly of the giant console. Cords and fittings draped, coiled, and snaked on the floor beneath all the electronics. He kept a wary eye out for anything sharp enough to slice through the neoprene that protected them. But neoprene sure as shit wouldn't stop a speeding bullet.

The other door was diagonally across the room. Not optimal for escape when he had no fucking idea what lay *behind* that door. But he wasn't taking Callie through two people determined to kill them. And *others*.

"That way." He pointed with his free hand. She nodded, moving crab-like in the low space.

"Jo-nah? Come out so I can talk to you," Anndra cooed. But the seductive tone was ruined as two more shots hit the metal bench with loud pings that reverberated through the room.

Callie crawled out on the other side, putting the giant console and monitors between herself and Anndra. Jonah got off several more shots, covering her until she reached the door, then raced to join her. All he could see were Callie's trim ankles and the curve of her ass as she crouched low to get across the room, keeping the console between her and the Spanoses.

He got off two more shots, heard Kall's shout of pain, and bolted into to a low crouch of his own. "Go!"

Hidden well below the top of the console, Callie sped crab-like on all fours. Jonah stayed on her ass.

"I'll hold them off. Try the door." He sent up a prayer that it wasn't locked.

Reaching up, Callie twisted the heavy handle. The door opened a crack. Jonah got off another shot. The answering fire was a hell of a lot closer—he saw two pairs of feet beneath the console. "Go!"

Callie pulled the door open just wide enough to slip through. Jonah fired his last shot then followed her, slamming the heavy door shut behind them, blocking the brother-and-sister duo.

They both straightened. Callie handed him the gun she'd somehow managed to hold on to. He checked the clip. Twelve bullets.

"Can you lock it from this side?"

"No." There was nothing around them to block the door or wedge beneath the handle. Jonah ripped off his water shoes. Folding them into thick pads, he shoved them under the thin door crack.

"Your feet . . ."

"The cement looks smooth enough. That won't hold them long. Move!" They had less than a minute to get away from the door before the Greeks came through it, guns blazing. He grabbed her hand, all distrust and hurt gone in the face of their mutual survival. "Haul ass."

The tunnel was a smooth tube of gray cement. Human-made, six feet across, ten high, and an unidentifiable length that zigged and zagged at crazy angles. The air smelled stale, and the slap of her rubber-soled shoes on the hard surface sounded dangerously loud.

Metal-caged bulbs every twenty-five feet kept the path dimly lit. Other than the two of them, the tunnel was empty with no indication of where it led. No one else shared their wild dash to wherever the hell they were going. But that wasn't going to last long if Spanos actually had the friends with him that his sister had ordered.

Suddenly the whole tunnel vibrated, followed by an undulating roll beneath their feet. Callie's steps faltered as she staggered, slapping a hand on the wall for balance as the lights overhead swayed. "God, is that a quake?"

Jonah grabbed her other hand, keeping her tethered to him, not to keep her moving—she was doing that on her own—but he had a sudden, terrible fear that they'd become separated. That she'd need him and he'd be fuck only knew where. He tugged her against his side. "They wouldn't be stupid enough to start a quake while they're in here with us—"

The quake continued, rolling beneath their feet like a waking beast as they ran. "Shit, maybe they *are* that stupid." He spared a moment of concern for his dive team, who'd be surfacing to wait it out.

Jonah kept the momentum as best he could. They'd turned several corners, still with no fucking idea where they were, and when they might reach a destination. But any second now that door back there was going to bust open and someone was going to be right on their asses. "Keep moving."

The opening slam of the door behind them made them put on more speed. There was a sharp corner ahead about ten feet . . .

He heard the passing of the bullet before he felt the wind as it grazed his cheek. Jonah tightened his fingers around Callie's.

"Unless they each brought another clip," she told him, her breath raw and uneven as she ran, "they have ten bullets between them."

"You counted the bullets?"

"I couldn't tell who shot what, but together, yeah." She shot him a smile. "Where would the 'others' come from? Are we going to run smack into them, do you think—Oh, my God, look!"

They almost fell over a kid-sized jeep as they rounded the next corner at a dead run.

Jonah started squeezing by it; there was only a couple of feet. "We can run faster than a golf cart! Come on."

Callie hung back, tugging his hand. "We can go faster in this. Ry—my friend has one. They can usually travel at about twenty miles an hour, thirty feet a second, Jonah. *Faster* than we can run. Come on."

What the hell? Incongruously, the cart was plugged into an outlet near the floor. Jonah yanked out the cord. "Let's do it." He didn't fucking need a reminder that Callie had betrayed him and worked for his family's enemy. But that was a conversation for another time.

It took moments to climb on and start it up. He wanted the beefy roar of a Harley engine; what he got was the pissy purr of a battery-operated golf cart. The vehicle took up most of the passageway, but once it got going, it did seem to travel at a fast clip. At least they were putting distance between themselves and whoever was following them.

There were no more gunshots. That was a blessing. However, there was another danger. The quake continued, shaking the walls and ceiling. The cart had a hard top. But it wasn't going to last long as huge chunks of cement started fracturing from the top of the tunnel to pummel them. They winced every time a rock made a dent in the roof. Any minute one of the sharp projectiles would slice through it, and then they'd be screwed.

A chunk the size of a loaf of bread thunked off the top, continued its downward trajectory, and sliced open his arm before shattering on impact on the ground. Jonah hissed out a curse.

"Ho-w b-ad is it?" Callie yelled over the din of crashing cement. Her teeth clicked together with the vibration of the floor.

The slice in his favorite wet suit pissed him off more than the hot trickle of blood. "Scratch."

There didn't appear to be an end to the labyrinth of tunnels. And he was fucking done with shit falling on them, gaps in the floor, and the potential of Anndra, Kall, and "others" right on their asses. When he got out of this fucking hellhole he'd have nightmares about this little trip through a rockfall of cement with gun-wielding Greeks after them. He floored the pedal. None of this made any damn sense.

"What has that room got to do with cosmetics? And who built it, for what purpose?" Callie raised her voice over the din, reading his mind, although with the vibrations and sound of crashing cement it wasn't that easy to understand her.

"When? Why? And fucking how? Hell if I know." Large chunks of cement continued to rain down as the thick tires of the golf cart spanned an inch-wide crack in the floor.

Callie applied the nonexistent brake on her side of the floorboard as Jonah took that gap, gunning the piss-poor engine so it went a millimeter faster. Callie's elbow bumped his shoulder as she rested her arm on the seat twisting to see behind them.

"The tunnel's collapsing in on itself." Other than the vibration of her voice she sounded calm and matter-of-fact. Thank God she was cool under pressure, because Jonah was scared enough for both of them. "No one could be sneaking up behind us. The entire ceiling back there is now on the ground, and the floor has fissures a foot or more wide. Someone's setting off this quake. Clearly they have no idea of the consequences of this kind of unnatural disruption."

"Or they do, and don't give a flying fuck."

The ceiling still crashed around them. Bigger slabs broke apart in a cacophony of noise, and clouds of dust and debris, causing them to cough as they squinted to see through the thick air.

The collapsing tunnel was going to bury them alive.

Nineteen

Callie let out a startled scream as, one-handed, Jonah grabbed her arm, yanking her down off the seat of the golf cart while it was still in motion. She barely had her feet on the ground when he pulled her into a flat-out run. The cart careened into the wall behind them.

He had the gun in his right hand, although she had no idea who he planned to shoot. Everyone behind them must be dead beneath the rubble by now. Breaking her out of a nanosecond reverie, he jerked her forward when she didn't move fast enough.

"If they were the *bad* guys," she shouted, trying to keep up with his long, *running* strides, "and the bad guys are *dead*, who's causing the earthquake?" Her voice jiggled like Jell-O as her entire body shook. Somewhere along the way she'd lost one water shoe, and her braid flapped on her back as she ran. It wasn't easy. He was taller, stronger, and more athletic than she was.

"Does it fucking matter? Don't waste your breath talking. *Run!*"

Callie didn't argue. This was Armageddon. The ceiling, walls, and floor imploded around them as the quake continued to shake, rattle, and roll beneath their feet. An enormous grinding crash, like thunder, only a hundred times louder, rocked the floor. The noise came from behind them.

Reactively, Callie tuned to look. "Oh, God, Jonah—the tunnel's sealed with debris."

She didn't expect a response, and she didn't get one.

The major damage might be behind them, but fractures snaked along the walls nearby. Small chunks of cement dropped down on them like dark, heavy snow as the ceiling crumbled.

She'd never been a runner. Or a jogger. All her exercise was under the water. Swimming used different muscles. Pulling up an energy she didn't know she had, she matched Jonah's speed, assisted by his brutal grip on her hand. She practically flew.

They ran a lethal obstacle course. No going back. And at this rate, there'd soon be no going forward, either.

Jonah skidded to a stop. She bit her tongue as she slammed into his arm. "Now what?"

Twenty feet ahead, the ceiling crashed down in enormous chunks with the earsplitting noise repeating as it broke into smaller pieces that bounced and skittered around them. On either side the walls rippled, then imploded with stunning force. Jonah took off at a full-out run, dodging debris in his path, helping her when the going got tough. At one point he picked her up by the waist and threw her over a six-foot roadblock, then scrambled down the other side, grabbing up her hand again as she staggered to her feet, dazed.

"Go. Go. Go." Walls cracked, veins opening like spider webs on the ceiling as the roof broke open above them. Destruction was hot on their heels.

"Don't *look*. Run!"

"Excellent advice," she yelled, barely able to hear herself.

The noise was hellacious, the dust choking and hard to see through, the path treacherous with boulder-sized masses of cement. Enormous spears of rebar protruded from many of the immense fragments falling around them.

The going was a minefield, treacherous and terrifying. A spar of rusted rebar snagged on her calf, gouging through the neoprene. No pain, just an intense burn, minor compared with everything else going on around her.

The only reality was Jonah's painfully tight grip on her hand. Callie put on more speed to match his longer strides. Her choppy breathing, coupled with the dust-thick air, made her chest and throat ache, and her eyes stream. One foot in front of the other. One foot in front of the other.

Why—God, *who*—was doing this? Destroying the tunnel to the water just to kill a handful of people seemed over the top.

"Go. Go. Go—Fuck!" Jonah almost wrenched her arm from the socket as he swung her behind him, and they narrowly missing being squashed like bugs by a ton of flat slab as it peeled off the wall to their right.

Callie gagged on the cement dust as Jonah choked out, "Keep moving."

Numb, she kept moving.

His hair and wet suit were gray, powdered with cement dust. Bonded with the sweat on his face and neck, it had formed a paste to form deep rivulets of tanned skin beneath gritty streaks. The tight, prickly sensation of her skin told her she looked just as bad.

Callie's side burned like the fires of hell. Pressing her elbow into the wound, she prayed she wouldn't pass out. *Breathe.* They had enough crap to deal with without Jonah having to carry her. Or maybe he was pissed off enough to leave her right where she fell. Both lousy options. Like a sore tooth, she explored the small hole in her wet suit with the tip of her finger as she ran. Oh, crap! That freaking hurt like nothing she'd felt before, but then she'd never been shot before. "Wow, lucky me, this whole trip has been a cornucopia of firsts."

"What?"

He had ears like a bat. "I'm good." Shocking, bright-red blood smeared her fingers; for a moment her steps faltered as black spots danced dizzyingly in front of her eyes. Scrubbing her hand on her upper thigh, she forged ahead. Wrapping on arm across her middle, she pressed her hand firmly against her side, hoping to hell it stopped the flow of blood.

Passing out was. Not. An. Option.

"There's a door up ahead—*¡Dios!*" He jerked her against him. "Watch out for *that*!"

"*That*" was a chunk of concrete the size of a car, with spikes of rusty metal sticking out of it like a kid's *Star Wars* toy. It bounced twice, screeching metal joining crashing cement, before landing four feet away.

Jonah guided her lagging feet around the obstacle, then resumed running, sure she'd stay with him. Only one of them had that kind of confidence in her stamina. And she wasn't it. The layer of sweat between her skin and the neoprene made her itch. It stung as it ran into her eyes, making her eyeballs burn and water. And *now* the pain in her calf joined the sharp pain in her side.

Through blurred vision she saw the huge metal door ahead and almost sobbed with relief. Whatever was behind that door couldn't be worse than this.

Jonah grabbed the ornate, wrought-iron handle. "Fucker better not be locked!"

It wasn't locked. Jonah bust through the door, dragging Callie with him. Slamming it behind her, he took a moment to catch his breath. At least it was dead quiet. Gun in one hand, he braced his hands on his knees, head down, wheezing in clean air as his heartbeat slowed.

The almost-silence on this side of the door throbbed in his ears. After several moments, he straightened to see how Callie was doing. "Good job back there—"

His heart lurched. She lay on her back on the floor, spread out flat, eyes closed. She wasn't dead. Her chest rose and fell erratically. Liberally covered in gray dust from her still-neat braid to her one water shoe, she breathed like a beached fish.

Jonah did a visual inspection. Dust, sweat, a rip in the leg of her suit shone shiny. Blood. Fuck. She *was* hurt. "You going to make it?" His heart hammered. It was hard to remember just how pissed he was at her when she looked so vulnerable, and heartbreakingly beautiful, despite being covered in the dust.

"I appreciate your concern," she muttered sarcastically, not opening her eyes. "Other than a bullet hole, a gouged leg, exhaustion, dust inhalation, and terror, and probably a dislocated shoulder from being yanked around like a tug toy? I'm just awesome."

It took a second. "*¡Dios, Callie!*" Jonah dropped to his knees beside her, his side burning as if it were being eaten by fire ants. He ignored the discomfort. "You buried the fucking lead! Why didn't you tell me you'd been shot?"

"I was waiting for just the right moment."

A quick glance at her leg showed it was no longer bleeding. A gunshot took precedence. "Show me."

Without opening her eyes, she used her opposite hand to point to the small hole at her waist. Blood seeped out of it. Slowly, but *seeping* wasn't good.

For the first time, Jonah looked around to see where the fuck they were. Another computer room? What the hell *was* this place? Stark white—a *clean room*. Smaller than the other chamber and vastly different in appearance. This was filled with state-of-the-art, high-tech equipment from some futuristic movie.

Everywhere he looked was a hard surface. All he had to stop the bleeding was his swimsuit or hers. Panic filled him. She could die right before his eyes, and he was helpless to stop it. He didn't know where he was, or who else he was dealing with. He had one gun, six bullets, no clips. His fist wouldn't stop a hail of bullets. Fucking hell.

Gently he pulled down the zipper of her dust-encrusted wet suit. Her skin was pebbled from the chill in the room. Not good. "Talk to me."

"I begin my life, with the beginning of my life, I was born."

Easing the neoprene off one shoulder and then the other, he bared her to the waist. "You want to quote *David Copperfield. Now?*" Hard little nipples poked through the thin black nylon of her swimsuit. Cold was good to stop bleeding. That was, if not great news, *news*.

He released the straps and peeled her out of the top half of her swimsuit to her waist. The wound was about two inches long, bleeding, but the edges had already crusted. Carefully he slid his hand under her to the small of her back, looking for an exit hole. He didn't find one. Her skin felt sweaty and shockingly cold.

There was too much going on to know if it was a graze, or if the bullet was in her. *He* went cold.

Callie hissed as he carefully inspected the wound. "I love *David Copperfield*. I could probably quote quite a bit of it, if you like?"

"Pass." He had to clean the wound. She required stitches, antiseptic, bed rest. And if the bullet was still in her—surgery . . .

"Can we talk about Rydell?"

"Jesus, Callie—" Standing, he pulled down his own zipper, his fingers clumsy with speed and worry. The room was cold enough to cause goose bumps on his over-heated skin. He peeled the wet suit off, then hooked his thumbs in the band of his swimsuit.

"Can we talk about us, then?"

He knelt beside her again. She still hadn't opened her eyes. He wished to hell he knew more than basic first aid, because the loss of blood was going to put her in shock sooner than later and he had fuck-all to help her.

Gently he lay his own wet suit over her. Better than nothing. "This is neither the time, nor the place."

Wadding up his cotton swim trunks, he gently pressed the fabric to her side. She hissed in another sharp breath.

Shitfuckdamn. "Sorry."

Opening her eyes, she held his gaze and said softly, "Me, too." Her expression lightened beneath the grime and sweat. "Oh, God, Jonah—"

Shit. He scanned her face, checked the cloth over the wound. "What's the matter?" What the fuck *wasn't* the matter?

"No matter where you are, you're always naked."

For a second the fear leaked out of him. But it didn't stay at bay long. "Callie, we have to find a way out of here. The room's soundproof obviously. But there must be people about. I need to get you medical attention."

"I was just resting." She used one hand to push her up-per body off the floor, then sat there panting, legs out-stretched, eyes closed, clutching his wet suit to her naked chest. "I'm good." She looked at him and extended her hand. "*Really.* Help me up. I can walk."

Stubborn as hell. Precious as hell. What the fuck was he going to do about her? "I'll carry you."

"I'll walk," she told him firmly as he lifted her to her feet, holding her around her shoulders until he was sure she was steady. "You need your gun hand free. Okay. *That* sounds insane. Your *gun* han—" She let out a huff of surprise, and her gaze skewed behind him, and her eyes went wide.

Bare-ass naked, he spun toward the threat, gun raised.

Three familiar black-robed men. Standing silently, ten feet away. "*Kyrie* Cutter, *Doktōr* West." Achaikos Trakas's greeting cut through Callie's words.

There'd been no indication of their presence. They'd appeared out of thin air, as if by magic. Or elevator.

With Tall were Short and Medium. Trakas, Eliades, and Demetriou. Whatcha know.

Jonah shifted Callie behind him. She said, "*Excuse* me?" in dire tones and moved to his side, his wet suit held flat against her chest to cover her nudity. Jonah tucked her against him, wrapping a supporting arm around her shoulders. She didn't shake him off. In fact a fine tremble traveled through her body as shock set in. He held her more tightly, willing his body heat to warm her.

She was half naked. He wanted a doctor, a hospital, IVs, and a herd of trained medical professionals.

What he had was bare-ass naked, a wounded woman beside him, bad guys in front, and a gun out of fucking reach.

The old men didn't move from the dark opening behind them. The gates of hell, or an elevator to somewhere not buried beneath the ocean. Jonah figured he was game. Callie might be standing, but for all her bravado, her knees kept dipping, and it was only his implacable hold keeping her upright.

Since they didn't seem to be bothered by his nudity,

Jonah wasn't, either. "Dr. West's been shot. She needs medical attention right away."

Eliades, his face shiny and flushed, extended a plump arm in invitation. "This way, *Kyrie* Cutter. We will take care of both of you."

"That sounds like a threat to me," Callie said under her breath, echoing Jonah's thoughts exactly.

"Or they're inviting us to tea," he told her just as quietly, his tone Sahara-dry, not believing a word of it.

Anything *this* elaborate, *this* expensive, this fucking *secretive*, was clearly worth killing for. What it had to do with cosmetics, or the price of tea in fucking China, Jonah had no idea.

Tucking her wet suit up around her shoulders, he helped her stuff her arms into the sleeves, moving her backward by inches, until he touched the gun with his bare foot.

The color drained from her face beneath the dust and grime, making his balls pinch to see her in such pain, but he got her covered and the zipper pulled up to her throat.

"Your swimsuit . . ."

He didn't give a shit about his trunks—

"Pick up the damn gun, Cutter!" she hissed under her breath, eyes hard.

He scooped the gun and wad of black cloth up at the same time.

She swayed, and, against her feeble protests, he scooped her up. She fit in his arms nicely. She adjusted the gun, concealed in the crumpled black cloth of his swimsuit on her lap.

He strode over to the old guys. Short handed him a blanket. Among the three of them, the old man, Jonah, and Callie, they managed to wrap her in the scratchy wool and get her settled in his arms.

As soon as they stepped into the glossy white box,

overhead lights sprang on. Callie lay her head in the curve of his shoulder, sliding one arm around his neck. Her hold was weak. The three men, smelling a little of oregano and ancient dust crowded inside with them, and the elevator smoothly ascended. There was no control panel. No UP or DOWN button. No one had said a word. The elevator just moved on its own.

"You better be taking us to whoever's in charge, because we're done with being shot at, running through miles of tunnels, and being cut off from our ship."

Take me to your leader.

Someone must run this place, and that someone, please God, would be rational and sensible enough to allow him and Callie to leave. And he believed in unicorns. What he did know was that someone had used fucking overkill to prevent anyone from using the tunnel to the lava cave ever again. What must've taken decades, if not centuries, to build had been destroyed in less than an hour.

Yeah, no. They wouldn't be leaving anytime soon. Not unless he came up with a viable plan PDQ.

As the elevator slowly rose, Jonah tried to figure out where the hell they were. The only place that made any sense was Fire Island. Right now, that was all he had to work with.

Keeping his eye on Tall, he figured Trakas was in charge of this group. Between keeping half his attention on the men, and making a quick glance or two at Callie, his mind ran like a gerbil on a wheel.

He presumed they'd pop up like rock rabbits in the small village, but that might not be the case at all. Logically, he figured they couldn't be anywhere near Fire Island. The distances just didn't match up. But since that's all he had until further notice, Fire Island it was.

Mentally he reviewed what he know of the island's

topography, the distance from the small village to the water. There were at least two boats there that he knew of. The old fishing vessel, and Anndra's fancy *Astondoa* yacht. Either would do. Of course it would help if he had a fucking clue of his location right *now*.

"The Guardians have been here for a millennium, *Kyrie*." Eliades's scalp shone pink beneath the spare white hairs of his comb-over. The lights in the ceiling shadowed his hangdog features, making his trout-like mouth appear grotesquely large. Like the others, his hands were folded inside his sleeves.

"Did Guardians build this elaborate system of tunnels, and the tech labs, and the steps down to the water?"

"Yes." Trakas was apparently the spokesman Guardian for the group. "For millennia Guardians have maintained the tunnels, and updated the technology as necessary."

"Are the Guardians *also* responsible for precipitating the earthquakes?" Callie asked from beneath his chin. Jonah thought she'd dozed off. "Because that's an incredibly dangerous thing to do intentionally. The tectonic plates—"

"They know," he murmured against her hair, and felt her jaw clench against his chest.

Yeah, they knew.

Trakas touched the wall beside him, and the elevator slowed, then glided to a stop. He turned hooded black eyes to Jonah as the door slid open soundlessly. "The system was designed to deter visitors."

No shit. "Effective, but not good for stock growth, shaking your own facility to ruins, is it?" He followed the tall black-garbed man and was in turn followed by Small and Medium.

A short, brightly lit, cement-lined corridor led to a small room. It looked like a storeroom, with piles of crates stacked neatly along one wall. But it was now set up as a medical facility. Other than the boxes, it gave the appearance of any modern, well-equipped doctor's exam room. A high, cloth-covered table, lights, instruments on a tray. Small vials of God knew what.

His arms tightened around Callie. He didn't want to be there. He didn't want *Callie* there. He reminded himself to be careful what he wished for, because this was it, and seeing all those sharp instruments, and these three old guys, made his heart pound and his scrotum contract.

"Place her here, Mr. Cutter." Trakas motioned the draped table with his lantern jaw. "Eliades is a medical doctor. *Doktōr* West has been shot. Her leg cut by ancient, rusted construction materials. You, too, are injured. Both of you must be attended to immediately. Questions must wait."

"No. Questions *cannot* wait." She'd rather start digging the bullet out herself than let any of these old men use their shiny instruments on her. Nothing was happening until she got some goddamn answers. And just because she was being told the guy was a medical doctor didn't mean it was true. Eliades was so fat he could barely toddle, let alone wield a sharp instrument.

No thanks.

She slid the cloth-wrapped gun off the juncture of her thighs, beneath her butt and out of sight.

Callie wrapped her fingers around Dr. Eliades's plump wrists as he came at her thigh with a large hypodermic needle.

"Help *Doktōr* West get comfortable, Trakas," he said over his shoulder. The other two old men had stepped back to give him more room. Jonah was near them, putting his arms into his wet suit. Dear God, the man loved to be naked. The parts that hadn't been covered were vibrant, tan, and delectable. But she wasn't admiring his physique.

His side looked like hamburger meat, raw, and angry, and already bruising. He had cuts on his throat, his face, and his feet.

They both required medical attention. But this wasn't where they were going to get it.

Trakas came to "help" her. Giving him the evil eye, and through gritted teeth, she snarled, "Stay the hell away from me." He didn't move, but he didn't come any closer, either. His intensely focused black eyes remained on her face. His fixed stare made the hair on her body go on full alert.

She used the heavyset man's wrist as a fulcrum to leverage her upper body off the table. She might feel like crap and hurt like hell, but every fight-or-flight sense shouted that these guys were *not* trying to help her.

Whatever they were doing, whatever they protected, was important enough to kill for. She and Jonah would not be the exception.

"If comfortable means take off more clothes, no thanks." It wasn't easy, but she managed to sit up and fling her legs over the side of the high bed, putting her knees between them to hold Eliades at bay. Holding on to the edge of the thin mattress with a two-handed death grip kept her from blacking out and keeling over.

The pain in her side was so intense she didn't even feel the rest of her aches and pains.

Jonah, who'd been hastily pulling his wet suit over his nakedness, lunged across the room to grab her by her upper arms as she swayed. "Lie down. Let him help you."

Callie gave him a pointed stare. These guys had just killed *how* many people? Did Jonah think they'd just allow the two of them to waltz out of here? She so didn't think so. There was absolutely no reason to give them medical attention. Instinct and keen self-preservation told her their intention was not to let them leave at all. Which meant this whole "*Eliades is a medical doctor*" was bullshit.

"We don't know what's *in* that needle," she said fiercely, sotto voce. "Keep him the hell away from me."

She saw by the darkening of his eyes that the thought had crossed his mind as well. He gave a short nod, then helped pull her wet suit up her back and over her shoulders. He faced the old men. "I'll get her back to *Stormchaser*, and have her flown to Heraklion if necessary." He helped stuff her arms into the sleeves. With even that careful movement, pain shot a fiery bolt from her side to her brain, then spread to every atom in her body.

She breathed through it. Going face-first through a windshield had been a lot worse. She rested her sweaty forehead on Jonah's chest for a moment, gritting her teeth as she rode it out. He cupped the back of her head, holding her there. "Tell me when you can stand," he whispered.

Mouth dry, pain-sweat trickling down her temples, she stayed where she was. Having him holding her, solid and bullet-free, helped her to focus for a moment. She gritted her teeth, and tears stung her eyes; the pain wasn't dissipating. "Minute."

"So it's you who've been trying to deter us? Not the Spanoses?" Buying them time so she could gather her strength, he cupped her hot cheek in his cool palm, stroking her thumb back and forth in a soothing gesture that didn't alleviate the pain, but tugged at her heart.

"It is not us, but *your* actions that have caused this catastrophe. It was you who precipitated disaster by removing precious and vital pieces of the city, *Doktōr*." One of the men—the quiet one, Demetriou?—said, sounding more afraid than annoyed. "They must be returned with all haste."

"I recovered a lot of artifacts and took them on board the ship for preservation," Callie rebutted, still leaning on Jonah but turning her cheek so she could speak more clearly. Ah, crap. Shouldn't have moved. The room swayed. She froze before resuming speaking. "What exactly are you referring to?"

"You have in your possession three mosaic tiles. Humankind is not ready."

The three little iridescent mosaics she had in a bowl of water beside her bed? She frowned, not opening her eyes.

"I don't follow," Jonah said over her head. "Humankind isn't ready for—*mosaics*?"

"There are seven hundred and seventy-seven separate mosaics pieces strategically placed throughout the city. Each quarter-inch piece of glass is a piece of the . . . jigsaw puzzle, as it were. Each glass mosaic is electron-infused with nanotechnology. Each nanobot is a part of the whole. The nanorobotics form macro-scale robotics with sensing. Powerful communications—nano manipulation with computational replication—" He sighed with frustration. "Every tile *must* remain in place. Each is integral, and part of a whole."

Callie's brain spun with the implications. "Is that what's been interfering with our communications devices?"

"The low-frequency hum is the robotics' signature. They *communicate* with one another in perfect synchronization. All part of a harmonious whole, which, when the individual parts are brought together, will one day fulfill our prophecy. But if pieces are removed, as you have done, it disrupts the pattern."

Callie couldn't wrap her brain around any of it. Nanobots? The possibility was intriguing, fascinating, really. At another time and place she'd love to sit down over a cup of coffee and discuss nanotechnology with a man old enough to be her grandfather, all freaking day. But this wasn't the day.

"*Nanotechnology?*" Jonah's chest shifted beneath her cheek as he gave an incredulous laugh. "What do these bots do?"

"Now? Nothing but wait, bide their time. In the future the components will form a beacon, a powerful communications device—"

"To who or what?" Jonah demanded.

"I cannot answer that."

"Can't?" Callie demanded. "Or won't?"

"It is the same, *Doktōr* West."

"No," Jonah said drily. "It's not. You're saying that someone three thousand years ago had technology that we're just *learning* in the twenty-first century? And they placed seven hundred bits of glass a hundred and fifty feet underwater?" He tried a different tack. "And who were they trying to attract with their beacon?"

Twenty

The men were blowing smoke. Did they really think she and Jonah were that gullible? The implication was too sci-fi and implausible to be real. The mosaic nanobots weren't what they were protecting. As far as she knew, the engineering discipline of designing and building nanorobots was still in its infancy stage.

Drugs made more sense. Maybe a drug smuggling operation? The hidden cavern wouldn't be detectable underwater . . . Actually, at this point, she didn't really give a shit what they wanted and why they were doing what they were doing. All she wanted was for her and Jonah to be back on board *Stormchaser*, where she could lie down in a cool, dark room.

She suspected Jonah had pretty much the same desire. He was naturally curious, but she bet he'd rather be on board his ship right now than here listening to the old men's technobabble. He was giving her time to gather her strength so they could make a run for it. Which she appreciated.

"The technology was not placed *under* the water, *Kyrie* Cutter." This time she recognized Trakas's clipped tones. "The Sacred City was built around the individual pieces. Was built specifically to house and protect her nanorobotics."

"The Sacred City, and that technology, is what Guardians are privileged to protect, our entire lives. At all cost."

Jonah's stroking thumb stilled. "You're claiming this technology came from three thousand *years* ago?"

Trakas made an affirming clearing of his throat. "It's imperative the three missing components—the mosaics—be returned to their correct GPS location immediately."

"It's a big ocean," Jonah said drily.

Putting something *back* meant they were being taken to a boat, and back to *Stormchaser*. Although no one had requested that *they* return anything to the ocean floor. Just that it had to *be* returned.

Callie put a hand on Jonah's wrist, loving the feel of his cool skin, and the tensile strength there. "Everything is documented. I know *exactly* where they came from." *Now ask us to return the mosaics for you and let us go, so we can do it.*

"There's no need. They will be deposited back to the sea. They will transmigrate to where they were originally placed."

Callie lifted her head, ignoring the blizzard of black snow. She could just see Trakas around Jonah's supporting arm. "Could you be more specific on the *how* of their return?"

She looked up to meet Jonah's eyes. They were pissed off and had just added another layer of anger. They both knew precisely what the men really meant.

Kill them, and scuttle the ship.

Jonah mouthed *Fuck* then said so low, Callie barely heard him, "Ready?"

No. She wasn't. She nodded. Counted through the pain until it was bearable. A few more minutes would help. If not, then yes, she was ready.

Jonah's fingers tightened in her hair as he turned his head and demanded, "Dr. West needs water."

Yes! That would help.

A moment later he held a glass to her mouth. Looked like water. She sniffed. Was she being paranoid? She didn't think so. She took a tentative sip. No odd taste. Lukewarm, tasteless water. With Jonah's help she drank the entire glass. It was as if every parched cell in her body was flooded with life-giving moisture.

"Hell," Jonah said, keeping his attention on her. The problem was—Well, shit, there were *myriad* freaking problems here. But she knew that to leave they'd have to dispatch the three old men. To leave they'd have to run. And right this second running wasn't in her cards.

"If what you say is true, this knowledge could advance science and medicine by *decades*."

"It is too soon for mankind to have this knowledge and technology," Eliades intoned, his voice reflecting his hangdog expression and demeanor. "We are merely the Guardians."

"Do these *nanotechnology* mosaics have something to do with the interference to our electronics underwater?" Jonah asked, leaning away just enough, while still supporting her shoulders, to pull up the zipper on the front of her wet suit. That done, he tugged up his own. *Shoes?* he mouthed.

She shook her head. One wasn't going to do it.

"Jamming your radio frequency, producing the fog, the quakes, and the sand trap—all deterrents. You refused to go."

Jonah twisted his head to look at Trakas. "That *sand trap* broke my friend's leg in three places."

"Your man was meant to *die* that day." Eliades refilled the glass, handing it to Jonah. "That section is the entrance to the Sacred City. Not even Guardians are permitted to enter, unless under the most dire of circumstances." He sounded appalled and horrified that anyone had the temerity to even *attempt* entering.

"The city is *that* important?"

"It is *more* important than any one being."

"Were you aware that the Spanoses were in the control room when you instigated the earthquake? Of course you were. Is that what they were doing? Going into the Sacred City uninvited, so you killed them?"

Medium's dark eyes narrowed, his face flushed with anger "Entering the Sacred City uninvited?" he whispered, his voice filled with fury and horror. "Worse, *much* worse. They raped and pillaged sacred material to use in frivolous pursuits. Kallistrate was *warned*, but that was our error. He was only an initiate into the order, not yet a full Guardian. He had not yet earned the right to go into the city. The brother was not the one in charge. It was his sister who was the mastermind behind their nefarious doings.

"They ignored repeated warnings to cease and desist— and requests to leave the island. Instead they came more frequently, and brought professional divers to assist them, and men with guns to protect them. They *had* to be stopped."

Jonah held the glass, but Callie took it from him and drank again. "What did they have to do with any of this?"

"Kallistrate was born here. Raised to be a Guardian. A high honor. But he went away to England to get an education. Then he became too sophisticated, to *Western-ized* to want to come home where he belonged, to follow our ways."

"Then what were he and his sister doing here?"

"They used to come once a year for our Sacred City's orichalcum. For the past three years they have come twice in a twelve-month period. But this was their third time *this* year."

Callie swung her feet between Jonah's legs. The pain was manageable. "Orichalcum is a myth."

Demetriou pinned her with a glare of disdain. "No. It is very real, *Doktōr* West. It was mined here on the island for thousands of years. It was a main component in the nanotechnology used in the mosaics. An integral part of the Sacred City. The vein was depleted a century before the Big Eruption. The only place this precious metal can now be found is in the vaults of the temple inside the walls of the city."

She eased her butt forward. Knowing Jonah would catch her if she fell. "What do they want it for? Is it of great monetary value?"

"In today's market?" Trakas asked. "With its rare properties? *Yes*, multimillions of American dollars. Kallistrate procured it from inside the walls, taking a few bars at a time. They only required a minuscule amount for processing. The dust is added to the creams and lotions he sells worldwide."

"Orichalcum?" Jonah slid his hand to her upper arm, then closed his fingers around it to support her as she slid her feet down to the floor. She wobbled, but his hand remained steady.

"A metal Plato described as unique to Atlantis," Callie murmured.

His eyes never left her face as he addressed the men

behind him. "Why put an obscure metal into lotions and potions? What's its claim to fame? Nanobots again?"

"Its application in medicine, or for topical use, is that it works at a cellular level—it is the main ingredient in their Fountain of Youth products. Dramatically reducing all signs of aging."

Women would pay *anything* to get their hands on a product like that. "If it's been deep underwater for thousands of years," Callie asked, "how did they even *know* about it?"

Trakas hesitated. "Kallistrate was trained in the ways of the Guardians from the day he was born, until he fled. Orichalcum has been an integral part of the Guardians' diets since the beginning of time."

"*Eating* orichalcum makes you look younger?" Jonah sounded a little left of incredulous.

"Not just *look* younger, *Kyrie*."

Callie leaned her hip against the table, wondering what the hell she'd just ingested in those two glasses of water.

"Just how old *a*—"

Jonah tightened his hold on her upper arms as Callie listed to the left. Her sudden lack of balance had nothing to do with her knees being too weak to stand from blood loss. It was another goddamn *earthquake*.

The floor beneath his bare feet buckled, walls rippled and shuddered, sending a cabinet sliding halfway into the small room. Instruments chattered across the surface of the nearby metal tray, then clattered to the floor.

Wood and metal screeched and groaned as the building torqued violently. Bracing himself with one hand on the shuddering wall, he held Callie against his chest as the high narrow window shattered, spraying glass into the room.

Trakas yelled at the other two men in rapid-fire, incomprehensible Greek.

"Big surprise, guys?" Jonah yelled over the din. Oh, yeah. This was going to be as bad as what they'd just come from. Outside would be safer than in. Time to get the hell out of Dodge.

Trakas and the others stood in the open doorway, swaying and bucking with the quake as if they were standing on a surfboard riding the waves. Deciding to run for it, or stay there so he and Callie were trapped?

"You'll be safe here." Trakas's voice vibrated as he lied straight-faced.

Yeah, right. "Does that mean you're going to turn the damn thing off?" Jonah demanded. "I'm all for it."

"There is no switch for this, *Kyrie*," Trakas said grimly as Demetriou and Eliades slipped behind him. The old man blocked the doorway, holding on to the jamb with both gnarled hands as the floor continued to rise and fall in uneven waves.

"Then we're going with you."

The Guardian's face turned a deep plum color as he burst into a spate of Greek too frantic for Jonah to follow.

He put up his hand to stop the outpouring of fear. "Whatever the hell you're saying, we're not staying in this room. So get us out of here, or get the hell out of our way."

Dios. He didn't want to kill a defenseless old man, but if it came to a choice between the Greek, or himself and Callie, there was no contest. Even though he'd never shot a man, this was life or death. There was a first time for everything.

His stomach churned as he accepted that today would be the day that changed him. He'd have to figure out how to live with it . . . later.

The room filled with shadows. A quick glance at the

high, narrow window through the broken shards of glass showed the sky darken from brilliant blue to dark, ominous gray in seconds.

Sliding his palm under his bunched-up shorts on the table behind Callie, he palmed the gun, adjusting his grip, then brought the weapon out in the open, pointing the muzzle at Trakas's forehead.

"Give her your shoes," he instructed Eliades, figuring the smaller man had the smallest feet of the three. "Move it! *You*—" He motioned to Trakas with the barrel of the gun inches from his chest. "Hand 'em over."

"It's too late, *Kyrie*," Trakas muttered, but something in Jonah's expression convinced him to get the lead out, and he crouched to unbuckle his sandals. Demetriou helped Eliades, who was having a hard time reaching his feet.

"It's *not* too fucking late." Jonah handed the gun to Callie, kept her an arm span away from Trakas, and hastily slid his feet into the sandals. "We'll die here together if you don't hurry." Crouching, he did them up. Too small; his toes hung over the front edge. Better than barefoot. Rising, he took the gun back from Callie.

Once the fat guy managed to get down, he and Demetriou fought with the buckles, sweat running down their red faces.

Once the sandals had been handed over, Jonah shoved them at Callie. "Hurry."

"You don't have to tell me twice." She retained her dry sense of humor—a woman used to keeping cool during tense situations. He couldn't think about the fact she'd been shot. She had guts. Heart. And a deceitful tongue. Couldn't think about that, either.

"Out of the way," he told the three men, voice grim. "Last warning."

They parted, and he and Callie pushed past them, clustered just outside the door. "You're fools. Run!"

He didn't wait to see if they were smart enough to leave. He and Callie raced out into the corridor and turned left, running flat-out. Opposite from where they'd been brought in. He knew what was in that direction, and it didn't lead *out*. He hoped to hell left was freedom. At this point they had nothing to lose. Yet another gray cement corridor, and up ahead, dusk-like daylight.

Moments later, like a giant beast waking from a centuries-long nap, another quake rippled beneath their feet. Jonah held Callie tightly against him as they slammed into the wall. His shoulder and side throbbed with the impact. He shot a concerned look at her. Stoic as ever, jaw clenched, gaze focused. Lines of pain bracketed her mouth.

"Don't stop for anything!" he yelled, scooping her under his arm as the floor continued to undulate.

"Does that feel like an aftersho—" An incredibly loud percussion cut her off. Whether this one was human-made, or nature was simply pissed at the previous interference, this quake put the ones before it to shame. A series of thunderous pops and bangs sounded like a combination of heavy artillery and industrial-grade fireworks.

Bursting through the narrow door, they jettisoned into the great outdoors, onto a dirt road, and into the jaws of hell.

The long-dormant volcano, reactivated by the human-made earthquakes, shook and spewed. Turning day to night, filling the air with dust and flaming projectiles. The fragments, semi-molten when airborne, landed still smoking hot around them.

The stink of sulfureted hydrogen saturated the heavy

air. The sulfur instantly made his eyes water. The shrill screams of terrified men, running like ants at a picnic, joined the cacophony of falling projectiles and the horrendous creaking of the earth splintering. The sun should be shining. Instead, a dense black cloud cover hung suffocatingly low over the small village.

Jonah recognized the path leaving the village. "Windward." Confused, frightened Guardians ran up the mountainside, arms protecting their heads, black robes billowing around them while shit flew in the air around them. "Damn fools! They should be running down toward the sea to escape."

"Watch out for fumaroles," Callie cautioned, indicating a smoking hole opening up six feet in front of them as they ran. She pulled him sideways, so they narrowly missed being hit by molten volcanic bombs.

"Come with us!" Callie tried to grab a man's arm as he ran passed them in the wrong direction. He shook her off, yelling invectives.

"It isn't the stink of sulfur that's going to kill them, it's the CO_2—" They crested a hill, the ocean spread out below them. At least two miles away. But it wasn't the distance or the view that captured her attention. She'd turned to look back at the Guardians' progress up the mountainside. It was a gentle slope to the top of the—"Oh, my God—look at that!"

An eruption column.

The top of the volcano spewed a three-thousand-foot black mushroom cloud of smoke with a fiery base. Projectiles peppered the way as they skidded and slipped, hauled each other upright, and kept running. "Is that it?" Jonah shouted as there was a momentary lull in flying projectiles.

"That's just the warm-up! This could go on for days." A powerful explosion lit up the underside of the smoke cover.

"Then we better be long gone by the time that happens."

They held each other as the earth shuddered beneath their feet, and as soon as it settled enough for them to run, they did so.

"There's laundry on the line," Callie shouted, tugging him off their path to investigate. "We should cover our faces as best we can. Water would be great . . . The goat trough will do. Grab that robe."

Jonah pulled it off the rope line. It was still damp. Taking it to where Callie bent over the trough trying to catch her breath, he started tearing it into pieces.

"Those stupid bastards set off all those damn tremors, and now those human-made quakes are setting off natural quakes, and their tame little molehill has morphed into a mountain about to erupt!" Callie yelled over the sound of animals squawking, bleating, and crying, and the percussion of rocks falling.

A rough tremor shook the ground as they soaked the strips in the water. "That smoke cloud must be at least two hundred feet, and she's shooting stone bombs now, but in minutes the magma is going to start bubbling up through all these cracks and we're all in deep shit!"

Squawking chickens ran across their path, and a dog barked frantically nearby. "Don't see any sign of magma. Not yet anyway." He scanned the area as he wrung some of the water out of the cloth.

"A red glow up that way." Callie pointed while covering her nose and mouth with her free hand. "Could be the dome waiting to crest and blow. Magma's not far behind."

Taking a handful of wet strips from him, she wrapped her head and face then bent to cover her feet as best she could. Jonah did the same. Callie's eyes lit up with humor. "We look like the Mummy."

"Hands, too." He wrapped his own.

A blizzard from hell, gray ash swirled around them, dense enough to fucking chew. The stench of sulfur permeated the air. The terrified, agonized screams of the black-garbed men running up the street, some with robes in flames, was just part of the nightmare of fleeing humans and animals.

"Hurry, neoprene doesn't degrade until after two hundred degrees. Right now the worst we have to deal with are boulders and ashfall and the smaller falling debris." Anything else, and they, and all the islanders, would be toast.

"Great. About a hundred times less than the temperature we're going to run in if there's a magma flow!"

"One thing at a time, all right?"

She didn't need to explain to him the inherent dangers of being this close to an active volcano. Lava tubes networked beneath the island. Fissures would open up, dome fountains—this was bad, and hell was going to rain down on their heads, and open under their feet, at any moment.

"One stray spark . . ." The wet suits weren't going to protect them from falling rocks or molten lava, but they'd protect their skin from some of the fallout. It had to be enough.

"What's our risk?" he yelled, heading over a small rise.

"Right now? We're in the medium-risk zone . . . But in the next fifteen minutes? I'd say high-risk. Or kiss our butts goodbye. The lava, when it comes, will most likely follow the ancient flows to the sea."

"When we get to the windward side, we'll stay as close to shore as possible. First boat we see, we get the hell outta Dodge and head out to the *Stormchaser.*"

If the insane fucking Guardians hadn't sunk his ship while he'd been busy.

He tangled his fingers with hers, both wrapped, so it wasn't skin-to-skin. But he needed the contact. "Then haul ass."

"Keep going, I've got you," Jonah yelled. Sweaty, dizzy, and numb, Callie kept pace alongside him.

She ran without seeing where they were, or what she was stepping on, or through. She ran because Jonah refused to let go of her hand. He flew down hills, up hills, and down a steep incline without breaking stride. Smoldering, burning shrubs and grass were no deterrent, Jonah plowed through anything in their path.

Yelling *stop* wasn't an option.

She smelled the heat creeping behind them. The stink of sulfur filled her world. Overpowering, her fear even more so.

Her steps faltered. Jonah pulled her upright, kept her going. She was vaguely surprised her shoulder wasn't dislocated. It was the same arm Jonah had yanked, tugged, pulled, and grabbed all day.

The stitch in her side took over her entire body. Or that could be the bullet wound in her side. Was she bleeding to death with every step she ran? Gritting her teeth, determined to keep going, to keep up, she suddenly felt her knees buckle and she dropped, a painful skid along the rocky ground.

The abrupt cessation of movement jerked her hand free from Jonah's, radiating pain up her arm. Chest heaving, she sat back on her haunches, struggling to suck in a breath. God, it was hot, so hot the air was hard to breathe, searing her nose and throat on the way to burning through her lungs. The earth was on fire. The air was on fire. She was on fire.

"Get up."

Callie tried, but her body refused to move. Depleted. Done. She blinked streaming eyes, to see Jonah standing about six feet away, magical and mystical shrouded in swirling dust and smoke. "Minute." It took everything in her to push out that one word.

Darkness, not from the swirling ash and billowing smoke alone, crowded out the clarity of her field of vision. She'd lost too much blood and she knew it. This was it. Endgame. "Go ahead. I'll catch up."

"Stand the fuck up. *Now*, Calista."

She'd never heard him use that tone. She lifted her head.

Stabbing a finger at the ground between them, he raised his voice, sounding furious and terrified at the same time. "See that?"

A fissure had formed between them, a glowing lightning-bolt-shaped glint of dark bubbling red that opened so quickly, they both had to jump back and retreat. The snake-like crack split the ground in a long jagged line from the volcano behind them, and made a crazy zigzag path to the sea in the distance.

In the crevasse, bubbling magma pulsed like the living heartbeat of a demon beast struggling to escape.

The heat scalded her skin, made the moisture in her eyes dry out, made her lungs burn. The frantic pounding of her heartbeat almost blocked out the crackle of the grass burning and the loud thumps of smoking projectiles plummeting to the ground nearby.

The rift went from a foot to two feet wide.

"*Jump*," Jonah shouted, voice cold and lethal.

Callie staggered, sweat stinging her eyes, side on fire. God. His feet were inches from the edge. She put up both hands. "Go back! Please, Jonah—" Sandals, already dry rags, no protection between him and the magma.

His gaze held hers. Like hers, his eyes were bloodshot, streaming. But the blue was still vivid and compelling as he held out his hand. "You have to be on *this* side." He walked backward as the gap widened, four feet wide, jagged and fiery between them. "Do you understand, Callie? You have to jump over, and come to me. Now!"

Even as she looked, the fissure grew at an alarming rate. Five feet. The earth rumbled, the rolling vibration like an ultrasonic cleaner beneath her feet. "I can go around," she shouted desperately.

She was in no shape to jump that distance. Even fighting fit and well rested she wasn't sure she could jump—

Oh, God. *Six* feet.

They were right in the epicenter. If they got out of this alive it would be a miracle.

"No," he told her grimly. "You fucking well *can't*. Look where it is. Jump before it gets too wide. You can do it, take a running jump and you'll be in my arms. I'll catch you. For fucksake, *now*."

She needed a minute. An hour. A month. She took several steps back as the fracture crept toward her toes. The heat was intense; it burned her skin and snaked a scorching path down into her lungs.

"*Dios*. This is no fucking time to be indecisive. I'm making the call for you! Jump, goddamn it." There wasn't an iota of gentleness in his voice. "Time's run out. I'm not leaving you there. Jump, or I'll come over to you and we'll both be trapped."

She knew better. She was the only one trapped. He

could walk away now and live. If he waited they both would die: Her for trusting him. And him for being a damn fool idiot trying to save her ass. "Give me one good reason to trust you." She trusted Jonah. It was herself she didn't trust. Afraid, deathly afraid, she knew she was making excuses, trying to buy time so she could think it through.

Jump to my death.

"I can only think of one."

Be with Jonah.

She had to move back. So did he. The distance between them widened. A nearby bush burst into flame, the grasses around it sparking in the breeze she couldn't see or feel.

Run like hell to see if there was another way around the problem . . .

She smelled her burnt hair. "We'll be burned to a crisp?"

"Okay. Two reasons. That and I love you. Everything else can be worked out."

The longer she waited, the more intense the heat became, the wider the gap. The more in danger they both were. "It's about damn time you told me, Jonah Cutter." Crazy talk. Oh, God, she had to jump, she knew she did. If she kept debating the pros—being safe in Jonah's arms—with the cons—falling into the molten magma . . .

"I've been a little busy, Calista. Now damn it, run and jump to me before that gets too wide for you to cross."

She looked up and down the length of the wide fissure, at the lava oozing up around it. "I suppose you're expecting me to say the same?" She paced. *Could* she jump that distance? If she jumped short . . . if she didn't jump at all . . .

"That you love me? Hell yes, you do. Fuck it, Doctor! We can discuss that later when we're the hell off this misbegotten island. Right now I'd rather you moved your ass so we can both *do* that."

Callie turned and used every ounce of energy she didn't have running back up the hill. When she figured she was a reasonable distance away, she turned and raced back as fast as her legs and momentum would carry her.

She leapt across the hot river of bubbling lava.

Twenty-one

Heart in his throat, Jonah willed Callie to make it as she practically did the splits to jump from her side to his. It probably took her seconds, but to Jonah, too afraid to blink, arms outstretched, feet braced, it felt like her movements were caught in slo-mo.

Arms and legs flailing, she wasn't graceful, but she got the job done. When she slammed into him, nearly knocking him to the ground, he closed his arms fiercely around her, staggering from the impact, sucking in air. *Dios*, he'd never let her go.

His skin already felt as though he suffered from an intense sunburn. Callie's face, under the dust and sweat, looked red and painful. Helping her when she staggered, he took a firm grip on her hand. "We're going to have a chat about your inability to make fast decisions, but we'll save that for another day. Now run, damn it!"

Angling away from the crack in the earth, he made a beeline for the small inlet he remembered seeing when he'd come with the guys, a lifetime ago. Not far. Steam rose in giant, billowy white plumes with a magnified hiss as magma hit water up and down the coastline.

"Almost there." He jumped with her over a small fiery vein, then another. The grass and shrubbery farther up the mountain burned, adding to the powerful, choking stink of charred wood, oregano, thyme, and sulfur. His stomach roiled in protest.

The going was harder on the soft sand, especially given that they'd already used up most of their reserves. "Shit." The magma had already beaten them to the water. A slow-moving bubbling black-and-red tide ate up sections of beach, then hissed and steamed as it kissed the waves.

Turning in a half circle he spotted the *Astondoa* moored at a small jetty beneath an overhang.

"There!" Callie pointed to Anndra's fast motor yacht at the same time. A giant, red-hot boulder the size of dive tank hit the sand. Close enough for them to feel the heat. More followed.

They ran.

Maura and Gayle had seen the dense black eruption column of smoke and headed south. A call from the *Astondoa* to *Stormchaser* gave Jonah the location of his ship some sixty miles south of where she'd been anchored. After doing a cautious circuit of the island in the hope of finding any of the Guardians, they headed out to sea at full throttle.

An hour later they were on board *Stormchaser*. Callie wanted to drop to the deck and kiss it. Jonah helped her onto the dive platform, then up the ladder to the first deck where everyone waited. He held up his hand as crew and dive team pressed forward, clamoring for answers. "We'll fill you in later. Bring the first-aid kit to my cabin in twenty minutes," he instructed Maura.

"Shower or bed?" Like two drunks, she and Jonah went down to his cabin. "I don't care if we get the sheets dirty, I'm not sure I can move."

"You'll feel better after a shower. Then we can look at your assorted injuries. How's your side?"

"As exhausted and beat up as the rest of me," she murmured as they entered his cabin. She knew she should insist on showering in her own room. But she didn't want to be apart from him. Not until she absolutely had to be. And since he didn't suggest she cross the corridor, either, Callie followed him inside and shut the door behind her.

"I can't tell the difference at this point." The room was cool, dim, and clean. "Everything looks weirdly . . . *normal.*" Tears pricked her eyes. God, she needed normal right now.

"*We* don't look so normal." Jonah's smile was very white against his dirty face. "Come on." Without touching her, something Callie desperately needed, he headed to the bathroom.

"I'd advise you not to look at yourself in a mirror until we're done." His tone was dry, but she couldn't summon the energy to smile. The bathroom was small, and she was all elbows and knees as she grappled with the zipper down the front of her wet suit with fingers made clumsy by exhaustion and a sudden spate of nerves.

"Don't make any sexy moves, Cutter," she said, only half joking. Jonah looked as exhausted and wiped out as she felt. If *she* hadn't forgotten his anger about her involvement with Rydell, she knew *he* hadn't, either. Their life-and-death race to safety merely postponed the completion of *that* conversation. "I don't have one ounce of energy in me."

Now that it was over, now they were safe, and not fighting danger together out of necessity, they were right back in the control room, everything still unfinished. It was easy to claim to love someone when you were about to die a fiery death, but back in their real world, Rydell Case still stood between them.

Naked, Callie opened the shower door and pressed the dial for water. Set to Jonah's preference, the water shot out cool. Eyes closed, she let it sluice over her without moving. It stung against her burnt skin, but gave relief at the same time.

After a moment she felt Jonah's fingers working at the back of her head. His touch in her hair, no matter how impersonal, proved that she wasn't too tired after all. But he wasn't coming on to her. Just his hands made impersonal contact; his body stayed well away from hers. The ache in her chest grew into a painful ball, making it hard to breathe, and harder still not to let the tears, so close to the surface, fall.

She rarely cried; there was never any point to it. But the sadness of impending grief was almost too much to contain. She should've gone back to her own cabin. "I can do that," she whispered, not moving as his fingers snagged in the dusty, damp, nasty mass as he loosened the braid.

"I've got it." He worked through the long skeins, then nudged her directly under the water.

She groaned as her parched skin sucked up the cool liquid. Tilting back her head, she drank until she was satiated, as Jonah started lathering her hair with soap that smelled like an ocean breeze. Heart heavy, she hummed her pleasure.

Opening her eyes to find his chest inches from her nose, she put her hand out. Pouring a dollop in her hand, he went back to washing her hair, his strong fingers massaging her scalp until she wanted to melt into a puddle at his feet.

Rubbing her palms together, she stared at his throat,

as far as she could reach with his hands in her hair and his arm surrounding her. From the neck up it would take a concerted effort to get the thick paste of caked-on dust-turned-mud washed off.

Gently but firmly he pushed her hands aside. "Later." Lifting her chin, he met her eyes as he carefully washed her face as if she were a child. Callie desperately wanted to lean against him for the last time. Wanted to store up every memory so she could take it out for years to come, and relive every moment they'd shared.

Locking her knees, standing still as a statue, she let him bathe her as her mind drifted. Maybe she fell asleep.

"Turn."

His hands seemed to be everywhere at once, and she turned so he could rinse her hair. The soap suds tickled her skin and ran down over the globes of her butt. Bracing her arms against the tiled wall, tears of exhaustion stung beneath her closed lids as Jonah carefully and impersonally washed her back, and down her legs.

"Callie? *¿Querido?*" he murmured softly against her cheek. Groggy, she blinked open her eyes. "Get out and dry off. I'll be right with you, I have to chisel this crap off myself, too." He nudged her out of the shower stall.

Cool air pebbled her skin as, dripping on the floor, she stumbled into the bedroom and dropped face-first across the bed.

Jonah sat on one side of his bed, Maura and Gayle on the other. Callie, sprawled facedown between them, hadn't moved a muscle since he'd emerged from his shower. He'd swept her wet hair out of the way and draped a towel over her naked body for modesty's sake. They needed full access to see what the damage was.

"Let's do this by committee," Gayle said efficiently. "I'll take care of her feet, then I'll work on yours, Jonah."

"The gunshot on her left side takes precedence over assorted singed body parts." He pulled the towel aside to expose Callie's left hip, which was on the women's side of the bed.

"Right side?" Maura ran her hand down Callie's rib cage, then down over her hip searching with eyes and hands for the wound.

Since the sight of the blood was still crystal-clear in his mind's eye, Jonah said emphatically, "No, *that* side."

Maura gave him a sympathetic look and said evenly, "Let's take a look on the right side anyway, okay?"

Jonah slid the towel down so it covered just her ass and bared the long line of Callie's back. There wasn't a mark on her, just smooth, lightly tanned skin without a blemish. He ran his hand from her nape to her ass cheeks. "That's impossible. I saw the wound myself."

"Then she's a quick healer," Gayle said cheerfully, gathering salve from the first-aid kit to treat Callie's burns.

Except—"Was she wearing fireman's boots?" the first officer asked with a slightly puzzled frown as she held Callie's foot in her palm.

"Same sandals as I was—"

"I see your burns, Jonah." She gently placed Callie's foot back on the bed. "But look at her feet and hands." Gayle caught his gaze across the bed. "Not a red mark on her. Anywhere. Now look at you."

Yeah, he didn't need a mirror to tell him he was a mess. His skin was red and blotchy; fiery pain throbbed in his hands and feet, across his cheek, and down his side, which was raw and black and blue. "I don't give a shit about me. She must have internal injuries—maybe the gunshot wound was more to the front than the back—"

Gayle put a hand on his arm. "*She's* fine. Exhausted, but uninjured. Let's patch you up so you can conk out, too, okay?"

Callie woke to find Jonah beside her, ankles crossed, chest bare, propped up against the pillows. Only the night-lights on the above decks shining through the window illuminated the dark cabin. "Is it morning?"

He didn't move. "Just after midnight. You didn't sleep long enough. Go back to sleep."

"I feel wonderful." Surprisingly, she did feel great. Rested, energized, and wide awake. "How are *you* doing?" He must be as wiped out as she'd been. Why hadn't he slept? Was he sitting here in the dark plotting her punishment for being in cahoots with Rydell? It seemed unlikely that Jonah would be that cruel. He was more a walk-away-and-never-look-back kinda guy.

"Fine. A few dings here and there, nothing major."

He was looking at her as though he expected . . . she had no idea what. "Where are we?"

"Still heading south. Maura and I agree, the whole area is unstable. No point hanging around. We're heading back to Cutter Cay."

She sat up, pushing the long, damp strands of her loose hair out of her face. She was naked, disconcerting when things were still unsettled between them. Since she lay over the coverlet, there was nothing to pull over herself. She brazened it out, pretending she was fully clothed. "Can we see the eruption from here?"

"Yeah, starboard side. Want to go up and take a look?"

Swinging her legs over the mattress, she stood, then plucked a towel from the foot of the bed to wrap around her body. She nodded. "I need to go to my cabin for a sec."

"You'll need this." When he turned to reach over and

get something off the bedside table, the meager light limned his bare hip, showing he was completely naked. *Ah. Jonah.*

He picked up the master key. Their fingers brushed as she took it, but if he felt the same zing of electricity at their touch, he didn't show it. "Meet you on deck."

Callie hastily dressed in khaki shorts and a white tank top, then carefully emptied the small bowl of water beside the bed into the sink with the stopper closed. Fishing out the three iridescent tiles, she held them in her open palm under the light in the bathroom, staring at them intently for a moment. "What secrets could you tell me? What wonders could you teach the world?"

Closing her fingers around them, she left her cabin and made her way to the top deck. The slider was open to the balmy night air. A half-moon emerged from behind the cloud cover—smoke from the volcano, Callie figured.

Jonah was leaning over the aft rail as she walked across to him. "You don't have a mark on you," Jonah said softly.

Since she was barefoot, and hadn't made a sound, Callie wondered how he'd known she was behind him. Coming up beside him, she pushed her loose hair over her shoulders as the breeze danced the long strands around her face and arms. "I noticed. The fact should scare the hell out of me, but strangely I'm okay with it."

"It beats digging a bullet out of you while we ride the high seas," Jonah said drily, not looking at her.

"It beats even thinking I ever *had* a bullet in me," Callie responded with utmost sincerity.

He gestured to the orange glow across the water. "It's a pretty spectacular show. But I feel for those poor bastards dying for their cause."

"Maybe it was part of their prophecy. Whatever the

reason, they believed in it fully. And acted on those beliefs." Her voice carried, and she lowered it as she draped her wrists over the railing, mimicking his posture and casual attitude.

Even from a hundred miles distant, she smelled the volcanic smoke and saw the molten flares shooting high into the night sky. Fiery orange reflections danced on the dark water between *Stormchaser*'s wake and the small speck of Fire Island. Soon to be extinguished as the entire island sank beneath the water. Just as the Sacred City had done three thousand years before.

"They sacrificed themselves to keep their city safe." Standing several feet from him, her body listed toward his as if he were magnetic and she couldn't stay away. Since he wasn't looking at her, she drank in his strong profile, his unshaven jaw, the curve of his cheek. And ached inside. Her fingers itched to comb through the shiny, silky length of his hair, being teased by the slight ocean breeze.

She inhaled the unique scent of his skin, sea and Jonah. She'd never see the ocean again without wanting him. It was going to be tough as hell in her line of work.

Instead, she stayed where she was. And yearned.

"The lava is flowing in the same paths it did three thousand years ago, depositing where it did then," she said quietly, voice strained. "The city and everything in it will be buried under millions of tons of magma. No one will ever be able to find it now, even if they know its location."

"An irreversible way to preserve its secrets," he said just as quietly, staring straight ahead.

"Obviously they felt strongly enough about preserving those secrets to take such drastic action. They knew when they activated all those quakes that this would happen. Do you think it was foretold in the manuscripts?"

"Maybe. We'll never know."

He'd said *Stormchaser* was heading back to Cutter Cay. He hadn't said if she'd be there when they made port. She couldn't imagine him wanting her with him for the entire journey back to Cutter Cay. Did he plan to drop her off in a nearby port, and have her fly back to Miami?

Yes. She was sure that's what he'd do.

This, then, would be their last night together.

Or as together as two people who had unresolved issues could be.

"How did the Guardians even *know* about nano-technology?" she asked, because it was safe, and non-inflammatory, and hearing his voice was going to have to hold her forever. "Fire Island was so isolated. No phones, no TV, the only books we saw were thousands of years old. It's pretty hard to make up something if you don't at least have a vague knowledge that it exists."

"I believe them." The long line of his back caught the moonlight, which highlighted the shift of his powerful muscles under bronze satin skin. At least he wore shorts.

Callie swallowed thickly. "You do?"

"Yeah. But no one is going to believe *us*. We have dozens of artifacts. The pictures we got of the pages . . . Of course, you're right. No scientific, irrefutable proof that was Atlantis."

She brought her hands back to the deck side of the railing and opened her fingers. "These . . . ?"

The nano-infused mosaics would be irrefutable evidence. Showing them to the world would bring everyone to the location to delve into all the secrets the Guardians had spent millennia preserving. "I wish we could take them down," she said regretfully. "It would be fascinating to watch them migrate. Here, do you want to—?"

His eyes ate the light, looking more black than piecing blue as he shook his head. "You do the honors."

Callie closed her fingers around the glass squares for a moment. They seemed to warm against her skin. "Whatever your secrets, whether we call the Sacred City Atlantis or not, your secrets are safe with us."

Turning her wrist, she opened her hand over the water. Together they watched the small pieces of ancient history return to where they were supposed to be. The tiny glass mosaics picked up the orange glow of the volcano, and the stark white of the moon, as they turned end over end, then disappeared soundlessly into the water without a splash.

"Which pretty much makes *us* the Guardians of the Sacred City's secrets now, doesn't it?"

"Yeah. What I'm thinking, too." Turning his back to the rail, he faced her. "What will you tell Case?"

"I'll tell Rydell the truth," Callie replied, knowing the it-was-interesting-having-sex-with-you-goodbye speech was moments away, and tried to brace for it. "We discovered a Sacred City and it was consumed for all time by the volcano that put it under the water three thousand years ago." Dragging in a breath, she kept her gaze steady as her heartbeat raced, and her breathing became impossible because her entire body hurt just looking at him. "And you? After all that, in the end you have nothing to show for this salvage. A few silver coins, a handful of artifacts we can't authenticate—will your brothers be pissed off that you didn't find your treasure?"

His eyes reflected the glow of the volcano, and he startled her when he slid his hand under her hair to cup her nape.

"You're wrong, Callie. I found my treasure. A priceless treasure that I *can* authenticate. You."

Her heart leapt. "But—"

"No buts," he murmured firmly as he drew her to him, his chest hard and solid beneath her palms, his heartbeat strong and even as he lowered his mouth to hers. "*Eres mi todo, mi amor.* Enough said."

You are my everything, my love, said it all.

Get swept away in Cherry Adair's
next Cutter Cay novel!

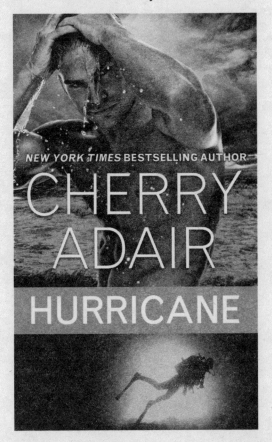

NEW YORK TIMES BESTSELLING AUTHOR

CHERRY
ADAIR

HURRICANE

Available April 2017 from St. Martin's Paperbacks

4829